THE IMMORTAL MARRIAGE

by Mrs. Atherton

HISTORICAL:

> The Conqueror
> A few of Hamilton's Letters
> California: An Intimate History

WAR BOOK: The Living Present

FICTION: [CALIFORNIA]

> Rezánov
> The Doomswoman
> The Splendid Idle Forties (1800-1846)
> A Daughter of the Vine (The Sixties)
> Transplanted (The Eighties)
> The Californians (Companion Volume to Transplanted)
> A Whirl Asunder (The Nineties)
> Ancestors (Present)
> The Valiant Runaways: A Book for Boys (1840)
> Sisters-in-Law (The Present)
> Sleeping Fires (The Sixties)
> The Avalanche

> [IN OTHER PARTS OF THE WORLD]

> The White Morning
> Mrs. Balfame
> Perch of the Devil (Montana)
> Tower of Ivory (Munich and England)
> Julia France and Her Times (B. W. I. and England)
> Rulers of Kings (Austria, Hungary and the Adirondacks)
> The Traveling Thirds (Spain)
> The Gorgeous Isle (Nevis, B. W. I.)
> Senator North (Washington)
> Patience Sparhawk and Her Times (California and New York)
> The Aristocrats (The Adirondacks)
> The Bell in the Fog (Short Stories of Various Climes and Places)
> Black Oxen (New York)
> The Crystal Cup (New York and New Jersey)
> The Immortal Marriage (Ancient Greece)
> The Jealous Gods (Ancient Greece)
> Dido: Queen of Hearts (Tyre and Carthage)
> The Sophisticates

THE
IMMORTAL
MARRIAGE

BY
GERTRUDE (Horn) ATHERTON 1859-

"Life is the gift of nature; but
beautiful living is the
gift of wisdom."

LIVERIGHT PUBLISHING CORPORATION

PUBLISHERS   NEW YORK

COPYRIGHT, 1927, BY

ATHERTON COMPANY

First printing, April, 1927
Second printing, May, 1927
Third printing, August, 1927
Fourth printing, March, 1929
Fifth printing, February, 1931
Sixth printing, November, 1933
Seventh printing, August, 1937

PRINTED IN THE UNITED STATES OF AMERICA

Lines to a
Bust of the Fifth Century B.C.
that MAY have been intended for
Aspasia.

It is not awe that holds one—'tis not love,
    Too friendly to be strange, yet strangely cold;
Like night, enfringed by steadfast stars above,
    She veils her beauty, lest one prove too bold;
Divine, austere; nor dare one venture far
    To plead a human longing to possess—
Pride set upon her brow a barrier!
    And yet what tribute could one offer less
Than love and to be loved? Her pouting lips
    Are chastely silent, sweetly eloquent:
The nectar of the gods no mortal sips
    And only Zeus himself commands consent!
A GODDESS she—no lesser loves enthrall,
    And humbly man remains devotional.

                         J. D. P.

THE IMMORTAL MARRIAGE

THE MORGANATIC MARRIAGE

THE
IMMORTAL MARRIAGE

BOOK I

I

Axiochus of Miletus was dead and in the dark hour before dawn the doors of his house were thrown open, the flute boy gave signal, the professional dirge-singers raised their voices in lamentation and issued into the street beating their breasts. The male relatives and friends followed, immediately preceding the body on its couch borne by slaves. Behind the bier walked Aspasia, the only child of the dead man, with a white lekythos in the bend of her arm and a few paces ahead of her aunts and cousins: a symbolic divarication that made her supple back a target for resentful eyes. The procession was closed by a number of slaves carrying a table loaded with garlands, lekythoi, and other votive offerings. Torch-bearers lit the way.

The mourners wore the black funeral himation, a full mantle sweeping severely from neck to sandal, one point thrown over the left shoulder, but the corpse had been dressed in white with a chaplet of gold leaves on its head and covered with wreaths of flowers, olive, and parsley. Axiochus, austere in life, lay on silken cushions and Persian tapestries, but his arms were straight and rigid at his sides, his pointed beard upthrust as if in defiance of death. Between his lips, as gray and hard as slate, was a coin to insure the services of Charon across the Styx.

The funeral procession passed through the narrow streets of the city, across the Agora, or market-place, through the inner

gates, and down a broader way toward the outer walls. The
men were silent, but the women, their voices covered by the
wild high wail of the mourners, gossiped without restraint.
The day before they had washed and laid out the body, anointed
and perfumed it with unguents, then stood by the hour singing the family dirge; they felt they were entitled to relaxation
before reaching the pyre.

"Do you know anything of Aspasia's plans, Cora?" eagerly
asked Tecmessa. Both were sisters of the dead man.

"Not I. Who does? She cannot live alone. Has she invited
you? I have my family, thank Hera. So have Polyxena and
Jocasta. It will have to be you——"

"The gods forbid! Aspasia will always be mistress in her
own house, even as I in mine. She would not listen to me—
no, not in anything, spoiled as she was by Axiochus. Moreover,
she would expect me to sit at her feet and listen to her as if her
lips were the lips of a goddess, no less— Athenè herself come
down from Olympus to dwell in Asia Minor. Not I! Axiochus,
so hard with every one else! I never could understand it."

"But she cannot live alone," insisted Cora.

"Then let her hire some one. There is old Gylles."

"Perhaps Axiochus named some one in his will. Have you
heard anything of his will, Tecmessa?"

"I have heard that Hippodamus son of Euryphon is named
her guardian."

"But he goes soon to Athens to lay out the Piræus. Pericles
has invited him."

"Then he in turn may name Tellias, who should have been
named by Axiochus—his own brother!"

"But in bed most of the time with some imagined disease.
Her husband should be her guardian. Twenty-four and unmarried! It is scandalous! An Ionian woman! Who will
believe she has not had lovers?"

"Who will believe a woman has lovers who talks to men of
nothing but philosophy, natural science, rhetoric, metaphysics,
and history? Pindar and Æschylus, Herodotus, Sophocles?
Homer is too old-fashioned! No, she's got a fire in her head.
She's not a woman at all."

"Nonsense. Why are so many men mad in love with her if all her fires are in the wrong place?"

"Is she not beautiful? And her skin is so soft and white it makes men think of snow, not of marble from Paros—and snow melts. Still, I wonder any young man has courage to approach her, for she talks only to the old and learned."

"She is very sweet," ventured Theodotë, the daughter of Cora, who was plodding along, heavy with child. "I don't know why you fear to live with her, Aunt Tecmessa."

"Sweet, yes, why shouldn't she be, who has had her own way all her life? But there can be a sting in sweetness—when she merely smiles if you give her advice, and goes her own way as if you were an old woman selling fish in the market-place. And what do you know about it?" she asked sharply, for the way was long and she had her own weight to carry. "Sixteen last Hekatombaion!"

The girl's face flushed and she drew herself up proudly. "I am a married woman, as you are, O Tecmessa, and I shall soon be a mother, as you are. And my dear husband says that I grow wiser every day."

The elder women laughed good-naturedly but made no retort. The head of the procession was passing through the outer gates. Tecmessa heaved a sigh of relief.

"It is well," she muttered, "for we were late in starting; I feared the sun would spring over the mountains and be polluted by the sight of our poor brother's corpse. Alas, poor Axiochus—"

"Don't begin to wail now. You will need all your breath at the pyre."

But there was still half an hour before the sun would rise over the harsh Asiatic mountains. The dome above the funeral pyre—erected on the Sacred Way, that led to the ruined temple of Apollo Didymæus—was still almost black, its vastness broken by a line of white eagles, drifting slowly, awaiting the coming of day.

The silence as the bearers lifted the couch to the apex of the pyre was as deep as death itself. In that windless void not even the pines on the lower slopes had begun their morning dirge.

Aspasia, her relatives and friends, stood near the head of the pyre, the slaves and mourners at a more respectful distance. The torch was applied, the flames from the resinous wood sprang upward, blotting out the mountains, throwing the nearer tombs, one of them the great statue of Chares of Teichiussa, into sharp relief, and the silence was rent by a loud, piercing, but rhythmic wail. The hired mourners beat their breasts, tore their hair and clawed their cheeks, the pain lending a more sterling note to their professional screams. The relatives and friends of the dead took up the refrain in a high monotonous chaunt, lifting their faces to the top of the pyre where all that was left of Axiochus of Miletus had disappeared in the consuming flames.

Only Aspasia was silent. She lifted the lekythos as high as her long arms would reach and poured the libation, then withdrew to the other side of the pyre and stood with her arms hanging listlessly, her eyes beneath her straight frowning brows bent to the ground. Although she had all the Asiatic Greek's love of pomp and ceremony she hated the discordant noise that violated the beautiful solemnity of the hour and place, resented the superstition that the sun would have been offended at the sight of her father's still majesty. Wickedly she wished that solemn file had lagged and the mighty orb of day challenged to do its worst.

The pyre fell to ashes. The bones were gathered by reverent hands, placed in a marble urn, and carried to the family tomb that stood in a grove of cypresses. All the votive offerings, some of great value, as well as the garlands and lekythoi, painted with familiar scenes, were grouped about the funeral urn, libations were poured, and the tomb was sealed: a treasure house for the ardent archæologist some twenty-four hundred years hence. The wailing went on unintermittently until the sun, blood-red, stood suddenly above the hard high rim of the mountains; unheralded by rosy fingers, full-born, hot, arrogant, the emblem of Olympian Zeus.

The tired cracking voices ceased. The white eagles swooped

to the forest. The procession re-formed and wended its way back to the city, leaving Axiochus with his ancestors, a handful of bones that a few months before had been a proud and independent, an arrogant and masterful man, a familiar figure in the market-place. The women chattered without restraint, and even the men, their solemn duty done, walked with heads erect and indulged in animated conversation. All moved rapidly, for they were hungry and the funeral feast awaited them in the dead man's house.

Aspasia lingered at the tomb, Hippodamus near by. She joined him in a moment and they walked together to the city, the beautiful light graceful Ionic city, white and dazzling under the strong rays of the sun.

"I do not feel like talking now," she said at length, "but I wish you would linger—or return—after the others have gone. I have—there are things I wish—to discuss with you."

"Certainly, dear Aspasia. I am your friend as well as your guardian, and you must ask my advice in all things. And do not grieve too much. Remember that death is death. What is done is done."

Hippodamus was little over thirty, but already famous as an architect of novel ideas. It was later in life that he developed an interest in politics and would have had the cities he laid out governed by a constitution invented by himself; at this time he was interested in architecture and ground plans only. Tall and imposing in appearance he looked older than his years, for he cultivated an expression of serene gravity—often shattered, however by the quick excitement of the Greek—and his features were as mathematically regular as the cast of his mind; the only eccentricity he had so far displayed was to wear his hair and beard longer than the fashion. Practical and logical as most Greeks, he had a cold passion for straight lines and rectangular thoroughfares. Pericles, who would have permitted no desecration of the ancient irregularities of Athens, had chosen him to rebuild the town on the harbor of Piræus, which was quite another matter. He was also a shrewd man of business, and for that reason Axiochus had asked him to be guardian of his daughter and her large inheritance.

As they passed through the gates of the inner walls Aspasia paused and pointed to the thin line of smoke rising from the Prytaneum, or Town Hall.

"The Public Hearth," she said softly. "Our Public Hearth! For six hundred years it never went out—not since Neleus son of Codrus brought fire from the Public Hearth of Athens to found our city of Miletus—how I hate the Persians!"

"Well," said Hippodamus soothingly, "the Persians are conquered and terrified. The Delian League protects us. They will never put out our fires again. And it was only for a few years—"

"Yes, but those years! When the Public Hearth was cold and empty! Thank the gods I was not alive to see it."

"Nor was I. But my father has told me of the day when Athens sent fire to kindle it again. That was a day of wild rejoicing in Miletus."

"Athens!" said Aspasia dreamily. "Athens!"

"Not to be compared with Miletus," said Hippodamus proudly. "A mere huddle of houses in which her fine public buildings and temples look out of place. I would that I could tear it down and rebuild every inch of it."

But Aspasia would not answer this challenge and they went on in silence to the great house of Axiochus, where the mourners were impatiently awaiting them.

II

The funeral feast was over, the guests had departed, and Aspasia sat alone in the aula or central court of the house. Hippodamus had gone home for his afternoon nap, a rite with which nothing was permitted to interfere. But the shadows were lengthening; he would arrive presently, bathed and combed and anointed.

Aspasia, who had laid aside her mourning robe, wore only a white chiton, a long straight garment girdled loosely, and sat on a marble bench in the shadiest corner, gazing pensively about her. She was no longer grieving for her father, for as Hippodamus had said, death was death, and she was a Greek. Facts must be faced and accepted. Moreover her father's

illness had been long and painful and the summons of Pluto
not unwelcome. But she sighed as she looked about that
beautiful court, with its fluted slim Ionic pillars, its statues and
tapestries and painted urns, where her father had sacrificed at
the altar, and she had held converse with brilliant men since
she was a girl of fourteen.

The house had been razed when the Persians sacked Miletus,
but rebuilt on its foundations by Axiochus, and she knew that
in this same court Thales and Anaximander and Anaximenes,
Cadmus, Pythagoras, Perecydes, Hecatæus and Anacreon, had
met and discussed the great subjects that made them immortal:
for in Miletus science and philosophy and prose-writing,
geography, geometry, arithmetic and history were born. It
was hallowed ground, and a proper frame for the most ambitious woman intellectually in all that little world of the Fifth
Century B.C. But she sighed again, and then rose. Hippodamus had entered.

She stood smiling but gave him no other greeting. The
Greeks bowed only to the gods and shook hands only to seal
a compact.

His eyes, bright after his nap, smiled in return and he
seated himself on a bench opposite. "You must forgive me,"
he said; "but after that long feast and so much talk—gods,
how those women did chatter! But you are not alone? I
expected to find Tecmessa with you."

Aspasia lifted her shoulders. "Perhaps she expected to be
invited, but I told her to go home and rest. She was very tired;
nor do I think she was anxious to remain."

"But she will return?"

"Doubtless to-morrow," said Aspasia indifferently.

"But—my dear—surely to-night. You cannot live alone."

"I cannot? But I think I shall, O Hippodamus. My
aunts are very kind, and I love them—dutifully—but I cannot
have them about the house. They would stifle me."

Hippodamus stirred uneasily. If he had belonged to a later
time he would have filled a pipe; as it was he broke off the
leaf of a palm and shredded it carefully. "But Aspasia—you

are young and very beautiful. Men seek your society constantly. Scandal would not spare even you."

"I am indifferent to scandal. Besides, I shall not remain in Miletus." She sighed once more as she glanced about that beautiful court. "I shall go with you to Athens."

"What?" Hippodamus dropped his palm leaf. "But that is impossible."

"Is it? I think not. My father had promised to take me, and it has been the goal of all my ambitions. The great men of Athens! The men here can teach me nothing more. I would talk with dear Anaxagoras again, and our old friend Herodotus. And with Pericles, Damon, and Zeno, and a young man of whom I heard much named Socrates. And Sophocles! Euripides! I would not only talk with those great poets but witness their tragedies in the Dionysus—"

"But Aspasia! Aspasia!" Hippodamus, his serenity rudely disturbed, was striding up and down; he knew at once this was no caprice with which he had to deal, and how was he to control this independent creature in Athens? "I cannot take you there. It is true that Zosmë goes with me, but we shall live in the Piræus, for a time at least, and that as you may know is thirty-six stadia from Athens; and those great men of yours seldom visit it—the home of sailors, petty merchants and bankers—*Metics!*"

"Oh, not for a moment should I think of living in Piræus. I shall take a house in Athens."

"Take a house in Athens! O gods on Olympus! Are you mad?" Then he faced about and looked at her hopefully. "Have you relatives there, perhaps?"

"An old sister of my father. She has invited us often to visit her."

"Possible—barely possible. Why didn't you say so at first? If you had sprung this on me before my nap you would have upset my digestion for the day."

"I'll go to her for a short time if you will not live in Athens, but I certainly shall not remain with her. I shall have a house of my own."

"And be classed with the hetæræ! You know nothing of

Athens. It is utterly unlike Ionia. Here even the respectable
women are free. There they are little better than slaves.
They never go outside the house without their husbands' permission—rarely at all save to take part in the great state
festivals."

"I am not going to Athens to see the women."

"O Axiochus, why did you die?" Hippodamus raised his arms
to the blue vault above, although he believed his friend was
crossing the Styx at that moment. "If you would spoil this
girl you should have lived until you had coaxed or forced her
to marry." He dropped his arms and strode toward her. "Do
you think *he* would have consented to your living alone in
Athens? O Zeus! Why did he make me your guardian? You
will be called a hetæra and I be blamed by all Miletus!"

Aspasia smiled. "Do you think so? I know Miletus and
Miletus knows me. She will hold no one else responsible."

Hippodamus growled. "True enough! But she will not
forget that I am your guardian—Ha! That reminds me!
What if I refuse to take you? Even an Ionian woman is not
allowed to control her property. I'll seal your money-chests
and leave just enough with your steward—"

"Oh, no, you will not, Hippodamus! No! No!" Aspasia
clasped her hands and raised her eyes—"the sea-gray eyes
of Pallas Athenè"—swimming with tears to his, and he melted
immediately. Never had he seen the famous Aspasia, the idol
of intellectual Ionia, in tears before; although no doubt she
had turned them on often enough for the benefit of his poor
old friend.

Nor, in his anxiety for her future, had he ever thought her
as beautiful. Her thick straight hair, twisted into a great knot
at the back of her proud little head, was the color of a copper
ingot from Cyprus, while her narrow brows and long lashes
were many shades darker. Her features, in spite of their classic
regularity, had a certain piquancy, impressed upon them by the
lighter side of her versatile mind, and were set in a rarely perfect oval. Her mouth had the voluptuous fullness and ripeness
of Ionia, but curled upward at the corners; one rarely took
count of the firm chin and hard line of jaw. Her long slender

body had been compared by the poets to an Ionic column infused by the gods with life, and her hands and feet would have been modelled many times had she listened to the appeal of sculptors. She could be feminine and frivolous or she would not have been an Asiatic Greek, but when presiding at one of her father's more intellectual symposia she looked as wise as Athenè herself.

And this siren alone in Athens!

Why in the name of Zeus and all the rest of the gods, thought Hippodamus irritably, couldn't she have been born ugly? How did intellect ever wander into such a temple? Would that Zeus would sweep her up to Olympus where she belongs and keep her there!

He controlled his agitation and sat down beside her. "Listen, Aspasia," he said, choosing his words carefully. "It was your father's will that I take his place when he left you for the dark realm below. I understand, of course, your longing for Athens—the intellectual center of the world. I would that Axiochus had gone there to live, for you have as much to give to Athens as that great city of Pericles would give to you. But he did not. He never would have left Miletus, save possibly for a brief visit, even to please you, whom he honored as much as he loved. I know he would wish you to live here after him, in this sacred spot that was the home of his fathers. And I know that his bones would rattle in their urn were you to become the butt of the comic poets of Athens; as you would be if you lived alone and received men at your house—yes, even if Tecmessa went with you, for such things are not understood in Athens. The good women, the wives, cannot read or write. The only women of whom men make companions are a few, a very few, of the hetæræ, who have educated themselves for that purpose. You would be misjudged, publicly lampooned in the theatre— Oh, remain here and live alone if you will! At least Miletus knows you, knows that you are above suspicion."

Aspasia smiled provokingly. "Now that you have done your duty your serenity should be restored," she said sweetly. "And my father's bones will never rattle as long as my own conduct is above reproach."

"Your conduct will *not* be above reproach if you live unmarried in Athens and are classed with the hetæræ—Ah! That gives me an idea." He sprang to his feet again and strode up and down the marble floor. "I will go ahead and find a husband for you. It should not be difficult, for you are very beautiful, you are the daughter of a family long distinguished in Ionia, and you are worth many talents—how many I do not know yet, but you are wealthy—"

"I will marry no Athenian," said Aspasia sharply. "I have married no man here for one reason: the young men do not interest me. They think of nothing but pleasure and their idea of love is lust. I shall not marry in Athens for quite another."

"Well, what now?" Hippodamus sighed and seated himself, with as judicial an air as he could assume, in a marble armchair of state; resigned to another argument and uneasily conscious that he would not get the best of it. "Be kind enough to explain why no citizen of the City of the Violet Crown is good enough for Aspasia of Miletus."

"Ah! You would disparage Miletus?"

"Not I. She is, herself, the mother of many colonies and in her day was as great as this Athens of Pericles. Beneath us are the stones of another Miletus founded by Crete—perhaps two thousand years since. But, beautiful as she is once more, her glory has departed; without the protection of Athens she would be the footstool of Persia. I love her, but as you know, I never delude myself. Once more I ask: why should the Milesian despise the Athenian?"

"I do not despise the Athenians. Far from it. But there are things I resent." She paused for a moment and fanned herself slowly. . . . "You have said that the Athenian women of my class are uneducated, ignorant. They have husbands only because every Greek wishes for sons to carry on his name and pay ceremonial honors to his corpse. Therefore if any Athenian marriage is happy it is by accident; if any Athenian loves his wife it is because she is a good mother to his children, amiable, and an excellent housekeeper; but even so he does not make a companion of her, unless he is more stupid than most Athenians, and his conversation is not desired in the market-place or the Lyceum. And any other wife equally docile and comforting would suit him as well. Love! And when a man is sought after by other men, he treats his wife kindly, no doubt, for she has her uses. If she were an educated and intellectual woman—but no, his father would not have chosen her, even if by chance such a phenomenon had appeared in his own class. You know this, Hippodamus, and yet would have me believe that you can find me a husband in Athens!" And she fixed her bright scornful eyes on her uncomfortable guardian.

But he retorted quickly: "The greater reason you should remain in Miletus. But I had hoped to find the exception. All men are not precisely alike, Aspasia."

"Admit that you merely wanted to gain time—and leave me behind. Admit it, Hippodamus, admit it."

"I deny it," he said stoutly, although his fine face had flushed. "But by your own reasoning . . ."

"I have given only one reason and the least." Again she paused and this time regarded her slender bare foot in its sandal; then turned her powerful gaze full on his. "The Athenians worship beauty and wisdom above all other men in the history of Earth. Also, they must experience love and companionship in one in order to be happy; that exaltation of mind and sense which constitutes this passion that made Sappho immortal. And for whom can they feel this double-sweet passion of love? Not for their wives, certainly. Not for the hetærae, whom they must also despise, if for another reason. No, it is for the young men they reserve this great and sacred passion. For those beautiful youths, the most beautiful the world has ever known, who are trained to bodily perfection in the gymnasia until they look like young Apollos, and whose minds, as carefully trained, are brilliant and plastic and companionable. On them is all this wealth and ardor of love expended—they are exalted and idolized as only women should be—"

"Aspasia!" Hippodamus was thoroughly shocked. There were limits to even an intellectual young woman's knowledge of the world. "How do you know—you, a girl—"

"Girls know everything," said Aspasia coolly. "Even in Athens, no doubt. But you mistook my meaning. I was not thinking of depravity. It does not interest me. Many of those love affairs, as you well know, are a sort of godlike friendship—although I don't think much of the ways of the gods. Let us say pure and beautiful, exalted and self-sacrificing, and of an incomparable white-hot ardor. They would die for each other, those lovers; the elder seeks to improve the mind, the character, of the youth he loves; he would give him his last obol, and protect him from the wrath of the gods. They fight like gods not men on the battlefield if they may fight side by side and die together. It is sublime! Sublime! And from one man to another! What irony! It is women who should be loved and exalted and worshipped. It was not always so. Did not women rule in Athens before Cecrops? Are there not goddesses? Athenè, Hera, Aphrodite, Artemis, Demeter? Is not Athenè titulary goddess of Athens? Do not philosophers refer to virtue and reason, men to great cities, with the feminine pronoun? Something has gone wrong in Athens. I would I could set it right. I shall talk to those women—"

"O gods on Olympus!" cried Hippodamus. "And do you suppose I shall take you to Athens to start a revolution? That is a man's world, and women are of less account than the bees on Hymettus. Those men of Athens will brook no interference. The poor women would get a sound whipping—that would be the result of your meddling."

"Oh, I shall not be sudden and tactless." Aspasia's eyes were no longer flashing. She was smiling roguishly.

"Yes! Your first undertaking would be to bewitch the men, and give those poor wives more cause for tears than they have to-day. Do you think it will console them to hear that their husbands are flocking to the house of Aspasia—for the sake of conversation! They will believe anything but that. They will remember only that you are as beautiful as Aphrodite. And the comic poets! The scandal-mongers in the Agora! O gods! O gods!"

"I can take care of my reputation," said Aspasia serenely.

"I shall move in a world of my own. And I shall make friends of the comic poets. They are men, are they not?"

"They would not spare their own mothers. They respect not even Pericles himself. On the contrary, their sympathies are all with the oligarchical party. They hate the very word democracy. And what more democratic than a woman living alone? Knowing that you are of the same class as their own Eupatridæ, they will regard it as an insult to the class their mean souls worship—and such men must resent the very existence of a woman both intellectual and learned. No! I shall not take you! That is my last word."

"But not mine, O Hippodamus; and I go with you to Athens."

And in the middle of the following month they set sail out of Theatre Harbor, one of the four fine harbors of Miletus; and Aspasia looked her last upon the famous city of her birth, its white tranquil beauty jealously hidden from the rest of Asia by its grim rampart of mountains.

III

They sailed in two long galleys, placed at their disposal by the Captain of the Athenian garrison, one accommodating all but three of the servants, and many chests. Hippodamus, his wife Zosmë, and Aspasia reclined on cushions under an awning on the deck of the smaller galley. Little Archeptolemus played about under the eyes of his anxious nurse, and the handmaids of the two ladies sat with the rowers: stalwart sailors-of-fortune from all parts of Hellas.

The geometrical features of Hippodamus were as serene as his mind; he had done his duty and exhausted every argument, but who could have his way with Aspasia daughter of Axiochus of Miletus? He had capitulated with resignation and grace.

Moreover, a compromise had been effected. He would take a house in Athens instead of the Piræus and Aspasia would be a member of his family; his wife was a woman of wisdom and dignity before whom even the comic poets would blench. It was an arrangement by no means to his liking, for it meant a long journey twice a day, and his sacred midday meal, his afternoon nap, taken the gods knew where; but to permit the daughter of his beloved friend to live alone was inconceivable. Better she had been exposed at birth on Mount Latmos and devoured by wild beasts that prowled on four legs. He had accepted an irksome responsibility and must make the best of it.

His wife, one of the few women with whom Aspasia was intimate, had been delighted at the prospect of companionship in a strange land where she would see little of her husband by day; and, while affecting to share his dismay, had subtly led him to his destined goal.

"There is one thing to be considered," she had said musingly, while Hippodamus still thought himself obdurate and Aspasia was calmly superintending the packing of her chests. "You will entertain, of course. It will be expected of you, and you could not live without the society of men. There is no society for women in Athens, and unless I am permitted to attend your banquets and symposia, and talk with your friends in the aula, it will mean that I spend my days and nights in the women's quarters, and all my beautiful embroidered chitons and himatia wasted. I should weep without end and pine for Miletus. But I contemplate nothing of the sort—nevertheless I should welcome the assistance of Aspasia. I am not fond of talking, as you know—except to you, dear Hippodamus—and she cares for nothing else."

"Women do not attend symposia in Athens," said Hippodamus feebly.

"We are foreigners and may do as we please. And I would have your house as brilliant as any in Athens—for we must live in Athens if Aspasia goes with us; more brilliant, if possible, to show those proud Athenians what Miletus can do. You are a great architect, greater than their own Kallikrates and Ictinus and Mnesicles, and you must impress them in every way. Aspasia would be a great help to us both. Yes, dear Hippodamus, I fear we must think it over—what can that child be screaming about now?" And she smiled a farewell into his adoring bewildered eyes and left him for the women's quarters, where she gave her own servants orders to pack.

She lay comfortably on her cushions, looking speculatively at Aspasia, whose luminous eyes were staring into the distance as if even now she beheld the glory of Athens.

She wondered if this day-star of Ionia never secretly dreamed of a husband. It was unthinkable that a girl of so much beauty and fire should be content to go through life asking nothing of any man but talk. To be worshipped for her intellect was all very well, but it was far more satisfactory to be loved. A barren life truly. She had cultivated her own mind and no friend of her famous husband despised her, but she would no more have given herself to the intellectual career as Aspasia had done, than she would have lived for frivolity and sensuality in the fashion of so many of her friends. She wished that Aspasia could have found a Hippodamus and that he were one of their little party. Then there would have been no flaw in her content.

For she was a trifle uneasy and if conscience had been invented in those Pagan days it would more seriously have disturbed her tranquillity.

She remembered what her busy husband had forgotten. Several years ago Pericles had brought about the passage of a law depriving all aliens of the rights of free-born Athenians, pronouncing all marriages with foreign women illegal and the children bastards. That decision had created the greatest consternation in Athens, for many men had taken wives from Ionia, Æolia, Syracuse, Magna Græcia, and even from the other City States of Hellas proper. And now these wives and children were legal outcasts. It was a cruel law, but Pericles had met with little opposition. The Athenian's pride in his city had grown so inordinate that he would willingly have banished all Metics had they not been essential to the prosperity of the State.

The Athenians would give no countenance to the legend that their remote ancestors were wandering tribes from somewhere north of the Euxine Sea; or from anywhere else. They were autochthonous, sprung from the sacred soil of Attica herself; the seeds sown, no doubt, by Almighty Zeus, gold-haired

Apollo, fleet-footed Hermes, Ares god of war, vine-wreathed Dionysus, and Poseidon, "ruler free of cliffs Ægean and the gray salt sea."

Many of the Eupatridæ (families of noble blood) claimed descent from one or more of those gods—and for all their contempt of kings and practice of democracy—a democracy with an absolute ruler in Pericles the Alcmæonid-Bouzyges—thought Zosmë with a silent laugh. She had her own pride of birth, but she resented the absurd pretensions of Athens, its airs of superiority over Asiatic Greece, which had contributed so much to the intellectual power of that haughty and exclusive little peninsula.

And these "foreign" wives no doubt were superior in education and accomplishments to the native Athenian women, trained only in the domestic virtues of housekeeping, management of slaves, spinning and weaving. She wondered if some jealous woman had not been at the bottom of that law. Not the wife of Pericles, for they were notoriously mismated. But no doubt there were other women in Pericles' life. His name had never been connected with the hetæræ nor with pæderastia; but he had married late even for an Athenian, and no doubt Athenian ladies, secluded though they were, had their ways of eluding indifferent husbands.

And Aspasia? Was she dreaming perhaps of a husband in far-off Athens, since she would have none of Miletus? Should she have told her? But Aspasia would merely have warned her not to remind Hippodamus of what he had mercifully forgotten, and added coldly that she wanted no husband of Athens to shut her within four walls and order her not to leave the house without permission.

Zosmë shrugged her handsome shoulders. That certainly was no life for Aspasia, and she had never heard of an indulgent Athenian husband. Let the question lie where it belonged, on the knees of the gods. Aspasia would seem to be a favorite of those august capricious deities. No doubt they would look after her. And perhaps, after all, she was not as other women.

The sailors rowed steadily and swiftly; there was no wind to fill the sail. The Ægean Sea was as deep and rich a blue as the sky above. It was the month of Mounichion, in the Christian era to be known as April, and the heat was not oppressive. Under the awning both eyes and complexions were protected from the fiery rays of the sun. Hippodamus made notes on his tablets. Zosmë nodded and slept. The nurse took the restless Archeptolemus down to the hold and sat beside one of the rowers. Aspasia withdrew her gaze from the horizon and looked about her with interest.

It was not her first sea journey. She had gone with her father to Lesbos to worship at the shrine of Sappho, and again to Ephesus and Halicarnassus. But this was her first journey toward the west, and its goal shed an enchantment on a beauty that needed no aid from the imagination.

They passed little islands, single and in groups, some inhabited, others deserted, their temples in ruins; and once more she anathematized the Persians. Marble fanes dotted one near by, and shepherds sat on the hillside among their flocks. An olive orchard on one of the slopes looked like a sheet of silver. The more distant islands were a misty blue, as if pale emanations from the deeper blue of the sea, but those they passed were wooded and fertile and richly colored with the wild flowers of spring. Far in the north was a shaft of flame, an Island volcano in eruption, its angry light hardly dimmed by the sun.

"I hope that does not mean another series of earthquakes." Hippodamus had put aside his tablets to gaze at this display of Vulcanic temper. "You have heard of the great earthquake in the Peloponnesus, some twenty years ago, when Sparta was laid in ruins—one of the most terrible disasters of modern times."

"Would that an earthquake would drop Sparta into the Styx," said Aspasia viciously, "for she is ever a menace to Athens."

"Yes." Hippodamus sighed. "Pericles has effected another peace; truce would be a better name for it, although it is called the 'Thirty Years' Peace.' But will even he be able to enforce it? All Hellas hates Athens, the hate of envy and jealousy. But none with the deadly venom of Sparta, who, until the Persian War, when Themistocles made Athens the greatest sea-power in the world, was the leader of all the Hellenes. Now Athens is the head of the Delian League—an Empire, although officially called a confederacy!—and even the treasure chest moved from Delos to the Acropolis. The land empire is gone and there is unrest and resentment in many of the islands, and in the towns of Asia Minor, as well as in the north; for, with justice or not, they regard Athens as arrogant and oppressive, and pay an unwilling tribute. And Corinth's hatred is second only to Sparta's. If the reins should fall from Pericles' hands! I fear there would be no place of refuge but Crete or Italiot Hellas, and perhaps not there."

"What is the secret of his power?" Aspasia had but a general idea of the politics of the various City States; she determined that Hippodamus should instruct her fully before their arrival in Athens. "I do not like all I have heard of him. To me he seems little removed from the old Tyrants—Pisistratus, for example, and whom he is said to resemble. Why do they elect him Strategos year after year, when other Strategoi rarely serve more than one? And permit him to exercise absolute power in a democracy—he, a Eupatrid, a descendant of kings and of the Tyrant Cleisthenes of Sicyon—and one of the wealthiest men by inheritance in the State?"

"His resemblance to Pisistratus exists only in the imagination of the comic poets," said Hippodamus severely. "And as for Pisistratus he is much maligned. He loved Athens and built not only the aqueduct which furnishes the city with water— a reform that enables the Athenians to practice the virtue of cleanliness—but many beautiful temples, as you would see for yourself if the Persians had not destroyed his work. . . . Pericles is a great and remarkable man, Aspasia, of godlike calm and unfailing wisdom. Most Greeks in public life, I regret to say, are self-seeking and dishonest. There have been few like Solon and Cleisthenes (of Athens), Aristides and Kimon. But Pericles is of a transparent integrity. He possesses no more formidable weapon in the eyes of his enemies. He is a rich man who lives frugally, to set a good example. He is an enemy of oppression and a true friend of the people. He makes their lives as easy and happy as possible, protecting them from the rich, building constantly to find them employment, and enlivening the monotony of their lives with many state and religious festivals—some of an unparallelled magnificence. The Heliæa, or law courts, is an institution from Solon, but its real power dates from the rise of Pericles, for the jurors are now increased to six thousand and adequately paid; and so are the soldiers for the first time. He has diverted certain public moneys into the hands of the poor that they may be able to attend the theatre. They are as familiar with the tragedies and comedies as the rich man who pays for the chorus. His advice—and his generosity—keep many out of trouble. He is reëlected in the Ecclesia as a matter of course, for the people know there is no such statesman in all Hellas, and that there has been none greater in the past."

"He sounds to me like—like—" The word prig had not been invented, even by the Ancient Britons. She searched and found her comparison. "A grape that the sun has forgotten to kiss and never will sparkle in a goblet of wine."

"Nothing of the sort!" cried Hippodamus indignantly. "He is a man of men. A reckless fighter, and a great General who has erected some eight or nine trophies; which means that so many times did he lead his armies to victory. You should know as much of our present history as of the past, O Aspasia. And that is not all, as you would learn if you could hear him speak in the Ecclesia. He has a voice as golden as your hair, and it coils about his hearers in that assembly until they are enmeshed and spellbound, although he despises grand phrases and never stoops to flattery. But he illustrates from the vastness of his knowledge, and although his Olympian calm has been derided by the comic poets, when need demands he is vehement and passionate. But generally he is content to be persuasive, to use logic not fire, and he does not hesitate to be scornful or peremptory. It is said too that when he ascends the Pnyx to the Bema he prays that he may not forget one of his carefully written-out and memorized sentences."

"He is religious, then?" Aspasia's lip curled. She had her

opinion of the gods, created by man in his own image and as full of mortal faults.

"No one knows what lies behind that masklike face, but he pays the gods due reverence, and, as I told you, is said to invoke their aid."

"But not Apollo's, I think, if he is as wise as you say. Apollo, when he spoke through the oracle at Delphi on a certain occasion, advised the Athenians to submit to Xerxes. I doubt if they have forgotten that ungodlike mistake."

"Apollo has lost caste, no doubt. But those temples are nests of political intrigue, and, although I sigh to admit it, I am afraid those priests of Delphi were either bribed by the Persians or, sure they would win, were anxious for their favor."

"Well, I shall never go to Delphi and ask advice of a woman dressed up as a priestess and sitting on mephitic vapors until her brain is poisoned and she shrieks like a woman in travail—"

"Aspasia," interrupted Hippodamus, looking at her anxiously and forgetting Pericles. "More than once I have heard you say things that argue a disbelief in the gods—or, what is equally impious, a lack of respect for them. I implore you to guard your tongue in Athens. We Asiatics have grown somewhat careless, and you are too deep a student of Xenophanes, Heraclitus, and Parmenides; but the Athenians take their gods almost as seriously as all did in ancient times—when Agamemnon sacrificed his young daughter Iphigenia on the altar at Aulis at the command of Artemis—"

"Do you mean they would do that to-day—in this enlightened modern age?"

"Certainly I do not," he said tartly. "They have grown humane and wise and reject ancient superstitions; but they revere and love the gods nevertheless—attributing those old abominations to a time when men were little better than savages, and were continually murdering somebody—anybody. Their untutored minds would drive them to the most brutal interpretation possible. Oracles are often vague and it takes a wise man to translate them. But it is time for our midday meal. We will stop at this island."

And he walked to the end of the deck and signalled to the following galley, while Aspasia smiled and unfurled her parasol.

They slept that night on the island of Icaria. Silken tents were erected in a grove of firs, and they wrapped themselves in closely woven rugs of Miletus and lay as comfortably as might be. There was a village on the harbor but no inn, and tents were preferable to the narrow deck houses of the galley.

Social intercourse between the islands and the mainland was rare, and Hippodamus had friends only on Delos. But although the Asiatic Greek loved luxury and many cushions, there were no complaints, for all, even Hippodamus, doubly calm and stately since his defeat, were excited and happy. Travelling was no habit with women in those days, and rarely thought of, but the intelligent mind has welcomed change and variety in every age.

And they felt as secure as behind their own solid walls in Miletus. They heard the snorting of wild boars in the forest and the barking of many dogs, and once there were angry cries in the village, where sailors, no doubt, were drunk and fighting; but slaves armed with spears patrolled the grove and no harm approached them.

That journey was a succession of long dreamy days steeped in warmth and beauty, and untroubled nights. They were never out of sight of the islands, and the open sea was lively with broad trading ships and triremes—tall warships with three banks of rowers.

In the evening and early morning Hippodamus and Aspasia walked about the islands—mountainous more often than not. Zosmë seldom accompanied them; she had no love of exercise for its own sake, although, followed by a slave holding a parasol over her head, she took a daily promenade when at home, visiting the bazaars and her friends. But Aspasia was as active of body as of mind, as lithe and evenly developed as any youth in the gymnasia of Athens. When Hippodamus, during one of their morning climbs, told her that she could not walk abroad in Athens she merely laughed.

"Would you have me lose my complexion and grow fat?" she asked him. "And my mind grown as torpid as my body?"

"By no means. But—I will confess it has caused me some anxiety. None but the hetæræ and the women of the people—or the Metics—are ever seen on the streets of Athens, save during the great festivals; very rarely a lady, heavily veiled, accompanied by her husband. . . . You promised me, Aspasia, that you would do nothing to scandalize those people so different from our own. But what shall you do for exercise? Would that they had gymnasia for women."

"I shall exercise if I have to rise before dawn and climb Hymettus. You can make no objection to that, O Hippodamus, for if the men of Athens talk all day in the open air they must sleep like the dead at night. And my tall Thracian slave Xanthias shall accompany me."

"But you will lower your veil if you meet any countrymen?" Hippodamus thought this a dubious compromise and hoped she would forget it.

"Certainly," said Aspasia indifferently. . . . "How odd it is that in this little world of even greater Hellas all the City States should be so unlike one another. Nothing but a rampart of mountains separates Attica from Bœotia, and I am told they are like each other in little but language and the worship of the gods. In Sparta the girls exercise naked in the gymnasium with the youths, and in Athens they never see even the man who is to share their bed until the betrothal ceremony. I wonder if the world will ever again know so intensely jealous and individual a race."

"Never!" said Hippodamus confidently. "Only the Persians can unite us; even then we quarrel bitterly among ourselves; and jealousy often breeds treachery. Time seems to teach man little. He is often as unreasonable and unpatriotic to-day as when Achilles sulked in his tent because Agamemnon had offended him. Under wise guidance like that of Pericles each City State may keep peace with itself, but it is ready to spring at another's throat even on the battlefield with the common enemy opposite. If Themistocles had not outwitted the Spartans at Salamis we should be the slaves of Persia to-day. And Themistocles, ostracized, died at the court of Artaxerxes, conspiring against Athens. We are a great and accomplished people, but the gods know we are not perfect."

"Ah, but we are Greeks! We are Greeks!" She was standing on the brow of a hill and she lifted her arms exultingly and then pointed them toward the northwest; for they were on the island of Naxos, a sudden wind having driven them off their course. "And we go to Athens, the greatest city in all the world—and the hearth-mother of Miletus. What does she hold for me, I wonder?"

"Yes, what?" said Hippodamus sharply. "What? I would give a talent to know!" And once more he was assailed with misgivings and wished that he had locked her up in the house of her father and sped from the harbor at midnight.

IV

Aspasia stepped from beneath the awning that her view might be unimpeded. They were approaching Point Sunion, the southern outpost of Attica. On the height above stood what the Persians had left of the temple of Poseidon, against a background of pines. Smoke was rising from the sacrificial altar beside it, and priests, their pomp sadly blurred by the distance, stood with arms upraised to the invisible but omnipresent goddess. They were the only signs of human life. That green wall shut off the silver mines behind it, where thousands of slaves toiled for the glory of Athens.

As the galley rounded the point and sailed toward the open roadstead of Phaleron, Aspasia's eye was caught by two points of light far away and high above the surrounding plain. She knew at once what it was, for the fame of that glittering metal was as wide as all Hellas. Pheidias, at the bidding of Kimon, had erected on the Acropolis a gigantic statue of Athenè Promachus, made from the spoils of Marathon; and the point of her spear and the crest of her helmet were visible to mariners far out at sea. Returning sailors always gave that symbol of victory a joyous welcome, and Aspasia heard the harsh voices of the rowers below.

A wave of hot blood surged over her body and seemed to break in her throat almost choking her, and then icy points pricked her spine. Her life had been intellectual not emotional but for a moment she was lost in a swooning ecstasy. Athens. . . . Yes . . . but why should a city, even Athens, make her feel as if she were racing across the heavens in a chariot of fire, her singing blood calling to the pursuing god to hasten and overtake her?

She shook herself angrily and turned to her companions, who were also gazing at the "mariners' welcome."

"Athens!" she said lightly. "We shall sleep there to-night."

"If the wind does not drop," replied Hippodamus. "Pray to the gods—if you ever so condescend—that our sail will remain full."

"Oh, I never hesitate to pray for what I want," said Aspasia gaily. "Gods exist, no doubt, however unlike they may be to our limited mortal conception of them, and it is well to conciliate them with sacrifice and prayer. I hope your steward has already procured a goat!"

Hippodamus laughed. "Be sure he has, for he at all events walks in fear of the gods."

"He has had many things to think about," said Zosmë anxiously. "I have heard little good of the houses of Athens, but I hope he has found one in which we can exist in decent comfort."

"Hæmon has had nearly a month," her husband reassured her, "and, he knows how to lay out drachmæ to the last advantage. Be sure if he found nothing on the market he has bribed some worthy family to spend the rest of the year in the country."

"We must rent a country-place for the months of Hekatombaion and Metageitnion, for the heat and stenches will be abominable in Athens."

Hippodamus groaned. "Well, let us hope we can find one between Athens and Piræus or all the flesh will be shaken from my bones. The roads in Attica are the worst in Hellas and the dust chokes and blinds the very horses."

Zosmë took his arm and pressed it fondly. "If we cannot we will remain in Athens," she said in the cooing voice she reserved for her husband alone. "I have come with you to make you comfortable and happy, dear Hippodamus. Remember I was willing to live in the Piræus; and if Archeptolemus falls ill we can send him to the country with the nurse."

Aspasia walked to the end of the deck as Hippodamus bent and kissed the dark glowing face raised to his. Domestic bliss bored her, and she was thankful she had no husband either to defy or to manage with the subtlety of Zosmë. She lost herself in anticipations of the imminent hour when the illustrious men of Athens would hasten to visit her.

But she forgot to pray to the gods and the wind died suddenly. They did not sail into the great harbor of Piræus until the following morning, and it was another hour before they beached.

That harbor was an animated scene. It was filled with trading ships from all ports of the civilized and barbarian world. From all the harbor towns colonized by Hellas even to Massilia on the sea-edge of the wilderness of Gaul in the west, the shores of the Pontus in the north and the southernmost islands of the Ægean; "Barbarians" represented by traders from Phœnicia, Egypt and Carthage. Swarthy men swarmed the decks shouting in foreign tongues and every Hellenic dialect, pointing their prows toward the harbor's entrance or racing for the beach. The galleys had been hard-pressed as they steered between the towered moles of masonry, and there had been loud vituperation from their rowers: excited at the prospect of their own hour in the town where it was always possible to escape from the eye of the captain and find joyous welcome in wine-houses.

Shattered was the peace of that long and lovely voyage. Serenity dwelt only in the blue vault above. Children swarmed about the dwellings on the slopes of Munychia and Acte; their parents, no doubt, foregathered in the Piræus, which tossed like a varicolored sea in a storm. Even the road in the wide valley between Piræus and Phaleron was crowded with mule carts, and slaves bent double under sacks of merchandise or of silver from the mines of Laurion. The masters shouted and cursed, for they were in haste to buy and sell and add their voices to the din.

The galley approached the beach slowly, the captain's eye

searching anxiously for a vacant place in one of the shipsteads, and Aspasia had time to look ahead with lively curiosity before her senses were stunned by the noise and rough contacts. Her eyes dwelt on the "Long Walls," built by Pericles and joining Athens to Piræus. Five miles to the south was another wall converging from Phaleron to the capital, but as there was marshy ground between where an enemy might land at night, Pericles had built the second of the Long Walls some three hundred yards from the northern; and Athens could now defy her foes by sea as with her own city wall she could defy them by land. As long as those walls lasted she was secure from hostile navies. The danger lay in that strip of land that joined the Peloponnese to Attica by way of a now adverse Megara. If Sparta could have sunk her jealousy it is possible that the sun of Athens would not have set for centuries to come and that of Rome been but a pale and humble reflection.

The comparatively narrow space between the Long Walls was even more crowded than the road beyond. Carts piled high with goatskins filled with wine, sacks of onions, olives, and garlic, kegs of olive oil, baskets of pottery, bags of silver for purchase, running slaves almost equally laden. The drivers screamed and the slaves and mules panted, their tongues hanging out.

"And every one pushing and cursing in the narrow reeking streets," said Hippodamus contemptuously. "Knocking one another down to get to the corn market or the slave market or the sea-captains first. A pest-hole of a town. But Pericles has shown his wisdom once more, and two years hence this chaos will be a gracious city with wide streets, temples, and porticoes, public buildings and great warehouses on the beach; and the inhabitants more decent in consequence— Ah! There is Hæmon."

A tall man in a gray chiton had detached himself from the mass and lifted his hand in respectful salutation, then caught the eye of the captain and pointed to a shipstead near by. The captain needed no second hint and a few moments later the galleys were beached. Hippodamus helped his charges to descend and handed the child to Hæmon, then tossed a bag of obols to the rowers and ordered the household slaves to follow closely.

The steward leading with the delighted Archeptolemus on his shoulder, clinging to his thick gray curls, they pushed their way through the crowd of merchants, traders, and sailors—far too democratic to make way for wealthy travellers who had no place in this mart where gain was god.

Aspasia and Zosmë drew their mantles over their heads and protected their young and beautiful faces from the vulgar gaze, each clinging to an arm of Hippodamus but momentarily threatened with submergence. Men shouted, dogs barked, women screamed, babies howled. A lost child had been lifted by some casual philanthropist to a statue of Hermes, and, clasping the neck of that impartial deity with his legs, jabbered happily at the turmoil.

There were few native Athenians. Piræus was the paradise of the Metics, Greek "foreigners," encouraged by Pericles to pour gold into the veins of Attica.

After a few breathless moments the Milesians reached the Place of Commerce, and although the four sides were swarming, where merchants showed their wares in gay bazaars, and bankers changed money, the middle of the square was comparatively empty. There were many women here, not only housewives but singing girls, garlanded and scantily clad, their dark bright eyes glancing appraisingly from one strange face to the next.

Hippodamus paused and waved his hand vaguely toward the promontory of Alcimus. "The grave of Themistocles," he began, but Zosmë interrupted him firmly.

"This is no time for sight-seeing. On some quiet evening perhaps, if there is such a thing in Piræus."

They walked slowly under the hot bright sun to the head of the square where chariots awaited them. Just beyond was the slave market where enterprising sea-captains were selling their captured or kidnapped wares to the highest bidder. Even Aspasia and Zosmë did not pause to throw a glance of pity at the tired and terrified wretches; many with skins no darker than their captors', for there was little traffic with Africa. Theirs was a civilization built upon slavery; any without it was inconceivable, and even the speculative mind of Aspasia had never dwelt on the subject. Kind to their slaves, like all well-bred—and law-abiding—Greeks, they were as little given to pity of others as of themselves. Pity was an almost unknown sentiment. What was was. It was a part of the mission of the tragic poets to purge the mind of pity as well as of terror. They were a humane people, but guided by the light of reason, not by an organ sometimes mentioned by doctors but as yet unclaimed for symbolic purposes.

v

"I think, O Master," said Hæmon, "it were better not to try to approach Athens between the Long Walls—"

"Certainly not. We will take the old road. It is bad enough, but at least we shall not run the risk of being flung against solid masonry and our brains dashed out."

A moment later they were in the chariots and making their way slowly from the town. Zosmë and Aspasia sat together; Hippodamus and Hæmon, the latter with the boy on his knee, led the way. The nurse and the handmaids with the jewel caskets followed in a mule-cart, the other slaves on foot behind them carrying the chests. The charioteers, standing erect behind their patrons, guided the horses deftly through crowds and narrow streets until they reached the broad road beyond the city gates and then incited them to breakneck speed.

The road now was almost deserted, for the men, mules and slaves that had choked it would not return until late afternoon. And once more they were surrounded with beauty. There was no dust. It lay biding its time under a late spring shower. There were five miles at this point between the Long Walls and the old Wall of Phaleron and all the plain was filled with wild flowers: white and pink asphodel, bright poppies, blue hyacinths, purple crocuses, pale narcissi, iris, and anemone, under the plane trees and pines. In the gardens of country-places and farms there were roses and violets, the air heavy-laden with their perfume. The long line of Hymettus towered above them, bare, gray, gullied, and austere, under the blinding light of day, her lower slopes terraced for vineyards. Small marble fanes had been erected since the Xerxes invasion and statues to Hermes and Pan.

Although the Greeks gave little conscious observation to natural beauty, and even their poets were inspired to put appreciation into as few words as possible, their quick devouring minds were colored with it nevertheless. It enriched their vocabularies and fertilized their idealism. They might not rhapsodize over a wild-flower, but wide plains of delicate color filled them with an equally delicate serenity. Did Athenians find themselves on the Acropolis at sunset they gazed with a deep inward peace—and pride—at the glory in the west beyond Salamis and Ægina. They rarely spoke of it, but each was privately convinced that the sun in his rising and setting reserved his extremest majesty for the City of the Violet Crown.

The chariots covered the four miles and more in a quarter of an hour, and, racing through the suburbs, entered Athens by the Itonian Gate in the great wall of Themistocles that encircled the city within a radius of five miles. The horses, breathless, their nostrils red and distended, were permitted to walk, and two shaken Milesians, almost as breathless, sat back and looked about them eagerly.

Aspasia was invaded by a sensation of blank dismay. Athens had been described to her by unfriendly critics but she had been unprepared for such ugliness as this. Like all people of her time she saw no beauty in ruins—a decadent taste reserved for the Christian era—and the broken columns on the Acropolis offended her sight and filled her once more with hatred of the Persians. Only the superb brazen statue of Athenè Promachus stood out in perfection, looking like a lost but defiant goddess, who had lifted herself haughtily above an unseemly world. The Acropolis for all its fame was little better than a barren rock, sanctified only by its history. And on the left were other barren rocks, a ruined fane on the nearest.

The charioteer pointed his whip. "The Hill of the Muses," he said, for he had driven many curious travellers. "Its temple will shortly be rebuilt. And on the other side are the great temples of Hercules and Demeter and Artemis, restored and beautiful as in the day before the invasion of the Persian host." He spat over their heads. "Were it not that I have orders to follow closely I could show you many beautiful temples—and other great works erected by order of Pericles the son of Xanthippus

—whom may the gods preserve. I lament that I am forced to drive you through a deme that has less beauty than a gully on Hymettus. Even now, if you will say the word—"

"No! No!" exclaimed Zosmë. "Follow closely, as you were told, and take us to our house as quickly as possible."

They left the squat dwellings of the carpenters and masons and other workmen of Athens, and turned into a long narrow street, where, they were told, men of wealth and distinction made their homes. But there was nothing to please the eye here: rows of houses with party walls, built of sun-dried bricks, their flat surface broken only by a shallow porch or a statue of Hermes at the door, and here and there an upper window; (behind one Aspasia caught a glimpse of a woman's wistful face). Doubtless there were beauty and luxury within, but if so they were jealously secluded. The driver pointed to a house larger than the rest and standing apart, a welcome break in that uninspiring monotony.

"The house of Pericles the son of Xanthippus," he said. "Built by his father after the return of the family from exile. It is said that he would live in a smaller dwelling, for although an Eupatrid he is as simple as I in his tastes. But he would not offend the shade of his father; nor would his wife consent, for she is the wealthiest woman in all Hellas."

Aspasia glanced at the house with faint curiosity, and asked indifferently: "Why is the street deserted at this hour? I see no one abroad but ourselves."

"The men are all in the Agora—and, yes, on the Pnyx." He pointed with his whip. "I had forgot the Ecclesia was called for this morning."

"Our house, I believe, is on the other side," said Zosmë, who was holding a bottle of perfume to her delicate nostrils. "Let us hope its street will not be as evil-smelling as this—also that they have finished throwing out their refuse for the day and nothing will descend on us. . . . And if you will draw such a long face, Aspasia, remember that you would have travelled through the black waters of Hades if they had led to Athens."

Aspasia smiled. "I am unable to help recalling those lines of Pindar's: 'Oh! The gleaming and the violet-crowned, and the sung in story. The bulwark of Hellas, famous Athens, city divine!' I see little but the bulwark, and the walls are certainly imposing. However, as you say, dear Zosmë, it is Athens—why is Hippodamus stopping?"

"To listen to the orator on the Bema, no doubt," said their friendly charioteer. "We will do likewise."

They entered the pass between the Areopagus and the Pnyx and the horses were brought to a halt. The Pnyx, a walled rocky eminence with levelled surface, was covered by some six thousand men sitting on stools and listening attentively to a man who stood facing them on the Bema. He was a tall man, gracefully and lightly built, the outlines of his slender figure unconcealed by the white mantle wound closely about him, leaving one arm free, and flung over the left shoulder. The cold grave features under the crested helmet would have looked as lifeless as ivory but for his flashing eyes and darting glance. Other dignitaries, similarly attired, sat on a flight of steps behind him and flanked him on either side; several sat on the lower steps of the Bema, their necks craned as if fearful of losing a word.

Aspasia forgot her disappointments as the voice of the orator filled the silence; a rich golden voice, although his utterance was quick and authoritative.

"We are now at peace with the world, Men of Athens," he was saying. "And although we have already erected many splendid buildings, and temples to the gods, still have we much to accomplish before Athens is the envy of all Hellas for incomparable beauty; as she is to-day for the genius of her great men —her statesmen, philosophers, sculptors, architects and poets; and for the highest standard of intelligence and of living the world has ever known. To realize our highest aspirations, however, we must rebuild the temples on the Acropolis; even more to glorify our beloved goddess, Pallas Athenè. We have restored other temples, but until now we have had too many uses for money, to erect for her worship a shrine befitting the mighty daughter of Zeus—less than her due, for you all believe that she protected us at Salamis.

"Our chest is now full, Men of Athens, and we need spend

no more for the present on our navy. Our great annual surplus must go to gratify the ambition and the religious devotion that dwell in every soul present. Our city must be the wonder not only of the present but of the ages to come—"

Here the Men of Athens broke into wild cheering. Hippodamus signalled and the horses trotted forward. Aspasia sat staring at the littered street, hearing nothing of Zosmë's acid comments on the vainglory of Athenians. She felt curiously tired, almost frozen, and would not lift her eyes to the imposing beauty of the Agora as they passed it, in spite of their voluble charioteer.

They turned into another narrow street and drew up before a house of two stories with party walls but by no means contemptible in size.

"That was Pericles!" exclaimed Hippodamus as he lifted them down. "A rare piece of good fortune on your part, as you will probably never hear him again—even so, I fear you were observed. But I suppose," he added quizzically to his wife, "you are even more interested in your new house?"

"I am!" said Zosmë. "I am!"

He led the way under the little porch which the pious Hæmon had decorated with laurel wreaths, thus invoking the protection of Apollo; through the court door and down a narrow hall to the aula. The sky above was as rich a blue as Ionia's own, but Zosmë drew a sharp breath and set her lips. The resemblance to her own aula in Miletus ceased with that blue roof, although it was spacious enough. No tapestries here, nor painted walls, nor statues of the gods. The heavy Dorian pillars that separated the court on all sides from the portico and the rooms beyond, were clumsily fluted. Where marble tiles should have been was hard-pressed earth set with a rude design in pebbles, and two lone palms stood on either side of the door at the upper end of the court leading into the pastas. The only other objects to break the chill expanse were a few marble benches and the inevitable altar. Beside this altar, on which a fire was burning, stood a slave holding a goat in his arms and a knife between his teeth.

"Never mind," said Hippodamus, who knew exactly what she was thinking. "Remember the contents of our chests. And if you need other things that cannot be bought in Athens we will send to Miletus. Now I must sacrifice."

"What shall I do with Archeptolemus, O Master?" asked Hæmon. "The mule-cart has not yet arrived, and it is not seemly that one so young should witness a sacrifice. It might give him bad dreams."

"No, indeed!" exclaimed Zosmë. "Take him out to the kitchen and give him a honey-cake."

At this moment a slave girl entered the aula from the rear, bearing two lekythoi of wine and two garlands, one of roses, one of violets.

"A violet crown for Aspasia!" cried Hippodamus. "A good omen and a fit welcome."

He wreathed the indifferent heads of his ladies, handed the protesting Archeptolemus to the girl, and retired with Hæmon to an inner room. Zosmë and Aspasia exchanged glances, shrugged, and planted each a lekythos on the left hip. As the shrieks of Archeptolemus died away in the distance, Hippodamus, arrayed in his priestly robes, returned to the aula. Hæmon, dismissing the slave, turned the goat upside down, gathered its feet into one hand, and with the other held back its head. Hippodamus slit the throat deftly so that the blood shot into the flames, then cut a slice from the back and laid it on the coals. Zosmë and Aspasia poured the libation, the master of the house, with head thrown back, arms outstretched and upraised palms, invoked the favor of his household gods, Zeus and Apollo Patroos, and the new home was consecrated.

VI

"And now," said Zosmë, "we will go to the women's quarters and wash off the smell of Athens. And after that, I hope, to the andron, for I am hungry."

"Lunch will be ready, O Mistress," said Hæmon, "and I will now conduct you to the gynækonitis."

They followed him through the alcove called pastas and he inserted an enormous key into a door that might well have served in a prison.

"The thalamos," he said reverently, for the room of the master and mistress of the house was a hallowed retreat in the eyes of slaves. He pointed to a door at the right. "And your room, O daughter of Axiochus. I will await you here and conduct you to the andron."

He closed the door and Zosmë sniffed. There were no rugs on the floor and the walls were bare. The only pieces of furniture were a wide couch with a flock mattress scantily provided with cushions, two low wooden chairs and a marble bowl on a pedestal. The room was dimly lit by a bronze lamp burning olive oil, and a brazier of glowing charcoal stood in a corner: the sun shone without but the house was cold. A door on the left opened into a small private court. The other bedrooms were aired, lighted, and entered from the central aula.

"Thank the twin goddesses, Zeus on Olympus, and Pallas Athenè that I am not married to an Athenian," said Zosmë, as she lifted a jug and poured water into the marble basin. "And one of the slaves shall go back with the galleys and return with furniture as well as tapestries. I suppose we can buy cushions, and curtains for the doors, even in Athens."

"I shall take the front room upstairs." Aspasia had opened the door indicated by Hæmon and was regarding her own cell with disfavor. "At least it has a window."

They performed their ablutions, and Hæmon led them through the pastas to the andron, a large room with a circular hearth where the master of the house gave his banquets and dined with his family when alone. The ceiling of this room was painted with nymphs sporting among the reeds of a lake, and the couches were inlaid with mother-of-pearl.

A fire of pine cones burned on the hearth, the smoke escaping through an aperture in the roof. Hippodamus reclined on a couch, his arm about Archeptolemus. Zosmë and Aspasia took their chairs beside him, and Hæmon, Phila the nurse, and the handmaids brought in the little tables. The other slaves were still panting between Piræus and Athens.

Zosmë's cook being old and full of pains she had left him in Miletus, and the new one had provided, under Hæmon's directions, an abundant repast for hungry travellers, although lunch was a slim meal in Athens. There were mullets and quail,

barley-cakes, olives, lettuce, spinach, honey-cakes, dried fruit
and figs. The wine, freely mixed with water, was brought in at
the end of the meal; which was eaten with the fingers, bread
being used as napkins and then thrown to the floor.

Hippodamus discoursed about Pericles, Zosmë made caustic
remarks, although her amiability was quite restored, and
Aspasia smiled sweetly and admitted that the crownless king
had a voice of astonishing beauty and seemed born to command.

"No doubt he will get what he wants in this case as in others,"
she said. "I hope he does, as I have never seen anything less
inspiring than the famous Acropolis in its present condition."

Hippodamus chuckled. "Of course he will get what he wants,
although there will be opposition from Thucydides the son of
Melesias and other members of the oligarchical party—on general principles. But the people are with him. They are vainer
of Athens than Minos ever was of Knossos and would give their
last obol to erect a proper temple to Athenè; would obols build
temples. I would I could have the designing of those glorious
fanes—there will be more than one! But my hands are full;
nor would Pericles invite resentment by ignoring Ictinus,
Mnesicles, and Kallikrates. He rules with wisdom not force."

"I imagine he loves power too much to make any mistakes,"
said Aspasia drily. "But in the old days he would have ruled
with force not words."

"Or deeds, O Aspasia. He is the best as well as the wisest
friend the gods ever gave to Athens."

"But he is an autocrat in the secret places of his mind. Deny
that if you can."

"No one knows what he is in the secret places of his mind,"
said Hippodamus testily. He resented any criticism of his idol.
"Pericles knows the minds of all men but no man knows his.
And what matter? His deeds speak for him. Why speculate
on what he would have been in ancient times? A strange remark from you, O most logical of women."

"It is a woman's privilege to be both logical and intuitive,
O Hippodamus." Aspasia's tones lost something of their sweet

suavity for a moment. "And it is always amusing to speculate about the great—in the light of history."

"When are we to meet this paragon?" asked Zosmë languidly.

"I am afraid you will never meet him. He finds no pleasure in society and is never seen in public except when he speaks on the Pnyx or transacts business in the Agora. He goes to no man's house, and of course his symposia—rarely given—are attended only by men. I shall see him daily, but in his own house."

"He is still cleverer than I thought," observed Aspasia. "He cannot persuade even the Athenians that he is a god, but no doubt they believe that a being at once so remarkable and so aloof must be the result of some ancestral indiscretion with Almighty Zeus; and therefore if not quite a demigod, of an immortal inheritance. Are we permitted to go to the pottery shops?"

"Certainly not! But I will select the finest specimens in the Agora and send them to you for inspection. Be sure to drive a hard bargain."

VII

That night Aspasia had a dream she never forgot.

Athenè, a radiant figure of ivory and gold, resting one hand lightly on a shield, a spear held erect by the thumb, and an image of Medusa on her breast, her golden hair escaping from a golden helmet, stood at the foot of the bed and filled the room with light. Her "sea-gray eyes" dwelt with a mingling of kindness and severity on the beautiful young mortal asleep on the couch.

"Awake and arise, Aspasia," she said in a voice of liquid silver but in a tone of command. "I would speak with you."

Aspasia, in certain after moments, when she permitted her imagination to escape from that crystal intellect of which she was justly proud, was inclined to believe she had obeyed that command and opened her own gray eyes and looked upon that radiant vision. Also that she slipped from the bed and bowed her flexible body almost to the floor.

"I listen, O Pallas Athenè," she said humbly. And then she

slowly straightened her long body until it matched that of the goddess in height. "And I listen without fear," she added proudly; "although I am deeply honored and awed, O daughter of Zeus."

A faint smile crossed the calm features of the goddess. "It is well," she said musingly. "I would have it so. Men have said you resemble me; is it not true?"

"So they have said when they would pay me vain compliments, O Pallas Athenè daughter of Zeus."

"The mind of man is finite, but from time to time he has pale glimpses of dark truths, and expresses them vaguely. But one truth you alone of all mortals shall hear, and to-night. You *are* the daughter of Pallas Athenè, Aspasia of Miletus; as you will be known in Athens and in history."

"But you are a virgin!" murmured Aspasia in protest. "I was taught at my father's knee what all the world believes, that you are and ever have been immaculate, inviolate; even as Artemis fleet-footed daughter of Zeus."

"Nevertheless," said the goddess calmly, "you are my daughter. Like many another virgin, I, even I, Pallas Athenè, goddess of wisdom and the arts, goddess of the fields and the hearth, deity, loving and beloved of the immortal city of Athens, longed for a child; and after countless ages—ages of which man to-day knows naught—Almighty Zeus granted my wish. When you were begot I swept through the body of your mother, and I, not your mortal parents, informed you with life. Not with the sap of my body—which must ever remain inviolate—but with the flame of my soul and my mind. But only in a limited measure, my daughter. Had I ordained that you should be Pallas Athenè in mortal form you could have risen to kingly power, but I did not so ordain, for there is little happiness in the life of a ruler of men. And unless a woman is also a goddess it is well she should not aspire too high. But I endowed you with gifts of intellect that no woman in all Earth's history has ever possessed before. I withheld the gift of poesy, which the gods gave unto Sappho, for I wished your mind to be balanced and logical and undisturbed by wanton flights. And I gave you an indomitable soul that would fear no man, nor hesitate at the loftiest excursions into the godlike realm of thought."

She paused, and Aspasia, too bewildered to speak, made another obeisance.

The goddess continued.

"I dowered you with beauty, Aspasia daughter of Pallas Athenè, for intellect without it inspires no pæans of gratitude. And with all those lighter charms that conquer men when intellectual preëminence may leave them unmoved. I wished you to conquer all men, not merely philosophers, that your understanding of creatures so different from ourselves should be wide. A woman must have subtlety as well as wisdom. But I would that you remain a virgin."

"But I have never considered union with any man, O Pallas Athenè daughter of Zeus. I have lived for twenty-four years surrounded by men young and old and many have loved me; and never once have I been invaded by those tremors that seem to be so necessary to the happiness of other women. My emotions are mental—goddesslike! And now I understand why! They shall never be otherwise, O Pallas Athenè daughter of Zeus."

"You are a woman as well as an intellect," observed the goddess none too cryptically.

"But not as other women." And Aspasia drew herself up even more proudly. "I shall never forget that I am the daughter of Pallas Athenè, who sprang full-bodied from the head of Almighty Zeus."

The eyes of the goddess dwelt with both sadness and affection on that vital and far more lovely replica of herself.

"I repeat that you are a woman, Aspasia, and I would warn you there are men whose powers over women are as potent as if they had the ichor of the gods in their veins. And a few of them have, for the gods in the past descended to earth more often than was wise, or agreeable to mortal husbands. I did not warn you in Miletus, for I saw no man there who could conquer your proud spirit or liberate your mortal inheritance. But I foresee danger here in Athens. I may do no more than warn you, for the gods are no longer permitted by Almighty Zeus to interfere in the individual lives of men. We may only advise through the oracles; and often in our consecrated temples we are misinterpreted—or worse. Once and once only I have been granted permission to transgress the law, and I have descended from Olympus to put you on your guard, O my daughter.

"I do not affirm that you will find unhappiness in union, but I would have you remain a virgin, as I am, and ever shall be. I would have you in all things attain to an immortal ideal: stainless, spotless, as untarnished of body and soul as you are unparalleled in intellect—an ideal that will be beyond not only the attainment but the comprehension of other mortal women until Earth is consumed in the furnace of the sun.

"That is my wish. It is your wish—now. See that it remains so."

She shook her spear slightly and paused. When she spoke again there was alternate pleading and menace in her deep tones.

"If you obey my behest, I promise you, my daughter, that when you come to the end of your mortal span, you shall not cross the black and roaring waters of the Styx. I will sweep you up to Elysion—yes, even were Pluto and all his dark minions hovering over your bed of death.

"But if you hang your girdle on the altar of Aphrodite you shall descend alone to the House of Hades, and flit forever a pale shade on the shores of Acheron. Mortal love will not avail you there.

"I have spoken. Remember my words, Aspasia of Miletus daughter of Pallas Athenè daughter of Zeus. I go."

And the gold and ivory vision grew slowly transparent, hovered, vanished.

VIII

Aspasia awoke after what seemed æons of struggling out of darkness toward light. She was in the upper chamber and had opened the shutters of the small window before going to bed. The full moon almost filled the aperture. The room was very cold.

She shivered and sat up. The woolen bed cover was on the floor and she lifted it absently and wrapped it about her. Odd that she had been restless, for as a rule she slept too profoundly to toss, and the couch was soft with her own cushions.

And then she remembered the dream.

She had often been vaguely aware upon awaking that her sleep had been enlivened by dreams, but she had never been able to recapture them; merely a flying glimpse as they scampered down the end of a long perspective. But this dream rose in her consciousness as sharply defined as if it were a scene in a theatre. All it needed was a chorus!

Was it a dream, or a visitation? She had only to close her eyes to see that solid figure of ivory and gold standing at the foot of the couch.

But why ivory and gold? There was no statue in Hellas even of Pallas Athenè as extravagant as that. . . . And if she were the daughter of the goddess of wisdom would that not account for what had been a mystery to herself as well as to others? Her father and his father and their fathers before them had been men of superior attainments, but, as far as she had been able to discover, their talents had lain in their appreciation and patronage of men far greater than themselves. Her mother, she had been told, was a typical Ionian, gay, pleasure-loving, and with the dark beauty of her race. Blonde beauty was almost unknown in Asiatic Greece.

Nor were the men of her mother's family notable for anything but valor, achievement in games, deep drinking, and making love to many women. A dissolute lot. And the women were not much better. From whom then had she derived that austerity of body, and those superlative gifts of mind that her admirers called manlike—godlike?

And then she laughed aloud and addressed the old man's face in the moon, grinning at her mockingly.

"Yes! Yes!" she assured him. "I do not believe it. Would that I could, for I should be vainer than ever, and I have noticed that the most contented women are the vainest. . . . And how cold it would have been standing on that floor in my bare feet!"

She shivered again. Her feet were very cold.

Her levity deserted her for a moment and she frowned, recalling Athenè's warning of the menace in Athens. She remembered also that moment of hot suffocation on the galley at her first glimpse of Athens, and the strange weariness that had invaded her being as she listened to that wonderful voice on the Pnyx. But sensory impressions with her were always fleeting; she had not thought of them since. She shook off their memory now and once more addressed the moon.

"Not I! Not I! I call you to witness!" And as the grin seemed to expand she cried wrathfully, "If you had a beard I would pull it, as I often pulled my father's when little, and was sandalled thereafter."

She swung from her couch, her eyes still on that unsympathetic grin. "Of one thing only am I certain at this moment," she confided. "There is no more sleep for me to-night. I shall go to the roof and see if Athens is improved by your kindly beams."

She dressed herself quickly, wrapping about her the dark mantle she had worn at her father's funeral. As she was about to leave the room she saw a flash of light and heard the sound of voices raised in drunken revelry. Lifting her cloak over her head and concealing her face as much as possible, she leaned out of the window.

Six or seven young cavalry officers were passing on foot, their way lighted by slaves carrying torches, for the narrow crooked street received small benefit from the rays of the moon. They were singing a ribald song and reeling against one another. One carried a flute girl over his shoulder, and in spite of her uneasy perch she managed to produce a few liquid notes.

The beasts, thought Aspasia. *Persians!* And I had been told it is bad form in Athens to drink too much. *Their* wine was certainly undiluted. And then she laughed and clapped her hands. A party of footpads had darted round the corner and fallen upon the revellers.

There ensued a wild scrimmage, during which the flute girl took to her heels, and the young wastrels were getting the worst of it in spite of the rallying of their loyal slaves, when a tall figure, helmeted, and clad in a dark cloak, suddenly appeared at a corner of the street. Aspasia recognized him at once.

There was no mistaking that perfect balance and grace, and awe-inspiring dignity.

"What does this mean?" he demanded, and his rich authoritative voice filled the narrow street, drowning the angry cries. The footpads gave a yell of terror and fled. The slaves scrambled for the fallen torches. Only the young revellers stood defiant and sullen.

"Go to your houses," said Pericles sternly; "where you should have been hours ago. Would you disgrace Athens, known throughout Hellas for her sobriety? To-morrow you shall appear in the courts and be fined."

"You are out late yourself, O Pericles son of Xanthippus," said one of the young men impudently.

"But not drunk. And I should take no notice of you if you were sober. A citizen in time of peace may walk abroad at any hour. But the laws of Athens do not permit drunken boys to disturb the rest of decent men. Now go, and if you do not appear in the courts to-morrow I shall see that you are summoned with ignominy."

"That is naught to Hippoclides!" cried one of the number. And the others, as they swaggered off, echoed the popular retort of one of the contestants for the hand of Pericles' ancestress, Agariste, when her father, Tyrant of Sicyon, had decided that a young man whose idea of amusing his host was to stand on his head on a table and kick his heels in the air, was no son-in-law for him; and the rich and handsome young Athenian had laughingly defied him.

Aspasia fancied she saw a smile flit across that severe countenance as he walked on with measured tread. He certainly shrugged his shoulders.

Now, I wonder what he *is* doing abroad so late, she thought. But perhaps he takes his exercise by night, as he thinks it politic to seclude himself from the public gaze by day. But, like Hippoclides, that is naught to me. I will now, O Moon, to the roof.

The upper story covered all the rooms of the lower except the andron and kitchen, for smoke must escape. The slaves that had come with them were sleeping in cell-like rooms on this floor, the women's quarters separated from the men's by a heavy locked door. Hippodamus had been horrified at Aspasia's decision to room in such company, but the front upper chamber was not only larger than the one apportioned to her, its window was a luxury not to be foregone for a mere convention.

"Does not my handmaid do my hair and dress me?" she had demanded. "Shall I be polluted because she sleeps on the other side of my wall? Remember I had a window cut in my room in Miletus, for I, like my door closed at night that I may not be disturbed by people crossing the aula, and I cannot sleep without air." Zosmë had upheld her and once more Hippodamus had succumbed.

She went down the narrow passage skirting the aula below, walking softly past the narrow open doors of the rooms where the women slept heavily after a long and weary day, and ran up a short flight of stairs to the roof.

The house faced the Acropolis and its ghostly ruins. She crossed to the opposite end and looked down upon the Agora. And then she drew a deep breath and extended her hands palm upward as if mutely begging pardon for her harsh judgment of Athens.

In a sea of silver, marble temples and pillared porticoes, statues to gods and heroes, great halls for the Council of Five Hundred and for the jurors and prytanies, carved portals, pedestalled busts—of the famous living, no doubt—made a scene of such exquisite beauty that Aspasia almost wept.

A line of Hermæ separated this gracefully irregular quarter into two parts, and the spaces were set with plane trees whose shade must be welcome in the hot noonday. It was surrounded by colonnades, and at the northwestern end rose the noble fane dedicated to Hephæstus, the god of fire and of arts wrought in metal—not until the Christian era to be called The Theseum. It was a Doric structure, massive and severe, but almost Ionic in the moonlight.

In the neighborhood of the Agora were other public buildings, softly white and of celestial architecture, and above the circular roof of the Prytaneum rose a thin line of smoke from the Hearth of Hestia, whose embers had relighted the fires of Miletus!

About this vision of loveliness the dwelling-houses in the narrow crooked streets seemed to have bowed in shame and humility their heads to the ground; but harboring safely those passionate lovers of Athens, who lived in the open by day environed by the beauty their great men had given them, and looking upon houses merely as places for sleeping and eating and secluding their women. It would have been almost a sacrilege to divert money to the adornment of mere homes, which, to their own everlasting fame, should go to the making of Athens the glory of Hellas and the wonder of the world.

And surrounding all was the great wall of Themistocles, so wide that two chariots might drive abreast, and set with towers and great gates. On her left she could see the Dipylon Gate and beyond it the Sacred Way lined with tombs and leading to Eleusis: where the festival of the Mysteries was celebrated once a year in honor of Demeter.

And beyond all, far beyond, across the Saronic Gulf, were the mountains of the Peloponnese, like a brooding menace to the fondest hopes of Pericles. She felt the chill of the night air for the first time; and then, turning her head, saw a long line of triremes riding slowly on the Bay of Phaleron. Those galleys had devastated the coasts of Peloponnese before, making Sparta shriek with consternation and rage, and could do so again.

On all sides was the Attic plain, a long belt of olive orchards east of the city as silver as the moon; far to the north towered the mountains of Parnes and Pentelicus, whose quarries supplied the marble for the monuments of Athens.

She walked lightly about the roof to keep herself warm, pausing occasionally to gaze at the Agora once more, or to hang over the eastern parapet and look with amused interest at the low hill of Ares, where Orestes, who had killed his mother, who had killed her husband, who had killed his daughter, had been tried by the Court and defended by Athenè: sympathetic with the avenger of Agamemnon, and with small use, virgin though she was, for any woman who had murdered her husband. On this low mound, generation after generation, the court of the Areopagus had sat in awesome authority and administered the law, until Ephialtes, instigated by Pericles—less overtly powerful then than now—had curtailed their ancient powers and been assassinated for his pains. Their hatred brooded over the mighty Strategos, but he could afford to laugh at them now. They could only scheme and play politics.

Aspasia found interest in recalling the history of Athens, ancient and modern, that morning as she waited for the sun to rise.

It came at last, a pink glow above Hymettus, as translucent as water, like the reflection of some lake in the fields of Elysion. She fancied she could see the goddesses bathing, then flitting across the brow of the mountain.

She lifted her shoulders. Athens has made me imaginative, she reflected. And imagination plays no part in my life. That is for Sophocles and Euripides. I wonder when I shall meet them!

The pink deepened to rose, to fiery crimson, to flaming gold; the sun-god mounted slowly and with surpassing dignity above the ridge of Hymettus. It was day in Athens.

House doors opened and slave girls came forth with water jars on their heads, laughing and chattering. They walked swiftly to the spring houses, and lingered for a time in the little temples; indulging in household gossip, no doubt.

And then the gates in the wall were thrown open and the market carts came clattering in with the day's produce, while that end of the Agora devoted to the necessities of life filled rapidly with men and women, arranging their stalls. Bakers arrived with cartloads of bread, fishmongers with baskets of eels, lobsters, herrings, pilchards, mullets and sardines; farmers with spinach, lettuce, onions, garlic and fruit, or driving pigs and lambs for sacrifice; charcoal venders; bee-masters with honey from Hymettus; women carrying stacks of flowers on their heads to be made into garlands.

Bands of milch-goats were driven from house to house. Slaves came running to the market to buy bread for the master's breakfast. Shrill voices rose bargaining.

Aspasia, mindful of her promise to Hippodamus, went below before a shout should go up at the sight of a lady on the roof of the foreign architect.

IX

"Zosmë," said Aspasia, later that morning, "I must call on my Aunt Daphne. She is as old as Hymettus, and no doubt blind and deaf and cross, but she is the sister of my father and the eldest of the family. I must show her respect—but I wish you would come with me."

"I will, dear Aspasia," cried Zosmë, "for I have not been out of the house for twenty-four hours. Hippodamus has gone for the day to the Piræus with Pericles and what we do in his absence he need never know. Where does Daphne live?"

"On the other side of the Agora. I sent my slave Xanthias to find out and to announce my visit."

"Ah!" Zosmë's eyes sparkled. "We shall walk through the Agora, if only to see if it is as beautiful by day as you say it is by moonlight. Of course we must go veiled, but after all we'll not lose much in the way of fresh air. I suppose we'd better dress plainly, although I'd like to show one of my embroidered himatia to your aunt."

"As I said, she is probably blind, and of course we must not attract too much attention. I should put on my saffron that I wore travelling, but I don't think I shall; I prefer white."

She clapped her hands and sent a slave with orders to her maid. Zosmë went to her room, draped a frog-green himation over her tunic, and covered her blooming face with a dark veil.

When the handmaid brought the white mantle she wound it about her exacting mistress no less than six times. As the sleeves of the chiton fell below the elbows it was finally draped over the right hip and left shoulder whence it descended in soft sloping folds to the right foot. The white veil, a large square, was pinned to the crown of the head and hung to the knees.

"Can you see my face, Thera?" asked Aspasia anxiously.

"No, Mistress, and the gods know it is a pity. You might be as ugly as I am."

Aspasia sighed. "This is Athens! But I feel as if I were stealing out from a harem in Susa."

Followed by their handmaids and Xanthias they turned the corner of the street and a moment later had entered the Agora. Here both gave an involuntary gasp and not at the noble beauty spread before them. Never before had they been in a public place in which not a woman but themselves was visible. Men, men, men, everywhere.

Behind the columns of the stoas, or porticoes, under the plane trees, in the open, regardless of the sun on their bare thickly-thatched heads, sitting on the edge of the fountains, overflowing the barber shops, disputing before the tables of the bankers, but for the most part talking in couples or groups, were hundreds of men wearing mantles of white, green, wine-red, blue, brown, a few affecting the Spartan himation of coarse gray wool with no chiton beneath.

These, with few exceptions, were the gentlemen of Athens whose leisure was infinite. Metics carried business, trade, and commerce on their capable shoulders, and the workmen and slaves did the rest. Athenians of varying degrees of wealth—some poor enough—were free to cultivate the graces of the mind and the perfections of the body, and to indulge in those long conversations and arguments on politics and the arts, on philosophy (a term that included all knowledge), the iniquities and the complaisances of the gods, the affairs of every City State in Hellas, the rivals of Athens in commerce and military power, the last sensational lawsuit and the decision rendered by the dicasts, the prospect of continued peace with Sparta, the policies of Pericles and the strength of his rival, Thucydides son of Melesias, the ethics of using the annual surplus in the Delian Chest for the embellishment of Athens, the beauty or defects of the last monthly festival, the merits of the tragedies and comedies given at the recent Dionysia, the latest bit of scandal or gossip, or even on the impertinence and extortions of the fishmongers whose stalls they had visited earlier with their slaves, that made them at once the most profound thinkers, the most passionate politicians, the most nimble-witted conversationalists, and the most myriad-minded men in their interests the world has ever known.

There was a group of young officers near by, wearing broad hats, high shoes, and short coats of bright color pinned on the shoulder with a large brooch. Aspasia wondered if she had seen them last night. For the most part the men were older, ranging from the middle twenties to graybeards, and all of an exceeding dignity of carriage.

Zosmë knew little of nerves, but for the moment was overcome. "They are all staring at us!" she exclaimed. "It would have been better to have skirted the Agora."

"Well, we are here now, and if Hippodamus hears of it he'll lock us up on bread and water, and we'll never come again. At least they'll know we are not hetæræ, as we are veiled."

"They'll guess at once who we are, and some one will tell Hippodamus." She was well aware there was a limit to her husband's indulgence. "You know what gossips men are. And they've only to describe your walk; your feet never seem to touch the ground."

"Be a philosopher, dear Zosmë," said Aspasia impatiently. "We have this hour of liberty at least."

"Very well. No doubt you are right. . . . I notice the men here wear their himatia longer than in Miletus. I must have Hippodamus' altered, for I would not have him look provincial. The chiton, too, is rather shorter; it does not quite reach to the knees. Suppose we buy cushions? That will give us an excuse. There must be other foreigners besides ourselves in Athens; they will think we have come here to buy, knowing nothing of their customs."

They entered a booth, and after Zosmë had prodded and weighed and questioned and bargained, she bought six cushions, and Aspasia told Xanthias to run home with them and return as swiftly.

Then, almost jostled by the young officers, and still the target of all eyes, they entered a perfumery shop and chose several crystal, silver, and gold jars, and gave them to the maids to carry.

As they left the perfumer's they saw that all eyes were turned in another direction and that another ripple of excitement pervaded the Agora. Even the young officers had forgotten them.

A band of some twenty youths and young men had entered, crowding about one of their number who seemed to be the object of an eager, almost fawning, devotion. He was a tall boy of fifteen or sixteen and of a surpassing beauty. The sun seemed to concentrate its beams on his golden curls and classic features, his skin was as pure as an infant's and his expression both modest and sweet. He moved with grace and dignity, and, like all his companions, wore a white mantle which revealed the perfection of his long supple body.

"Xanthias!" exclaimed Aspasia. "Go and ask what that means." But she guessed.

Xanthias returned in a moment. "It is the new beauty, O Mistress," he said. "Acestorides the son of Diophantes. They are just come from the palæstra where they have been exercising."

Aspasia stamped her foot. "Abomination!" she cried. "A boy! I suppose they would never follow and almost prostrate themselves before a beautiful girl, even if they ever saw one!"

"Well?" asked Zosmë. "What did you expect? Is not Athens notorious?"

"But it is outrageous! Infamous! I've a notion to throw back my veil."

"For the gods' sake do nothing of the kind!" cried Zosmë in alarm; she knew that Aspasia was quite capable of it. "Be grateful that ridiculous boy has made them forget us and there is a chance Hippodamus will never hear of this escapade. Come. Let us go. Daphne will wonder what has become of us."

She steered the still seething marvel of intellectual Ionia toward the northeastern end of the Agora, while the very shopkeepers were running from their booths to stare at the mortal Apollo.

"The new beauty!" muttered Aspasia. "The new beauty! O gods, what irony!"

"Well," said Zosmë soothingly, "wait till the picked men of Athens come to our house. They will see a new combination, and you will have your revenge."

"Oh, I am not as personal as you think," said Aspasia crossly. "It is the principle of the thing that maddens me. If that Acestorides were kept in his proper place I should admire him myself, for I adore beauty in any form. If he were in love with one of those poor girls hidden in the women's quarters of her father's house I'd do all I could to further his suit. But of course he is only in love with himself, and no doubt laughs at the men prostrate at his feet. O gods! O gods!"

"What is this? Some joke of Poseidon's?" said Zosmë under her breath. "I thought I heard some one pattering after us. It would seem that you have one admirer left, Aspasia."

A young man with a flat nose, wide mouth, and bulging eyes like a crab's under an immense brow, was blocking the way. He stood, a grotesque figure in a short Spartan cloak, with his palms upturned as if saluting a goddess, his eyes fixed on Aspasia. His large bony feet were bare.

"Stand aside!" said Zosmë imperiously. "You forget yourself. If you are begging—"

The absurd figure drew himself up and his height at least was respectable.

"I am Socrates the son of Sophroniscus," he said calmly. "And if I beg it is only a word with Aspasia daughter of Axiochus, O Zosmë wife of Hippodamus."

"You know us!" cried Zosmë in consternation. "Then every one else does, I suppose. O Zeus! But what did I tell you, Aspasia?"

"We could not fail to recognize Aspasia of Miletus, and we knew that she had arrived in Athens yesterday with Hippodamus."

"But she is veiled!"

"No veil can disguise a woman who walks on air and with the fleet grace of Artemis, and whose bearing has the authority of Pallas Athenè. More than intellectual fame has preceded Aspasia from Miletus to Athens."

"But at least," said the exasperated Zosmë, "you should have waited for Hippodamus to ask you to the house. Is it the fashion then in Athens for men to introduce themselves to ladies in the street?"

"No men in all Hellas are as punctilious as Athenians," said Socrates proudly. "But I was carried away by eagerness. I am, alas, the least conventional of men. My feet directed me here against my will, for I am not wanting in courtesy and all due respect, O wife of Hippodamus."

"Strange conduct for a philosopher," said Zosmë sarcastically. "I have heard of your aspirations, and that you seize men almost by the nose and compel them to listen to you. But we are not men, and I, at least, am not a philosopher—"

"Do not be harsh, dear Zosmë," interrupted Aspasia, who had been inwardly convulsed. "Let us appreciate the compliment; and the originality of Socrates son of Sophroniscus, for he, at least, did not run to gape at a mere boy."

"Oh, I admire beautiful youths, and above all Acestorides," said Socrates naïfly. "But who could remember even such godlike beauty as his in the presence of Aspasia of Miletus?"

"The entire Agora!" exclaimed Zosmë. "Deny it if you can."

"But you are both veiled," said Socrates diplomatically. "And I fear you exaggerate, for many men were too deep in philosophical discussion to turn their heads. And do not be severe, O Zosmë; remember that the men of Athens worship beauty, and are permitted to look upon the beauty of young men only; and boys in the sweet bloom of youth—"

"And whose fault is that?" demanded Aspasia. "Not the girls'—"

But Zosmë firmly interrupted her. "No argument here. I know what that means. We'd not get home before Hippodamus. And now, Socrates," she added more kindly, "let us pass, and I will see that my husband asks you to the house."

"Oh, yes, Socrates," said Aspasia. "You must come to us very soon. I have long looked forward to discussion with you." And then she did a rare thing for a Greek. She held out her hand.

Socrates stared at that hand as white and shapely as if modelled by Pheidias, and grasped it in his hairy paw, while his face turned purple and he trembled from head to foot. Then he stepped aside and bowed as if before the sacred wooden statue of Athenè in the rude makeshift temple on the Acropolis. He seemed incapable of further speech.

"I congratulate you on your new victim," said Zosmë as they hurried on. "He looks like something thrown up from the sea by Poseidon, who could endure the sight of it no longer."

But Aspasia shook her head in reproof. She might hate ugliness, and rubbed her hand surreptitiously against her mantle, but she could both endure and forget if the brain behind inspired her with respect.

x

Daphne, who had married a Cretan while the family was in exile and buried him in Athens long since as well as most of her children, lived in a large house in a quiet and more secluded quarter not far from the Agora. She was very old, and her doorman still more ancient and stone deaf. He stood with his hand on the pedestal of Hermes peering with rheumy eyes down the street. Zosmë groaned inwardly.

Xanthias ran forward to announce the visitors. The old man grumbled but stood aside for the ladies, and waved the slaves into his little room beside the door.

Zosmë and Aspasia threw back their veils and walked down the hallway to the court where they could see their hostess sitting near the altar sunning herself. She rose as they entered, a very tall straight old lady with black eyes still bright, and her scant white hair carefully arranged in one of the prevailing modes. She wore a black woolen chiton high in the neck and long in the sleeves, and a girdle of massive gold. Her cheeks were sunken but she had retained her front teeth. She was an imposing figure; and, thought Zosmë, she has a good handmaid.

She smiled a grim welcome and offered her cheek to Aspasia to kiss. "Sit down," she said, motioning to a marble bench opposite her chair. "I hope the sun will not be too strong for you, but my old bones need it." Her voice was harsh with age but still modulated.

Both would have preferred the shade of the pastas after their walk, but could hardly remonstrate; and while Aspasia described her father's last days and funeral to her aunt, Zosmë glanced about her with satisfaction.

This aula was still far short of Milesian standards, but a vast improvement on her own. There were no tapestries, but fine statues of Athenè, Apollo, and Artemis, the columns were beautifully fluted, and the walls of the portico painted with colors once bright but now faded to soft and harmonious tones. There were many marble chairs and benches and the altar was richly carved. In each corner stood an olive tree, planted no doubt when the house was built, in compliment to Athenè.

"I am admiring your house, O Daphne," said Zosmë, when the hostess turned to her politely. "I am sure that mine is the ugliest in Athens."

The old lady shrugged her bony shoulders. "What would you? The Athenians have little taste in anything but temples, and the people from whom you rent none at all. Moreover, they are as poor as charcoal burners, and lived, so gossip says, on olives and sardines. The father, who built the house, inherited many talents, but squandered them all. The rent you pay will enable them to live in comfort for years and have eels once a week for dinner. I hear they are charging you an outrageous price."

"Hippodamus has not told me," murmured Zosmë, who was suffused with a glow of pleasure at listening to gossip once more. "But if you never go out, O Daphne, how is it that you know so much of your neighbors' affairs?"

The old lady laughed maliciously. "Everything is known in Athens. What else have we women to talk about?"

"But I thought the women of Athens never visited one another? Never left the house save under the escort of the husband, and seldom then?"

"That is what the husbands think, and the world believes what men tell them. But as a matter of fact we slip in and out of one another's houses every day in the month; and as the men are talking eternally in the Agora, or the Lyceum, or some other of those sculptured resorts built in beauty for men only, and are never at home save to eat or sleep, and slaves for the most part are faithful, we visit whenever we choose. Of course we do not go far, rarely out of our own quarter, but the better streets are always deserted at certain hours, and a man does not spy on his wife unless he suspects her of misconduct. How is it, Zosmë, that you were allowed to come so far and without your husband?"

"Hippodamus is in the Piræus," said Zosmë demurely. "We too have faithful slaves. And of course we were veiled." She concluded it were wise to say nothing of the Agora, for she fancied this stern old lady would condone no violation of the major proprieties.

Daphne turned to her niece. "Why are you not married?" she demanded abruptly.

"I have been asked that question for nearly ten years," said Aspasia smiling. "I have only one answer: I do not wish to marry. My father understood and did not urge me."

"Then he was a fool. A woman may addle her brains with philosophy and still have a husband and children. It is her duty to the State. I had sixteen. Have you had lovers? Our Ionian women are notoriously voluptuous."

"I have not!" Aspasia's white skin turned scarlet and her eyes flashed fire.

Again the old lady shrugged her shoulders. "Then you too are a fool. What in the name of Aphrodite are you made of? And why did you come here? You cannot marry respectably in Athens, for that villain Pericles has placed all alien women, no matter what their birth and breeding, on a level with Metics, or worse. I am too old to care, but I have two daughters left and they weep all day. Their husbands are kind to them, and their friends faithful, but they are outcasts nevertheless. Our only hope is in Thucydides son of Melesias. If he succeeds in accomplishing the ostracism of Pericles, and the oligarchical party returns to power, that abominable law will be revoked."

"Is there any da—hope of that?" asked Aspasia.

"We pray and offer sacrifice to the gods that Pericles may be driven out of Athens. There is no telling what he will do next. He is mad for power and his only passion is its exercise. The greatest aristocrat, so he thinks, in all Hellas, he assumed the leadership of the Demos—with which he has as much sympathy as I have—because it is the most numerous and the strongest, and by flattering and coddling it he could rise to almost kingly power. They think he loves them and they are no more to that cold aristocrat than the puppets in a marionette show."

"I hear he hates his wife," said Zosmë, who cared little for politics and longed for more gossip. "Surely he cannot be too cold to care for some woman, and he must be sought by many."

"He cares for no woman—for nothing but power. If he were human I'd like him better. Perhaps one reason he is not," she added viciously, "is because he would have to take off his helmet if he made love to a woman, and he is never seen without it. His head is almost as high as the helmet itself. The comic poets have made all Athens laugh with the squibs that head has inspired."

"But he has a figure and a voice, O Daphne. Women are susceptible to both; and that voice would charm the snakes out of their holes."

"It is true, Zosmë, that women gossip about him eternally, even when they hate his politics, and I don't doubt he could have his pick if he chose. Many think him little short of the gods on Olympus, but not I. I've boxed his ears many times in this very aula. He was a passionate boy and a domineering one. He and my son Cadmus were always fighting, and are bitter enemies to-day— Ah! Here comes Zenophile, looking like Niobe as usual."

A tall woman in black had entered the aula. She came forward swiftly, casting curious glances at the strangers, and kissed her mother on the cheek. Daphne performed the introductions.

"My daughter Zenophile wife of Agelaus son of Nicanor, to Zosmë wife of the great architect Hippodamus of Miletus; and to Aspasia daughter of Axiochus—your cousin."

Zenophile gave each a wintry smile and took a chair beside her mother. She was not yet forty and had been very handsome, but her face was ravaged with grief, and her hair, twisted into a ragged knot, was streaked with white. She looked with cold disfavor at her beautiful cousin.

"So you have come to Athens to find a husband and enter the ranks of the hetæræ, even as I," she said. "Well, at least you will sin with your eyes open and not bear children in all innocence to be classed with the bastards in Piræus. I wish I had exposed mine on Hymettus! Now three have children of their own to blush for their grandmother, and my beautiful Galatea sits all day at her spinning-wheel and weeps because if she marries at all it must be with a Metic. And that she shall never do!" she added passionately. "Not if I strangle her with my own hands!"

"Why don't you take her to Miletus?" asked Aspasia. "You have many relatives there and she would soon find a husband."

Zenophile laughed harshly. "Do you suppose Agelaus would leave the Agora, and the excitement of politics here in Athens? Or that he would let me, who am so necessary to his comfort— and to nothing else!—go alone? The law has not affected him and he has already forgotten it. When an Athenian has men to talk to, beautiful youths to look at, and hetæræ to wanton with, what does he care for the tears of his wife, and one daughter more or less?"

The visitors felt exceedingly uncomfortable, and the hostess interposed hastily: "Galatea is only fifteen. Before her bloom fades Pericles may have fallen, and Thucydides is our friend. Has Agelaus brought home any news?"

"They do nothing but plot in secret. Pericles had another great triumph yesterday on the Pnyx. He would use the tribute money in the Delian Chest to build temples on the Acropolis, and six thousand men cheered him when he proposed it. But the Oligarchs are already whispering among those men that he merely wants control of that money to increase his own power, perhaps to make himself Tyrant in Athens; and that if Sparta— backed by all Hellas—declared war there would be no money in the treasury to equip and feed the army. Our only hope lies in his ostracism and on that hope we live. Pray Zeus it may come before Galatea fades."

Aspasia, forgetting the prerogative of her married friend, rose abruptly. "We must go now, dear aunt," she said, "for it is nearly noon."

"You will eat luncheon with me," said the old lady imperiously. "I have given the order. It will be served presently in the portico."

Zosmë, who was enjoying herself hugely, sent Aspasia an imploring glance, thanked her hostess sweetly, and accepted the invitation.

Aspasia, who liked neither her aunt nor her cousin and longed only to flee their presence, sat down with unruffled brow and murmured her pleasure.

"But I should like to see Galatea," she said. "Does she never leave the house even to see her grandmother?"

"Certainly she does. Zenophile, go bring her, and if she is in tears wash her face."

Zenophile frowned but rose obediently and departed. It was evident that Daphne wielded a Periclean power in her family.

XI

The conversation was desultory until Zenophile returned with her daughter. The girl was heavily veiled and Aspasia looked at her with interest, longing for the sight of a young face even if sad. But the face of the girl as her mother removed the veil and she approached to salute her grandmother, showed no evidence of tears. There was a roguish sparkle in her large black eyes and her cheeks were pink and rounded. She was small but well made and excessively pretty. Her black hair was confined with a blue ribbon, and as she threw off her mantle she revealed soft dimpled arms. Her white tunic, confined by a blue girdle, gave glimpses as she walked of one bare shapely leg.

The introductions were performed ceremoniously. Galatea returned Zosmë's smile shyly, and kissed her cousin with a gasp of surprise.

"Oh, but you are beautiful, Aspasia!" she whispered. "All the women and even the girls have been talking of you since yesterday, but I did not dream any but a goddess could be so lovely."

Aspasia, inured as she was, blushed at the girl's sincere admiration.

"May she show me the pastas and the paintings?" she asked her aunt. "I would see more of your beautiful house."

"Go," said Daphne, ignoring her daughter's frown. "But see

that you put no ideas into her head. Learning is not for her. She has enough to overcome without that."

"Not I!" said Aspasia gaily. "I had other young cousins in Miletus and I sought no pupils among them. I have had enough to do to fill my own head."

"And are you unhappy, dear Galatea?" she asked as they lingered in the pastas, the family gathering-place when the sun was too hot or the weather inclement. The chairs and sofas were cushioned and they sat down, grateful for the cool shade.

"Not always," said the girl, still staring at that white and copper beauty in stark admiration. "Why are you still so lovely, Aspasia? They say you are twenty-four. That seems very old to me."

Aspasia shrugged. "Because I have used my mind, not my body, I suppose. If I had married at fifteen and had eight children I should look like other women of my age."

"How old is your friend Zosmë? She looks older than you but still young, and is quite beautiful. I hear she has only one child. How is that?"

"You apparently hear everything! Zosmë is three years older than I. She was delicate in youth and did not marry as early as other girls. The great physician Hippocrates came from Cos to cure her. And then it was several years before she had a child. Little Archeptolemus is only four."

"But tell me why you have never married, Aspasia." The girl's eyes were brimming with curiosity. "You—who could have married many times over? And in Miletus where there are no cruel laws."

"O Zeus! How many times have I been asked that question?" She pinched Galatea's vivid cheek. "Because I did not want eight children, and prefer to talk to wise men. That you cannot understand, of course, so let us talk of something else. Are you pining for a husband yourself as you sit at your spinning-wheel?"

Galatea made a face at the spinning-wheel in the corner but answered frankly. "Of course I think of nothing else. I'd be quite willing to marry a Metic, if he were handsome and young and as rich as they say all Metics are. What difference? A girl must have a husband or why should she live at all?"

"Why indeed!" But Aspasia looked not unsympathetically at that eager pretty face, so ingenuous and yet so wise in the wisdom of her sex. She had received many confidences from her young cousins in Miletus and had shown an understanding of their primitive aspirations and desires that would have astonished the men who knew her only as a worshipful intellect. She was sometimes astonished at herself, but concluded that the mind needed variety and rest after too much exercise, lest it turn sterile.

"You could not marry a Metic," she said musingly. "Your parents would never consent."

Galatea glanced about her fearfully and approached her full fresh lips to the ear of this cousin whom she had trusted instinctively. "I'd run away," she whispered. "My slave Chloris is devoted to me and weeps at my fate more than I do."

"But Zenophile thinks that—ah—Pericles may fall and the law be revoked."

"I know naught of politics," said Galatea frowning, "except that Chloris, who gossips with the other slaves and has a lover, tells me that Pericles is popular and powerful and could laugh at his enemies if he ever laughed at all. Of course he might be assassinated—but the gods may protect him and I cannot wait. Oh, Aspasia, you are free to do as you will and Hippodamus must go daily to the Piræus! Will you not go with him and find me a husband?"

Aspasia laughed outright, then repented as the girl's face went blank with disappointment and two large tears rolled down her cheeks. "Do not weep," she said kindly. "I will consult Zosmë." She had no idea of committing herself, and rose thankfully as she saw her aunt walking slowly toward the eastern portico where the chairs had been arranged for luncheon.

But Galatea caught her hand. "Promise me!" she exclaimed passionately. "You can if you will! Any one may read in your face, in your proud bearing, that you do what you wish and laugh at authority. You look like a goddess, not a mere woman.

You—you look as Pallas Athenè must have looked when she walked the earth."

Aspasia flushed and stared. "But—Pallas Athenè is not the goddess of love, you know. I hope you do not pray to her, but to Aphrodite."

"Oh, do not quibble, Aspasia! Promise that you will find me a husband. I will hang myself with my girdle if you do not!"

She looks quite capable of it, thought Aspasia, who hardly knew which way to turn. It was all very well to encourage girlish confidences, but she was not a professional matchmaker.

"Listen," she said, as she took the girl by the arm and led her toward the portico where the slaves were already bringing in the tables. "It may be that I shall be able to arrange to send you to Miletus. My Aunt Tecmessa would welcome you, for all her children are married and she is lonely. I will speak to Hippodamus. But you must be reasonable and patient, and realize that it cannot be done in a day. Now I ask that promise of you. Do you give it?"

"Oh, yes, dear Aspasia, I will be patient! Oh, yes!" Her face was radiant again and she met her mother's cold glare with a laughing defiance.

XII

Zosmë's fears were groundless. Hippodamus heard nothing of their visit to the Agora. But two evenings later as they were all sitting on the roof watching Hymettus deepen from violet to purple, he said abruptly:

"It seems your presence in Athens is already known, Aspasia, and I think it strange, for I had spoken of it to no one; and of course Hæmon could not have gossipped, for when I sent him from Miletus I had not made up my mind to take you with us." (Zosmë and Aspasia lifted their fans.) "But this afternoon on my way home from the Piræus I stopped in at the Lyceum in the hope of meeting some of my old friends, and they had barely greeted me before they asked when they were to meet the celebrated Aspasia daughter of Axiochus of Miletus."

"The world is small," said Zosmë, being perhaps the first to utter that profound truth. "No doubt the slaves run from house to house with gossip. And after all we rode in chariots from the Piræus to Athens and had forgotten to put on our veils."

"So I noticed when you arrived at the house, but omitted to reprove you as it was a trying moment for all of us. But you surely met no one? The road and the streets were deserted, and every eye on the Pnyx was turned toward Pericles. Even he knows you are in Athens, Aspasia, and would converse with you."

Aspasia frowned. "I once had a wish to meet Pericles, but no longer. I called on my Aunt Daphne—"

"When? You should have waited for me!"

"But you are in the Piræus all day, Hippodamus, and my aunt is very old and would have been deeply offended if I had neglected her. Zosmë went with me and we were attended by two slaves besides Xanthias. Of course we were veiled, and, as you know, the streets are deserted during the morning hours. At her house I heard for the first time of that abominable law, moved by Pericles, whereby all who had not the honor of being born of two Athenian parents were cast out from the phratry and reduced to the level of Metics. And I witnessed the tragic results of that law. Zenophile, my cousin, who must have held herself proudly when she was one of the lawful matrons of Athens, now looks as if she had been cursed by the gods, and her pretty young daughter, Galatea, who has no hope of marrying in her own class, threatens to hang herself with her girdle if she cannot find a husband. I have no wish to meet a man so tyrannical and so unjust."

"I had forgotten that law," muttered Hippodamus, and once more he wished he had been firm in Miletus; until this moment he had cherished the hope of marrying Aspasia in Athens. "But you must not blame Pericles. He could not get any law passed if it were not agreeable to the Demos. It is safe to say that he knew of their wish to keep the ancient blood of Athens pure. The city owes its present greatness, its supremacy over all Hellas, to men born on the soil of Attica. Even Themistocles, although a plebeian, was born to an Athenian father. I do not approve of that law; but remember that Pericles is a profound politician as well as a great statesman—"

"And instigated that law to enhance his own popularity and power! I doubt if he cared an obol whether Athenians had foreign wives or not. As little as he cares for the misery he has inflicted. Nor do I believe for a moment that he could not have dissuaded the Demos even if the most determined among them had risen in the Ecclesia and expressed their desire to pass such a law. He could make them believe garlic is honey. You once said yourself, Hippodamus, that when they are under the spell of his voice he can sway them as he will. They seem to worship as well as fear him and I doubt if they ever have an idea he does not plant in their heads—"

"You are mistaken, Aspasia! The politics of Athens are peculiar to herself. Nowhere in all Hellas are the people so powerful as here; they think of little else than politics, and they think for themselves. It is fortunate for Pericles that he thinks with them. Great as he is, and superior in intellect and character to all men, even as Almighty Zeus is greater than he, he would be reduced to the rank of a mere citizen did he desert the Demos and ally himself with the Oligarchs."

"Oh, I have not impugned his wisdom, Hippodamus. He is as crafty as Pluto, to whom it is more fit to compare him than to Zeus—"

"You are unjust!" cried Hippodamus in wrath. "Like Pluto indeed! When he thinks only of the good of his fellow-citizens, and would save them not only from the wrath of the beneficent gods but from that dark journey across the Styx if he could— even as he has curbed Sparta and given them peace. And it is quite possible, O Aspasia, that he had profounder reasons than we know of for instigating that law. He is not the man to be cruel merely to gratify Athenian pride. As soon as I have time for a morning in the Agora I shall ask the opinions of my friends on the subject."

"Do," said Zosmë. "And meanwhile advise us about Galatea. Aspasia believes she should be sent to Miletus where Tecmessa could marry her properly. I cannot endure the horrible thought of that lovely young girl swinging like Phædra with her girdle about her neck. Surely you, dear Hippodamus, who always contrive to get what you want, can manage to rescue this poor child."

"I will speak to Agelaus." Hippodamus, appeased, took his wife's hand. "Even Pericles would approve, for he is the last man to wish the young to suffer, and if her father is obdurate I am sure he will reason with him." He was inspired diplomatically himself and added: "Pericles will be more inclined to interest himself, Aspasia, if you put the case before him yourself, and ask him to intercede with Agelaus."

"I do not wish to meet him," said Aspasia obstinately. "I dislike being rude and I could not refrain from telling him I think it absurd that a democracy should suffer a Tyrant in all but name, and that he takes a base advantage of his power. He no doubt would order me to return to Miletus forthwith, and I wish to remain in Athens."

"He would do nothing of the sort!" said Hippodamus indignantly. "Whatever he may be he is not vain and petty. He is frequently abused in public and has never yet deprived any one of the right of free speech. Moreover he is used to the tempers of women. He has had sufficient experience with his wife, and with Elpinike, sister of Kimon and daughter of Miltiades, a woman with a tongue and who hates him and does him what injury she can. He merely smiles when she seeks him out and abuses him, and tells her to go home and spin wool. He would smile at you also, but as at a beautiful spoiled child—Elpinike is old and ugly—and change the subject—"

"Oh!" Aspasia sprang to her feet and walked to the edge cf the roof to stare at the glory of amber and gold in the west.

"I am sorry Aspasia has conceived this dislike of Pericles," said Zosmë, "for I have a curiosity to meet him. And is it not time for you to give a banquet? Or must others pay you that compliment first? What is the etiquette in Athens?"

"I have been invited to banquets and symposia on three successive evenings, beginning to-morrow. I could not refuse although I should have been glad to do so, for I shall feel little like work in the Piræus on the following mornings. Athens has a reputation for sobriety, but they often drink many bowls of wine at symposia, and even wine mixed with two parts water when drunk in quantities does not make men feel like gods next day. But to decline would have been folly, for personal popularity means much in Athens and is not to be lightly foregone. Only a Pericles is strong enough to let it be known he will attend no symposia."

"What shall you tell him if he asks again to meet Aspasia?"

"That she is indisposed—until this fit wears off. This is quite unlike Aspasia. I have always believed her to be the most reasonable of women. Why should she assume this personal attitude to Pericles?"

"I have no idea. But you cannot ask to the house others who wish to meet her if she is supposed to be ill. Pericles might hear of it and visit his displeasure on you."

"O women! women! Such a thing would never occur to him —but you might let her think so; and that until she is prepared to meet him it would be wise not to invite others."

Zosmë dropped her fan and bent down to conceal a smile. Another clash of wills between Aspasia and Hippodamus. She wondered which would erect the trophy.

XIII

But certain men of Athens were determined to meet Aspasia, and as Pericles seemed to have forgotten his request, Hippodamus concluded to invite them. He was not yet prepared to outrage the proprieties of Athens by introducing women at a banquet and symposium, and merely let it be understood that on a certain morning he would be in the aula of his house with his wife and famous guest. Even this was unconventional enough, but they were foreigners, and Aspasia of Miletus was not as other women.

It was Aspasia's habit when about to appear in public to sit for an hour before her mirror of polished bronze while the anxious and often despairing Thera arranged and rearranged her hair, then to try on one mantle after another until convinced there was no further room for improvement. When she left her chamber she dismissed the subject from her mind.

She wore to-day over a linen chiton that swept her high instep, a long mantle of fine white wool wound closely about her body and leaving both arms bare, save for the lower left arm which supported one end of the garment. Thera had finally arranged her thick hair in a massive projection some two inches above the base of the head, and crowned it with a diadem of beaten copper. The thin clinging material of the mantle—a mere oblong of wool—showed every line and curve of her slender but statuesque body. As she took a final glance at herself in the mirror she arranged her classic features, so often lively and mischievous, into an expression of lofty and intellectual composure, and then went slowly down the stair to the aula.

Hippodamus, in a purple himation clasped on the shoulder with a large brooch of heavily wrought gold, and Zosmë in a tunic of yellow silk—a fabric novel even in eastern Greece—that fell in narrow pleatings to her feet, and was made with a shorter tunic curving above the waist and drooping on either side, her black hair rolled from ear to ear just above the base of the head and confined with three bands of gold, awaited the guests in the eastern portico; the sun was already high and hot although it was not yet eight o'clock.

Zosmë knew better than to ask Aspasia what she thought of her new frock, when that friend, so often as feminine and frivolous as herself, wore what she called her immortal expression; but she sighed and wished that one or two women, to whom she might exhibit her finery, were to be among the expected guests.

Socrates was the first to arrive. He had risen early and gone to the bath, arrayed himself in a new but still Spartan himation, and, on the advice of a friend, wore a chiton beneath it. Both were of unfashionable cut, the mantle barely reaching to the bony knees and the chiton (borrowed) falling too far below them. But he had oiled his hair and beard and even encased his feet in sandals.

Hippodamus, who respected intellect however housed, gave him a cordial greeting and presented him with as much ceremony as if he had been of the Eupatridæ, not the offspring of a humble sculptor and a midwife.

"Socrates the son of Sophroniscus to my wife Zosmë daughter of Hexæmerion, and Aspasia daughter of Axiochus of Miletus."

A warning glance flashed above Zosmë's smile, and Aspasia, regarding him steadily with no smile on her own lips, said formally:

"I have looked forward to this day, Socrates son of Sophroniscus, and hoped to meet you before now. But Hippodamus has been engaged in the Piræus, and we have been obliged to remain without company—in the house."

Socrates was no fool. Moreover he longed to assure her that it had been agreed among the friends of her guardian that no hint should be given him of her innocent breach of the conventions. He had also wrestled with his sudden infatuation for one so far above him, and concluded sadly that it were enough to be a philosopher and measure his intellect with hers.

He therefore replied with a certain humble dignity: "I have waited impatiently for this day, O illustrious Aspasia, since I heard some five days since that you were come to Athens, for I would discourse with you on many subjects. I have little knowledge of any and am ever seeking enlightenment. Let us then, O Aspasia, if you will, talk on one of profound interest to all seekers after truth; and which one so learned as you must have considered far more deeply than I. I tremble in matching my poor wits against yours, but I take my courage in my hands and ask you this: Can he be true who is also false?"

"O heaven!" said Zosmë to her husband from behind the shelter of a bunch of peacock feathers. "He has her by the nose already! Dialectics at eight in the morning! I'd rather cut a lock from my head and split the hairs. Is Socrates as modest as he pretends? I suspect him of irony."

"Perhaps you are right." Hippodamus drew her further along the portico. "I saw him frequently on my last visit to Athens—a year ago, is it not? But modesty is ever disarming, dear Zosmë, and as he has no intention that any man with whom he wishes to split hairs, as you call it, shall escape him, he is clever enough to pretend that he would learn and not teach. They always get the worst of it, but that does not prevent them from being beguiled. No doubt he learns something, but I have a suspicion, shared by others, that he aims to be ultimately known not only as the master dialectician but as the greatest philosopher of his time. Some scoff, and regard him merely as a bore; others would cross Athens in the hot sun of noonday to sit at his feet. Who knows? He is still a young man, hardly twenty-five. Personally I am little interested, being merely a practical architect and a man of business—"

"Thank the gods!" cried Zosmë with fervor. "And of one thing I am certain. If Aspasia ever marries it will not be with a dialectician. She likes those mental gymnastics, but when and where she chooses. She would not rise and go to bed with them. But looking at her now, who would think she was a woman who was also a girl, and often as mirthful as I?"

Hippodamus glanced at his difficult ward, and the sight set his mind at rest for the moment. Her eyes were glowing with the ardor of mental conflict, but the rest of her face was immobile, and her body had a curious stillness as if the life principle had deserted it to possess the brain alone. She stood erect near one of the columns, her hand touching it as lightly as if arrested in flight, and that still form, oddly enough, was not dwarfed by the pillar and looked like sculptured marble even more.

After all, he thought, that is her true self. A woman who can look like that is incapable of being wayward save in mere trifles. Of passion she has none.

Zosmë interrupted his complacent reflections. "Here come more of your friends—and these Athenians do know how to wear their clothes. Who is that one who looks as if he were already on a pedestal in the Agora?"

"That is Sophocles son of Sophilus, warrior, statesman, and tragic poet, and the handsomest man in Athens."

"Is he married?" asked Zosmë eagerly.

"He is. And remember," he said warningly, "no matchmaking. Aspasia cannot marry an Athenian."

He went forward to greet the group of men who awaited him at the entrance of the court. They were men of varying ages, although only one was elderly and one still in his twenties. Sophocles, now fifty, was the most remarkable in appearance. Tall, even for an Athenian, he was as straight as a "good ashen spear," and he wore his dark green mantle with an ease and grace that no dandy could rival. His features were calm and benignant, but the eyes keen and often humorous. Like other men of his day he wore his hair and beard short.

Beside him stood his inseparable friend Herodotus, the historian, born in Caria but now a sworn resident of Athens. His face was wrinkled and weather-beaten for he had travelled in many climes, but he possessed a merry eye.

Another, whom Hippodamus welcomed to his house, was Anaxagoras, also an Asiatic Greek, who, long since, had introduced Ionian philosophy to Athens and founded a school. He was the intimate friend of Pericles, and popular rumor credited him with having taught that ambitious statesman in his youth the advantages of a passionless countenance, and a lofty style of oratory devoid of flattery and humor; besides instructing him deeply in philosophy. He shared the unpopularity of his pupil with the oligarchical party and the priests of the temples, although they did not suspect that he had routed long since what superstitious fears of natural phenomena may have lingered in the astute mind of Pericles: referring them to a fixed and universal code of laws, not to the humors of the gods.

But he was too old a philosopher to give a thought to unpopularity, certainly not while under the ægis of Pericles; and his fine face, although furrowed with thought, was calm and kind. He glanced over the shoulder of Hippodamus at Aspasia, still absorbed in Socrates.

"I long to see her again," he said, "for I not only held her on my knee as a child—and even suffered her to pull my beard!— but I was the first to instruct her in philosophy. She knows my work, *On Nature,* as well as I myself. I would greet her— and your wife, Hippodamus, whom I also remember."

"I should have sent for you before this, O Anaxagoras, if I had not known you were in the country until to-day. Nor did I need to be importuned by Aspasia, dear friend of my father and of my own youth. Let us go forward."

Anaxagoras strode ahead, and after greeting Zosmë put his hands on Aspasia's shoulders, turned her round and kissed her brow. She was too exalted by intellectual converse to smile, but she flushed and her eyes filled with tears as she returned his kiss warmly.

"O dear Nous," she murmured, "you bring back my father. How I have longed to see you."

But Hippodamus was already introducing the other callers; not Herodotus, who was well known in Miletus, but Sophocles and men less famous but of consequence in Athens: Pausanias son of Zegræus, and Diophantes son of Artaphanes, men of learning and wealthy patrons of art; Cephalus of Syracuse; Prodicus, the great rhetor from Ceos; Polygnotus, whose fame as a painter had begun under Kimon; Ion of Chios, historian, tragic poet and lyricist; the three great architects, Mnesicles, Kallikrates and Ictinus, who remained but a moment; and the younger man, Thoron son of Timotheus.

Aspasia murmured her greetings, and as her eyes swept those distinguished faces she perceived a phenomenon not new in her experience. These men carried the intellectual and artistic torches of Athens, but their eyes radiated an intensity of admiration that was due not to what they had heard of her mental endowments, but to that spontaneous acknowledgment man ever gives to beauty and youth. That uncompromising masculine note drove straight at her feminine consciousness. A gay smile shattered the gravity of her face, her red mouth, like painted marble a moment before, broke into curves, and her luminous eyes flashed a mischievous response.

Once more Socrates shivered. He knew that every man present longed to kiss her; and so, alas! did he. He retired to the altar and endeavored to lose himself in philosophic meditation.

"You are come for discourse, O most illustrious men of Athens," said Aspasia. "But I fear Socrates has exhausted me. He is an expert at dialectics, and my mind felt as if turned into a two-edged sword to meet and clash with his. The release has made me feel almost frivolous—remember I am an Ionian!— and the pleasure of meeting those to whom I have long wished to listen has raised my spirits so high that they dance mockingly above what intellect I possess."

"A charming greeting to your humble admirers of Athens, O divine Aspasia," said Sophocles smiling. "We should have hastened to come here before this had not Pericles claimed Hippodamus by day and others by night. It was not even known you were coming until your arrival set all Athens on the tiptoe of excitement; but we are here now and shall come daily, to discourse or not as you wish. If Hippodamus must be absent, then your old friend Nous, his senior by so many years, shall take his place. Is that satisfactory, Hippodamus?"

Hippodamus nodded. Nous (Mind), as he was called familiarly, could take his place beyond doubt, and solve a problem that had given him anxiety; he knew that Aspasia would not long consent to remain in seclusion and he could not neglect his work. But uneasiness had returned. Intellect had apparently folded its wings for the day in that lovely head, turning on its round white throat from one to the other of these new and ardent admirers; most of them old enough to know better. Aspasia looked to him suspiciously like woman incarnate. And that young Thoron, once a "beauty," but now past his bloom, was staring at this human enigma of his as if he would eat her alive. The others, at least, had abated none of their natural dignity.

Thoron was the son of a rich landowner, and, as far as he knew, an estimable young man. He could drink deeply enough at symposia, but had never been accused of anything worse. When seen in the Agora it was always in the train of Socrates, or hanging on his words in the barber shop. At the last Olympic games he had won the foot-race. No more desirable husband could have been found for Aspasia if Pericles had not proposed that infernal law. For the moment he was inclined to curse his hero.

But he was not the man to lament the immutable, and meanwhile here was this handsome young man with his eyes of desire, and a young woman who looked by no means unapproachable. He determined to put a stop to it at once.

He strode over to the bemused Thoron and said amiably: "Will you walk about the portico with me, son of Timotheus? I would have a few words with you."

The young man frowned, for he had not yet had a word with this girl more beautiful than any youth in Athens, but he turned politely and walked down the gallery with his host.

The Greeks were nothing if not direct. "Thoron," said Hippodamus, "I see that you have fallen under the spell of Aspasia, as so many other men have done. But she is not for you, for she will marry no man—"

"She shall marry me!" cried the young Athenian, smiting his hand against a pillar. "I swore it by all the gods the moment I saw her—as she stood there looking as if she had descended from Olympus, and before she raised her face to old Nous and was suddenly human and tender. And when she smiled at us all—O Zeus! The blood in my veins turned to fire!"

"That has happened before—in Miletus. Many times!" said Hippodamus drily. "It was the real Aspasia you saw first. Her lighter mood is shallow and passing."

"That I'll not believe—nor doubt she has moods deeper still. She may be the most intellectual woman in Hellas—what of that? She is still a woman and the most beautiful I have ever seen."

"But remember that you have seen few women."

"I have seen them in the processions—women and young girls —and caught the sly glances of more than one. There is none to compare with her. I shall marry her—I swear it by Zeus and Poseidon! My father shall visit you to-morrow; in the Piræus if necessary. He denies me nothing, for I have not squandered his money and forced him to borrow of the bankers. If she will not listen he will ask Pericles to intercede for me—"

"Yes!" cried Hippodamus triumphantly. "And what will Pericles say to him? That Aspasia is a foreigner and cannot legally wed an Athenian."

The young man seemed to crumple visibly before his eyes. His legs shook and his face turned ashen.

"O Zeus!" he muttered. "O Zeus!"

"Aspasia will be no man's 'companion.' She is as proud as Athenè herself. So be warned and go now and do not see her again."

"And I cast a white bean into the jar for that law!" cried Thoron wildly. "I in my insensate Athenian pride! And thought Pericles greater than ever when he proposed it on the Bema, and told us—Oh, what did he not tell us! They are talking of ostracizing him, and if he goes Thucydides son of Melesias will revoke that law. I'll be the first to scratch the name of Pericles on an ostraka—"

"Thucydides could not revoke that law, for the Demos voted for it as one man, and the Demos would be as numerous under him as under Pericles. Nor do I believe for a moment that the Oligarchs will succeed in ostracizing Pericles, in spite of their machinations. Face the facts, young Thoron," he added coldly. "Aspasia is not for you."

"I'll not believe it!" He was once more erect, his face flushed and his eyes blazing. This time he smote his hands together, and with such force that a slave came running. "I will exile myself to Miletus and marry her there."

"And if Aspasia will not leave Athens, O Thoron, what then? For years she has wished to come here, to live here, and here she is determined to remain. She is not the woman to forego the conversation of the most brilliant men in all Hellas for a brief dream of love—"

"She was made for nothing else. And if she wants intellectual converse, am I not a pupil of Socrates?"

Hippodamus was too polite to laugh, but he turned his face aside.

"Aspasia is not the woman to be content with one man's converse," he said after a moment. "She has an insatiable mind, and she came here because she had exhausted every mind in Miletus. But let us be practical, Thoron. Even if Aspasia consented to marry you—and I know of nothing more unlikely—do you not realize that if you exiled yourself and married a foreigner, your father would disinherit you? He may deny you nothing now, for he is proud of you, and you have not been wild and extravagant. But you are his only son, and if you went into exile and begat children there who could not carry on his name and pay honor to his corpse when death claimed him, do you think he would ever forgive you? You would be an outcast and penniless. Would you invite the fate of other men, who, without fortune themselves, have married rich women and been treated like free-born servants in consequence? We all know of such marriages. It is not in woman to respect the man she houses and clothes and feeds."

"O Zeus!" cried poor Thoron. "O Zeus! Curse Pericles! There is no hope save in *his* exile. I'll begin my share in his undoing to-day!"

And he almost ran across the court, nearly overturning Socrates, and out of the house.

Hippodamus shrugged his philosophical shoulders. Pericles could take care of himself. And at least he should have no trouble with Aspasia on the score of this young fool. If she ever lost her own head it would not be over an undigested mass of impulses and passions, who showed as little control over himself as a boar running wild in the forest; she had dealt with too many such. If he had estimated the young man correctly in the first place he would not have put himself out to warn or dissuade.

XIV

Meanwhile—for Zosmë, handsome and sparkling, in spite of the dignity she never relaxed in public, was receiving her share of attention from men far too courteous to neglect the wife of their host—Anaxagoras had managed to draw Aspasia aside.

"My dear child," he said, "I wish you to meet Pericles, and shall bring him here to-morrow. You are my two best beloved pupils, and although it is unusual in Athens, I would have you become friends. Like all Athenians, he wishes to hold converse with Aspasia of Miletus—and he saw you on the day of your arrival when he stood on the Bema—"

"He saw me?"

"Yes, and would know you. He has asked me to be his ambassador, for Hippodamus, unaccountably, has extended no invitation. You will express your wishes to your guardian—"

"That I'll never do!" Aspasia's face had lost its gaiety and looked rigid. "I do not wish to meet him and I shall not."

"What!" He added sternly: "Your reasons, Aspasia. I have never known you as a woman of caprice."

She gave her reasons with due emphasis, her sweet voice hard and metallic.

When she had finished he said severely: "It is not for a Milesian, not even for you, O Aspasia, to come to Athens to pass judgment on the policies of a City State so unlike your own. Nor, above all, on the acts of Pericles, the greatest statesman of this or any time. I shall not condescend to explain his motives. It is enough that what he does is for the good of Athens—"

"But you too come under that law. You too are branded a foreigner."

"Foreigners may still come and go as they will; their liberty is in no way curtailed. If they may no longer vote that is naught to a philosopher who has never ascended the Pnyx. If they may no longer hold property they may rent—and be received in society. My little revenue comes from my birthplace, Clazomenæ, and I am still the chosen friend of Pericles."

"Oh, men! And they can take care of themselves. But what of the women?"

"Women?" said Anaxagoras vaguely.

"Yes, women, who were once legal wives and are now without status, and girls who cannot marry? Have I not told you of Zenophile and Galatea?"

"It is the fate of women to submit to the law as it is their fate and their duty to submit to their husbands."

"Yes, in Athens. Do you forget that you are an Ionian? You have lived too long in Athens, dear Nous. You were only in Miletus at intervals, and rarely visited any house but my father's. But surely you are human enough to pity those women who were born noble and are now on a level with the hetæræ."

It was the first time in her life she had used the word pity, and she paused and wondered at herself. Was it really pity, or merely anger—resentment against any infringement of personal liberty?

Anaxagoras echoed her almost as vaguely as before. "Pity? That is no sentiment for philosophers, nor for any reasonable Greek. We must accept life as we find it and be thankful it is no worse. Is a law which makes a few people unhappy comparable with the natural ills of our brief existence? Worse than old age and death? Your cousin and her daughter are still inmates of the house of Agelaus and treated no doubt with the same kindness as of old. If the girl cannot marry there are other ways of making herself useful, and youth soon passes. Statesmen do not take the foolish desires of girls into account when devising new laws for the good of the State. This is the first time you have disappointed me, Aspasia, and I pray it shall be the last. I am proud of you even as I am of Pericles, and you are the only one of your sex for whom I have ever had respect and admiration as well as love. I would have you become his friend, for your minds are in harmony and he is a very lonely man. I shall bring him here to-morrow, and you will greet him as one great mind greets another, putting aside prejudice and crude judgment as unworthy of you. If you fail me—and that is unthinkable—I shall cast you out from my affections and see you no more."

Aspasia shrugged her shoulders. "Very well," she said coldly. "I shall receive him for your sake, and because only a fool sacrifices friendship on the altar of personal prejudice. I shall also conceal my dislike. And now, dear Nous, we had better walk back; I have neglected the other guests too long. And at least eight more of your adopted compatriots have arrived."

xv

But on the whole it was a highly satisfactory day. Anaxagoras had restored the balance, and Aspasia permitted herself to be seated on a thronos, or chair of state, and discoursed for an hour on the rationalism of Xenophanes, that pioneer of Greek thought, to whose teachings and to those of his disciple Parmenides the Hellenes owed their deliverance from the dangers of the Orphic cult, and their progress toward reason and truth.

The lecture was followed by a sharp discussion between Aspasia and the irrepressible Socrates on the metaphysics of the great Elean, but the morning concluded on a lighter note. The guests were invited to remain for luncheon, served in the portico, and Herodotus related several of his incredible adventures while travelling in Tyre, Babylon, and Egypt. Sophocles, a rare honor from him, recited the third chorus in his forthcoming *Antigone: "Blest is the life that never tasted woe,"* his round deep voice filling the court and thrilling his hearers. Zosmë thought he might have selected something more cheerful, but on the whole was too sleepy to care.

As the guests were leaving for their homes and siesta, Socrates had a word alone with Aspasia.

"The Xenophanic argument in favor of one god has interested men little in comparison with his other teachings," he said. "I noticed, Aspasia, you ignored it to-day. Has your mind ever dwelt on it?"

"It is reasonable if not so picturesque. But somehow," she added musingly, "I cannot reject Pallas Athenè."

"Nor I when I look at you, O goddesslike Aspasia. But I have pondered sometimes on this theory. One can conceive of a god imperial and almighty, who created the world and all things in it, who exists in a form beyond the imagination of mortals; and I find him more comprehensible—more acceptable—than a Zeus, who, if he exists at all, is too like men in his lusts and caprices, superior only in power and immortality. There have been men of Earth more admirable than he: Solon, Aristides—possibly Pericles. Why should a creature so fallible, and often contemptible, be worshipped and feared? Would it not be more dignified—and rational—to believe in one god of infinite wisdom, and superior to the best of men below?"

"Yes, but the time is not ripe, Socrates. Take heed that you do not utter this heresy in the market-place, or you will be stoned."

"I have never spoken of it to any but you, Aspasia. Liberty of thought, as of speech, prevails in Athens, and the comic poets are allowed to hold the gods up to ridicule; but even here it would not be wise to hurl at the public what it is unable to digest. Even Xenophanes, save to a chosen few, did not press the point; he merely identified the one god with the cosmos, and his audiences were far more interested in his attacks on the Orphic mysteries and his warnings of their future enslavement to the Oligarchs and the priests of the temples did they obtain a firmer hold on the minds of the people. But this idea of one god, supreme, omnipotent, incomprehensible, made in his own image and not in that of man, haunts my mind now and again, although I like nothing I cannot analyze in the light of reason. But we will talk of this again, Aspasia, for discussion with you sharpens my wits."

Aspasia smiled faintly. She too was feeling the need of siesta. "Whenever you wish, Socrates. Go now with the others and return to-morrow."

XVI

Aspasia, after a dreamless night, rose before dawn, encased her feet in high shoes of soft leather, wrapped herself in a violet himation, and stole down the stair. She had carried out her program of taking a morning walk while Athens still slept, but had not thought it necessary to remind Hippodamus of that plan so suddenly conceived on Naxos.

Xanthias awaited her at the door with a lantern, whose light shone faintly through its sides of translucent horn as they walked briskly through the silent streets and left the city by the Diomeisan Gate; its keeper amenable to three obols.

Aspasia had made a discovery during her first walk beyond the walls that gave her even more pleasure than exercising her healthy body. In describing the glories and shortcomings of Athens no one had thought to tell her of the Attic air. It was of an incredible lightness and clarity, so buoyant that it seemed to lift the feet from the ground and to etherealize the blood in the veins. When the sun rose it was felt in all its perfection, but even in this dark moonless hour it surely was drier and finer than air could be anywhere else in the world. Even the gold and the silver and the green of the stars were brighter than eastern stars, and looked as if they would dance did Pan blow his pipes. On these fleet morning walks Aspasia never indulged in philosophical reflections and doubts. She preferred to believe in the gods and habited them in her favorite stars.

The road lay toward Marathon, and as Xanthias panted after her he was beset with alarms, and finally ventured to remonstrate; favorite slaves were permitted many liberties.

"You will not go to the battlefield, O Mistress? Ghosts of the dead, both Persians and Hellenes, haunt it from darkness till light. They say that the cries and the clash of arms, the groans of despair and the terrible roars of the victors freeze the blood—"

"Nonsense. Such things are not. They are old dames' tales told about the hearth on winter nights."

"Oh, no, O Mistress. There are many who have seen and heard—and been smitten with dread diseases that no physician can cure."

"Have you seen these victims? I thought not. And if you must be superstitious, remember that when Pluto gets hold of a shade he never lets go. The dead cross the Styx not to return. But be at peace. Marathon is too far even for me. I shall turn shortly."

"Better now, Mistress," he exclaimed excitedly. "I see a man approaching."

"Well, what of that? Have we not met many husbandmen?"

"But you have forgotten your veil. And this is not a husbandman, Mistress. He wears a helmet—O Zeus! It is the great Strategos Pericles! Turn, Mistress!"

"Why should I turn? Will he blight me?" But her voice shook slightly and her light step faltered. She raised her head higher and went on.

"But Hippodamus, O Mistress! What will he say if he hears? Here comes a mule-cart—another! The market-place will seethe with gossip within an hour. Draw your mantle over your face, O daughter of Axiochus—"

"Keep quiet!" said Aspasia imperiously. "I'll box your ears if you don't."

The sun had risen and glanced on the bronze helmet of Pericles, walking slowly toward them. His hands were clasped behind him, his eyes bent to the ground. If he had heard their voices he gave no sign. It was not until both he and Aspasia stood aside for a market cart and were within a foot of each other, that he raised his eyes and said softly:

"Pass on quickly, Aspasia. I would not have you the subject of gossip."

Another cart was approaching, but although his words sent a curious ripple over her nerves, she gave it a contemptuous glance, caring nothing for a power to harm that lay wholly outside her experience. Moreover the varying impulses inspired by this man were suddenly overwhelmed by curiosity.

"The mischief is done, O Pericles," she said lightly, "if mischief it be. What are such to us?"

"No one in Athens questions the sourccs of gossip if only he be given something to gossip about. The husbands who buy in the market listen to the gossip of the vendors, and the women to the gossip of their slaves."

But he did not attempt to pass and stood regarding her with his steady powerful eyes, dark brilliant eyes that were oddly alien in that cold passionless face. "How is it," he asked, "that Hippodamus permits you to walk abroad attended only by a slave?"

"I am not an Athenian woman to be dictated to," she answered haughtily. "And I have the habit of exercise. If you object to women walking abroad, even in the early morning when there are few eyes to see, why do you not build a gymnasium for them? They need exercise and fresh air as well as men."

Something strangely resembling a twinkle appeared in Pericles' eyes. "A good idea, for confinement sometimes makes women irritable. But I fear our Athenian husbands would not vote the money."

"Why not—if it would add to the peace of the house? Or is confinement conducive to torpor as well, and they fear that with blood flowing freely the women of Athens might begin to think?"

"Very likely." She had turned and they were walking toward the city, Xanthias almost groaning aloud in the rear. It is possible that if Pericles had faced the opposite direction he would have walked on, but he had had more or less experience with the determined caprices of women.

"And are you, Pericles," said Aspasia, unconsciously dropping the more formal address, "in agreement with these house tyrants?"

"Oh, I assure you, our Athenian husbands are kind to their families and exercise little tyranny. We have more happy marriages than possibly you believe, Aspasia, who come from Ionia, where women have far too much liberty. You must admit that the standard of behavior is lower in Eastern Hellas than in Athens, where women are protected."

"Women should be free to choose for themselves whether they will have lovers or not," said Aspasia coolly. "And at least the women of Ionia are not hypocrites, as your women must be—not for a moment do I believe there are no whispered scandals in Athens. My Aunt Daphne intimated as much."

"Quite true, Aspasia, but there would be more if women were permitted to run about the streets and the Agora, and meet men of whose existence they are now barely conscious. We pride ourselves on few divorces in Athens. Moreover the wife has many duties that keep her quiet and content for the most part. The house is a little world in itself, and there she has a power with which the husband seldom interferes."

"And that is all you think women are good for!" she exclaimed passionately. "I find it abominable. Women should be as free as men, and—I repeat—be in a position to choose for themselves."

"A singular doctrine, Aspasia, and one which I cannot endorse, women being what they are: ignorant and stupid for the most part. There is only one Aspasia."

"And why are they ignorant and stupid?" she demanded, unmollified. "If you would send the girls to school with the boys you might discover they were even more intelligent. But that would not suit the men, I suppose?"

"Probably not!" And for the first time he smiled, and his statuesque face was transfigured. His heavy mouth curved, lifting at the corners, and points of light danced in his eyes. He looked suddenly younger and more human, as if he had opened a window on a private sun to let its radiance dazzle the beholder. It was a smile seldom seen and like his golden voice never forgotten. "Do not preach revolution to these women, Aspasia," he said. "I have enough on my hands with the men."

Aspasia had drawn a sharp breath and dropped her thick eyelashes. "Is your task then a hard one, Pericles?" she asked softly.

"Yes, it is hard." The smile left his face. "The Athenians are the most difficult people in all Hellas to manage, for they are the cleverest and the most restless, the most fickle, energetic, and insatiable; they want something new to interest them every day. One secret of my power is that I keep their minds occupied, and they know that the Oligarchs have little resource."

"Is that the reason you will rebuild the temples on the Acropolis?" Aspasia looked full at him, now that she could do so undazzled.

"One—but not the only reason! I am not a poet and cannot express in mere speech my desire to see noble temples and statues rise once more on 'the city,' as we still call the Acropolis. Not only will they give work to hundreds of freemen as well as to slaves—slaves not all owned by the State, but by citizens who permit them to work for hire that one day they may be enabled to buy their freedom—but it will elevate the meanest politician among us to gaze daily upon those lofty and exquisite works of art I and my architects and sculptors have in mind."

He hesitated, then met her rapt gaze and continued:

"And I too, Aspasia! I walk at night in the Agora or among the groves and columns of Academe when I cannot sleep, and peace comes to me. When I may look up to an Acropolis more awe-inspiring in its beauty than it ever was under the old kings or Pisistratus, my *self* perhaps will pass into that immortal beauty and become one with it. The wasp-stings of life may be forgotten for a few exalted moments, and I shall ask no more."

Aspasia felt herself stirred by a deeper sympathy than any she had ever experienced. Indeed, sympathy had rarely stirred her, for the people with whom she had passed her life had been fortunate, and content enough; with all of ease in their private lives and given to few public plaints save of the exactions of the Athenian garrison and the large sums demanded for the Delian Chest. Even her response to Galatea had been little more than excited interest.

"Are you lonely, Pericles?" she whispered. "Would you have my friendship?"

His eyes flashed round to hers, so soft and alluring, but there was no smile in their impenetrable depths.

"Yes," he said, "I would have your friendship, Aspasia. I had not dared even to hope to hear you talk, for until last night Hippodamus had not asked me to his house, and I knew he had asked other men. I had thought that possibly you, like many others, might be prejudiced."

"I hated you," she said frankly. "Some day I'll tell you why, but not now. But I hate you no longer, for I see that I have misjudged you. Friendship is the most sacred bond that may exist between mortals, and only the Greeks know its deeper meanings. I would have your friendship, Pericles, and not because Nous wishes it, but of my own will. This is a compact. Shall we shake hands?"

He took her hand in his, while Xanthias looked wildly up and down the road. He did not tremble as Socrates had done, but grasped it firmly and looked steadily into her glowing face.

"You are very innocent, Aspasia, in spite of your wisdom," he said sadly. "But I shall value your friendship more than any gift the gods could bestow, and shall keep it—if they permit."

"Why should you not keep it? And how much do you believe in the gods?" she asked gaily, escaping instinctively from that brief mood of solemnity.

He smiled slightly. "As much as you do, I imagine, O pupil of Anaxagoras. But the old forms come naturally to the lips; nor would it be wise in Athens to forget them. And they are very graceful. When we dismiss the gods from our vocabularies language will be the poorer."

She made him talk of Athens and the temples and buildings he had already erected. But she exclaimed with sudden irrelevance:

"Is the air so light anywhere else in the world? I feel as if my feet were winged. Is it true, Pericles, that you saw me from the Bema?"

"Yes. I fear that for a moment I saw no one else. I also saw you at your window and on the roof that night."

"Ah? How could that be? I had pulled my mantle over my

face. How could you guess that was my room? Or that I would walk on the roof at night?"

"A man has sometimes intuitions, and the moon was very bright. And now, Aspasia, we are approaching the gates and I shall leave you. We must not walk through the streets together. I shall present myself at the house of Hippodamus this morning, but, I fear, later than the others. I have a consultation with my architects that may detain me."

She nodded and entered the city. Xanthias' agonized voice reached her.

"For the love of Hera, Mistress, draw your mantle over your face! We have never been so late. You walked as if you had wet clay in your shoes."

And this time Aspasia indulged him.

XVII

There was no one in the aula but Archeptolemus, who was racing up and down dragging his toy cart and shouting at the top of his voice. Two house weasels, exterminators of mice, were almost as excited.

The boy took no notice of Aspasia and she went directly to the bath, a room behind the pastas containing a marble trough and a tripod upholding an apparatus for heating water. Thera was peering anxiously from the door.

"You are late, O Mistress," she said, while Aspasia began to disrobe hastily. "I feared that boy would awaken the household. And you forgot your veil. Did any one recognize you?"

But Aspasia would not answer. She took from the maid a handful of the refined earth imported from Cimolus for those wealthy enough to dispense with ashes or lye, scoured her body delicately, and Thera poured hot and cold water over her from two large jars. The day for luxurious bathing was yet to dawn, and ablutions were perfunctory and hurried.

When she had been rubbed dry she gave her handmaid a curt order not to disturb her until summoned and went up to her room.

It was her habit after her walk and bath to lie down until it was time to join the family at the morning meal, but to-day she felt no inclination to rest, and walked aimlessly about the room. She was vaguely dissatisfied with herself and it was a sensation to which she was unaccustomed. Had she succumbed too quickly to that unique personality, forgetting her well-founded dislike and disapproval? Had she been momentarily enslaved by the magic of that voice—and smile!—or by something noble and infinitely superior in the man which put to shame hasty prejudice?

But to offer him her friendship—a gift she had reserved for a few chosen spirits! When she had shaken hands with Socrates it had been merely a good-natured impulse, not with any intention of admitting him to intimacy. But when she had placed her hand in Pericles' it was to cement the most sacred human bond known to the Greeks. Love between men and women was either a transitory thing, founded mainly on lust, or a calm affection between husband and wife, and of no importance save for comfort and service to the State. But friendship glowed with an immortal fire, even though the clear-sighted Greek was never blind to its advantages.

And it should be founded on long knowledge of the character of each, and mutual soundings; not offered and accepted recklessly by two people superficially attracted. She might on further acquaintance find much in Pericles to dislike and distrust, and he in her: she had never assumed complete virtue in herself, knowing that she was wayward and capricious and sometimes fickle. He might weigh her in the scales of his cold calm judgment and decide that she had nothing to give him but philosophical converse, and she might come to hate him as a supercilious, arrogant, too-aloof, and wholly detestable man.

What unprecedented impulse had moved her to invite him to enter into the most hallowed and complicated of human relationships? And what had moved him to respond with equal spontaneity? Was it mere courtesy, reluctance to snub a young and beautiful woman?

She turned hot from instep to brow at the thought.

But hardly. He too knew the sacredness of that compact. Moreover had he not talked freely to her of his trials and aspirations, given her a glimpse of his secret life? That was not like

Pericles as he was known to the world. No, he must have recognized something secret and responsive in her that commanded his confidence as well as his liking; and once more a glow suffused her, this time more agreeably. And of course he knew that mentally they would meet on common ground.

But of what use, after all? How often would they talk alone? If he came every morning to the house—very unlikely, for he appeared to be the only Athenian of his class who had more to do than amuse himself with intellectual converse—he would be but one of many. And if they met during their morning walks it would soon be all over Athens. She had no desire to be the subject of vulgar gossip and innuendoes, not only for her own sake but for that of her amiable guardians. She forgot her willingness to live alone in Athens. What had been too remote then to consider seemed a very concrete and active principle to-day. And she had dwelt on a pedestal too long.

Life had seemed very simple before to a girl whose highest pleasure had been discourse with wise men, and whose every need was supplied by slaves who came running when she clapped her hands. She had had her way always, stepping lightly over such obstacles as disapproving aunts or envious acquaintance would have reared in her path. Her experience had been that if she set her mind on a goal she had but to saunter toward it, unless indeed it rushed toward her. Other women might be thwarted by jealous or unpleasant husbands, or unfaithful lovers, or unmanageable children, or empty money chests, or bodily ills. But she dwelt in a world apart. Nor had she been balked in her friendships. In her father's aula she had talked with men alone and searched the inmost recesses of their minds.

But this could not be done in Athens.

Even if Pericles called in the afternoon Zosmë would be there for convention's sake, and no doubt would send a slave running for Anaxagoras.

She stamped her foot, angry and at a loss. Of all the men she had met she desired to fathom Pericles, whether she ultimately hated him or not. Why could he not have been born a Milesian? But then he would not have been Pericles. No city but Athens could have bred him. Why could she not have been born in Athens? She stamped her foot again as she realized that her thoughts were flying about like some silly girl's who had no reason to guide her.

She clapped her hands and Thera entered promptly.

"It is time, O Mistress," she said; "the Master is crossing the aula. I must twist up your hair quickly."

Aspasia boxed her ears.

XVIII

If Hippodamus suspected that Aspasia indulged in morning walks he thought it wise to make no inquiries. Like many family men who trust in all important essentials the women of their household, he found it a good plan to be blind to what might affect his peace should he feel it his duty to remonstrate.

As he stood by the table in the portico eating his frugal breakfast of fruit, and bread dipped in wine, he remarked casually that he had obeyed her behest and sent Hæmon the night before to invite Pericles to call as soon as he found it convenient.

"He replied that he would call this morning," he added. "How is it, Aspasia, that you have decided to receive this monster?"

"Nous threatened never to speak to me again," she replied indifferently. "And that, of course, left me no choice."

"I shall meet his wife Olympias," said Zosmë with determination. "She inspires me with curiosity, and I long to see if her clothes are finer than mine. Pericles can manage it. Daphne says that women see far more of one another in Athens than we were led to believe."

"Ah!" said Hippodamus. "Ah. Well, that is harmless enough."

"You will go with me, will you not, Aspasia?" asked Zosmë.

"I have not the slightest curiosity to meet Olympias," said Aspasia coldly. "And I cannot understand your own. Have we not the greatest men in Athens to talk to? I find them even more interesting that I expected. What have secluded women to talk about?"

"Gossip, dear Aspasia, gossip. You know you enjoy it yourself."

Aspasia shrugged her shoulders. She was in a mood to forget there was anything feminine about her.

"Have you spoken to Agelaus about Galatea?" asked Zosmë of her husband; and Aspasia blushed, remembering she had forgotten her young cousin earlier that morning.

"He attended my banquet night before last and I had a word alone with him. He did not seem inclined to take my suggestion favorably, especially as he knew of no one with whom to send her. And, like other fools, he is a follower of Thucydides and believes that Pericles will be ostracized in the eighth prytany of next year."

"Next year!" said Zosmë lightly. "Anything may happen between now and then. Anthesterion is ten months hence."

"The public agitation for his ostracism will begin two months earlier—in all public places, but I am told that the secret machinations of the Oligarchs are incessant. If they are successful, Aspasia," he added with a smile, "you will bear your share of the blame."

"I?" Aspasia threw her bread to the dogs, who were prowling about, it being their mission to clean up the floor. "What do you mean?" Her dark narrow brows bent in a frown that hid the sudden fear in her eyes.

"That young fool, Thoron, is mad for love of you, and vows that Pericles shall be driven from Athens."

"Love of me? I was barely conscious of his presence."

"But he was of yours! It is a wonder you did not hear him shout."

"You should have reasoned with him."

"I did, and made as much impression as on Hermes at the door. You made one more enemy for Pericles, and a strong one, for he is popular with his friends. But no doubt that rejoices you."

Aspasia was thinking rapidly. She had offered this man her friendship. "Tell Thoron to return," she said. "I will engage to turn him from his purpose, or at least keep him quiet. Pericles is the protector of Nous," she added hastily. "I cannot have my old friend driven out."

"Fire is a dangerous plaything. Better let Thoron go his way.

I do not believe that Pericles is in any danger—and I have discussed the matter—"

"Send for Thoron," said Aspasia imperiously.

XIX

She was in no mood this morning to sit on a thronos and discourse on Truth, Excellence, Justice, Courage, Honor, Friendship, Rhetoric, Beauty, or any of those subjects Athenians loved to argue over hour upon hour. Moreover it had never been her habit to monopolize the stage too often, knowing that man was usually more ready to hear himself talk than to listen.

She started a discussion between Socrates and Protagoras, the Thracian sophist, now in Athens and reaping a rich harvest among ambitious young men who desired to shine in politics and dialectics; to learn, so it was rumored, for sophists were unpopular, "how to make the worse appear the better cause." These two men inevitably drew a group of listeners. Sophocles was induced to recite his *Nausicaa*, in which he had taken the part of the Phæacian princess, and, with a still larger group, was safely disposed of for an hour. Herodotus was always sure of an audience and always willing to talk.

Damon, the distinguished sophist, now an old man returned from exile, who had instructed Pericles in music and the art of political contest, and Zeno the Elean, and disciple of Parmenides, who, with Anaxagoras, had bent the youthful mind of the great Strategos to philosophy, were two of the many newcomers this morning, and Aspasia engaged them in conversation, artfully demanding to be instructed in Athenian politics, and learning much of Pericles.

Hippodamus was away at his task in the Piræus. Zosmë had attached herself to the Herodotus group as involving the minimum of mental strain. Anaxagoras, who had arrived promptly at eight o'clock, and been hastily initiated into Aspasia's tactics for the day, walked with benignant mien from group to group, placating Protagoras when driven to desperation by the antagonist who could ask more questions than any man in history; applauding Sophocles; inciting Herodotus when even his well-springs threatened to run dry.

A group of young men entered and passed quickly from Zosmë to Aspasia. They were by no means attracted by her intellectual reputation, for, like the comic poets later, they were inclined to be resentful of this encroachment upon a strictly masculine prerogative; but Thoron the day before had rushed into the palæstra, where they were watching Acestorides, and poured out his madness. They were curious to see for themselves the woman who could provoke such a holocaust. It was new in their experience.

Aspasia recognized them as the same gaily-dressed young officers who had striven to penetrate her veil on that memorable day in the Agora. She also guessed why they had come, and gave them her sweetest smile, handing Damon and Zeno over to Anaxagoras after he had completed the introduction.

"We are come to offer our homage, O renowned Aspasia," said Pittacus the son of Olympodorus, "for your fame is great in Hellas."

"And I am greatly honored, O Pittacus; and made happy, for there are few of my age here to-day. Yesterday Thoron son of Timotheus, came, but left before I could exchange a word with him."

She looked guilelessly from one face to another and saw a glint come into that semicircle of eyes.

"It is true, O Aspasia, that he left quickly. A sudden illness attacked him."

"Illness? He looked so handsome and healthy. I hope it was not serious and that he will return."

"He will return no doubt if you wish it," said Pittacus coldly. "And I doubt if he recovers unless you do."

"Ah? I do not understand." Aspasia's straight brows assumed a curve. "I am glad he did not remain for luncheon, or Zosmë wife of Hippodamus would be distressed."

"His illness was not an indigestion of the body, O Aspasia. He would marry you and this unjust law of Pericles' forbids it."

"Ah!" said Aspasia again. "That was indeed a sudden madness—when he hardly had time to hear my voice!"

"But he had looked at you, O Aspasia," said another of the young men eagerly. "And now we understand, although we

laughed at him yesterday. Now we shall write the name of—"
A pinch made him finish lamely: "do all in our power to help
him."

Aspasia felt a sudden sensation of chill, but she smiled and
answered brightly: "Is it not unusual in Athens for a man to
choose his own wife? Even in Miletus it is the father who
selects the girl he would have his son marry, although he rarely
imposes his will if the son is not satisfied with his choice. But I
have heard of no such indulgence in Athenian fathers."

"True, O Aspasia, but Thoron's father denies him little. And
although he is young to marry, Timotheus son of Sopolis would
speak to Hippodamus to-day were it not for the law."

Aspasia appeared to muse. She said in a moment: "But I
had never cared to marry, even in Miletus, where no husband
would forbid me to hold converse with any man I wished—receive many, even as here." She waved her hand at her distinguished visitors, some thirty in number, scattered about three
sides of the peristyle. "I fear I could not live the life of
Athenian women—confined to the women's quarters when there
were men in the house."

She saw those hard eyes grow more friendly, and Pittacus replied: "If Thoron had the good fortune to marry one so illustrious be sure he would not expect her to live like other women.
His doors would be open, as yours are to-day, to all men of
Athens worthy to converse with himself and Aspasia."

"He is very handsome," said Aspasia musingly, her eyes on
her fan. "And young. And wealthy"; this last specification inducing no shock of surprise, for the Greeks were ever practical.

"He is all that," said Pittacus; "and more. He is a winner of
games and a philosopher and temperate—for he listens to Socrates. May I tell him he need not despair, Aspasia?"

She answered demurely: "But I had never intended to marry."

"That no man can believe. We are almost dumb with wonder
that no man's siege has been successful before this."

"But I am twenty-four. Think of all the beautiful young
girls!"

"*Fools*—when they *are* beautiful. And that no man knows
until he is wed to one of them. Thank the gods the law does

not force us to marry before we are thirty. We'd not marry at all did not the law and custom compel us—for there is only one Aspasia."

Again she felt as if the bright morning had turned cold: she had heard that same remark but a few hours since. And she was playing a dangerous game; there seemed nothing to do, however, but to go on with it and trust to time and her wits. She raised her eyes and gave a little sigh.

"Will you ask Thoron to return? I do not know—I cannot tell—that dreadful law—but at least I should like to discuss certain great subjects with him. And I am sorrowful to think that I have made any one unhappy. Will you ask him to come to-morrow?"

"I will, O Aspasia, and take the news to his father's country-place, where he fled on his horse yesterday—no doubt to beat his head against the trees!"

"Oh, go soon!" cried Aspasia gaily, "for I would not have him disfigured. Is not that Pericles son of Xanthippus entering?" She hoped that her tone was impersonal and her cheeks still white.

"May Zeus smite him!" she heard one man mutter, and another said with a laugh: "No doubt you recognized him by his helmet, for, peace or war, it never leaves his head. All Athens believes that he sleeps in it."

Aspasia restrained herself from breaking her fan over *his* head, and murmured vaguely: "Oh? How strange. But you will not forget my message, O Pittacus?"

"We go now, great daughter of Axiochus, and will return with our friend to-morrow." And they left precipitately, giving Pericles a wide berth and not glancing in his direction.

xx

Anaxagoras had gone forward at once to greet Pericles, followed by Damon and Zeno, and they held him in converse an unconscionable time.

Zosmë left the circle of Herodotus and joined Aspasia, who stood before the pastas and facing the entrance, alone for the moment.

"He comes, the great man!" she said. "And the diversion is welcome. Herodotus is now reciting Homer, and I had enough of him in my school-days. I am devoured by curiosity to see how you will greet this man whom you so much dislike."

"I have never failed in courtesy, I hope," said Aspasia coldly. "He is in our house, is he not?"

"You look rather tired. Are you going to receive this mob every day?"

"Certainly. For what else did I come to Athens? And I have learned much from Damon and Zeno this morning."

"Oh, learn! But if you think you will learn everything by talking to ugly old philosophers you are mistaken. They are permitting him to approach us at last."

She glanced down at her embroidered mantle, thrust out a sandal encrusted with gold, and gave a swift pat to her hair. Aspasia looked calmly into Pericles' eyes as Anaxagoras introduced him sonorously.

"I salute you, O Pericles son of Xanthippus," said Zosmë with warm graciousness. "And my husband regrets that he cannot be here to greet you in his own house."

"It has been my pleasure to greet him in mine," said the Strategos with equal graciousness and smiling with his eyes. "And I have enjoyed many hours with him in Piræus. He is a great architect, O Zosmë, and the most original perhaps of his time. His conception of laying out cities on straight lines is both new and practical, and, I doubt not, will be pursued for years to come. I have in mind a Pan-Hellenic colony on our Italiot coast to be called Thurii, and Hippodamus has promised to build it."

"O Hera!" exclaimed Zosmë. "That means I shall have to go too!"

"But not yet, O Zosmë, for he will be at least two years in the Piræus, and by that time you may be tired of Athens."

"But then I should like to return to Miletus, where I have many friends of my own sex. Here you have no society for women."

"That is unfortunate, but why should you complain when the most distinguished men of Athens will come here every day?"

"I do not delude myself. They come to see Aspasia, not me. And I like my own sex." She gave him a swift searching glance. He looked formidable in spite of his graceful courtesy. Nevertheless she ventured. "I should like greatly to meet your wife Olympias, O Pericles," she said with the smooth audacity of a beautiful woman. "Would the earth rock if I called on her?"

The smile left his eyes but he replied suavely: "Olympias no doubt will be glad to receive you. She receives whom she will. I'll send her a message when I return to the house."

"Do you hear, Aspasia?" she cried. "I shall call on Olympias to-day."

Aspasia turned from Anaxagoras and replied absently: "Yes? But you have given me no time to add my greetings to yours. I too would welcome Pericles son of Xanthippus, and would ask him which he considers the higher virtue, moral courage or courage in war?"

Pericles shot her a reproachful glance. Zosmë threw out her hands in despair.

"O Aspasia! Offer the Strategos a lighter fare! I know from Hippodamus that he has been hard at work all morning, and surely, like other mortals, he needs relaxation. Even the gods are said to play."

"I assumed that Pericles had come for discourse." Aspasia spoke rather sulkily; she felt curiously at a loss. "Perhaps he would rather listen to Herodotus."

"I know every one of Herodotus' stories word by word." Pericles looked as if on the verge of laughter. "And I shall be frank and say that I take no particular enjoyment in dialectics. I was duly instructed by Zeno and have found them useful, but I am too busy to keep myself in practice. But I shall come some morning and hear you discourse. This call must be brief, for I left two angry architects in my house."

"Oh!" To Aspasia's annoyance she heard the disconcerted note in her voice and felt appeal in her eyes. His answered hers irresistibly. Zosmë, as keen as women ever have been and ever will be, felt a vibration in the atmosphere.

Oho! she thought. I wonder what *he* has to teach?

She said aloud: "We are foreigners, O Pericles, and need not too ceremoniously observe the customs of Athens. Will you not dine with us this evening? Hippodamus says he will neither attend nor give symposia for the moment; he likes a long night for sleep when he has work to do in the day. But—if you will—"

Another light had come into Pericles' eyes. He looked grateful, almost happy. But he answered quietly: "Yes, I will come, Zosmë. I know of nothing that would give me more pleasure."

He looked at Aspasia, who was looking at her fan. She raised her eyes in a moment and smiled brilliantly. "You will make us believe we are again in Miletus," she said, "where friends often assemble for dinner and women are not locked up like children in another part of the house." Her eyes wavered. "But I see Socrates approaching. No doubt he would speak with you."

Pericles suppressed a groan. A passionate lover of beauty and art, he hated ugliness in any form; and although he was willing to concede that Socrates was the most remarkable young man in Athens, he found him an offense to look at, and the creature with his eternal probing bored him.

"I must go," he said hurriedly. "Until this evening then, O Zosmë and Aspasia."

XXI

The callers had drifted out one by one or in groups as the sun reached its zenith, for guests could not expect to remain for luncheon when the master of the house was absent. Nor had Zosmë, who was a thrifty housewife, any intention of feeding them daily. She did them the justice to believe they cared more for conversation than for eating, but prices were higher in Athens than in Miletus, and she and Hæmon had had a serious discussion that morning. Hippodamus was wealthy, and her own fortune, inherited from a family of merchant princes, even larger, to say nothing of that of Aspasia, who bore her share of the expenses; but that was no reason for not practicing economy in the right place. Once a week she would give carnal sustenance to these mighty intellects but no oftener.

Quite another matter possessed her mind however as she sat alone with her friend in the aula, delicately dismembering a quail with her fingers. When the slaves had left she said abruptly: "Where had you and Pericles met before?"

Aspasia knocked over a goblet of water on one of the dogs. "What do you mean?" she asked, startled.

"I am not to be deceived, nor is it like you to be deceitful, Aspasia."

"I am not deceitful. But this is the first time I have been alone with you to-day. I walk every morning before sunrise, and to-day I happened to meet him." But she frowned, for she had intended to keep that meeting as secret as she had kept her dream, although she talked freely to Zosmë of most things.

Zosmë's eyes were round. "A walk before sunrise! What energy! I hope Xanthias goes with you."

"Certainly. And until to-day I have met no one. But this morning I met Pericles beyond the city. He, too, appears to feel the need of exercise, and, as you know, rarely shows himself in public."

"But how did you happen to speak? Anaxagoras was not there to introduce you!"

"I hardly know." Aspasia's voice fell with too light a note on Zosmë's sharp ears. "We almost ran into each other as we stood out of the way of a mule-cart. It seemed natural to speak."

"What did you talk about?" asked Zosmë eagerly.

"Oh—I believe he talked about his other architects, and he told me something of the temples to be erected on the Acropolis."

"Are they to be Ionic or Doric?"

"Ah—if he said, I have forgotten"; and Zosmë smiled wisely. "I suppose he preferred to discuss Truth and Excellence, even before breakfast."

"What could be more interesting?"

"Not to him. He gave you to understand quite finally that he hated dialectics. It is pleasant to think we shall not have them at dinner to-night. Do you dislike him as much as you did before you met him?"

"I neither like nor dislike him," said Aspasia coldly. "And if Nous believes him to be a wise and just man, I am willing to wait until I have been longer in Athens before judging him my-self. Certainly his manners are fine and without arrogance."

"I think him the most interesting man I have ever met here, although he rather frightens me. He not only has kingly man-ners and dazzling eyes but he gives the impression that he re-serves his discourses for the Bema. It is wonderful to know there is one man in Athens too busy to talk."

"Did you invite him to dinner to look at him?"

"No, merely to see what he looks like without his helmet."

But she wondered just what had been her reason, and sud-denly felt apprehensive. Divorces were easily arranged. A man had but to send his wife back to her relations and restore her dowry; there would be no such match in all Hellas for Aspasia were it not for that law. . . . She made up her mind to watch him to-night, and if she concluded that Aspasia had roused some-thing less frigid than his intellect she would see that her charge did not meet him again.

The slaves brought in the honey-cakes, fruit, and salted al-monds. Archeptolemus, escaping from his nurse, came running for his share, and conversation was at an end.

When they were walking toward the pastas she said: "I go later to visit Olympias. Will you go with me?"

"You will excuse me, dear Zosmë," said Aspasia with elaborate politeness. "I have not unrolled a book since I have been in Athens, and before to-morrow I must read over a work of Phintias."

Zosmë made a grimace. "I prefer my way of spending the afternoon!" She waved her hand and disappeared into the thalamos.

XXII

Aspasia opened the chest containing her library and took out a roll at random; she had already forgotten Phintias, and merely wished to restore her poise, so unaccountably disturbed, by men-tal abstraction.

It proved to be a volume of Pindar, and although she was in no mood for poetry, and despised Pindar for his childlike faith in the gods, and his shrewd bargaining with victorious athletes, still he wrote greatly even on trivial subjects, and ignored the foolish emotions. Had the author been Sappho she would have flung the book back into the chest.

She leaned one elbow on the arm of her chair and began to unroll the papyrus, her eyes glancing idly over the Pythian odes until they were held by the lines:

" 'Son of Philyra, leave thy hallowed course and look with wonder at a woman's mighty spirit and power. See what a contest she is waging with undaunted head—this maiden with a soul that no fear can overwhelm. From what mortal being was she born? From what race has she been reft, that she should be dwelling in the hollows of the shadowy mountains? And she is putting to the test a strength that is inexhaustible. Is it right to lay an ennobling hand upon her? aye, and by consorting with her to cull the honey-sweet flower of love?' . . . So saying he prompted the god to accomplish the sweet fulfillment of wedlock. Swift is the achievement, and short the ways of the gods when they are bent on speed. That very day decided all, and they twain were made one in Libya's golden chamber, where she guardeth a city that is fair indeed and is famous in athletic contests."

Aspasia glared at the closely written characters without paragraph or punctuation; but not at the difficulties that strewed the ways of learning in those days. She was well used to that. Oh, no. A curious feeling of languor had overcome her, and an inclination to dream. And yet she had once read that ode to her father, she remembered, and thrilled to nothing but the music of the lines. Nor had Sappho, in that singer's most turbulent moods, ever disturbed her cold serenity, and she had laughed at the girls who knew those love-poems by heart and chanted them at their spinning-wheels.

She felt her eyes drawn to the lines again, and rolled down the top of the papyrus hastily, unrolling the other end.

"Ye hymns that rule the lyre! What god, what hero, aye and what man, shall we loudly praise? Verily Zeus is the lord of Pisa, and Heracles established the Olympic festival, from the spoils of war; while Theron must be proclaimed by rea on of his victorious chariot with its four horses. . . ."

She rolled up the book and replaced it in its metal cylinder. After all, why should she be interested in these Delphic and Olympic victories that no woman had ever been permitted to witness?

She took up her lyre and struck a few notes, her fingers sweeping the seven strings absently. Then she found herself humming a song of Erinna's, that girl-poet of Rhodes who had died in her promise. It was a melancholy little song of a bride whose "father-in-law, to the tune of wailing dirges, burned the girl on a pyre with the torches by whose light the marriage train was to have been led home."

Great Zeus! thought Aspasia. What is the matter with me?

The lyre flew across the room to the bed. She dived once more into the chest and brought forth a volume of Pythagoras on mathematics.

<h3 style="text-align:center">XXIII</h3>

When Pericles took off his helmet before entering the andron Aspasia experienced a feeling of subtle satisfaction. His head was certainly high enough to destroy the beauty of any face; and of beauty, save possibly his eyes, he had none, (straight noses were too common for remark). She recalled her aunt's words and smiled wickedly. Better he make love in the aula and prescribe darkness later. She suddenly felt buoyant and frivolous, and thought it possible that change of diet had heretofore disagreed with her.

The dinner to-night was served at one long table, Hippodamus and Pericles reclining at either end; Zosmë and Aspasia sat between them.

The talk for a time was of the plans for Piræus, for the men had not met for two days. Hippodamus waxed in eloquence as he dwelt upon the stately rectangular city that would arise from the débris of that "pest-hole," as he invariably termed the important town on the harbor, and Pericles listened attentively and occasionally threw in a suggestion. He ate little, and Zosmë, who had sent Hæmon to the market for lobster and out into the country for chickens, which the haughty freeman in the kitchen had made into a delicate mess with onions, olive oil, and saffron, thought less of him. She lifted her eyebrows at Aspasia, who, when that voice made her feel as if she were sinking in a golden tide, looked at his head.

Reclining on a couch gracefully was an art in Athens and men were sharply criticized who failed to achieve it. Whether Pericles had practiced that art in secret or not, neither sculptor nor arbiter of fashion could have found a fault in the disposal of his long finely-drawn body as he reclined supported by one elbow; and his white mantle fell in folds as harmonious of line as if disposed by his slave of personal service. His black hair was thick and fine, but the mark of the helmet further disfigured his too lofty brow.

His lids were heavy and his eyes half-closed. Zosmë doubted if he were giving her husband the undivided attention the direction of his glance would have them believe. But his eyes never sought Aspasia's, and whether this were a good or a bad sign she was too wise to hazard a guess. Perhaps he was meditating on affairs of state.

The subject of architecture ran dry and she took the conversation deliberately into her own hands.

"Olympias received me with much courtesy, O Pericles," she said, "and I spent an hour in her beautiful apartments. What tapestries and exquisitely painted amphoræ; and rock-crystal cups, blue glass, and alabaster from Egyptian tombs!"

"She has much taste, O Zosmë, and could hardly exist without beautiful things."

"She is very handsome herself," said Zosmë enthusiastically, "and sits and walks with grace and distinction."

Pericles, to her sharp eyes, looked as if he were trying to remember, but replied politely, "Yes, certainly."

"Your two little boys, Xanthippus and Paralus, came in while I was there, sweet children and well-behaved." And then both women saw his heavy lids lift and a warm light come into his eyes.

"Yes," he said. "Yes. They are good little fellows. Which did you find the prettier?"

"Xanthippus, although Paralus, perhaps, has an even more winning manner. Your wards, Alcibiades and Clinias, also

came in—rather noisily; Alcibiades, in fact, was dragging
Clinias by the hair and the poor child was screaming."

Pericles laughed. "Alcibiades is a little wretch, but very
fascinating."

"Olympias says he gives her more trouble than all the other
children and all the slaves, but that she adores him for his
beauty."

"He will give more trouble as he grows older," said Pericles
drily, "and his beauty will play no inconsiderable part in it.
I wish his father had left him to his brother Axiochus, not to
me—and to my brother. We are joint guardians, but Ariphon
has four boys of his own and says his nerves will not stand any
more!"

"A terrible old woman, Elpinike daughter of the great Miltiades, came in also and brought toys and sweets for the children, who seemed to like her—except Alcibiades, who made a
face at her and was sent from the room. I left when she began
to abuse you, Pericles. Why does she hate you?"

"I brought about the ostracism of her brother Kimon," said
Pericles indifferently.

Aspasia turned to him for the first time. "Why did you do
that?" she asked. "Surely Kimon was a great and good man."

"Both; but he was also too good a friend of Sparta. I thought
it necessary for the welfare of the State to get rid of him. Later,
when his services were needed by Athens, I caused his recall."

Olympian! thought Aspasia, remembering the epithet so often
hurled at him by the comic poets. He might be Zeus himself!
And that slender strong body, that face as cold as if already in
marble for posterity, seemed to have diffused a chill through the
room. It was true, she reflected, that whatever he called himself, he was on the way to becoming as powerful as any of the
old Tyrants. Democracy!

"Do you have any one you wish ostracized, O Pericles?" she
asked, her eyes clashing with his.

"It is a weapon seldom used, and a dangerous one. The man
who shoots that arrow may see it rebound and speed back to
the target he offers—himself."

"Do you never fear it—yourself?"

"Aspasia!" exclaimed Hippodamus, and even Zosmë looked worried.

But Pericles answered calmly: "All things are possible. It is natural for the Athenians to hate superiority. They will shout in the Ecclesia until they have elevated a man above his fellows, and shout again until they have pulled him down."

"But you have been in power many years now, O Pericles, and you seem to be more powerful and popular than ever. How is that?"

Pericles lifted one shoulder and dipped his fingers into the bowl of water passed round by a slave. "They hate Sparta and so do I. The Oligarchs do not. Or possibly it is merely because I succeed in keeping their minds occupied and they know that the Oligarchs have little resource."

He looked steadily into her eyes as he repeated his words of the morning, and Zosmë caught the flash in their depths.

Aspasia felt the blood fly to her face, and turned hastily to Hippodamus. "Do not frown at me so," she said lightly. "Pericles understands that I am merely interested in the politics of Athens."

Zosmë saw his heavy lids droop as his eyes continued to dwell on Aspasia. This is the last time they shall meet, she assured herself with emphasis. For some reason she now thinks she dislikes him and I shall find ways of increasing that dislike.

But Fate, in which the Greeks had so implicit a belief, took matters in hand. As the slaves removed the sweets and brought in the wine, Phila, the nurse, came running into the room, her face distorted with fear.

"O Mistress!" she wailed. "Archeptolemus has the croup and Hæmon knows of no doctor."

Zosmë with a word of apology almost ran from the room. Even Hippodamus turned white.

Pericles produced his tablets and stilus from some mysterious recess and wrote a line. "If you will send this to the State-physician Acron," he said to his host, "he will come at once, although as a rule he sees patients at his official residence only. He is a Coan and a pupil of Hippocrates. He has carried the children of my household through more troubles than I should try to remember."

A slave was dispatched in haste, and Pericles continued: "You must beware of quacks, who still practice magic. The Cnidian school is old-fashioned and carries blood-letting to extreme." And he launched into a comparison of the schools of Cos, Cnidos, and of Empedocles of Syracuse, diverting the attention of his host until Hæmon came in with a message from Zosmë that the doctor had relieved the child but would remain for an hour yet and she must remain with him.

When they left the andron for the court, where they sat after dinner, one of Hippodamus' assistants entered and begged for a short conference with the master architect. The guest graciously excused him.

XXIV

Pericles had resumed his helmet but Aspasia was determined to cling to her mood of disenchantment.

"There is something I would ask of you, O Pericles," she said as they strolled about the portico.

"Certainly, Aspasia." His tone was non-committal.

"I have a pretty young cousin, Galatea daughter of Agelaus, who would marry—girls seem to think of nothing else; and that law of yours (her tone supplied the adjective) forbids it in her own class here in Athens. She is very unhappy. I conceived the plan of sending her to Miletus, where she could marry suitably at once. But her father will not consent. Could you not influence him?"

"I know of no one who would have less influence with Agelaus than I. He is a follower of Thucydides and hopes to see me in exile next year."

"Ah! You know?"

He laughed shortly. "Certainly I know."

"And will they succeed?" She was annoyed to detect apprehension in her voice.

"I think not. But, as I told you, the Demos is ever incalculable."

"What are you doing to thwart the constant plotting of these men?"

"I am not imitating their secret tactics, if that is what you mean. But I have my own methods, and the Athenians, if fickle, are clever and reasonable. They know me and they know the Oligarchs. I rely mainly on that. And there is always the Bema. When it is known that I am to speak—and that is seldom—I am sure of a full Ecclesia."

"And then they are potter's clay in your hands! Well," she added lightly, "I cannot picture you otherwise than here, the uncrowned king of Athens. I too believe they will fail. But what about Galatea? If she is not sent to Miletus there is nothing for her but to marry a Metic."

"And why not? Some of the Metics are very wealthy, and have handsome sons, even if they may not exercise in the gymnasia. There is the family of Conon in the Piræus. He lives in a fine house on the slope of Munychia, and has two unmarried sons. She might find their manners less refined than ours, but she would enjoy greater luxury than in her father's house, and she is young and would soon forget."

"But one of the Eupatridæ may not marry a Metic!" cried Aspasia, angry that she had suggested it even in scorn.

"Girls should marry where they can, for the good of the State. Metics fight as well as freemen."

"Oh!" Aspasia stamped her foot. "I believe you are made of stone!"

"Not of stone, Aspasia. No—unfortunately. But the good of the State must come before all things."

"That is the reason you passed that infamous law?"

"You speak as if I alone were responsible for that law. All Athens with a few insignificant exceptions desired it."

She waited a moment, hoping he would explain himself further, but as he appeared to have no such intention, returned to the subject of her cousin.

"Agelaus would never consent to his daughter's marriage with a Metic."

"I am not sure. He is extravagant, and no doubt Conon would pay a large sum for the honor of allying himself with the

Eupatridæ. The Metics too divide themselves into classes, and such a marriage would increase his importance."

"I prefer to send her to Miletus."

"But will that be possible? Even with her father's consent it would be difficult to find any one to escort her. I am sure he would not. She could hardly go alone on a trading ship. Perhaps you, Aspasia, will return sooner than you had intended and take her?"

She darted a swift look at a face as unconcerned as if he had suggested the best place to buy ceramics in the market-place. A cold wind seemed to have blown down the portico.

"I have no intention of leaving Athens, O Pericles," she said frigidly. "These two mornings I have held court in the aula have been the most agreeable of my life. Not even for Galatea will I renounce the company of these brilliant and distinguished men."

"Athens would lose more than Aspasia," he said politely. "I think you had better let me speak to Conon."

"What is the young man's name?" she asked helplessly.

"Hagnias, I believe. And all the sons of Conon are industrious and sensible."

"A hideous plebeian name!"

"True, but a woman soon gets as used to her husband's name as to his face."

"Oh!" Aspasia, feeling an impulse to stamp her foot again, drew herself up with the dignity always at her command. "Talk to Conon by all means," she said indifferently. "I would not see Galatea dissolve at her spinning-wheel. Who will act as ambassador, since you cannot?"

"Like all Metics he has a patron among the citizens, who represents him in courts of law. This patron, whoever he may be, will of course be the one to approach Agelaus. You have only to say the word, Aspasia, and the marriage shall be arranged."

"Very well. I see no other solution. I thank the gods I have no wish to marry, for I shall live in Athens."

"No," he said heavily, "you cannot marry here. If you married illegally you would be in an abominable position. It is not to be thought of."

"And I have you to thank for that, O Pericles! You may lay it to the Demos, but you alone are responsible for that law."

"Yes! I could have prevented it!" he cried. *"O Zeus!"*

There was no misinterpreting the emotion in his voice. Her eyes expanded with terror as if she had stumbled on some awful rite at Eleusis, and her mouth was as dry as once when she had a fever. Then she took herself in hand angrily. Had not many men loved her hopelessly? What was one more or less, even Pericles? But—Pericles! A thrill of gratified vanity restored her equilibrium.

"But of course you proposed that law for the good of the State," she said, and there was more of friendliness in her tone. "I believe you think of nothing else."

"It is quite true that I have trained myself to think of nothing else. I have the work of Solon and Cleisthenes, Themistocles and my father to carry on; and as this power has been placed in my hands, what else should I do? Athens is and must remain the greatest State in Hellas—in the world, that means; for outside of Hellas what is there but barbarians? And only as the greatest and most powerful of its States can she retain her supremacy and defy Sparta."

They were passing the street entrance to the aula and she turned suddenly into the little hallway. "Let us do something quite wicked," she said mischievously. "Let us go out and walk in the Agora."

"Why not? The Agora is deserted at night. But Hippodamus—"

"Oh, I can manage Hippodamus. He is used to my vagaries."

There was no moon and the colonnades and temples and great buildings of the Agora looked ghostly, for the colors that enlivened their marble beauty could not be seen at night. But the stars were like open lanterns, the fountains splashed, the cicadas shrilled with their eager insistent notes, and a nightingale in one of the plane trees poured forth a passionate song to his mate.

It was the hour and the place for love, but Aspasia sternly dismissed the thought, and said in the cool silver tones she could command at will: "Tell me, Pericles, are you as ambitious as men say? Surely you may give me your confidence, for have we not entered together the sacred realm of friendship? I would know more of you. Such power as you possess must be more intoxicating than wine."

"*Friendship!* Your friendship! What more could a man ask?" He paused for a moment and then answered her deliberately. "Why should I not tell you, Aspasia? Possibly no more ambitious man ever lived. But if ambition has ruled my life no man can say that I have used it to further unworthy ends. It may be true that patriotism is enlightened selfishness, but a man who devotes his life to his country may in time grow insensibly to place it above himself. Not for a moment have I forgotten the fearful responsibilities of the Captain who stands at the helm of the Ship of State—as Alcæus of Lesbos so aptly called it. Do you believe that, Aspasia?"

"Oh, yes, I believe it, Pericles. Who could doubt it but your enemies? They even say that your indulgence of the working-class, the constant amusements you provide for them, the free tickets they receive for the theatre, the payment to soldiers for services once unrecognized, the increased numbers and power of this mass of paid jurors drawn from all classes—all this will make the common people fall into bad habits, become idle and licentious." She had called again on her Aunt Daphne.

"I know," he said. "But I have done what I thought best. The poor are human and entitled to relief from toil. I believe they are better, not worse for it, that the good outweighs the evil. I would educate men as well as boys, and, by beautiful works of art, some leisure, holidays for both amusement and sacred rites, attendance at the theatre and the Odeum—our hall of music—raise them to a higher level. The people for the most part are sober and reasonable, and their natural energy makes them good workers. The poor were formerly little better off than helots, and Sparta alone should be a warning to treat even helots decently. Hers are ever on the verge of revolt, and she has a legal massacre once a year to sicken them with fear; even then she is not always successful. I believe in the other ex-

treme, believe that if I can make our toilers happy and interested they will grow more upright, not less. There is always an
unruly minority. When those become troublesome I found a
new colony—as, too, when we have more workmen than Athens
can support—and invite them to emigrate. If they are unwilling there are other ways of inducing them."

Aspasia laughed. "And the more room for the others! And
the more prosperity and internal peace for the State. You are
wise, O Pericles, and no wonder the people love you and are
faithful. But—do you really believe that men may be made
happy by processions and attendance at the Dionysus?" She
looked at him quizzically. "I have a fancy that is but the last
subtle stroke of a policy deeper still."

His eyes glowed with delight as they met hers. "Of course
you would know!" He clasped his hands behind his back and
looked straight ahead once more. "As I believe you have
guessed, it has been my object to make every citizen of Athens,
no matter how obscure, feel that he is an individual, and, if but
a unit in the State, as important a unit as the wealthiest of the
Eupatridæ—because he has a vote in the Ecclesia and behind
that vote an active enlightened mind. In depriving the Areopagus of its ancient powers and increasing the power of the six
thousand dicasts—paid for their services that they may more
comfortably neglect their own work for the year and give all
their service to the State—the motive was not only to avoid
corruption as far as that is humanly possible, but to make every
man feel that he is as important a factor in his way as archon
or Strategos. Moreover, for such a responsibility every man
must educate himself and meditate on justice and honor. He
must know law and he must know men; for after the next election—which occurs once a year—he may be called upon to exercise his knowledge of both. And if self-importance makes him
happier, it also improves him mentally and morally. And what
is the result? Is not the collective intelligence of Athens higher
than that of any other State? . . .

"I have also many men of great genius to encourage—for it
would seem that all the stray rivers of genius that have wandered about the world since the beginning of time have gathered

into one mighty stream here in Athens to-day—and if I live and remain at the head of the State they shall have every opportunity to make Athens immortal. But I would also have the general level of intelligence as remarkable in its way as this mighty outburst of genius. If it were not there would be few to appreciate great drama and sculpture, architecture and painting, few to be made happier in the educated appreciation of beauty. Men who lead grovelling lives with minds unquickened, can find no happiness in the sublime. They can only envy and hate, or sink deeper into indifference. But when every citizen is lifted above his condition, and his opinion demanded not only on serious policies and points of law, but on the modelling of an arm and the turn of a phrase, and he is permitted to whistle an inferior play off the stage, surely he is not only a better citizen but a happier man than when his only duty was to fight when he was told."

He broke off abruptly. "I usually talk little except when on the Bema or when drawn by one of my friends into philosophical discourse—but there are many—many things I would have you understand." He was a master of delicate inflections.

"Yes," she said eagerly. "Yes, yes! And the more deeply I am permitted to understand you—whom so few understand—the more perfect our friendship. I feel as if that word had meant nothing to me before. And tell me one thing more, Pericles. You have admitted your ambition—a word to which you have given a new meaning—tell me, do you not also love power?"

"Yes, I love power," he said shortly. "What else have I?"

Fire began to tingle between her fingers. The nightingale's passion flooded the Agora.

"No love of woman could ever make you forget it? I am told you have never loved, Pericles, and that your marriage was a matter of such indifference to yourself—although you were in a position to marry whom you would—you permitted it to be arranged by your family that two fortunes of the same clan might be united—and the time had come when even you could evade the law no longer. That is true, is it not?"

"Yes, it is true."

"And you have passed forty. Surely you must have met many

women of your own class, for your clan is a large one, and even in Athens, I fancy, there are opportunities. Has none ever attracted you?"

"For the moment perhaps."

"And the educated hetæræ? They are said to be brilliant and companionable—and of course they are beautiful."

"There are few such in Athens. They abound in Corinth, where men are more licentious, and freer with money."

"But Hippodamus was terribly distressed when I threatened to live alone in Athens and receive whom I chose. He said I would be classed with the exceptional hetæræ, so there must be more than you admit."

"Few that are exceptional, and of course they are conspicuous. Certainly you would be classed with them! You must have been mad to think of doing such a thing. I believe you are a good deal of a child, Aspasia, in spite of your great gifts—perhaps because of them."

"Oh, I have grown quite wise since I came to Athens. One may learn much in six days. I shall be as careful as if I had been brought up by my Aunt Daphne, which, thank the gods, I was not!"

There was a moment of silence and then he asked irresistibly: "And if you should love an Athenian, Aspasia, what then?"

"I? Love? I? But that can never happen. I am twenty-four. I know myself, even as you know yourself, O Pericles. Nothing but the pleasures of the mind attract me. They are to me what power is to you, and I would not tempt the jealousy of the gods by asking more."

"Ah!" He bit the word out. "No, I cannot think of you as any man's 'companion,' for that would be your position in the eyes of Athens if you married illegally. I am glad you are what you look—at times—a woman of snow, and too high on the mountain to melt."

"O Mistress! Mistress! Mistress!" An agonized voice awoke the echoes of the market-place.

"It is my Xanthias," said Aspasia resignedly. "He is more fearful than I of scandal."

Xanthias came running up. "O Mistress," he panted, "the Master sent me for you. He is very angry."

"I will go back with you and take the blame on my shoulders," said Pericles smiling; and she detected a note of relief in his voice. "No harm has been done, and I knew we should meet no one. Unless at symposia, all Athens is asleep but ourselves. That is, all who would come here. No doubt there is revelling in another part of the city."

XXV

Hippodamus was striding up and down the street before the house, thunder on his brow. But it rolled off when he saw his ward's companion.

"Ah!" he exclaimed. "Pericles is with you! I thought he had gone and you had run out by yourself."

"Surely, Hippodamus, I would not have gone without seeking you," said Pericles reproachfully. "And as Aspasia desired to walk I took her into the deserted Agora."

"You might have been called suddenly, O Pericles. It is amiable of you to give us so much of your time." His eyes twinkled. "I hope she did not draw you into a dialectical argument."

"We talked politics," said Pericles promptly. "I believe we have both received enlightenment."

He looked at Aspasia for a second, then bade them both good night and, stately and unhurried as ever, walked down the street.

Hippodamus laid his arm affectionately about his ward's shoulders as they entered the house. "You gave me a fright, dear child. You should have sent me word of your purpose. Zosmë too is very angry. But you would not go out alone at night?"

"Certainly not, dear Hippodamus. I should be afraid of footpads."

"Yes! Yes! I should not venture myself unless attended by two stout slaves. The Strategos is without fear, and, indeed, inspires it. He goes where he will and has never been assaulted, even by his enemies."

"You would have been very angry if I had gone out with another man." Aspasia looked at him with some curiosity. "How is it you do not scold me for walking abroad with Pericles?"

"Pericles is Pericles," said Hippodamus solemnly. "He is not made of common clay."

"But if the gossips had seen us?"

"He would not have taken you into danger of that kind or any other."

"True. He seems to be cautious as well as wise. But I will go to my room now, dear Hippodamus, for I have had a long and active day!"

As she passed the pastas on her way to the narrow stairway in the corner Zosmë suddenly emerged.

"I would speak with you, Aspasia," she said, and there was a glint in her eye.

"But I am so tired, dear Zosmë!"

"Not too tired, I fancy, to stay out an hour longer if Xanthias had not gone for you. Hippodamus believed you had gone alone, but I knew you were with Pericles."

"Well, what of it? The footpads run from him."

"I am not thinking of footpads. Will you sit down a moment?"

Aspasia shrugged and seated herself on one of the hard chairs of the pastas. "As you will. But please make the scolding brief, for I really am sleepy."

"I never scold any one but Archeptolemus and the servants, but I feel it my duty to remonstrate." Zosmë, always prone to make herself comfortable, sat upright and looked with magisterial severity at the defiant face opposite. "You walked with Pericles before sunrise. You walked with him again to-night. You have seen him three—we may call it four—times to-day—twice alone."

"I have seen many men alone."

"You always avoided being alone with men who—" She hesitated, for she knew the swift and sometimes poisonous growth of an idea, once planted. But the time had come for plain speech. "Pericles loves you," she said abruptly.

"Does he?" Aspasia stared absently at the altar in the centre of the court, but hid her hands in her mantle.

"Hippodamus would never see it, for he believes that Pericles is above all mortal weakness, as serene and passionless as he looks. But there are some things in which women are wiser than the wisest of men. Pericles may look like an extinct volcano but he is not."

"What of it? And what if he does love me since I do not love him?"

"You have met no man like Pericles. Not only is he the greatest man in Hellas, whose love would turn the head of most women, but—even I, who am indifferent to any man but my husband, can feel that subtle power which emanates from him; a power that flows from more than his intellect—oh, yes!—and could be exercised irresistibly over women."

Aspasia suddenly recalled the words of Pallas Athenè, and changed her position to divert attention from the shiver that ran through her body.

"I am not as other women," she said sharply.

"I hope not. But I have never been too sure. Have you ever seen that thing called a magnet, or the 'Stone of Heraclea,' Aspasia? My father had one. He had only to hold it in the air near pieces of iron and they approached it irresistibly and clung to it."

"I am not a lump of iron, Zosmë." Aspasia laughed lightly. "I am as pliable as a willow-wand, with a calm calculating Hellenic brain at the top."

But Zosmë was not to be diverted. "Aspasia," she said earnestly, "do not see Pericles again. You may not be attracted to him yet, or, if so, only by vanity, but I believe that he is to you, and with the powerful impulse of manhood. Your intellect is but an added fascination. And what he desires he will have. His will is as strong as his genius, or he would not be the greatest power in Hellas to-day—forcing or cajoling even Sparta to accept a long peace."

Aspasia politely stifled a yawn. "Oh, Zosmë," she said wearily, "I would sleep."

"I ask you again, Aspasia, were you sleepy while abroad with Pericles?"

"His conversation was stimulating, but—forgive me, dear Zosmë, yours is not."

Curiosity got the better of vigilance. "At least you might tell me what you talked about. I doubt if it was architecture."

"Politics."

"Politics and nightingales! What a partnership! What sacrilege! I wonder they didn't fly down and bite you. Still, I do not doubt his caution. He is no Thoron."

"Has it occurred to you, O Zosmë, that he may also be honorable?"

"When love flies in at the window honor escapes through the door."

"Do you insinuate that Pericles would seek to make Aspasia daughter of Axiochus his 'companion'?" The lamp in the pastas was burning low, but not too low to hide the angry light in her eyes as she flashed them full on her mentor.

Zosmë hesitated again. But she was heavy with words and must needs deliver them. "I heard something to-night. Acron sat with me after Archeptolemus had fallen asleep and told me much gossip of Athens. It is said that Olympias wishes to marry another man and that she will meet with no opposition from Pericles."

Once more Aspasia presented her profile, and knew that it was rigid. "Well?" she asked after a moment. "What of it? You know the law in Athens."

"Yes! That is the whole of my anxiety! Men have taken foreign wives since that law was passed and invited their relatives and friends to the wedding ceremony, thus obtaining social recognition from those who hold that law in abhorrence—also hoping for its revocation. The authorities are indifferent, for they know the children will not be enrolled in the phratry, and the sons, if they may fill none of the offices of the State, may yet be useful as soldiers."

"I thought there were no love matches in Athens."

"Acron told me of two lovers who met on the roof at night; as you know one roof joins another more often than not in this

crowded city. And a young man may see girls in the Panathenea, and whisper to them in the temples. But these men I speak
of were married before and are the fathers of legitimate sons;
of course no man would make such a first marriage. . . . So—
should Pericles be free—"

"You think he would set his own law at defiance and be
laughed at by all Athens! Moreover that he would love a
woman and offer her as a butt to the comic poets in the Theatre!
Oh, Zosmë, where is your intelligence?"

"There is much in that." Zosmë looked relieved for the first
time. "He is the last man to do himself an injury, to set love
above interest. I doubt if an Athenian would exalt the reputation of any woman above his own desires; but Pericles has
trained these people to believe that he is devoid of human weakness and lives for the State alone. He would not descend from
his pedestal—and perhaps sacrifice half his influence. Still, I
ask you, Aspasia, to promise me you will not see him again. I
mean alone. Take no more morning walks—"

"That I'll not promise! I must have exercise or fall ill.
But—I think I can assure you that he will not seek me again."

"Ah!" said Zosmë. "Ah! Well, I too must sleep. We will
part now, Aspasia, and I shall not speak of this matter again unless you wish it. I hope you sleep well." And pray Zeus I
have not done more harm than good, she thought with drawn
brows as she went to her room.

XXVI

It was long before Aspasia saw Pericles again and meanwhile
several things happened of note.

Thoron returned, and she managed him with skill, consider-
ing it was her first attempt to play with a man and delude him.
She recognized before long that she could make no essay to
convert him to the cause of Pericles without rousing his suspicions, and, changing her tactics, extracted from him every
weave in the secret woof of the Oligarchs; and turned her knowledge to account with such of the great man's enemies as attended her morning assemblies.

Olympias left the house of Pericles—and her children, whom

the law recognized as his only—and shortly after took her third husband. Her first had been Hipponicus, now more agreeably married to another. Their son Callias became in his generation the rival of Alcibiades in extravagance and wild conduct.

Agelaus, a weak, selfish, sensual man, who gambled heavily at quail fights and kept a wilful hetæra, listened eagerly to the proposals of Aitatus, the patron of Conon. The alliance was concluded with as much haste as was consistent with dignity; and although the rich Metic laughed behind his eyes, he permitted the Eupatrid to patronize him and further gild the pill.

It was the custom for weddings to take place in winter, the month Gamelion being sacred to Hera, goddess of marriage, but neither side would brook the delay.

The shrieks of Zenophile rang through the house when the fiat was issued, but Galatea danced round her spinning-wheel. Daphne shrugged her shoulders.

"You are foolish," she said coldly, as Zenophile lay moaning at her feet. "You are still young, even if you have permitted yourself to grow ugly with grief. What is a blow to family pride compared with old age and death? If I were your age I would dye my hair, put red alkinet and white lead on my face, and revenge myself on my husband by taking a lover. When your bones ache with the weight of seventy-odd years, and your teeth drop out, and your eyes are dim, and there is nothing left but the urn and the dark embrace of Pluto, then, Zenophile, is the time to despair and wish you had died before you entered upon a life that promises so fair and ends so soon in this tragedy of old age and death. But one must not let the mind brood on even that worst of all ills, for Fate is Fate, and the gods like not those who question their decrees. The gods reign. We are helpless."

"O me miserable!" wailed Zenophile, and tore out a handful of hair.

"Get up!" said the old lady imperiously. "Go home and send Galatea to me. I would look at a young and happy face, and remember that I too was once young and beautiful and eager to be wed."

The wedding took place with as much pomp as had Hagnias

been the grandson of Elpinike: one of the guests, for that redoubtable old woman missed nothing.

Hippodamus, Zosmë and Aspasia, on the afternoon of the ceremony, were among the last to pass under the bay and laurel leaves and receive a sesame cake at the door of Agelaus. They found the guests assembled in the aula; a brilliant company, for Thucydides son of Melesias and other prominent Oligarchs were present with their wives. A wedding was a great day for women in Athens, for it meant sanctioned liberty of sorts and free social intercourse.

But the Eupatridæ stood on one side of the blazing altar, Conon, his family and friends on the other, and glances were inimical. There was possibly no more alkinet and whitewash on the faces of the ladies from Piræus than on the haughty Athenian dames, but they certainly were overdressed. Their husbands' trading ships brought gorgeous textiles from Barbarian ports and these they did not hesitate to put on their backs, as well as to hang themselves with rude chains, bracelets and earrings from the same source. And Conon had the impertinence to wear a purple himation! When Zosmë caught sight of it she wished she had laid out a white one for Hippodamus.

All the women of the Eupatridæ wore white, embroidered with stars, flowers, or the formal key pattern, and gold diadems or bands on their heads. They looked as statuesque—unless too fat from lack of exercise—as any sculptor could have asked of his models.

The men wore colored himatia, some flowing back from the shoulders and revealing embroidered vests over the chiton. Thucydides, Hippodamus and Conon alone wore purple.

"They are not even as tall as we are," said Zosmë with a glance of languid contempt at the self-conscious group opposite. "And if they remain too long they will sink with the weight of their clothes. It is a sad day for this house. But I doubt if they ever enter it again."

"Do not forget," said Aspasia, "that these august matrons are also looking at us askance. They are all of the oligarchical party and must know that we are friends of Pericles."

Aspasia, although long accustomed to be stared at, felt uncomfortable under that battery of critical unfriendly eyes; her beauty unenhanced by art being no passport to the regard of women who resented the liberty she permitted herself and the adulation she received daily from men.

"It is a new kind of white paint," she heard one woman whisper as she moved toward Daphne, seated on a thronos near the altar. "No skin was ever as pure as that even in Athens. And alkinet would improve her."

Daphne's eyes were glowing sombrely. "One change the more," she said to her niece. "And what is one more or less? I, who have seen so many! Skulking in exile when Hellas was running from Persia or fighting her. Hunted from place to place, chased by pirate ships, hiding in forests on islands when the enemy's galleys were scouring the Ægean. Then rest and unrest here in Athens. The mighty Themistocles plotting in exile. Peace with Persia and war in Hellas. Megara won and lost. Eubœa lost and won. Disaster for Athens in Egypt. Bœotia lost to the League and the Empire weakened. The blessed Kimon ostracized by that villain Pericles, recalled, and dead in Cyprus before he could have his just revenge. The sacred Areopagus shorn of its ancient powers. Democracy kissing the feet of a Tyrant in all but name. I may not have presented these events in order, Aspasia, for my memory is failing; I merely recalled them as they came to me, to give you some idea of the changes one may witness in so short a time as seventy years. The only lesson I have learned from life worth knowing, it sometimes seems to me, is that change is the one thing we may be sure of. I wonder how many Galatea will witness!"

"Galatea at least will be happy," replied Aspasia, for once not interested in history. "Where is Zenophile?"

"On her bed tearing the cushions with her teeth. She will not be present. Galatea's elder sisters are dressing her."

A young man crowned with a garland entered the court, dark, kind of face, wearing the short coat known as chlamys, red, embroidered and pinned on the right shoulder with a jewelled brooch. He held his head defiantly, and his figure, too, was erect, although with none of the lithe grace of youth bred in gymnasia. Aspasia heard an angry murmur at his presumption in wearing a garment sacred to the young aristocrats of Athens.

"Hagnias!" she said.

"Apparently, as he wears a garland," said the old lady indifferently. "I have not seen him before as I did not come to the betrothal. I certainly shall not see him again."

The youth took refuge beside his father and bridesman, to await the coming of the bride.

She entered in a moment, garlanded, heavily veiled, her pale pink himation of some gossamer-like material. Her step was buoyant, almost impatient, and Aspasia saw her turn her head toward the bridegroom.

Beside her walked her bridesmaid, also veiled, and Agelaus clad in his priestly robes. They were followed by a slave carrying a bleating lamb. The bride and bridegroom with their attendants stationed themselves on either side of the altar, while the master of the house made sacrifice.

After he had cut the throat of the victim he slit open the body, extracted the gall-bladder and cast it into the flames: thus exorcising bitterness from the lives of the wedded pair; then handed the lamb back to the slave to skin and roast.

After the invocation to the gods the company moved into the andron for the wedding feast, the men and women placing themselves on either side of the central hearth. Bits of the sacrificed lamb were passed and other roast meats, and an immense wedding cake made with sesame seeds and honey. A little nephew of the house, carrying a shoe-shaped basket, known as likmon, paced the room chanting: "Bad have I fled, better have I found."

The bride, still shrouded in her veil, within whose tight folds she had some trouble in satisfying her healthy appetite, was surrounded by her family, but after a time left her chair and took one beside Aspasia.

"He is handsome, is he not?" she whispered, her eyes on Hagnias, reclining on a couch opposite and talking with animation to his father and other Piraeans; Agelaus, although sharing a couch with Conon as politeness demanded, could find little to say to these traders and permitted his attention to wander to his friends.

"Yes, and young, and strong. I am sure he will make you a kind husband, dear Galatea; although I would have sent you to Miletus."

"Oh, no! That would have been too far from Athens and the beautiful processions; and now I may witness the tragedies in the Dionysus! When Hippodamus has made of the Piræus a beautiful city I shall be quite content."

"Your mother-in-law also looks kind. Have you spoken to her?"

"No—please hold my veil out, Aspasia, that I may get this under without soiling it—which is she?"

Aspasia rose and went over to the stout pleasant-faced woman who sat looking none too happy in her cloth of gold.

"Joy to you, Alcmena," she said. "Your daughter Galatea would greet you. Will you not sit with us?"

The woman rose to her feet with alacrity. "It is Aspasia of Miletus!" she exclaimed with a warm smile. "By the two goddesses, you are beautiful!"

"And Galatea is fortunate to have found a mother-in-law still young and so handsome," replied Aspasia, not to be outdone.

Galatea, unheeding indignant murmurs, stood up and offered her cheek to be kissed through the veil. "You will take my chair, O Alcmena mother of Hagnias," she said prettily. "I would serve you."

But Aspasia pressed Alcmena into her own chair and walked deliberately over and sat herself among the Metics. It was a gesture partly of defiant contempt, partly of kindliness, but she made valuable friends that day.

When the feast was over the company returned to the altar, a libation was poured, and the women crowded about Galatea expressing formal wishes for her happiness. Zenophile, who had appeared suddenly, arrayed in black, and looking more tragic than any mask ever worn in the Dionysus, handed Galatea ceremoniously to Hagnias, and he led her out to the bridal chariot, a wagon hung with garlands. The street was crowded with spectators from a humbler quarter, and they cheered when the young couple appeared and made jests which no doubt brought a blush to the bride's veiled cheek; although Greeks of all classes were used to plain speaking.

Galatea sat on a small bench, the groom and his chosen friend standing on either side of her. The driver stood in front instead of behind. The family, relatives and guests formed into a procession, and, to the music of the flutes and lyres of professional players, walked behind the chariot, singing the wedding-song—*O Hymen Hymenæus! O Hymen Hymenæus!* —the column led by the gaunt figure of Zenophile holding aloft the nuptial torches. The way led through the Agora to the Melitean Gate and between the Long Walls to Piræus.

XXVII

Aspasia watched the procession move slowly down the dark street and then went in to her aunt, who had asked her to take no further part in the ceremonies but remain with her until the return of the family.

"I shall wait here for a word with Zenophile," she said. "She alarmed me more with that desperate calm than when she was acting like a wild animal in the forest bereft of her young. She is a fool but she is my daughter and I fear she is ill. It is growing chilly here. How long will it take to walk to the Piræus?"

"More than hour, I should think, and as long to return. Why not go into the pastas?"

"I prefer to remain near the entrance." And Aspasia, who was never cold, took off her own mantle and enveloped the old lady.

The aula was dark, for the fire on the altar had burned out long since, and the stars gave little light. That part of the court behind the colonnade was steeped in darkness. Aspasia shivered suddenly.

"You are cold, after all," said Daphne irritably, for she was tired and oppressed. "Go to the women's quarters and get one of Zenophile's himatia. The slaves are probably all drunk."

"I am not cold, but I'll walk up and down if you don't mind."

The night seemed heavy with menace. The superstitious

beliefs of her childhood rose from the caverns to which she had long since consigned them and muttered. There was a distant roll of thunder, and thunder to the Greeks meant Zeus in an uncontrollable rage. Was there, perhaps, an old age even for immortals, and fury beset them at the sight of arrogant youth and too much happiness? The jealous gods! Were not mothers frightened and angry when they heard the beauty of their children praised? Was not that the secret of the caution of Hellenes, who rarely boasted, and, if too fortunate, propitiated the gods with sacrifice, prayer, and rich gifts? Instinctively she lifted her arms and invoked the protection of Athenè for the bride and her young husband.

She shook off the obsession and frowned angrily at herself. Strange conduct for a pupil of Anaxagoras, and of one unrivalled among women for learning—and then her restless pacing came to an abrupt halt and she craned her neck.

A shadow flitted through the entrance to the court and down the portico to the left.

"Who is that?" she cried sharply. There was no answer. The figure was running. She started in pursuit, although for the first time in her life she was frightened.

"It is Zenophile!" exclaimed Daphne. "Stop her!" She rose from her chair; but fell back, her legs giving way.

No one could run more swiftly than Aspasia, but the dark figure was too far ahead, and before she reached the pastas she heard the door leading into the women's quarters slam and a heavy key grate in the lock.

She beat on the door. "Zenophile!" she cried. "Open! Your mother is ill. Come to her."

There was no answer, but she heard the murmur of voices. No doubt a faithful handmaid had awaited her mistress. And then she heard a wild scream. It tore through the thin partitions, and other slaves came running.

"Break down the door!" commanded Aspasia. But it was suddenly thrown open and a girl ran out beating her breast.

"The Mistress has drunk hemlock!" she shrieked. "Oh, may Zeus smite me that I was not quick enough to snatch the cup from her hand!" And she fled through the house striking her head against the walls.

"Run for the doctor." Aspasia was cool and collected now that she was confronted with a tangible horror. "Run to the apothecary shop. Surely there must be some remedy."

"There is none, O Aspasia," said an old slave sadly. "Our Zenophile will be dead within the hour. O me miserable!" And he too beat his breast and the other slaves set up a terrible animal wailing.

Aspasia went into the room and stood over the woman lying on her couch, a slight triumphant smile on her pale lips. She was conscious and would be until she died, nor feel any pain.

"How could you!" exclaimed Aspasia in passionate disgust. Like all Greeks she hated death and despised the craven who confessed himself beaten. "Could you not think of your mother? Of poor little Galatea?"

"Married to a Metic! An outcast like her mother. I go willingly to the House of Hades, for whatever may await us in that dark realm of Pluto and Persephone it can be no worse— aye, better!—than being the neglected mistress of a husband and the mother of bastards."

If Agelaus had not left her for a younger woman I wonder would she have taken her legal downfall in the tragic mood? thought Aspasia with irresistible cynicism. She said aloud: "But you have darkened the fair first happy days of Galatea's marriage. At least you might have waited."

"The young are too selfish to grieve and she will forget me and my end in the arms of her husband."

"But surely she must have guessed something was amiss when you, her mother, holding the bridal torches, deserted your post! You could not have reached the Gate."

"I gave the torches to the bridegroom's mother—I never asked the name of either—and told her I had been ill and was too weak to walk to the Piræus. No doubt they were glad to be rid of me, for I heard some one say that I looked as if I had risen from the realm of shades, sent by Pluto to cast his shadow over the feast. . . . And for the first time in my life I have done what I wished to do. . . ."

Her voice was growing weaker and her lids heavy, but she looked resentfully at the beautiful face seen dimly in the light of the solitary lamp. "You know nothing of the dull thwarted lives of Athenian women, Aspasia of Miletus. Lives turned into tragedy when husbands desert their beds, and throw them casual kindness as they throw their bones at table to the dogs. Go back to Miletus!" she added with the sudden prophetic insight of the dying. "Go back to Miletus. . . ." Her voice trailed off.

Aspasia forgot her contempt and bent over the dying woman, stroking her damp hair and resolutely conquering a shudder of distaste. "Poor Zenophile," she murmured. "Poor Zenophile!"

"Go to my mother," whispered Zenophile drowsily. "You can do nothing for me. . . . It is many years since I have been so happy . . . a shade cannot feel . . ."

Aspasia had forgotten Daphne. She ran out into the court, and saw the old autocrat erect in her chair of state.

"Dear Aunt . . ."

"Take me home," said Daphne. "There is no daughter of mine in this house."

XXVIII

Aspasia was far too logical to blame herself for the part she had played in the final act of Zenophile's tragedy; and if sentiment was a mere glimmer on the mental horizon of the Pagan world, sentimentality lay so deep in the womb of distant centuries that if a god had descended and expounded its meaning no Greek would have understood him.

The gods, said the devout, had cursed Zenophile for some secret insult to their majesty. . . . She had gone the dark ways of Destiny. . . . Her friends blamed her husband. . . . Others in the same political straits blamed Pericles. . . . Galatea wept loudly for a day and then forgot. Agelaus too wept, and went to his hetæra for consolation. Daphne never mentioned her name.

Aspasia had many things to command her attention. Pericles had sailed with a fleet of triremes for the northern Ægean, ostensibly on a visit to his colonies in the Chersonese, the granary of Athens; and possibly to those on the Pontus; but both friends and enemies construed that voyage as a gesture of insolent defiance. Let the Oligarchs do their worst in his absence. He would not lift a finger to circumvent their plotting. But he left devoted and powerful friends behind him, even in his own class.

The Oligarchs were uneasy in spite of the weapons in their hands. They knew they had chosen an unpropitious moment for their attempt to drive him out. Athens was happy and care-free in its reaction from the gloom and anxieties of the preceding years; beginning after a short interval of peace, with the rude arrow Pericles had dispatched into Sparta's sensitive hide. Phocis was in possession of the great temple of Apollo at Delphi, and Delphi claimed it herself. Sparta sent a small army and gratified the ambitions of the Delphians. Phocis appealed to Athens, and Pericles went in person and restored the most famous temple in the world to its late owners. Sparta's interference had been unjustifiable, but that did nothing to assuage her mortification, and the Five Years' Peace was threatened. Obligations sat lightly on Sparta, and no one pretended to guess whether or not "The Sacred War" would rank as an isolated incident or as the prologue either to open warfare on her part or to subtle machinations amongst the more discontented members of the Confederacy, now known as the Empire.

They were not long left in doubt. Bœotia, the great City State beyond the northern mountain rampart of Attica, and whose capital was "Seven-gated Thebes," revolted. The exiled Oligarchs had returned and gathered about them all impatient spirits, affected both in pride and purse by the exactions of Athens. They overthrew the democratic government and announced the secession of Bœotia from the Delian League. Pericles, who had his own reasons for ignoring the defection, asked for time and a stronger army before marching against them; but he was overruled by the nine other Strategoi (Generals), and the eloquence of one of them, Tolmeides, a General of great ability, won the vote in the Ecclesia. Tolmeides was killed, and his force, including many of the young aristocrats of Athens, almost wiped out in the battle of Coronea. The secession of Bœotia was followed by the revolt of Locris and the ungrateful Phocis, states far enough north to feel safe from the vengeance of Athens.

Meanwhile, Pericles increased the army, assembled fifty triremes, and when the great island of Eubœa, lying along the coasts of Attica and Bœotia, revolted, marched at once to the new seat of trouble. He had no sooner crossed the straits, however, when he received word that Megara had massacred the Athenian garrison and declared its secession. This left the road open for Sparta, who, no doubt had instigated this revolt, if not the others, for her army, the greatest in Hellas, was already in the Megarid and on its way to Attica. Land would be laid waste and Athens besieged.

Pericles, ordering his Generals to remain in camp until his return, rode at top speed across the Attic plain and reached the small force he had left in the west just as the Peloponnesian army was marching into the Thriasian plain near Eleusis.

He demanded an interview with the young king Pleistoanax and his adviser Cleandridas; and the meeting took place in the royal tent. The Spartan army marched home, although Cleandridas avoided the Peloponnese, and Pleistoanax, after an unpleasant interview with his ephors, took refuge in Arcadia.

Pericles returned to his camp, and with five thousand hoplites (heavy-armed infantry) and his fifty triremes, soon reduced Eubœa, one of the most important of the tributaries, to her former state of submission.

Those had been dark days for Athens, and she did not breathe freely until the Thirty Years' Peace with Sparta was concluded. Another diplomatic triumph for Pericles, for although the land empire was lost and gloom still reigned, it was recognized that but for Pericles they would have been in a far more desperate case. Moreover if his advice had been taken the loss of Bœotia might have been the end of their misfortunes. There would have been no disaster at Coronea to demonstrate the weakness of the Athenian army; and his followers were quick to point out that whenever public enthusiasm overrode his counsel the result was calamity. Witness Egypt.

Not so the Oligarchs, and one of the accusations Thucydides

and his powerful coadjutor Antiphon would hurl at Pericles when the time came to open the battle on the Pnyx, was that he had bribed the Spartan King and his General with public money for which he refused to account. As head of the Board of Generals large sums passed through his hands yearly, and their disposition was rarely questioned, although he presented the statements to the Heliæa at the end of the year when his term of Strategos was technically at an end. If he merely announced that certain sums had been used for a "necessary purpose," there were no awkward questions. A very large sum was unaccounted for in the year of the Spartan invasion, and as he was not only a rich man and notoriously indifferent to the personal advantages of wealth, but of a political integrity that not even his enemies dared question, it required no uncommon sagacity to infer its disposal.

All this the infatuated Thoron told Aspasia; and although on the rare occasions when he had a word alone with her he would have preferred less impersonal discourse, he was eager to gratify every whim. Hippodamus had told him that her mind was insatiable, and if she would nourish it with the politics of Athens he, at least, was permitted to offer the dish.

He told her of the other charges and grievances. The use of the money in the Delian Chest—contributed by the allies and subject states on condition that the Athenian navy protect them from Persia—to build costly temples and statues, "decking out Athens like a vain and extravagant woman with the spoils of others." . . . The revolt of the City States would be laid to his oppressive measures. Athens would be warned that other states would rebel if he continued in power, and only his expulsion would save the Confederacy. Athens was still the head of a great maritime empire, or Sparta would never have come to terms; but if first one state and then another seceded owing to hatred of Pericles, where would she be to-morrow? A mere City State herself and trembling at every flash of bronze on her borders.

The last and most damning argument was to be that Pericles sought to make himself Tyrant in name as in fact. No word was so hated in Athens, who had suffered too much under Tyrants in the past ever to accept another.

"And will they succeed?" asked Aspasia, as they sat in the aula after dinner, to which the gratified Thoron had been invited; Hippodamus was detained in the Piræus, and Zosmë, who held this wooer in contempt, had gone to the nursery.

"Oh, beyond question, Aspasia." Thoron's voice was fervent and confident. Nor did he suspect that his idol had ever had a word with Pericles save on that morning when the Strategos had called formally at the house of the architect. "The Oligarchs under Thucydides and Antiphon are firmly united for the first time, and even sit by themselves in the Ecclesia. They grow more powerful every day and have great orators. I and my friends have hitherto taken little interest in politics, but we are now active members of that party, and, when the great day comes, shall write the name of Pericles on potsherds to a man."

Aspasia broke her fan but said sweetly: "You are wise, Thoron, to interest yourself early in politics, for who knows but that you may be the head of the State some day. . . . I wonder. . . . Do you believe that the Asiatic Greeks are likely to forget it was the powerful Xanthippus, father of Pericles, who insisted upon the League when others would have left them to the mercy of Persia?"

Thoron shrugged. "Past favors are forgotten in present indignities."

"True. What a monster this Pericles must be! I wish I had known more of him in Miletus, but the men who came to my father's house were little interested in politics."

"You can do much good in Athens, divine Aspasia," he said eagerly. "Whisper a word here and there among these men who come daily to sit at your feet and would deny you nothing. I overheard a few words of your conversation with Pausanias the other day, but he is a follower of Thucydides and words are wasted on him. Talk to Sophocles and Herodotus—and Socrates; he is beginning to have misgivings of democracy."

She wondered uneasily how much he had overheard of her conversation with Pausanias, whose arguments she had refuted by pointing out that the Empire owned its loss of Bœotia to the Oligarchs of that state, and that it was possible Spartan influence was at work to break down the democracy of Athens in order to inspire a still deeper distrust in the allies and pave the way for her own return to supremacy.

But it was evident that Thoron, who was as transparent as lantern horn, had received the impression she was merely extracting information from the Oligarch, and was slightly jealous that any one should instruct her but himself.

He continued, with rising color and unsteady voice: "You know, lovely Aspasia, what the downfall of Pericles would mean to us—"

But she interrupted him with a merry laugh. "You have promised not to make love to me while Pericles remains in power! And as you are so certain of his downfall why be impatient?"

"Impatient!   O gods on Olympus!   When every day is a year!"

"Why wait for the eighth prytany?   It may be raining in Anthesterion, and that would be regarded as a bad omen.   Could you not have your ostrakismos at once?"

"We observe the law in Athens," he said pompously.   "Athens is the most law-abiding state in Hellas, because she is the freest. But—Oh—Aspasia!"

She stood up and gave him a smile so sweet that he closed his eyes and lost his breath.   "Go now, dear Thoron," she said, "for I am very sleepy.   Only you could have kept me awake so long past my bedtime.   And I am to have a dialectical battle with Socrates to-morrow on the subject of Excellence."

Thoron groaned audibly and departed.

XXIX

Aspasia was sitting before her dressing-table staring absently into the bronze mirror, a lovely work of art upheld by a carved goddess and surrounded by flying cupids, and fingering with equal detachment the crystal, gold, and silver jars which had been presented on birthdays and festival days by her friends in Miletus.   They were designed to hold various mysterious aids to the toilet, but she kept them for ornament only; they were delicately carved and chased, and some were from far-off Etruria.

The slave sent back with the galley had returned on a trading ship months since, and her bedroom was both comfortable and luxurious. A Milesian carpet of blending purples hid the ugly floor and a violet coverlet of soft Carian wool the bed. Embroidered hangings obliterated the gray walls, and the low chairs were piled with violet cushions. On a carved stand was a large black vase or amphora on whose swelling sides, in the natural red color of the clay, was depicted the pilgrimage of a maid on the day before her wedding. Attended by her favorite slaves bearing graceful jars on their heads, she went to the temple of Artemis and hung her girdle on the statue of the goddess to whom all Athenian maidens were dedicated at the age of ten. Then, with her train, she proceeded to the fountain of Callirrhoë near the river Ilissus and the handmaids filled the jars with water from the sacred spring for the ceremonial bath on the night before the wedding.

Aspasia sometimes frowned as she looked at this notable work of art signed by Duris, the great vase-painter who had flourished before the Persian War, and she sat with her back to it to-day. It had been presented to her by Sophocles, and she had thought at the time it would have been a more appropriate offering to Galatea. She had acquired another object of art that she valued more highly. Xanthias had told her of an ancient piece that had been recently dug up in an old quarter of Athens and was on sale at a statuary's shop; and she had sent him to purchase it. It was a large marble basin, richly deepened in color, carved in the archaic style with figures as rigid and unlifelike as if arms were indeed, from shoulder to finger-tip, one with the body. Its lower part, which formed the pedestal, was also intact, and it now stood in one corner of her room and did duty as a wash-basin.

Thera sat at her feet performing the office of pedicure, for bare feet, however elaborately sandalled, must be as well kept as the hands.

The girl finished her task and rose lazily, her eyes heavy

with sleep; it was early afternoon and house slaves were permitted the luxury of siesta.

"Go now," said Aspasia kindly. She curled her pink toes and smiled. "You have done your task well. I'll knock on the wall when I need you."

When she was alone she sighed impatiently, then took from her library-chest a work that had never failed to interest her: that drama of Phrynichus on the conquest of Miletus by the Persians, which had so harrowed the feelings of the Athenians when performed in the Dionysus that he had been fined ten thousand drachmæ, nor ever permitted to give it again.

But it did not interest her to-day. The roll fell to the floor and sprawled there, once more in disgrace. She sat staring out of the window, over the housetops, at the purple mountains in the north; their sharp outlines as distinct in that clear brilliant air as if they were no farther away than Hymettus in the east. Not a sound rose from the sleeping city. Even the Agora was deserted.

The Agora! What had all those men talked of there earlier? Plotting, lying. . . . Socrates perhaps had discoursed in the barber shop to his increasing band of pupils, for he had not come to the house this morning. But not all who haunted the Agora daily were philosophers! Politics were the absorbing interest of Athenians, and she could guess that at this moment no name was more bandied about than that of the absent Strategos.

Pericles! Why did he not return to this seething city and show himself daily in the Agora, that the mere majesty of his presence might cement the loyalty of his followers and abash his lying enemies? But word came that he had taken his imposing fleet through the Propontis into the Euxine Sea, gratifying his flourishing colonies by that triumphant display of power and the light of his countenance. He had been gone five months and it was now Pyanepsion and autumn.

Hippodamus had taken a villa at Phaleron for the hot summer months and it was but two weeks since they had returned to Athens. In Phaleron his image had been less clear—although she had watched the horizon for the first glimpse of the return of the fleet!

And that was not all.

The Greeks had no "inner life," a deep-sea sounding the gods had neglected to invent. If ignorant they were guided by instinct or example. If educated they lived by the light of the intellect alone; when confronted by problems, abstract or personal, they turned on them the light of reason, and knew as little of morbid introspection as of soul dissociated from mind.

It would never have occurred to Aspasia to analyze and weigh her feelings for Pericles or attempt to delude herself. She missed him and longed to see him again; nor knew any reason why she should not. No man had ever so interested her, even in conversation; and until she met him the conversations of her habit had been on subjects he never broached. Except when engaged in suppressing troublesome wooers she had rarely indulged in personalities; and to anything pertaining to herself other than her intellect and her beauty she had never given a thought.

Therefore if her mind wandered so constantly to Pericles she was quite well aware that it was not his intellect alone that had attracted her. Even when discoursing and arguing in the aula below she had seen his shadowy figure more than once leaning against a column and regarding her with eyes half tender, half humorous. During the long days at Phaleron there had been few guests, and although in that irrelated setting his image eluded her, her thoughts had often wandered to the north and pictured him standing at the prow of his ship, his triumphant eyes roving over the new riches he had created for Athens.

She was not yet so far quickened as to dream of union with him, but she often dwelt upon the wonder of the thrilling quality of his voice, or mere presence; and this alone would make him to her unique among men. Nor was she likely to forget that moment when he had betrayed himself, and inspired her with terror—a sensation she made no attempt to define.

Nor did she deny that if the law permitted she would marry him. On love she had pondered little at any time, but when a woman had found one man out of many whose image, distinct or shadowy, never left her, for whose nearness she longed constantly, and whose voice was ever in her ears, what more could love be? Love and friendship in one was companionship perfected, a deeper appreciation of virtue and beauty. These Athenians, by what gradual process the gods only could explain, had deprived women of the power to give them intellectual companionship, and had found it one with the other, showering on the beloved all the wealth of their nature; for intimate companionship, reciprocal love they must have. And this would be hers with Pericles!

The eminent men, whose conversation and adulation she had anticipated with such pleasurable excitement, and who had gratified her to the full on that morning of her first reception, no longer interested her as individuals. They were a composite that gave her mental stimulus and the power to which she was accustomed. She had received them daily in Athens, and a few in Phaleron, and knew that her mind when with them had never been more lucid nor commanded a more gratifying respect. Nor did they fail to stimulate her agreeably. But for the first time in her life she knew what it was to be lonely.

He must return before long. What then? Should she sacrifice her haughty pride and marry him illegally? Much dwelling on that subject had disposed of some of its odium. The women of Athens, powerless and seldom seen, meant nothing to her. The intellectual men would still seek her. Hippodamus and Zosmë would be shocked and angry, but accept the inevitable. Miletus was too far away to consider.

There was no one to consider but Pericles. If such a marriage would fling another weapon into the itching hands of his enemies, destroy the confidence of the people, who looked up to him as a being of uncommon clay, it was not to be thought of for a moment. If she married him it would be for the happiness of both, and what happiness for either if his pride and his power lay trampled in the dust?

But would they? He ruled by his great gifts, by moral force as well as intellectual power. And what had morality to do with his private life? The public had never concerned itself with the private lives of its great men, if their integrity and their unselfish devotion to the State were beyond cavil, if in their hands the State was rich, secure, exalted.

Morality in its future extension played no part in her musings. She merely took no interest in women who were unfaithful to their husbands through frivolity or lust; she might live to the age of her Aunt Daphne without being tempted to enter their class. Not only had passion never troubled her but her pride would have revolted from certain appellatives sure to be associated with her name.

But Pericles? Could she not give him more than he would lose, if indeed he lost anything? She knew that his few friendships—for the most part with old men—could hardly be called intimacies; and sympathy his proud nature had never demanded. His intercourse with others had been purely intellectual; and she had been admitted to an understanding of intellectual paucities!

But it was for him to decide! Had he gone away to forget her? And succeeded? She turned cold at the thought, then smiled with secret wisdom. She had not been endowed by the gods with all but the mad gift of poetry to encounter resistance in the man of her choice. And what mate in all Hellas—which meant all the world—for Pericles but Aspasia of Miletus?

And then she sighed deeply. After all it would be as the gods had decreed long ago on Olympus. Mortals were puppets in their hands.

It was seldom she thought of her dream, and when she did now it thrilled her with the certainty that Pallas Athenè, knowing those ancient edicts, but believing herself powerful enough to influence the fate of one whom she had made demigoddess, had descended to warn her.

And then she laughed aloud. Once again she had been lapped in the old perfumed waters of superstition! If there was but one god, as Socrates was beginning to believe, he was far too magnificent and remote to concern himself with the individual lives of mortals. She shrugged her shoulders as she reflected that her fate was not in the hands of Olympians but in those of Pericles son of Xanthippus.

XXX

It was a week later that she stood on the roof and watched the fleet sail down the Bay of Phaleron. Every woman in Athens was on her roof that day and the city seemed to surge as if in the throes of a gentle earthquake. The Agora was crowded with men, their voices a pitch higher than usual, for Athenians cultivated low modulated tones and despised the ungoverned.

The women chattered like magpies and several ran over to the roof of the Milesian architect and introduced themselves to Zosmë and Aspasia.

"You are strangers in Athens," one of them cried, "but of course you know that is the fleet returned from the north and that Pericles is with it! I hope he will ride in triumph through the city for we have not had a festival for a month."

"Are you then a friend of Pericles?" asked Aspasia, looking with interest at the smiling pretty young woman, who had told them her name was Constantia.

"Oh, yes! My husband is Glaucon the son of Ctesias who fought with Xanthippus at Mycale. There is a plot to ostracize Pericles, but Glaucon says it will be defeated."

"Does your husband talk politics with you?"

"Yes, indeed! Although many husbands tell their wives to go and spin wool when they ask questions. But I have one who does not treat me like a fool, and although I was very ignorant when he married me, now I am quite wise. He sometimes sits with me in the afternoon instead of going to the Lyceum or the gymnasium."

Aspasia smiled at the lively clever face and wondered once more why Athenians were so blind to the possibilities of companionship in the house. They must be steeped to the very hair of their heads in the egoism of sex to believe that Greek intelligence could be confined to men alone; these men who were born of women who had fathers like themselves! But she shrugged her shoulders. That problem interested her little at present.

"Does Pericles usually make a triumphant entry when he returns from a voyage?" she asked.

"No, alas. Only when he returns from a great victory over the enemy. But he has been gone so long this time, perhaps he will yield to the desire of the people. Do not you hear them shouting?"

A faint roar was indeed borne on the breeze from Piræus, and both eagerly watched the road between the Long Walls. Aspasia, much as she longed to see him, hoped he would refuse to gratify his people; to make a public entrance into Athens, save at the head of victorious troops, hardly seemed to consort with his dignified reticence and the democratic simplicity of his life.

Her hope was realized. A mass of people surged back between the Long Walls, but the bronze helmet of Pericles was nowhere to be seen. Word came that he had remained in the Piræus to consult with his architect Hippodamus.

After luncheon, when Zosmë was safely asleep, Aspasia put on her veil and slipped out into the deserted Agora. She had committed this naughtiness before, but saw no reason why only men should enjoy that marble loveliness, and wondered that Athenian women had so little enterprise. Even the shops were closed, and the scolding bread-women and gossipping fish-mongers had left for the day. The jurors would not return for two hours and the Agora was as safe for women to play in as their own country gardens.

The sun was hot, but she raised her parasol, and despite her restlessness and inner perturbation enjoyed the white dazzling beauty of the colonnades and structures, built with that graceful massiveness peculiar to Athens, and always imposing and glorious. The Temple of Hephæstus, already deepening to the faint golden hue of Pentelic marble when exposed long enough to the atmosphere, seemed to brood over the city from its slight elevation like a beneficent god. She stood before it for a few moments admiring its pediment and the rich colors with which sculptors and architects were not too proud to enliven the sterner beauty of marble, but dared not venture within lest she rouse a sleeping priest. She drifted about under the plane trees, listening to the music of the fountains, the only sound in the Agora, for even the birds were asleep; and finally came to rest in the colonnade known as "The Painted Porch," where Polygnotus had reproduced, in gorgeous colors and with admirable technique, scenes from the great Battle of Marathon. An idealist, he made all men worthy to come under his brush little short of gods, for if they were not they should be. So elevated was his style and so sincere his idealism that Aspasia when troubled often went to him to be lifted out of the prosaic restless present with its mean political passions and its ever encroaching commercialism. Why were bankers allowed to transact business in these stately porticoes, and why were political discussions ever permitted to disturb the exquisite majesty of the Agora? She resented even the law courts, in spite of the beauty of those symmetrical buildings. If the Athenians were a hard-headed race, yet still with a passion for art, so much wiser would they be to segregate the beauty so necessary to their happiness from the defilements of common life.

She was sitting on a bench, absently regarding the great tragic poet Æschylus distinguishing himself, her mind far away from the triumphs of art and the clashing of arms, when she heard a light step in the portico and turned as cold as the marble about her. She would know that step on the battlefield.

But her recoveries were always quick, and she stood up and greeted Pericles with a faint smile. She had already thrown back her veil.

Pericles stood staring at her. "I thought—I am—I didn't think it possible," he stammered. And then his face broke into radiance. "O Aspasia! Aspasia! That it should be you, and so soon!"

"Soon!" echoed Aspasia. "And you have been gone five months! And for many days before you left you gave no sign that you remembered I had offered you my friendship!"

"Oh, friendship!" But the radiance was still in his face. "Surely you knew why I did not seek you—why I left Athens?"

Aspasia shrugged, and her gaze wandered to Æschylus. "To

forget me? Then as you have returned, no doubt you accomplished your purpose."

"I never attempt what is impossible of fulfilment. But I wanted to think—I dared not see you again until—I could not even believe you would care whether I went or remained—and before I knew I must think—I must weigh. . . . Perhaps I hoped you would have returned to Miletus. . . ."

She turned toward him and smiled again but this time her red mouth curved and tilted at the corners, although she put her hands suddenly behind her.

"And if I had?" she asked. "Would you not have followed me?"

Pericles came a step forward and she retreated. "Yes," he said. "I should have followed, for I have made up—"

There was a sound of running feet, and this time it was Thera who interrupted. "O Mistress!" she cried, staring at Pericles. "Come quickly! Zosmë wife of Hippodamus is asking for you. But she has not left her room. Come! Come!"

He covered the brief distance and bent his lips to her ear. "Be at your window to-night," he said imperatively, and sauntered down the portico. Aspasia and her maid hastened to the house, where Zosmë, mercifully, was still at her dressing-table.

XXXI

Thera ran upstairs with the telltale mantle, veil, and parasol. When Aspasia entered the thalamos, if her cheeks were pink this was to be expected after two hours of siesta. Her friend's cheeks were bright red.

"Do you wish to speak with me, Zosmë?" she asked.

"Yes." Zosmë regarded the back of her head with the aid of a hand-mirror. "I had a letter from Miletus just now, and in it I learned—O Hera! this knot is on one side; it must be done again—I learned that your friends are missing you terribly and clamor for your return."

Aspasia sat down abruptly on the tumbled couch. "Socrates says we should not use the adverbs 'terribly' and 'awfully' to express commonplace states of mind," she remarked pedantically. "His friend Prodicus, the great rhetor from Ceos, reproved him until he was broken of the habit."

Zosmë consigned Socrates to Pluto and replied: "I am not as interested in rhetoric this morning as at other times. What of your friends?"

"I have no intention of returning to Miletus. Nor would I travel on a trading ship." Aspasia stifled a yawn.

"A galley would be placed at your disposal. Hippodamus has great influence."

"You are tired of me then, dear Zosmë, and would be rid of me! In that case I'll take a house of my own and send for Aunt Tecmessa."

"Oh, no! Oh, no!" Zosmë sprang up, the beautifully chased hand-mirror clattering to the floor. "You would not do that, Aspasia!" She added firmly: "You could not. Hippodamus is your guardian and would withhold the money."

Aspasia rose, her eyes blazing with anger. "And I am to be sent back to Miletus as if I were a child, not a woman near twenty-five, because you fear I will meet Pericles again? I am not deceived for a moment."

"Yes—that is my reason, Aspasia. He may or may not seek you. I do not know. But if he does—"

"Once more, I am a woman not a young girl to be sent here and there by my guardian. I shall not leave Athens, nor at present this house—mine as much as yours, O Zosmë!" She walked toward the door, and Zosmë ran after her.

"Dear Aspasia! Not for all the wealth of Carthage would I have you angry with me. But I have been sick with anxiety ever since the news came this morning. And even before. I have offered prayers and sacrifice to the gods, and if Delphi were not so far, and the way beset with enemies of Athens, I would go there and consult the oracle. Oh, listen to me, Aspasia! I dare not hope he has forgotten you, for you are not a woman to forget. No doubt he has tried, but he has only to see you again. It all depends on you—and I saw a light in your eyes this morning!"

Aspasia leaned against the door and looked straight into the distracted eyes of her friend, her own calm once more.

"And suppose I did love Pericles, what then?" she asked. "Would you deprive me of what you hold dearer than all the resources of the intellect? Would you have me—"

"But you cannot marry him! Not legally!"

"Suppose Hippodamus had been an Athenian and you had met him here? Would you have gone back to Miletus?"

"Certainly," said Zosmë faintly; and she too sat down abruptly.

"I think not. You are a woman of much character and independence. You might have hesitated, for you have a horror of scandal and despise loose women, but you would have finally concluded that if you renounced the one man with whom you could find happiness the loss would be greater than the gain. And the wedding ceremony still takes place in Athens between citizens and foreigners, and receives countenance from many."

"But the children!"

"The children may not be enrolled in the phratry, but when the father is wealthy they may receive the same education as the others, and I doubt if the illegal sons of the Eupatridæ are denied the palæstra. When they are grown they will have made friends in their own class who would not think of excluding them from symposia, as they do Metics as a matter of course. And if they may not enter the cavalry they may still distinguish themselves on the battlefield—man's dearest ambition. And have not even Metics received the gift of citizenship for such services, and others, to the State? What greater spur to ambition? Moreover, no law prevents them from becoming philosophers, historians, poets, sculptors, sophists, if they have the endowment. Who more greatly esteemed in Athens to-day than Anaxagoras, Zeno, Herodotus? Even Damon has returned and established a school. And the sophist Protagoras? If that law had existed fifty years ago could it have prevented the rise and the power of Themistocles? No law can suppress genius, nor even cleverness combined with ambition. Of how little account are the majority of men who bask in the light of the law? They are nothing but a vote in the Ecclesia or the Council of Five Hundred."

"You have given this matter due thought," said Zosmë suspiciously.

"I have thought of little else. And I shall remain in Athens. Make up your mind to that."

Zosmë cast about desperately. "Remember Zenophile," she cried.

"Zenophile was a fool married to a fool. There are many such, no doubt. My place is not among them."

"And do you intend then to marry Pericles? O Zeus!"

"He has not asked me to marry him, dear Zosmë."

"But he will! He will! And I am distracted! To have your name bandied about the market-place, in every house in Athens, the very slaves running with gossip! I wish Pericles had ignored Hippodamus for his rivals and we had never come to Athens."

Aspasia had turned pale and twisted her hands together, but she answered in a moment: "The Athenians are never interested in one subject for long."

"It would give the Oligarchs a new weapon."

"Ah!" Aspasia opened the door. "That is the one thing to consider." And she closed the door behind her.

XXXII

But she was determined to think no more until she had talked again with Pericles. It was rarely that her mind escaped from the control of her will, and she read the most abstruse book in her library until it was time to descend to the andron for dinner.

Hippodamus bore the burden of conversation during that meal and his talk was all of Pericles, who had given immediate attention to the work his architect had accomplished in his absence. They had lunched together and the Strategos had told him anecdotes of his voyage, which, apparently, had been one of triumph and benefit to the State. He was too full of his subject to notice the abstraction of his wife. Aspasia gave him a flattering attention.

There was a moon to-night and he lingered later than usual

in the aula, but finally went to the thalamos and Zosmë went
with him.

Aspasia ran up to her room and leaned out of the window.
A dark figure was standing in the shadow of a porch opposite
and emerged immediately. The helmet of Pericles glittered in
the moonlight.

"Come down," he said.

Aspasia lifted one end of a dark mantle over her head,
brought it across the right shoulder and hip, over the back
and left shoulder; all in one swift practiced movement. It
would have been necessary to peer into her face in order to
recognize her.

She opened her door and listened, but there was no sound
in the upper corridor save the subdued roar of heavy sleepers.
She walked softly past the open doors and down the stair into
the deserted aula; and waited again. She feared no one but
Zosmë, although it was hardly likely it would occur to even
her alert mind that her charge would leave the house at night.

There was no sign of Zosmë nor of any one else. Aspasia
walked quickly down the portico and turned the heavy key in
the outer door. Fortunately the doorkeeper slept upstairs instead of in his little room beside the entrance. There were
burglars in Athens but they rarely took the trouble to pick
locks; they merely cut a hole in the walls and crawled through.

Pericles was striding up and down impatiently.

"I thought you would never come!" he exclaimed. "But we
cannot talk here. Will you come with me?"

He waited for no answer but walked quickly down the street,
and Aspasia followed him round to the western side of the
Acropolis and up the steep path to the summit. There among
the ruins of old temples and the palace of ancient kings Pericles
paused in the shadow the great statue of Athenè cast in the
moonlight and faced her.

"Aspasia!" he said. "Do you know why I have brought you
here?"

"Yes, Pericles," she said. "I know."

"You know that I love you and would marry you—and how
little—O Zeus!—I have to offer!"

"It is more than any other could offer—to me."

"Oh!" He turned sharply and strode from her, kicking loose bits of marble from his path. There was little left of his Olympian repose.

He stood before her again. "I told you once that if you married an Athenian your position here would be abominable. Do you remember that word? There is no compromise in it. The wedding ceremony would mean nothing to any but our friends. To-day you have the greatest position of any woman in Hellas—in the house of your guardian. If you came to my house you would be a hetæra in the eyes of the law—and of all who love scandal."

"I should be in your house! That is all that would matter to me. But to you? Have you thought well? The people now believe you to be faultless, without human weakness, with no thought for anything but the State. If you shake that faith, prove that you are as human as the humblest among them, may it not be that the Oligarchs will succeed, when, without that last argument, they might fail?"

"There is no question I have left unconsidered, Aspasia. If the Oligarchs have a strong enough case against me they will succeed without attacking my private life. And if I am ostracized I shall go to Crete where I have friends. A man is not deprived of his wealth when driven out; and if I must go I could endure exile and inactivity if you were with me. But I do not believe for a moment that I shall be ostracized, for I know the Demos better than the Oligarchs would know it after fifty years of power. Moreover it is quite possible that ours would be considered a mere alliance of intellects. . . . There is another thing. . . . You have not thought of it and it only came to me of late. The Greeks have a theory about extreme personal beauty. They believe it to be a mark of divine favor, and as such to be granted special privileges and removed from common attack. Your beauty would not curb my enemies; they would not hesitate to strike at me through you; but to the mass what you did would be right and I be the more exalted in their esteem that I had won you. So dismiss your fears for me, Aspasia."

"Ah!" she cried. "I had not thought of that! And I believed I had thought of everything!"

"Of everything?" he asked softly. "Then during these long months you have thought of me constantly?"

"Yes, day and night, Pericles. Why do you hesitate longer?" And she cast aside her mantle and opened her arms.

BOOK II

I

ONCE more Aspasia stood on the roof of Hippodamus, although it no longer sheltered her. But the house of Pericles was far from the Agora, and in the Agora the long-heralded ostrakismos was in progress. It would be late that night before the result was known, but by keeping a close watch she might receive some hint of the way the wind blew.

Pericles himself was in his office deep in consultation with Pheidias over the designs for the pediments of the great temple of Athenè, whose foundations were already laid on a vast substructure of masonry intended not only to level the summit of the Acropolis but to raise the most beautiful temple in the world slightly above its fellows.

The Agora was so densely packed with men they hardly could make their way to the immense urns placed near the row of Hermes to receive the oyster shells and potsherds scratched with the name of the man they would ostracize; and every street leading into the great enclosure was equally gorged. No name had been given when the announcement had been sent forth to the farthest confines of Attica that an ostrakismos would be held in the eighth prytany of the year, but every citizen was welcome to come to the city and write the name of any man whose exile he believed would be of benefit to the State.

Goatherds, shepherds, charcoal-burners, stone-cutters, fishmongers, carpenters, shoemakers, cobblers, tanners, smiths, potters, fullers, weavers, metal-workers, cabinet-makers, builders, masons, vase-painters, dyers, jewellers, statuaries, sea-captains, sailors (when freemen), manufacturers of arms and of wool and linen, actors, rhapsodes, diviners, schoolmasters, Agora booksellers, doctors, apothecaries, shopkeepers, bakers, cooks—

mingled with the great gentlemen of the Eupatridæ, Strategi, members of the Areopagus and the Council of Five Hundred, archons, magistrates of all degrees, cavalry officers, scholars, philosophers, poets (tragic and comic), painters, sculptors, architects, rhetors, historians; jostling one another good-naturedly in the free atmosphere of democracy. For that matter every free-born Athenian was an aristocrat in his own estimation whatever his social status, and every son of free-born parents was an Athenian under the law.

One name must be written six thousand times to secure the ostracism of the undesirable citizen, and there were some forty thousand free-born men in the State—as against twenty-four thousand Metics and eighty thousand slaves in whose lives politics played no part: it looked as if the entire citizenry were assembled in one section of Athens to-day and the Agora roared like a sea in a gentle storm.

Aspasia, who was seething with an almost uncontrollable excitement, had nevertheless forced herself to assume a statuesque calm; and even to look with amusement at Constantia wife of Glaucon who was almost dancing.

"Look! Look! There is my husband!" she cried, pointing. "He goes now to cast his shell into the jar. I made him let me write the name of Thucydides on it before he left the house. Oh, that we women could vote! All of us—all we young women—would write the same name and drive out the enemy of Pericles. Oh, Aspasia, what a lucky woman you are! Not one of us but would be in your place, whether the law recognized us as a true wife or not."

"But I thought you loved your husband!"

"Oh, yes, yes, of course. But after all Pericles is everything and a husband is only a husband. We envy you but we love you because you are so beautiful, and we believe the gods fashioned you on Olympus and sent you to earth to unite with Pericles. Is not that a poetical thought, Aspasia?"

"Very." Aspasia blushed slightly, and forgot the Agora for a moment in a warm wave of memory. And then she added hastily, "What does Glaucon think of the prospect?"

"Oh, he has little fear for Pericles. So many men have

private hatreds that it will hardly be possible for any one man to receive six thousand ostrakæ—I would that it were! The Oligarchs have been at work for nearly a year. They have sent smooth-tongued emissaries up into the mountains to talk to those ignorant goatherds and shepherds and make them promise—bribed them more like—to come to Athens and cast their ostraka to-day. They must have left the goats and sheep with young boys, for I am sure every man old enough to vote is in the city. It is a great day! But what are those mountaineers and the few workmen the Oligarchs have persuaded? They cannot drive out Pericles."

But Aspasia was by no means sure of the failure of the Oligarchs. She knew that many of them sincerely believed that democracy was unwise and even vicious, and sincerity is a powerful aid to eloquence. Thucydides, a fine orator, to whom even the Demos, lovers of oratory, were always willing to listen, had stood on the Bema ten days since and drawn a harrowing picture of the future of Athens if left to the mercy of a man who sought tyrannical power; who not only had incurred the hatred of the allies but wasted their money, merely to add to his own fame in Hellas; indifferent to the dangerous jealousies he was exciting in other City States.

He had used every argument and denunciation in the abundant repertory of his party, and any, however extravagant, that occurred to him at the moment. But to Pericles' sensational marriage he had made no allusion. Perhaps because he had thought it best to ignore an event that had proved surprisingly popular with the common people, perhaps merely because he was a gentleman.

The Demos had cheered his eloquence as heartily as any of his followers, sitting haughtily aloof on the Pnyx; but that might mean little, for all classes were proud of their power to appreciate art in any form. Or they might have taken an ironic amusement in deluding him.

When Pericles had stood on the Bema three days later the Oligarchs were reminded once more of the famous reply of Thucydides to Archidamus, the elder of the two kings of Sparta. "Pericles? I used to wrestle with him in the gymnasium. Even when I threw him he denied that he had fallen, gained his point and talked over those who actually saw him fall. It is the same in politics."

Pericles, as he had looked down upon those six thousand and more rapt faces—for even the Oligarchs never denied themselves the pleasure of hearing him speak—had not for a moment the air of a man defending himself. He made no reference to the charge of bribing the young King of Sparta and his General, and, indeed, he knew he was safe there: the Demos was quite aware that he had saved Attica from invasion and cared not a whit what his methods had been. Nor did he condescend to refute the accusation that he purposed to make himself Tyrant; he brushed that aside as too silly for an intelligent Demos to consider.

He dwelt on the prosperity of Athens and the complete resignation of the allies and subject-states to the payment of large yearly sums to insure their protection by the Athenian navy from the ambitions of Persia. He was in constant communication with his captains and agents and not a word had reached him of any symptom of unrest. He kept nothing from the people. If revolt threatened the news would be proclaimed in the city at once. And he reminded them that it was to another oligarchical party they owed the loss of Bœotia and the destruction of the land empire; nor was the useless death of so many young. Athenians at Coronea any fault of his. If his advice had been taken there would be fewer families in mourning to-day. His desire was for peace and the preservation of lives valuable to the State. Was peace the desire of the Oligarchs? Was it a secret that they longed for a renewal of the war with Persia? And if Athenians were so ill-advised as deliberately to enter upon a war which they now had it in their power to avoid, was it to be imagined the gods would protect them as they had at Salamis and Platæa, when they were invaded and innocent of any desire for ruinous warfare? More certainly there would be wrath on Olympus and they would be left to their fate.

Moreover the men who were now busy at their various tasks, happy in the secure knowledge of a long peace and the prospect of growing rich, would be forced to drop their work and march to the battlefield; and even if they escaped conquest and slavery would return years hence to face ruin and possibly starvation in an impoverished State. It might be that sometime in the future they would be driven into war with Sparta; they must have a long period of rest and recuperation meanwhile, and add to the population of the State.

But Pericles' triumphant moment came when he stepped to the edge of the Bema and raising his arm pointed to the Acropolis. "I have been accused of wasting the money in the treasury, O Men of Athens," he said, and there was a deep note of indignation in that golden voice which had held his hearers spellbound. "Of decking our city out like a vain wanton instead of letting a great surplus—a surplus annually almost doubled—lie idle when no better use could be designed for it than to make Athens the fairest city in the world. The tributary states, far from resenting it, will flock to Athens to gaze and worship, for Athens will be the shrine of Hellas.

"I have not heard a word of protest from any of them. Why should they question what we do with the talents they pay into the Delian Chest as long as we fill our part of the contract and enable them to live in peace and increasing prosperity while Persia dares not lift her hand as long as the Athenian navy exists? During my recent voyage when I sailed up the Propontis as far as Byzantium, I heard only expressions of pleasure at the prospect of witnessing more and even greater works by Pheidias, who has already enriched Hellas by his genius. Should the word go forth that we have changed our minds because we fear that noble temples will make a wanton of Athenè, there is danger of inspiring an uneasy misgiving in our allies that we are grown weak-minded; and with the loss of respect we could not hope to hold their allegiance.

"And that is not all. The wrath of Pallas Athenè, our beneficent goddess, would be profound and disastrous. We have waited too long to keep our promise, made in days filled with foreboding and terror, to rebuild her shrine on the Acropolis; for as you well know I hoped that all the States of Hellas involved in the war with Persia would keep their own promises to the gods and raise new temples up there on the ruins of the old. But you know just how sacredly they regarded those promises when the invader was driven out and our navy was the bitter envy of neighbors as well as of our enemies.

"It is the glory of Athens that she is able to raise these lofty tributes to our goddess unaided. But if you have been induced to change your minds, so deeply do I feel this obligation to keep a sacred promise and to avert the wrath of our goddess, I myself will pay for those beautiful temples Pheidias and our architects have designed. As you know, my fortune is large and my wants simple. You have only to say the word and all that I possess except a bare subsistence shall be turned into the chest of Athenè on the Acropolis. But Athens shall not be the laughing-stock of the world nor suffer the wrath of her proud goddess. I have spoken, Men of Athens. Do as you will."

He had left the Pnyx amidst stupendous applause and cheers of "Pericles," while the Oligarchs had hastened with drawn brows from the hill talking and gesticulating excitedly with one another.

But the applause for Thucydides had also been great, and the Oligarchs had had five days to seek out those men and turn the tide.

If she had had her way she would have remained at home on this fateful day, alone with Pericles, diverting him from apprehension and expending on him all the richness of a nature, whose resources, seeemingly without end, inspired her with a wonder almost naïve. She had taken her intellect as a matter of course, but she now found herself as well as life far more interesting than she had ever found philosophers and discourse.

But her husband, apparently, was not suffering from apprehension and had laughed and told her to go to the roof and witness a sight she might never see again. Pheidias, like all great artists, was as difficult to handle as a woman, and if he put him off to-day he might sulk for ten. Whether Pericles was sincere in his unconcern she could only guess, and the doubt piqued her a little. If not, then it was the first time he had failed to take her into his confidence for he could not give her enough of himself.

II

"Look! Look!" exclaimed Constantia. "Do you see that big red-faced man—there! He is lifting the little man with a face like an owl on an obol to the pedestal of Apollo. That is Cratinus, the great comic poet, who has written so many outrageous things in his plays about Pericles. How I hate him! He came to our house once to a banquet and I watched from behind the door. Does he go to yours, Aspasia?"

"No, he does not come to the house of Pericles. I have never seen him before."

She looked with interest at the large ruddy countenance framed in freshly barbered curls of the man whose plays were the most brilliant ever heard in the Dionysus, and whose scorching wit, in its impious mood, must cause great Zeus to writhe on his throne. Pericles had admitted to her that when he was the victim he felt like having a surgical operation performed on his head. When he had built the Odeum, that unique hall of music shaped like the royal tent Xerxes had left behind in his flight, Cratinus had compared its lofty dome to the headpiece of the great patron of art, and that had been but one squib of many.

Aspasia caught sight of Socrates, and he was making his way to the row of urns. She drew her breath sharply and then drove her will at him with all the force of her being. She had drawn him into a political argument, hoping to trip him into mentioning the name of the man whose exile, in his estimation, would advantage the State, but he had eluded her. She was by no means sure of him. He still came to her house and talked to or at her by the hour, and was on as friendly terms with Pericles as that Olympian would permit, but she knew that his distrust of democracy was increasing, although he had no friends among the Oligarchs.

She saw him pause and talk with Cratinus, for whose genius he had the highest admiration; then—and the wondering Constantia saw her eyes blaze and her lips stretch back from the

glistening teeth—he held his bit of shell against the shoulder
of the poet, scratched something with a sharp-pointed instrument, and lifting it as high as he could reach, flung it over the
intervening heads into one of the jars.

"O Socrates!" she cried aloud. "If you have written the
name of Pericles I'll have vengeance and you never shall enter
my presence again!"

"O Hera!" exclaimed Constantia. "Here comes that terrible
old woman. She is always running into our house, for she is
a friend of my grandmother-in-law—and always abusing
Pericles."

"Who?" asked Aspasia indifferently, her mind still on
Socrates.

"Elpinike, sister of the great Kimon— By Hestia, she is
coming here! Do you know her then, Aspasia, that she comes
to the roof of Hippodamus?"

"I saw her at the wedding of my cousin Galatea daughter
of Agelaus, but did not meet her."

She turned and looked with some curiosity at the little old
woman who had been a famous beauty in her day, albeit a
mere female, and who had never accepted the convention of
seclusion for her sex. She came and went as she would, and
not even in her youth had condescended to veil herself from
the public gaze.

Her face was covered with a thousand wrinkles, but although she disdained artifice and leaned on a cane, it was
evident she had not outgrown her love of dress; her himation
was richly embroidered and draped with style and grace; a
scarf of black and gold tissue protected her head. As she
approached Aspasia, her eyes twinkling malevolently, a wave
of Eastern perfume preceded her.

"Joy to you, Aspasia of Miletus," she cried in a shrill voice.
"You are wise to take your last look at Athens from this
eminence, and on so beautiful a day!"

"I salute you, O Elpinike," said Aspasia sweetly. "I hope
you do not find this winter air too harsh, and regret that Zosmë,
wife of Hippodamus, is not here to greet you; her little boy
has measles."

Elpinike's eyes snapped. She was apprehensive herself, and ready to put forth all the resources of her famous tongue to shatter the goddesslike calm of this woman who had won the man whom she hated and admired above all men. If she had been a young woman, she often told herself, she would have married and converted him. That a man, long invincible, had fallen victim to the wiles of this foreign woman on whom the napping gods had bestowed both beauty and intellect was an insult not to be borne, and she longed to see her bowed in humiliation. When—if!—they were driven from Athens, she would follow them in her chariot to the Piræus, nor cease to gloat until their galley had disappeared on the horizon.

She waved her hand, a shrunken claw, toward the Agora. "Athens is out in full force! Casting its vote to a man to expel one who has thought himself omnipotent too long."

"Ah?" said Aspasia. "I had not heard that Thucydides was so full of conceit. That is he by the Gate of Athenè, is it not? He has an authoritative mien but is not wanting in modesty."

"I was not thinking of Thucydides and you know it as well as I," exclaimed the old woman, who wished she had not lost her front teeth, for the hiatus made pitch uncertain. "The Demos is awake to the truth at last, Aspasia the Milesian."

"And what is truth, O Elpinike? Is it what man thinks to-day or to-morrow? Is it what he feels or reasons? Is it light from within or without—"

"To Hades with your dialectics! The only truth I am concerned with to-day is that the vicious and ridiculous policies of Pericles have failed and that he will be on his way to exile ten days hence."

"I have heard that the climate of Crete is very fine," said Aspasia, serenely. "And that there are many wise men there. Of course Anaxagoras, Damon and Zeno would go with us, and Pericles would be able to devote himself to philosophy. He regrets he has so little time for it now."

"He'll need all he has—a man like that, who thinks that, like Zeus, he was born to rule—stagnating in exile! No woman will console him, Aspasia the Milesian. Do not flatter yourself. And when youth and beauty go, what then? Pericles is a Greek and like all Greeks he hates old women."

"But old age is so far from me, O Elpinike. How can you expect me to cast my thoughts so far into the future when the present is so kind? I fear I lack imagination." As the old woman grew warmer the young woman grew cooler.

"But you would hate exile," cried Elpinike in futile wrath. "You would hate it for yourself as for him. Deny it if you dare."

"You forget I am a Greek, if not of Athens, and shall accept the decrees of Fate. But I do not anticipate exile, O daughter of Miltiades. Perhaps because I lack imagination."

"You mean you are not in fear of what is doing down in that Agora?" Her voice cracked on its high note and increased her rage by breaking into a mumble on the shrunken reef of her gums. Why had not some genius invented false teeth?

"None, O Elpinike, for I cannot know Pericles as I do and not believe the gods love and protect him. They created him to rule and rule he will."

That was the private opinion of Elpinike, but to hear it expressed so confidently by this goddess whose serenity Pallas Athenè herself might have envied was too much for what remnant of self-control a disappointed old age had left her. She raised her cane and would have struck, but Aspasia caught it deftly, and after regarding her for a moment calmly, without scorn, returned it to the trembling hand of its owner.

"I would not have Elpinike, daughter of Miltiades and sister of Kimon, do aught so great a lady would remember to-morrow with shame," she said gently. "My only regret is that we are not alone." The women near by had forgotten the ostrakismos and were staring with open mouths and suspended breath.

Elpinike flushed a dull purple, then drew herself up with exceeding dignity.

"You have reproved me justly, Aspasia wife of Pericles," she said quietly. "And before all I ask pardon of you. I also ask pardon of the gods and of the shades of the great men of my family, that I, Elpinike, daughter of Miltiades, sister of Kimon, widow of Callias, and the descendant of kings, should so far forget myself." She paused a moment, and added with more effort: "And if Pericles goes forth to exile—which I must still hope—he is still to be envied of all men. Farewell, Aspasia, and forget the sad folly of an old woman." Holding her head high in disdain of eyes shocked, disapproving, gloating, she walked across the roofs and descended the stair of the adjoining house.

"Oh, Aspasia, but you gave that old eumenide a lesson!" cried Constantia in ecstasy. "All my life I have longed to see some one tumble her off that pedestal silly people who are afraid of her tongue have permitted her to roost on, and you—*you* have done it! Oh, I could dance! She'll never dare look at me again. How Glaucon will laugh when I tell him!"

But Aspasia waved the subject aside and returned to the edge of the roof. She soon forgot Elpinike.

"You know so many of these great men, Aspasia," said the eager voice of Constantia at her side. "They say that every illustrious man in Athens goes to your house to talk with you, even men who are followers of Thucydides son of Melesias. Will you not point some of them out to me?"

"Do you see that one over there with the sad weary face? That is Euripides of Salamis, born on the very day of the victory that made his birthplace immortal in history. He is the great tragic poet, as great, some think, as Æschylus or Sophocles, although others execrate him for his modern scientific attitude to life and men and his critical attitude to the gods."

"And you have met him? Oh, again what would I not give to be you! I have never seen him before even in the Dionysus, although I thrilled and wept and almost screamed when I witnessed his *Pleiades*. If I had my way he should take all the prizes."

"Yes, he is leaving the elder dramatists behind in advanced thinking and human understanding, though it would hardly be possible to rival Sophocles in form and style and Æschylus in grandeur. I have met him but once, for he seldom leaves his house, but Socrates brought him one morning. I feel sure he has come to-day to protect Pericles! He told me that he knows little of politics but would welcome a long peace in Athens that he may have uninterrupted leisure to write all the tragedies 'buzzing in his head like bees about the wild thyme on Hymettus.' Were Pericles driven out who could say what would happen? War like as not, and poets must buckle on their armor like other men. . . . Do you see that young man just below us with a brow as solemn as if weighing the merits of two rival philosophers? That is Thucydides the son of Olorus. He comes often to the house, for he is a devoted adherent of Pericles, and my husband always welcomes him. He is very wise for his age, and although his mind is cold and dry it is of a remarkable lucidity. He is unrelated to our enemy and will vote as he thinks best for the State. It is a great countenance, is it not?"

Constantia shook her dark curls. "I like a little more gaiety in a countenance and eyes not quite so keen. I am sure he would never condescend to talk to his wife."

"Probably not! He talks little even to me, no more than politeness demands. He is a nephew of Elpinike, and perhaps she shut him up long since and gave him a distaste for our sex. But he listens to Pericles as if he were storing up every word he utters. I give no man a more cordial welcome!"

"Ah!" Constantia sighed. "How interesting your life must be! If other women would not be in your place it is not because you are not legally wed but because they are too ignorant to uphold such a position and talk to all those wise men. All the goddesses stood at your cradle."

"I wonder!" said Aspasia.

III

She lingered on the roof after the other women had gone down to sit with their husbands at dinner, for when that sacred hour approached the Agora grew perceptibly thin. She felt tired from standing and the long strain but walked about restlessly. Pericles had bade her remain until Hippodamus could escort her home, for while men were still abroad she might not be safe from insult even with a bodyguard of slaves.

He should not leave the house himself, for it was his policy on a day like this to hold himself coldly aloof.

What name had been scratched most often down there in the Agora? She had received not a hint. There had been arguments rising to a pitch of wild excitement, and several fights. Men with bloody faces had been dragged through the crowd by police-slaves. But although the name of Pericles had been shouted many times and that of Thucydides had come up to her like the hiss of a snake, she knew no more of the temper of the majority than when she had stepped on the roof that morning. She had made a number of important converts and they had promised to make others, but, alas, there were thousands with whom they could not come in contact.

Her eyes wandered constantly to the circular roof of the Tholos, for under it those fatal mites of shell and pottery were being counted—and it would be midnight before a town-crier ran through the streets shouting the name of the man whose exile his fellow citizens had decreed.

Unless, as Glaucon believed, private as well as public hatreds would prevent any one man from receiving six thousand indictments. And what then? Pericles would not be fully exonerated nor his enemies subdued. He must continue his daily struggle against the powerful Oligarchs, subjected to constant annoyance, even thwarted; calling on this resource and that to accomplish his purposes in spite of them, when he should be able to devote all the powers of his mind to the higher demands of statesmanship.

And if they were driven out? Could a man like that be happy in exile even with the woman he loved so completely? She shook her head sadly. Passion had not clouded her intellect, dislocated those clear logical processes she had trained for so many years. Pericles, under that godlike calm, was a volcano of energy. His mind worked like lightning and must ever have something to strike. Work was his play, and although when in the mood he would argue with one of his philosopher-guests by the hour, his body in complete repose, his eyes betrayed the restless impatience of his mind—perhaps a second train of thought that had leaped to the morrow. Such a man in exile would consume himself, burn to ashes in a year. And she would be left alone with her intellect and the conversation of wise men!

A deep shudder shook her from head to foot, and she lifted her arms to the heaven of the gods, forgetting her unbelief.

"O Pallas Athenè!   O Pallas Athenè!" she prayed.   "At least you promised no vengeance on earth.   Give Pericles Athens and power, and do as you will with me in the lamentable hour of death."

Then she steeled herself once more to accept the decree of Fate and sought distraction in the changing beauty of Hymettus.   Gaunt and forbidding in the sunlight, as the evening hour approached she became a long-limbed goddess whose admiring handmaids arrayed her in the robes she scorned by day: robes of lilac, amethystine, heliotrope, lavender, mauve, violet, deep purple—until the afterglow behind Salamis went out and she sank in dark slumber.

Hæmon appeared at the top of the roof stair.   "The Master is come, O wife of Pericles," he said, "and will shortly go to the andron."

"Have you heard aught of the counting?" she asked sharply.

"Naught, O Aspasia.   But we offered sacrifice to the gods this morning before the Master went to the Piræus.   The Mistress left Archeptolemus to pour the libation and all the household slaves were bidden to attend.   Every house in Athens made sacrifice to-day!"

"Yes, and many for Thucydides the son of Melesias!   How is the child?"

"Better and better, Acron has just left him and the Mistress will go to the andron."

"Very well."   And Hæmon standing aside, she ran down the stair and into her old room, where a thoughtful maid had left a jug of water by the basin.

When she descended to the aula, dark and cold on this winter night, she lingered for a moment before passing on to the andron.   Here she had married Pericles, and with as much pomp as if blessed by the law.   Excepting the extreme Oligarchs all families of distinction in Athens had attended that wedding, whatever their motives, and every man who had made her morning receptions famous—save Thoron. He had attempted to assassinate Pericles, and was at present rusticating in the country, the humiliation of failure in no way assuaged by the contemptuous refusal of the great man to prosecute him.

Galatea had come to the wedding with her young husband looking happy and already maternal. "He is mad for a son, of course," she had whispered to Aspasia, "but has promised me that should it be a girl he will not have it exposed. I asked him what he would have done for a wife if I had been put in a pot and left in the market-place."

Hæmon had gone to Daphne with an invitation and returned with a hearty curse.

The young daughter of Pericles' brother Ariphon had been her bridesmaid and Pheidias bridesman. The sky had never been so rich a blue nor the air so warm and caressing, for they too had not waited for winter and the blessing of Hera. All the professional lyre and flute players had clamored to do honor to Pericles and had stood before the door of the pastas making their entrancing music from first to last; nor ceased for an hour after she had entered the house of Pericles.

What Pericles had said to Hippodamus she never knew, but her guardian sacrificed the lamb and cast the gall-bladder into the flames with the dignity and pride of a father giving his daughter in marriage to a legal husband. Zosmë, the matter out of her hands, had shrugged her shoulders and accepted the decree of the gods. She had handed Aspasia to Pericles and carried the nuptial torches through the streets, thankful that for once the common people were too awed to make unseemly jests. Pericles had walked beside the chariot, congratulating himself that on a man's second marriage he was not expected to wear a garland. His sister Agariste had awaited the wedding-party at the door of his house and presented the bride with the ritual bitter-sweet quince.

Aspasia sighed deeply. Three months of such joy as no mortals had ever experienced before! Were the jealous gods restive and launching their bolts?

She heard the voices of Hippodamus and Zosmë in the pastas and went forward swiftly, hoping he had news for her, although if the slaves were ignorant of what was passing behind those closed doors it was not likely that a whisper had reached the ears of a foreigner.

He had no encouragement to give her and the meal for a time was eaten in silence. Hippodamus was visibly depressed in spite of his faith in the star of Pericles, and Zosmë reflected his mood. A fire burned on the central hearth, but a rising wind blew the smoke back into the room, and the cook—a freeman like all of his profession—had lingered too long in the Agora and burnt the fish. The atmosphere was altogether so dismal that it affected Aspasia perversely and she began to laugh. To her friends' astonished queries she replied that many amusing things had happened in the Agora which she must have noted unconsciously; and she could do no less than relate them. All felt in better spirits when they left the andron.

IV

"We will go now, Hippodamus," she said; "for the streets must still be deserted, and later, no doubt, many will go again to the Agora. Come with us, Zosmë, and wait for the news in my house."

Zosmë went to the nursery. Archeptolemus was sleeping, the faithful Phila in attendance. She sent for a warm mantle, and the three went out into the silent city. Slaves before and behind carried torches.

They reached the house of Pericles ten minutes later, and were obliged to knock twice before the great double doors behind the pillars were opened a few inches and a gruff anxious face peered out.

"Who are you and what do you want?" growled an old voice inhospitably, for doorkeepers were not chosen for their amiable qualities but to discourage unwelcome callers.

"It is I, Marcus," said Aspasia impatiently. "You should know it would be no other at this hour."

The doors were flung open. "I am distraught to-night, O Mistress, and there are many who would be as willing to send

Pericles son of Xanthippus to Hades as to exile. And he only laughed when I begged him to offer sacrifice to the gods to-day."

"Where is the Master?"

"In the andron with Anaxagoras, Pheidias, Damon, Zeno, Menippus, Thucydides the son of Olorus, and Sophocles, all of whom came unexpectedly to dine. Lambo is cursing the gods in the kitchen. There was only one lobster and not enough bread. Molon had to run out and borrow——"

"Well, close the doors, and send no message to the Master. We'll await him in the pastas."

The rooms in this house, built by Xanthippus, were uncommonly large and had been furnished with taste and expenditure. The pastas, lit to-night with three lamps by a slave as soon as he heard the voice of his mistress—high bronze lamps exquisitely wrought in three tiers—was hung with Eastern tapestries, the spoils of war, and furnished with chairs, tables, and sofas fashioned with the loving care cabinet-makers lavished on their work in those days of friendly rivalry and pride in their chosen art. A portable stove of terra cotta, painted with the death of Achilles, shed a friendly warmth, and a deep rug from Carthage covered the stone floor. On a long shelf were groups of the statuettes made in Tanagra, as full of life as if they had danced from the hands of their joyous creators; and in each corner of the large room was a superb amphora of unusual size. On two were portrayed scenes from domestic life in Athens, on the others the Dionysiac revels of the vintage. This house, indeed, was a museum of beautiful things, not all collected by Xanthippus; Pericles, as a patron of art, could do no less than encourage it by offering prizes for the highest achievements, and gratify the ardent but business-like craftsmen as well as himself, by giving their choicest amphoræ, lekythoi, kraters, jugs of pottery or metal, cups and lamps, a place in his mansion.

But as he had a reputation for austere living to maintain, and, indeed, cared little for personal comfort (Olympias had rarely left her own luxurious apartments, furnished by herself), Aspasia had found the couches and chairs uncushioned. She had sent Xanthias to the Agora to buy out a cushion shop, and Pericles had discreetly ignored the innovation.

Zosmë sank on a sofa and looked about her with delight. "It rejoices me to come to this house," she said, "but it also makes me homesick. Save for that great bare aula with its cold white statues and Doric pillars, it is almost as beautiful as any in Miletus."

"Never mind," said Hippodamus with nervous humor; "you may be in your own house this time next month. The Oligarchs do not look with favor on the talents spent in Piræus."

Aspasia wandered restlessly about the room. It seemed an eternity since she had left Pericles that morning. A gay laugh came through the door connecting the pastas with the andron. "That is Pheidias," she said impatiently. "I wonder will they have a symposium and sit there all night?"

"It is your duty to go in and greet Pericles, Hippodamus," said Zosmë. "You might tell them we are here. Of course we shall not be invited in but they might have the politeness to come out."

As Hippodamus opened the door Aspasia saw Pericles. The others, reclining, were dipping their cups into an immense silver krater passed round by a slave, but he was leaning against one of the columns that surrounded this beautiful room. His eyes were bent to the floor and there was no smile on his face. The wind had evidently gone back to the Ægean, for the charcoal on the hearth glowed brightly and the atmosphere was clear. Sophocles was finishing a story that made manifest the symposium was not as intellectual as might be expected in this house, and a shout of joyous laughter covered the entrance of Hippodamus. She heard another shout, this time of welcome, as he closed the door.

"If they're telling their wicked stories they'll sit there till the town-crier runs through the streets," said Zosmë disgustedly. "They might come out and distract our minds. I care little for your old Nous and Damon and Zeno, and that young Thucydides makes me feel like an obol, but I delight in Sophocles; and Pheidias when he is in a good temper is amusing."

"You haven't mentioned Pericles," said Aspasia demurely.

"Would he look at me?"

Aspasia turned with a slight expression of alarm. "What do you mean? He never looks at me in public."

Zosmë gave her rich throaty laugh. "I have observed his dignified aloofness when in your presence, dear Aspasia! He tries hard, but there are times when eyes escape the will. When even a Pericles is in love he is not always master of his eyes. He must be a tremendous lover, Aspasia!"

But Aspasia blushed and turned her back and picked up a tanagra.

"Shall you take back a collection of these?" she asked.

"Hippodamus has promised to take me to Tanagra in the summer—if we are still in Athens! What time shall we hear?"

"About midnight, I should think. Would it were over!"

The door opened and the men came in. There was excitement in every face save that of the host, but the wine they had drunk had drowned anxiety for the moment. Even the serious brow of Thucydides was flushed and his eyes bright. Pericles, as calm as if sitting to Pheidias for his bust, greeted Zosmë hospitably but avoided the eyes of his wife, although he caught her hand for a moment behind the broad back of Sophocles.

Pheidias, his fine sensitive face lit with wine and admiration of his hostess, seated himself beside Aspasia on a sofa and immediately began to talk of the great temple which was to be erected under his supervision, even though the celebrated Ictinus was its architect. A true Athenian, he took a lively interest in politics, but not when in the throes of creation. He had run to the Agora early in the morning and cast his shell, then dismissed the subject from his mind.

"Pericles was as enthusiastic as I over the designs for the pediments," he said eagerly. "Indeed it is in conversation with him that inspiration often comes to me. The gods have been good to artists and to Athens to grant us such a patron."

"Yes!"

"On one pediment Athenè springs full-armored from the head of Zeus. On the other she battles with Poseidon for her beloved Athens."

"Yes?"

"But that is not all, Aspasia." He lowered his voice. "I

told him for the first time to-day of the marvellous statue of Athenè Parthenos my imagination has conceived. O beautiful Aspasia! Would that you could be the model for that statue! Alas, that you cannot! They would call it a sacrilege and cast me into prison and give me a cup of hemlock to drink. But you and you only should reign in that temple which will make the names of Pheidias and Pericles renowned through the ages. And, alas, once more! Athenè may not even be beautiful, only serene and wise."

"Have you a model in mind?" asked Aspasia listlessly.

"I may have no model save perhaps for the figure—perhaps I shall not for that. It is difficult to use a model for a figure of heroic size, and this greatest of all statues will be little lower than the roof of the temple itself."

"Have you designed it?" She was straining her ears for the first sound that might penetrate the heavy curtains that hung between the pastas and the aula.

"It has not yet sprung from my head, O Aspasia, and it is cracking my poor skull. For the first time it is granted a mere mortal to feel like Almighty Zeus! And Pericles will be Hephæstus and split it with an axe!" He laughed merrily and she smiled in return.

"Tell me more, Pheidias," she said, anxious to keep him at her side. She was in no mood for the others.

"It will cost untold talents, but it will be a lesson to Persia, for it will be divine art combined with the costliest of materials; and with her the substance is all, the delicacy or grandeur of art nothing. This great statue then, Aspasia, that will stand in the cella of the magnificent temple on the Acropolis, and facing the eastern portals to greet the sun-god in his rising, will be not of marble but of solid ivory and gold— What has startled you, Aspasia?"

"Ivory—gold—" Aspasia was staring at him with open lips and dilated eyes. "Pallas Athenè—ivory—gold—" Until to-day she had not thought of her dream for many months and she wondered if she were dreaming now. But she heard Zosmë laugh and the deep voice of Sophocles.

She dropped her eyes. "It is a wonderful conception,

Pheidias," she murmured. "It took away my breath with its magnificence and its daring. And even the mere dream may enlist the favor of Athenè and bring us good fortune to-night."

"What a wonderful idea, Aspasia! And I must have been inspired to put my dream into words to-day. A chryselephantine statue in honor of a goddess! It should enlist the favor of even one so stern as Athenè."

"Hera may be jealous," said Aspasia smiling. "And you know that she can inspire even Zeus with fear."

"But Athenè is his favorite daughter—"

There was a sound of running feet in the aula, the curtains were flung apart and the white face of the doorkeeper confronted them. At the same time they heard a roar from the direction of the Agora.

"The name must have been announced, O Master," the man stammered. "I have sent two slaves running—I could not wait for the crier!" And he ran back across the aula and out the front door.

The silence of death fell on that little company but every eye blazed with excitement. Pericles lowered his lids and stood like a statue. Aspasia, who had sprung to her feet, went to his side. He moved his head and looked deep into her eyes. All others were turned toward the entrance.

"It must be one name after all." The nervous voice of Pheidias broke the heavy silence. "They would not shout if no ostracism had been accomplished."

"They are coming here!" cried Zosmë. "That mighty noise is nearer than it was! Oh, Pericles! Will they tear you to pieces if this terrible thing has gone against you?"

Pericles smiled. "I think not, Zosmë. That is not the way of Athenians even when excited."

"There is a hiss in that roar!" It was Sophocles whose voice was quick with excitement. "And your name makes no hiss, Pericles— Listen! That is the voice of the crier!"

A high powerful voice rose above the clamor and carried straight to those strained eager ears.

"*Thu-cyd-ides—Thu-cyd-ides—Thu-cyd-ides—*"

Anaxagoras, Hippodamus, Sophocles, Pheidias, Damon, Zeno,

flung themselves upon Pericles and embraced him, their tears raining on his calm face. He stole a quick glance at Aspasia and flashed his admiration and gratitude. She was as outwardly unmoved in that supreme moment as himself. Zosmë had dropped on a chair and was sobbing hysterically.

The old doorkeeper ran toward them again. "O Master!" he gasped and fell by the altar.

And then it seemed to Aspasia, who had gripped the carpet with her feet, that ten thousand men had forced their way into the court and were pressing forward to the pastas, where Pericles, who had managed to shake off his demonstrative friends, stood between the pillars. They were men of every class in Athens and a baker was arm in arm with Ariphon second son of Xanthippus. They were still shouting, but no longer the name of the fallen man. It was "Pericles" that flew up to chase the enemy among the frosty stars.

And Pericles knew that at last his power was unchallenged in Athens and the way clear before him. His was the only calm face in Athens that night, but his brain was racing. Immortal fame, dearer to the Greeks than all else the gods could bestow, would be his if life spared him. All other obstacles were swept from his path. The glory of Athens should increase tenfold and his name be linked with it indissolubly and for all time.

But when an hour later that shouting host had gone and silence once more fell on his house he thought only of Aspasia.

v

Socrates rose nervously as Aspasia descended upon him. He had not been one of the crowd that had filled the great aula this morning, when every public official from the Nine Archons and the Council of Five Hundred down to the magistrates of the Piræus, had come to congratulate Pericles; but he had not dared to stay away longer. He knew that if he did she would send two slaves to drag him before the bar of judgment.

As she swept down the portico she looked like Athenè about to come to grips with Poseidon. All she lacked was spear, shield, and helmet.

"You wrote Pericles' name yesterday!" she cried as they stood opposite. "Deny it if you dare!"

"How can you know——"

"Don't try to evade me. Did you or did you not?"

"I did, Aspasia. And unless your eyes burn me to cinders I will give you my reasons——"

"Reasons! Do you not imagine I have heard every 'reason' of Pericles' enemies until I know them as well as you do? I only see you for the last time to-day to tell you that you are a traitor and a disloyal friend——"

"Oh, no, Aspasia!" Socrates, always slow to wrath, was goaded out of the philosophical calm he had vowed to maintain. "Were you Athenè herself I would fling back those words. I love you above all women and have suffered intolerable tortures; and I admit and admire the genius of Pericles—who would not? But my first duty is to the State, and I believed—do believe—that his policies will ruin Athens in the end— You must listen to me, Aspasia," he said sternly as she moved to interrupt him. "You have received me to-day and you owe me that courtesy. If Pericles could live for ever I should fold my arms in peace and give no further thought to those affairs of state that distract the mind from philosophy. As long as he lives he will hold the Demos in the hollow of his hand, and now that the Oligarchs are prostrate there will be peace and prosperity in the State. If he keeps Sparta and Corinth at bay I do not doubt he will make Athens more powerful still and realize his ideal of all that he believes a great City State should be. Art, science, and philosophy will flourish as never before and our commerce put out the light of Syracuse and Carthage. But who is to come after him and continue his work? Can you point to any man in this State, Aspasia, whom he could train in his policies, who has the intellect, the moral force, the power over the minds and wills of men, the golden voice, the inimitable eloquence— any man who combines all these great gifts the gods have bestowed on Pericles alone? Is there any man in Athens whom he regards in the secrecy of his proud soul as aught but his servant? You alone in all Hellas are his equal, and no woman may rule the Athenians——"

"You talk as if he were a weakling." Aspasia could restrain her angry impatience no longer. "No man could be more healthy and strong—nor more abstemious. He may live for forty years yet—why not?"

"True, Aspasia, and he may die to-morrow. A man lives no longer than Fate decrees. But even if he should live to old age, what then? Old men as oft as not lose their powers of character and of mind. And their eloquence, Aspasia. It is difficult to preserve eloquence when the teeth are loose or missing and the voice cracked. And no man can keep his hold on the Athenians unless he can delight them on the Bema. Eloquence is the mightiest weapon in the quiver of the statesmen, the supreme gift of the gods—"

"Well, twenty years then. A woman may be old when she is past sixty—long before!—but not a man. And during the next twenty years what may not happen? Some one of his younger disciples may discover the needful gifts and be trained to succeed him."

"Such men do not appear in history as often as that, Aspasia. There is only one Pericles. We shall never see another."

"That I believe! But a man of lesser genius might still carry on his work. What of young Thucydides?"

"He has neither eloquence nor fascination. He would not draw a hundred men to the Pnyx. He is as cold as Pericles looks. I am told that the only occasion on which he was ever shaken was when he listened to Herodotus at Olympia read his description of the Battle of Salamis; and would write himself were there anything left to write about. He would make an excellent historian, with that cold lucid mind and his critical attitude toward statesmanship—but never a leader of men. . . .

"No, Aspasia, Pericles has no successor, nor will have. And when he dies the Demos he has educated into an exaggerated conceit and independence, love of power, and a demand for indulgence and pleasure, will pull Athens down about its head. Only Pericles can control it. Therefore, I would have had him go before it is too late."

Aspasia had been staring at the altar; she turned again on

Socrates and shrugged her shoulders. "I refuse to look beyond Pericles," she said.

Socrates smiled sadly. "You are but a woman, Aspasia, for all your great talents. But am I forgiven, dear goddess? It would have been easy to lie to you, and I was tempted, for the loss of your friendship was something I hardly dared contemplate. I did not sleep last night. It would be as if the sun and the moon and all the stars had gone out of the universe. And I feared my mental growth would be stunted. I was a mere tyro at dialectics until you came to cross swords with me and teach me all the resources and subtleties of that master accomplishment. Your old teacher admits you have left him and all others behind. They say that if no sophists had arisen you would have invented dialectics yourself. Every one notes my improvement, and there is much I would learn from you yet— yes, and much besides dialectics. The perfect intellect is the omega of life!"

Aspasia laughed. "I am certain the practical side of your mind did not sleep last night, although the rest of it might have been caught napping!" She darted forward and slapped him smartly on each ear. "You deserve that much—you *Spartan!* And you deserve more. I had intended never to see you again. But I value honesty as highly as I value intellect, and I know you will never stoop to plot secretly against Pericles."

"Oh, no!" exclaimed Socrates in horror and forgetting his tingling ears. "Now that it is decreed he shall remain and rule Athens and the Empire I ask of the gods only that his power may increase. And I would he could live for ever!"

"But you would have Athens another Sparta! As you look as if you had no idea of going we may as well sit down."

"You know that I wish no such fate for Athens. What hope for philosophers in a military state? But I do not believe in encouraging too much individuality in the common people. And I believe Sparta has shown wisdom in basing her prosperity on agriculture not on commerce—"

"Well, blame the decline of Ionia and the death-blow given to Phœnician commerce by the Persian defeat, not Pericles."

"True, Aspasia, but who took full advantage of those conditions before the rise of Pericles? Is it not to our own rise as a great commercial power that we owe those deformities of character caused by the love of gain? We have more Metics in Attica than in all the rest of Hellas together, and Sparta will not admit one within her borders. They have corrupted every Athenian forced to toil for bread—and others who are not but would increase their fortunes. Commercial prosperity breeds greed, and indifference to simple happiness—and philosophy."

"But not to politics and art, Socrates; not among Athenians. And as all men cannot be philosophers why not let them be happy and successful in their own way?"

"Because I look to the future, Aspasia. And not only because I would have men happy as nature decreed, but because Athens to-day is no breeding-ground for soldiers. Sparta has a great army, the greatest in Hellas. They may know nothing of pleasure, nor art, nor philosophy, and little of personal happiness, but every man is a great fighter and disciplined by Generals who live only for war."

"And what of our navy? The greatest in the world! And do you imagine Pericles does not know as much of Sparta as you do? He does not believe the Athenians will fail on the battlefield because they have not been stunted in all else and turned into thralls of war. Rather they will fight with more spirit and devotion because they have so much to lose and to protect. His foresight is as great as yours, and more famous," she added proudly, "and he will continue to do as he thinks best."

"I have no doubt of that," replied Socrates drily. "Nor do I question his foresight—but does it project its rays beyond his own span of life? That is the question, Aspasia. I fear nothing as long as he remains on earth. But death—"

"And I forbid you ever again to connect the name of Pericles with that execrable word! Death! A word we live to forget!" She sprang to her feet, the blood flying to her cheeks, her eyes glowing with sweet fire. "Would the gods would grant us immortality and I could live on with Pericles for ever!"

And then she felt her revenge was complete as she saw the

ugly great face of her hopeless adorer turn almost black with the blood that suffused it. He too sprang to his feet, overturning his chair and ran from her presence.

"O Philosopher!" she mocked. "O Philosopher! I have still much to teach you."

Socrates beat the air with his fists and disappeared.

VI

Aspasia, still laughing, left the aula and passing through the pastas and andron entered the court of the gynækonitis or women's quarters. This inner court was nearly as spacious as the outer, consecrated by its builder to the men of the family and their guests. It was two stories in height, and beyond the columned porticoes were the rooms for the women and children and for slaves when spinning and weaving. The thalamos was beside the andron, but opened also on the court—strewn to-day with balls, kites, marionettes, toy carts, and boy dolls from Tanagra. A swing hung between two columns. At the far end a door led into a garden.

From this shady enclosure came shrieks of fury and fright.

Alcibiades again! Aspasia shrugged her shoulders. Where can Amykla be?

The nurse of Pericles' wards ran out from one of the spinning-rooms and into the garden. The sound of hearty slaps invaded the marble peace of the aula, followed by more shrieks, and a roar of furious protest. Amykla reappeared, dragging a boy by each hand, Alcibiades kicking and fighting to be free. Xanthippus and Paralus followed, both dishevelled. Aspasia looked on in amusement.

The nurse caught sight of her and stopped in dismay.

"I thought you had gone forth, O Mistress," she stammered. "I would not have these naughty children disturb you. Alcibiades promised to behave himself if I let them play in the garden, and now he has been fighting all three and overturned a statue. I shall shut him up in the storeroom and give him no supper."

"I'll not be shut up!" Alcibiades composed his features, stamped his foot, and tossed his curly head. He was only five but he already had a presence. A difficulty with his *r's* gave a touch of picturesqueness to his commanding little personality, and his beauty was extraordinary. "I am Alcibiades the son of Clinias who fell at Coronea," he said haughtily, "and it is not for slaves to punish me."

Amykla administered another cuff and received a kick in return. She dropped his hand to lean down and rub her shinbone, and Alcibiades ran to the wife of his guardian; she had stood between him and punishment before.

"*Dea'* Aspasia!" he cried, flinging himself into her arms. "You will not p'lmit that woman to put me in the stolroom. It is no place for the son of Clinias, and I cannot endul to be shut in. I must have fleedom to come and go as I will."

Aspasia pulled a short bright curl that stood up like the crest of an angry cock. "But you must mind your nurse like a good little boy," she said, recalling the frequent advice of Zosmë to Archeptolemus. "You *are* a little boy, you know, and must do as you are told until you are grown to be a man."

"Why cannot I be a man at once? Why must I be a little boy—like those?" pointing a finger of scorn.

"That is the way of nature, dear Alcibiades. In two years from now you will have a pedægogus like Xanthippus and Paralus, instead of a nurse, and go to school. There you will learn many things you do not know now."

"And must I mind that pedægogus?" he asked anxiously.

"Yes, and your schoolmaster. Otherwise you will not know all that you must know to be a great and good man. The citizen of approved virtue is he who is able both to rule and to obey." Aspasia felt that she was discharging her vicarious duty as creditably as might be.

"I will mind no man and I will lule all men."

"But you mind Pericles."

"Oh, yes, I mind Pellicles, because he is in the place of my fath'l, and I tu'ln cold and shiv'l when he looks at me stulnly."

"He will do more than look at you if you do not obey Amykla and if you beat the other boys."

"They are fools," said Alcibiades loftily. "I despise them. So do you, Aspasia. I have seen it in you' eyes."

Aspasia looked into those keen luminous eyes with some alarm. "I love Paralus," she said with emphasis. "And you are quite wrong. I despise neither of the others. They would be good little boys if you would let them alone."

"They must know that I am mast'l," he said with dignity. "I have no one else to play with and they must obey me. I beat them just now because we were pletending I was the gleat Stlategos Miltiades at Malathon and they were my hoplites, and they said I gave too many oddles."

"I don't doubt it! A General is usually content to give one order and then let his hoplites charge the enemy. Too many orders would confuse them."

Alcibiades pondered this. "P'laps you are light, Aspasia." His brow cleared. "I will give only one oddle helafter, and if they do not obey beat them at once."

"A good General is always obeyed."

His eyes flashed. "You dal not say I'm not a good Gen'l!" he cried passionately. "I am all that I will be, O Aspasia wife of Pellicles. And I shall not love you if you deny it."

"Dear Alcibiades!" She was somewhat at a loss, for she knew little of children and this one was a problem to many of varied experience. "At least I am glad that you love me, for you sometimes obey me, and I would that you loved Amykla as well."

"I love you because you al beautiful and I hate Amykla because she is ugly," announced the eternal male, never more highly exemplified than in Alcibiades.

"You must go to her now. It is time for your supper."

"She would give me no supper and put me in the stolroom. I'll smite her if she touches me."

The nurse, who had approached, concluded it were best to relent. "You are forgiven, Alcibiades," she said coldly, "if you will promise not to be naughty again."

"I'll plomise nothing." He took refuge behind Aspasia. "Alcibiades does not give his word to slaves."

At this moment Pericles appeared in the door of the andron. "Leave the aula and go to your room at once," he said sternly.

Alcibiades met the eyes of the lofty helmeted figure fearlessly and squared his shoulders.

"Velly well, Pellicles son of Xantippus," he said with dignity. "I go as you command me. *You* may give oddles to Alcibiades son of Clinias, but no one else."

And he marched off.

VII

"If you would but take Alcibiades in hand yourself!" exclaimed Aspasia as they entered the thalamos. "No one else has the least influence over him, and he is terribly headstrong and should be taught to bow to authority before it is too late."

Pericles shrugged his shoulders. "I have no time to discipline children," he said. "I have too many grown-up children on my hands. And Alcibiades is much as I was at his age. I taught myself discipline and he must learn to do the same."

"But you spent your childhood in exile and that must have been discipline of a kind. Alcibiades is living in happiness and security."

Pericles smiled. "I would not have you worry about the children, Aspasia. It was not for that the gods made you. Our nurses are carefully selected and are usually from Sparta. My old pedægogus Zopyrus has recovered his health at the farm and will take Alcibiades in hand two years from now. He has had much experience with naughty boys and will know how to deal with him. What of Socrates?"

"He confessed he had written your name." She repeated the conversation. "I forgave him because he is Socrates and because after all it mattered nothing. But I boxed his ears."

Pericles laughed heartily. "No doubt he is now more your slave than ever." And then his face turned graver than was its habit when Aspasia alone was present. "He may be right—who knows? No man can exercise any wisdom save his own, and it seems to me that such gifts as I have and the great power the Athenians have placed in my hands, should be employed to make the State both prosperous and happy. Socrates has forgotten that the world does not stand still and that progress is a law of civilization. If opportunities were neglected what progress would there be? Is our Hellas the Hellas of Codrus or of Agamemnon, or even of Pisistratus or of Marathon? Man's vision is finite. What Hellas will be ages hence may depend upon what I make Athens to-day, and Zeus knows I am heavily conscious of my responsibility. But I can do no more than exercise my own wisdom."

He turned abruptly and went over to the "Master's Chest" that stood in a corner of the room. "Will you summon Euangelos? It is the last day of the month and there is money to disburse."

"You leave me little to do in your house, Pericles," she said after she had sent for the steward. "Zosmë and other house-wives exercise great authority and are occupied with domestic matters all morning and sometimes all day."

"Why should you of all women waste your time on household matters that are the sole resource of ordinary women? Euangelos has administered my affairs for twenty years and no woman could give him assistance. Nor would it suit you to bend your mind to such details. Confess it, dear head!"

Aspasia laughed and blushed. "I fear you see through me, O Strategos! I thought it only graceful to protest. I know of nothing I should like less, and confess that was my only misgiving when I married you."

Euangelos, a tall man of middle age and commanding appearance, who had been one of a family of consequence in Argos until taken captive by the Spartans after the Battle of Sepia and sold into slavery, came in and immediately entered into conference with Pericles. Aspasia remained, as there was a subject she wished to discuss with her husband, and while Pericles was counting out money and giving brief peremptory orders, she wandered about the room debating with herself how she could add to its beauty.

It had been a forbidding room when she had come to it three months ago. She had not yet forgotten her sensation of dismay when she entered it on the night of her bridal. A big square room with bare walls, it had been furnished with a narrow couch uncushioned, one chair, a small table for the lamp, a bronze wash-basin, and the great carved chest in the corner. Pericles had occupied it alone even during the years of his married life, and his idea of comfort was that of a soldier accustomed to sleep on the battlefield.

But when she had expressed herself warmly he had pulled her ear, called her a luxurious Ionian, and told her to do with this room, now dearer to him than all others, what she would.

He refused to part with his own bed, but it was pushed into a corner and hidden under a purple coverlet. A broad couch was heaped with her own violet cushions, and so were the chairs and sofa she had appropriated from other parts of the house. Her archaic basin stood high in one corner, and the magnificent amphora Sophocles had given her occupied the place of honor against the wall of the pastas. Her dressing-table stood between the court door and a high window, and sparkled with the mirrors, boxes, and jars she had brought from Miletus and with others that had been given her on the day of reception after the wedding. The walls were hung with linen dyed a delicate shade of lilac, and her own purple rug hid the floor. She had had a marble trough and a tripod put in a small adjoining room, and kept there also the chests that contained her wardrobe, library, and many small bags of gold darics and silver drachmæ. Hippodamus had handed her fortune over to Pericles, and although he would administer it with the same stern frugality that characterized the direction of his own and his wards' great wealth, no doubt he would yield to her coaxing when her present supply of spending money was exhausted.

But in a city where women were not permitted to roam among the bazaars there was little temptation to get rid of money. As fashions rarely changed, clothes lasted for years, and when soiled were washed or sent to the fuller's to be cleaned. Aspasia's extravagances had consisted in buying books, works of art, and long strings of rare beads itinerant venders sometimes brought from foreign ports; but, she reflected, as she wandered about waiting for Euangelos to go, the room needed nothing further to enhance its beauty, and Pericles' library was more extensive than her own. As for beads she had a string of every color. She was glad, on the whole, that it would be long before she must ask her husband for money. It would be rather more of an ordeal than commanding—not asking—her father or Hippodamus. And she wanted no sordid arguments with *him!*

When they were alone Pericles threw himself into an armchair, and Aspasia sat on a stool at his feet—a subtle expression of humility that gave her pleasure in this early stage of matrimony.

"Am I to go to the theatre?" she asked, smiling up into his eyes.

He plucked the gold pins from her hair and drew the copper mesh between his strong hands; hands that looked as if they could strangle a man with one turn of the wrist, although no one had ever seen him violent even on the battlefield.

"You wish to go, I suppose."

"Oh, yes! All my life I have longed to sit in the Dionysus, and Sophocles will give his *Antigone* on the first day! He has read it to me, but I would see it acted in the most famous theatre in the world. I did not ask to go to the winter performances— but the Greater Dionysia! Oh—Pericles!"

"But—you know—" He hesitated, and looked out into the now silent court.

"I know! The lawful matrons of Athens will resent it if I sit with them, and I must not sit with the hetæræ or the Metics."

He gave a short impatient sigh. "Yes. That is it."

"But we go veiled."

"Many of those women saw you at the wedding reception, and there is no disguise for Aspasia. Elpinike would rise in her seat and shake her stick at you. You must not suffer public insult, at least. And Olympias. She hates me. There is no telling what she would do."

"Why does she hate you so?"

"Because I saw as little of her as possible, I suppose. She had no love for me, but she is vain and imperious."

"Did she make unpleasant scenes?"

"There would have been many, but I merely walked out."

She laughed merrily. "And what would you do if I made a scene?"

"I should pursue quite a different method. Be sure I should not walk out."

Aspasia blushed. "But the theatre, dear Pericles? Am I never to sit in the Dionysus and listen to those marvellous dramas people come from all parts of Hellas to witness?"

"I think Agariste might be able to protect you. I have given the matter some thought. Many women are afraid of her. If you went with her . . . it is possible. . . . She is still a friend of Olympias. I fear only Elpinike."

"I wonder." She had recalled her interview with the terrible sister of Kimon. "Listen, Pericles." And she gave a lively description of that encounter, as absorbing a topic of conversation in the houses of Athens to-day as the result of the ostrakismos.

"Great Zeus!" he exclaimed. "You must have been inspired by Athenè herself! It is quite possible you made a secret friend of her, for she is not ungenerous. It is possible also she will take no part in the Dionysia, but remain in seclusion with other humiliated Oligarchs. I had not thought of that."

He twisted her hair into a shining rope and wound it about his arm. "Yes, you shall go," he said after a moment. "I would have you disappointed in nothing." And then as she caught his hand and pressed it to her breast, her eyes sparkling, he gave a quick sigh. "It is at such times as these, Aspasia, that the old superstitions return and I fear the jealousy of the gods. Complete power and perfect happiness! Even before last night I sometimes felt a cold wave of apprehension."

"Oh, Pericles! Use your foresight for the State and live with me in the present!"

VIII

Aspasia's morning assemblies were more crowded than ever, for many hoped to find favor with Pericles by paying court to his wife. But no man came a second time if his intellectual attainments were too meagre to enable him to hold his own in that company of high and varied accomplishment.

As the time for the greater Dionysia with its theatrical performances drew near, strangers filled the inns, and others more fortunate visited friends or relatives in the city. There was none this year from the seceded states; the visitors came from the colonies, the islands, and Asiatic Greece, a few from Carthage and Syracuse.

The guest-rooms in the houses of Pericles and Hippodamus were all occupied, and as not a few of the visitors brought their wives, Aspasia's mornings assumed a different character and the andron witnessed an innovation. Pericles would not dine without Aspasia and she would not hear of banishing the wives of their guests to the women's quarters. But although the news of this revolutionary departure from custom flew all over Athens it was the cause of more tears of envy than of vehement censure.

There was an atmosphere of gaiety pervading all Athens, and not only because of the approaching festival, the most important of the year; for the first time in many years there was not a cloud on the horizon of the State. With Pericles in power they were assured of a long era of peace. The potters, notoriously quarrelsome, smiled on one another. The other craftsmen sang at their work, and the drivers of the great ox-carts that brought the marble from the quarries of Pentelicus to the Acropolis. The men in the Agora were indifferent to politics for the moment; with but one party in Athens discussion was unfruitful. They talked mainly of philosophy and art, the rumored designs of Pheidias, and the chances of Sophocles for winning the first prize with his *Antigone*.

Or of the various lawsuits pending, for in their less intellectual moods nothing interested them more than litigation. If the dicasts held court in one of the stoas they were sure of a large audience, and the pleaders were stimulated to higher oratorical flights than the case perhaps warranted. The Court on the Areopagus looked down with scowling disdain, and lamented as ever the decadent condition of the times when every freeman, no matter how meanly born or ill-educated, could be elected by lot in the Ecclesia to decide not only the fortunes of his fellow-men (often his superiors), but to try the important cases of the nine hundred and more cities of the empire, forced by the conditions of the Delian League to bring their more serious troubles to Athens. The Nine Archons were elected by lot also, and at the end of their important services and considerable power, passed into the Areopagus for life, their jurisdiction, save in a few minor offenses, confined to murder cases only.

Until the rise of Ephialtes and Pericles they had been the chief power in the State, and the Areopagus was of an immemorial antiquity. And now they were relegated to the background and regarded as old fogies by these six thousand jurors who served in panels of five hundred and were all over the place. Their last hope had died with the ostracism of Thucydides and the elevation to uncontrolled power of the man who had brought them low. They grew even more stately and authoritative of mien, and imitated, perhaps unconsciously, his Olympian repose and grand manner.

Murders were rare in Athens, and as time passed and work for the lower classes grew more and more abundant they had little to do but try stray cases from the tributary cities and take part in the great festivals; very dignified and imposing in their robes of state. At the performances in the Dionysus they would as ever occupy front seats. No such honor was extended to mere dicasts.

But it is safe to say they were the only discontented men in Athens, save the fallen Oligarchs, who no longer counted, and, for the most part, had retired to their country estates. A few, less bitter or more philosophical, buried their grievances and gave loyal support to Pericles. Life was long and they had no desire for years of inaction. More and more of them went to his house.

They rarely saw him, however. He was on the Acropolis with his architects and builders, at the studio of Pheidias in the Altis, in the Piræus with Hippodamus, or in his office on the right of the entrance to his house: a sacred lair which not even Aspasia dared penetrate.

He had much to do and to think upon! The land empire was lost, but the power of Athens on the sea must be ever in the eyes of the world. Sixty triremes—giving employment to six thousand soldiers and sailors—patrolled the Ægean between the Piræus and the Propontis to strike fear into Persia and protect the trading ships carrying exports and imports; and his eye was ever on Sparta and Corinth. He had his agents in those cleruchæ, or colonies, he had planted on the tributary islands and created in the Chersonese and on the Propontis, but their reports so far were that all was peace and submission.

Corinth, once the great commercial city of Hellas, had long since been strangled by his subtle policy, but although the commerce of Athens had increased in proportion, the time had come to double the exports. He interviewed many Metics in his office at Piræus, and in Athens. Farmers were encouraged with loans from the State to produce larger quantities of wine and olive oil, dried fruit, and raisins for the foreign market. More honey was gathered and carefully prepared, for Attic honey was a delicacy that brought a high price in distant countries. Agents sent to Italy, Syracuse, Carthage, and Egypt returned with orders for pottery and metal-ware of the most expensive description, and there was joy in the Ceramicus. The force of slaves in the mines of Laurion was increased and larger quantities of silver exported. The little factories turned out in greater profusion shields, arms, and woolen fabrics for export; and imported raw materials were transformed in other factories into fabrics and articles for foreign consumption. Tons of marble were also exported.

He had sent that soothsayer Lampon of many resources to Italiot Greece to select a proper site—conveniently guided by the oracle at Delphi—for the new city to be called Thurii, and employed Protagoras to adapt the code of Charondes to the needs of a cleruchia of more importance than any he had yet founded. It was to be a Pan-Hellenic colony; envoys had travelled all over Hellas with his invitation to partake in the new venture and met with satisfactory response. Thurii was to be no excuse for getting rid of undesirable citizens, but such Oligarchs as found the glory of Athens faded would be welcome in the new city; to be laid out by Hippodamus with wide streets, splendid temples, a theatre and law courts.

He had experienced one bitter disappointment in his life and he would not suffer another if human powers counted for aught. He had cherished a sublime dream: the union of all Greek cities under the ægis of Athens, knit together by common bonds of religion, tradition, customs and language; even those semi--

barbarous states which it was neither possible nor desirable to draw into the Empire would feel her influence and bask in her moral and intellectual supremacy.

As a preliminary step he had invited every State that had been concerned in the war with Persia to send representatives to a Pan-Hellenic Congress in Athens to discuss the rebuilding of the temples, the payment of the votive offerings due the gods for their deliverance of Hellas from the yoke of the Barbarian, and to take common measures for clearing the seas of pirates. But Sparta loudly rejected a plan that would make Athens more famous and powerful than ever, and her voice was heard all over the land. The envoys returned to report humiliation and defeat. His dream of a brotherhood of States, with common interests and a determination to live in permanent peace with one another, vanished for ever. So, too, vanished the one opportunity ever given Hellas to form a powerful union of States that would have averted internal wars and been able to resist not only Philip and Alexander but the Romans of the future.

When Bœotia led the revolt of the States to the undoing of the land empire Pericles welcomed the loss, serious a blow as it was to both prestige and treasury. But he now knew where he stood. He had no desire for constant friction and petty warfare to deplete the population of his own City State, and certain of those unwilling tributaries had no seacoast at all, or none favorable for naval attack. Better to be rid of them at once; and a long peace with Sparta was worth more than their loss. Only in peace could he make Athens supreme in art and in commerce.

His navy swept the pirates off the seas, and unaided he would make Athens the intellectual and artistic centre of the world.

He was profoundly aware of his good fortune in being at the head of the State in an era that had brought forth such an unexampled outburst of genius, either born on the soil of Attica or irresistibly drawn to it. Poets, philosophers, sculptors, architects, painters, rhetors, sophists, vase-painters, flourished in a profusion for which even the legendary glories of ancient Crete offered no parallel.

Sophocles, Euripides, Crates, Carcinus, Xenocles, Ion of Chios; Cratinus, Hermippus, Pherecrates, Magnes, Telekleides

Myonides—alas, that Æschylus was no more. But he had left ninety dramas behind him, and many had been produced since his own rise to power.

Anaxagoras, Damon, Zeno, young Socrates, and others of less immediate fame, but attracting increasing attention.

Pheidias, Myron, Cresilas, Agoracticus, Polycleitus, Pyrrhos, Pythagoras of Rhegium.

Kallikrates, Ictinus, Mnesicles, Hippodamus, Korœbnis, Metagenes.

Polygnotus, Micon, Panænus, Onarsias, Cimon of Cleonæ, and young Agatharchus.

Prodicus, Protagoras, Antiphon, Tisias.

The greatest of the vase-painters belonged to the day of his father, Xanthippus, but there were now Dibutes, Cleophantes, Meidias, and others of such talent they might yet rise to the fame of Brygos and Duris.

And if there was but one historian of note at least there had been none greater than Herodotus.

What an array of already great names—and others putting forth shoots in the rich soil of Athens! Never again, he believed, would so many geniuses of the first rank come to fruition in one era. There must have been high words on Olympus before this supreme favor was granted to the city of Pallas Athenè!

But through the secret invisible workings of whatever hidden forces, this golden river had risen to full tide in his day. And if his sad ghost flits among the ruins of the Athens he loved and made beautiful beyond compare, it may console him to reflect that his own splendid genius directed the course of that river until it became a mighty fountain to dazzle and inspire the minds of men for all time.

Although in these days, save when talking with Aspasia, he rarely thought of himself, he was too clear-sighted and too Greek not to realize that without him these men of genius might never reach their highest fecundity; or would reach it elsewhere and the fame of Athens be in no wise enhanced. If the Oligarchs had come into power no money would have been spent on temples, statues and cities. The philosophers and other learned men too well known as his friends would have been driven out. Even the poets would have suffered if Thucydides and Antiphon had accomplished their unconcealed desire to renew the war with Persia. In his hands alone lay the immortality of these great men and of Athens; and his peculiar gifts of infallible artistic judgment, and imagination coupled with far-sightedness, gave him more than one glimpse of the appraisal of posterity on the Golden Age of Pericles. In this he was more fortunate than most benefactors have been, who often wonder gloomily whether their names and their efforts will outlive their little day. But Pericles possessed the Greek clarity of mind in a superlative degree and knew that in him alone lay the power to immortalize his city. Even *his* foresight, when exerted in behalf of the State, might fail, owing to circumstances none could anticipate, but in art no one ever surpassed him in judgment, and if he was aware of this it was not with conceit, but merely with a true racial acceptance of fact. If his taste had been at fault no man would have been more keenly aware of it than he. Others more gifted and accomplished would have been called in for consultation. But he stood alone in artistic perception as in statesmanship. And in all things! Until Aspasia had come into his life his loneliness had been almost intolerable. Now he had reached the acme of his ambitions, his hopes, his desires; as he had told her there were moments when he felt misgivings and terror. Then he would shrug his shoulders with true Periclean philosophy. Enjoy the gifts of the gods while they lasted. And he was very busy!

IX

The Festival of the Greater Dionysia lasted from the eighth to the thirteenth of the month of Elaphebolian, when the winter rains were over and the Attic plain was covered with a carpet more varied in hue than any ever wrought in Carthage or Miletus. The great amphitheatre on the southeastern slope of the Acropolis with seats for seventeen thousand people was cleared of all débris, the wooden benches mended, and back curtains painted to indicate the scene of the play.

On the first day the choregus—the rich citizen who had assumed the expense of the chorus—the actors, and the chorus itself, assembled in the theatre, the formal announcement was made of the lyric and dramatic contests to be given in the Odeum and the Dionysus, and the last rehearsal—in the presence of the First Archon, who had selected both plays and actors—took place.

The second day saw all Athens in the streets or on the house-tops to witness the procession in honor of the god Dionysus, whose ancient wooden image was carried from its temple, by the longest route possible, to the stage of the theatre. It was led by the great dignitaries, but female jugglers, acrobats and capering Pans, the lyre, the flute, and less seemly revelry accompanied the god of wine and pleasure on his triumphant pilgrimage; which lasted until the dignitaries, at least, were ready to drop from fatigue. The girls watched from the roofs or sang and danced in the courtyards. For six days all classes of free-men would be as light-hearted as children who had never known sorrow, care, nor invasion. These Athenians born in the spring-time of the world knew how to enjoy themselves. They danced and laughed and sang, gave rein to every wanton impulse, applauded and criticized, drank deeply, worshipped the gods, and almost loved their fellow-men.

Of all this Aspasia saw nothing; although sitting in the aula —alone, for her receptions were discontinued during this season of festival—she heard from dawn until darkness. Nor did she attend the performances on the third day at the Odeum where there were lyric contests between choruses of men and boys, chantings of Homer and Hesiod, songs of Pindar, Simonides, and Sappho; the prizes awarded by Pericles. She had agreed some-what reluctantly that it were best to reserve her first public appearance for the Dionysus. If nothing untoward occurred on the first morning she would also attend the second. The after-noons, reserved for comedy, were not witnessed by women— save possibly the hetæræ—as those brilliant and amusing per-formances were calculated to bring a blush to the most withered cheek; the delighted roars of the men could be heard all over Athens.

But on the fourth day she joined the mighty throng that

started shortly after dawn for the theatre. They came from all quarters of Athens, from the suburbs, the farms, Salamis, and the Piræus, and every man and woman wore a garland. Some seven thousand workmen and other poor citizens carried two obols in their fists, the dole of the government. The women were few in number compared with the men, for many matrons had long ceased to care for anything beyond their own walls, and girls were permitted to take part in nothing but the Panathenea and the Mounichia. Few Metics brought their wives, for tickets to their class were restricted, and no workman would have thought of doing such a thing. Aspasia caught a glimpse of Galatea—unveiled—who was hanging heavily on the arm of her husband. In her eagerness for life it was evident that she meant to quaff every cup her new estate offered.

Agariste, a masterful woman with a mustache and a figure almost as commanding as her brother's, flanked Aspasia on one side, Zosmë on the other. Both guardians experienced qualms, and, devoted as they were to the drama, wished that the day were over. Even if the morning passed without insult, the gods only knew what tale the night would bring them. A play of Cratinus was to be produced in the afternoon, and as he was a bitter enemy of Pericles, what filthy shafts might he not level at this wife of the Strategos unrecognized by his own law! Agariste, who feared no man, and kept her husband and sons in subjection, dreaded almost as much as she detested the comic poets, and although she had succumbed to the charm of this unwelcome sister-in-law, heartily wished she had remained in Miletus.

Aspasia was invaded by no tremors. Her spirits were soaring, and not only on the wings of universal gaiety; she was about to realize one of her most permanent desires and she was to hear three tragedies and a satyric drama by her friend Sophocles. There had been a furious controversy at her last morning levee before the festival on the relative methods of Æschylus and Sophocles—absent at rehearsal. Atrometus, an elderly Eupatrid of great wealth, who had been choregos for more than one of the dramas of Æschylus, and whose intellectual symposia were famous in Athens, and Pausanias, who had expended large sums on the chorus for this year, were the protagonists; and the argument had been listened to by every one present, sides taken, and more than one voice lifted in protest or applause. When Atrometus and Pausanias had had their full say and haughtily presented each other with a back, the argument had raged on until hunger emptied the aula.

The ultimate verdict had been for Sophocles. That Æschylus had grandeur, prophetic fire, no man would deny, and his *Agamemnon* was and ever must be unequalled in imagination and sublimity. But Sophocles had the sculptured perfection of Pheidias, a flawless artist of the drama, and each of his plays was complete in itself, not one of a trilogy unequal in merit. He was a master of concentration and complex unity. There was a perfect balance between the round development of his characters and the splendor of the story; a harmony that appealed to the educated love of form of the more critical Athenians of his day. As a mere master of stagecraft he had shown a new acumen in substituting three actors for two in portraying the several parts. And he was supreme in pathos; he could move even the gods to tears.

Socrates had raised his powerful voice in behalf of Euripides and been nearly annihilated. Euripides had his reputation to make. He was disrespectful to heroes and gods. He was no artist. It was an insult to such august names even to mention him. Aspasia laughed to herself as she recalled the angry faces —already too heated—pressing upon Socrates, and the perfect calm with which he had held his ground.

"What are you laughing at?" asked Agariste, and half wished she were an Ionian. True, racially, she was, but in these days Athenians were Athenians, and Asiatic Greeks were welcome to the designation. They were foreigners and who cared what they called themselves? "You surely do not expect to laugh at *Antigone?*"

"Oh, no, dear Agariste. I have already wept over *Antigone,* and no doubt shall be glad of my veil to-day." And she gave a brief account of that hot dispute.

Agariste shrugged her square shoulders. "I witnessed many plays of Æschylus—twenty, I should think—and I have witnessed many of Sophocles; and few of either that did not move and interest me. Why be so ungrateful as to dispute the respective merits of those great men? But the men of Athens must ever be disputing about something. The only time they ever keep their mouths shut is when they are asleep or engaged in hot fighting. Gods, what a crush! Be careful your veil is not torn off."

The vast theatre rose above them, already filling. Standing tantalizingly on a higher point of rock than the last semicircle of seats was a bronze tripod to be awarded the choregus if his chorus reached the usual high standard. Along the parapet might be seen a row of heads: the citizen-archers who guarded the treasure in the square ugly temple that held the sacred wooden statue of Athenè.

The altar and wooden image of Dionysus stood on the large circular orchestra—some sixty-five feet in diameter—where the play would be given. The drop curtain against the high wall at the back portrayed the entrance to the royal palace of Thebes. Scattered here and there among the tiers of seats were brazen vessels to reverberate the voices of the actors.

They gave up their tickets, rough disks of lead, and were escorted by the "cashier" to the seats reserved for their kind. The first person Aspasia saw was Elpinike, unveiled, and seated next the aisle; and for the moment her heart failed her. But she caught the flying skirts of her courage and paused in front of those snapping eyes that had penetrated her veil instantly.

"Joy to you, Elpinike," she said softly. "It will always give me pleasure to greet you."

"Doubly so now, no doubt!— But no, I'll not misjudge you, and your beauty has made my old eyes glad. You are triumphant, of course, but not over a defeated old woman. Go your way in peace. If Pericles feared I would make an unseemly exhibition of myself to-day he was mistaken for once—"

"Oh, no!"

"I thought so. But it will do him good to learn there are a few things he cannot foresee. Tell him I said so."

"Thank the gods for that!" exclaimed Agariste when they

had passed out of earshot. "But where did you meet that old eumenide? She must spend a fortune on scent."

Aspasia told the story absently as she looked about her with ever-increasing interest. All men and all women were in gala attire and the garlands on their heads made the grim rock of the Acropolis look as if it had burst into bloom to rival the wild flowers of the plain. She glanced over that sea of heads, never still for a minute, to the opposite side of the theatre where the hetæræ sat carefully segregated. Their himatia were more gorgeous than those of the Metics at Galatea's wedding, and their handsome unveiled faces full of gaiety and insolence. She watched them for a few moments to note if any of those roving eyes were searching for one, whom, no doubt, they had discussed overmuch and would be gratified to see publicly in their ranks. But they had no thought for any but the wild young bloods who sat as near them as possible.

Her gaze wandered from the theatre to the panorama spread beyond. Just below, the Street of the Tripods wound round the base of the Acropolis, lined with the pedestals, of varying magnificence, the victorious choregi had erected for their rewards. She hoped Pausanias would add to their number. He was a rather tiresome person, but he had done her good service in diverting certain followers from Thucydides to Pericles and she would have him rewarded by the State! In this part of Athens was the Altis or Sacred Grove and it was set with statues and little temples, altars and shrines among the scattered pines. Without the walls the colonnades of the Lyceum gleamed through its ilex grove; and just beyond the theatre rose the tentlike roof, flashing in the sun, of the Odeum, designed by Pericles for the city.

Although that incessant hum of many voices was in her ears she could *hear* the deep silence of the plain, and so clear and brilliant was the atmosphere she fancied she could see the bees on Hymettus. The mounting sun gave out warmth without undue heat and the rich blue sky above that transparent air must surely be the floor of Elysion. The only thing moving within the range of her vision was the classic Ilissus wandering slowly between its narrow banks, to join the Cephisus beyond the Long

Walls. Trees shaded it and it had its own statues and fanes. On a terrace above was an unfinished temple begun by Pisistratus, now a ruin.

She turned her head. The men slaves of the households had been given a holiday, and she had been told they would go to the roofs near the theatre. As she had expected, they were crowded there, contenting themselves with the prospect of a distant sight of the actors. She knew that many of them, like Euangelos, were educated men and had attended the theatre in their own countries. Cursed war! She prayed there would be none in her time. If Xerxes had conquered, these men about her might be slaves in Persia to-day. Even her Xanthias had been born in freedom.

"Here is Olympias!" whispered Agariste. "Pray Athenè she is in one of her loftiest moods and will not deign to notice us."

A tall rather heavily built woman wearing a yellow mantle and veil, a woman with a carriage of indescribable hauteur, paused as she was shown to a seat below, turned, swept the forms above her, and then focussed her attention on Aspasia— who could feel those hidden eyes burn her face.

"O Zeus!" muttered Agariste. "She looks as if she were going to speak." And Aspasia's heart missed a beat.

But Olympias continued only to stare, and, since she might not raise her veil save when all eyes were directed to the stage, contrived to make every other part of her ample person radiate scorn and contempt. Nor did she budge until she was gratified by a murmur, audible even in that louder hum of seventeen thousand voices, of "Aspasia." . . . "Aspasia." . . . "Wife of Pericles," and the craning of many necks. Then she shrugged her shoulders and sat down.

Agariste drew a deep sigh of relief. "I feared worse," she said. "Although I told her yesterday that if she made a scene I'd find some way to punish her. She laughed, and then asked me to remember she was a great lady. I told her she had been born one but too much wealth and a bad disposition had corrupted her. The interview was none too pleasant."

"She *looks* as if she had had three husbands and divorced two." said Zosmë. "I wonder will she divorce this one?"

"The gods only know, but I think not. She was in love with Cleander before they induced her to marry Pericles. He was away as Ambassador to Syracuse and fell ill and she forgot him and thought it would be a fine thing to be the wife of the first citizen of Athens. But when he came back! Well, if Pericles heard the gossip he was indifferent. He had the boys, and I fancy his only misgiving was that she would not ask him to divorce her—"

"Ah!" interrupted Aspasia, to whom this gossip was distasteful. "It is about to begin. I would miss nothing."

Trumpeters stood at either end of the curtain and peremptory blasts reduced the audience to silence. The priest of Dionysus walked majestically to the altar and poured the libation, then, kneeling with arms outstretched, lifted palms and voice in invocation. Every one present was reminded that, whatever the entertainment, this great festival was, above all, one of religious devotion to the fire-born son of Zeus. All heads were bowed for a moment and he took his seat in a solemn hush.

His was the seat of honor, a thronos in the very middle of the front row. Pericles sat on his right, the First Archon on his left. The seats near by were occupied by the priests of many temples, the rest of the archons, the members of the Areopagus, other dignitaries, distinguished strangers, and celebrated Athenians. Aspasia caught a glimpse of the profile of Sophocles and wondered if he were nervous.

A door on the left of the drop-curtain opened and the chorus, masked, and richly dressed to represent elders of the Theban court, entered the orchestra and grouped themselves. From the opposite door Cleidermides, the most famous young actor in Athens, emerged, in the guise of Antigonè the ill-fated daughter of Œdipus. By his side walked Telpolemus, next in distinction, to take the part of her sister Ismenè. There was a faint sibilant rustle in the audience as the women threw back their veils.

Masked faces cannot express emotion, and actors had practiced gesture, intonation, and eloquence of body, until they had reached a point of perfection that made mere features seem meaningless. Their voices were so clear, flexible, and sonorous, and possessed such carrying power, the brazen vessels were needed for the deaf only; and that light air alone was an unrivalled conductor. Even the slaves on the roofs, straining eager ears, caught now and then a phrase.

> *Own sister of my blood, one life with me,*
> *Ismenè, have the tidings caught thine ear?*
> *Oh, hath not heaven decreed to execute*
> *On thee and me, while we are yet alive*
> *All the evils Œdipus bequeathed?   All horror,*
> *All pain, all outrage, falls on us!*

The actor delivered the poet's words in tones of such poignant anguish, that a quiver ran through the most responsive—and the most intelligent—audience the world has ever known. They almost hissed at Ismenè's faint-hearted replies to her heroic sister's appeal to bury their slain brother in defiance of their cruel uncle's decree.

It was a play above any other to wring the heart of all Greeks; for not to bury and with solemn ritual those fallen in war was a bitter ignominy that even the enemy rarely visited upon the hated dead. When Creon declaimed haughtily and in accents of finality:

> *He shall have no lament, no funeral,*
> *But lie unburied, for the carrion fowl*
> *And dogs to eat his corse, a sight of shame,*

the men refrained with difficulty from uttering a cry of fury, and the women sobbed quietly. Agariste ground her teeth, and old Elpinike shook her cane.

But unless a play was of inferior quality, in which case they uttered cat-calls and yells of derision and whistled it off the stage, they rarely interrupted even with applause; reserving all demonstration for the end, when, if gratified, they broke into a tumult that could be heard a mile away. They listened with so tense and reverent an attention that the stillness in the vast auditorium was shaken only by short gasps, deep sighs of relief or despair.

And when hearing those tragedies in the Dionysus, unless the dramatist were Euripides in too modern a mood, in every heart, even the most skeptical, was a belief in the gods. The most irreligious mind cannot withstand sublimity of expression. The majestic rolling phrases of Æschylus or Sophocles evoked the very images of the immortals, and many believed the same power drew them down from Olympus to listen.

Antigone proceeded without intermission on its course of anguish, defeat, and relentless misfortune, until Creon's last words:

Intolerable destiny descends!

and the few concluding lines of the chorus—all that a chorus should be and a triumph for Pausanias—were lost in the storm of clapping, shouting, stamping, and roars of "Sophocles!"

x

"I am going," whispered Aspasia. "I could not listen to another tragedy even of Sophocles. I should faint, or have hysterics, or do something else to make myself conspicuous. And no one will notice. They are all moving—"

"Oh, no!" exclaimed Agariste, who could have sat through ten plays without leaving her seat. "Who ever heard of such a thing?" And Zosmë took hold of her mantle. Never had she experienced such delightful vicarious emotion.

"You need not come with me," said Aspasia impatiently. "But nothing will keep me." And she made her escape.

The women remained in their seats, chatting excitedly, eating the honey cakes and sipping the wine handed round by order of the generous choregos, but the men poured out of the theatre to stretch their legs and exchange enthusiastic comments on the play. A crowd surrounded Sophocles, and Aspasia saw the helmet of Pericles above the mass of heads.

No one noticed her—a veiled woman who might have been hurrying home to her children—for all were too excited over the great tragedy they had witnessed and too eager to express their opinions. In the last group she passed one man had dared to stigmatize Antigone herself, as "too masculine," and it looked as if blows were imminent.

The streets, with the exception of those immediately about the theatre, were deserted, and she could have made her way home swiftly and met no one. But she was in no mood for the house. She walked quickly to the nearest gate and passed through the suburbs and out into the peace of the country. Treading lightly a meadow of blue aloes she reached the Ilissus, and crossing a bridge sat down near a little ruined temple in a grove of pines.

The birds sang in the trees of the grove. The silence was perfumed with earth and flowers. Far away the blue mountains of the Peloponnese looked in that clear atmosphere as if carved on the horizon.

The tumult in her nerves subsided. The intolerable beauty and sublimity of those lines ceased to reverberate in her tired head. She fell to dreaming of Pericles. What was the excitement of a mere drama to that she had known with him? And what mattered the woes of a woman long dead in the transcendent happiness of one woman more alive than she had ever been and with years of bliss before her?

She was sitting on a low bench, her chin propped on her hand, seeing pictures in the waters of that narrow stream called by courtesy a river, when she heard a quick menacing step and looked up to see Thoron standing on the opposite bank and regarding her with hungry angry eyes.

She sat erect and drew her brows in a frown. She would have hated any one who interrupted her musings, and this was the last man she desired to see. No man but one had the right to love her.

"I thought you were in the country," she said coldly.

"There are horses in Attica," he replied savagely. "And I am no child to be told to go and hide my head."

"But you are a citizen of Athens and as such amenable to the law, O Thoron. If it were known you were here—"

"They may do with me what they will! I knew you would be abroad to-day and that I might have a glimpse of you, but I looked for no such good fortune as this."

He leaped across the river and stood over her, and she rose to her feet haughtily. He looked like a madman and they were hidden in the grove, but she despised him too thoroughly for fear.

"You will go at once," she said in the most cutting tone of contempt she could command. "I came here to be alone after witnessing a great tragedy. I wish to talk with no one and with you least of all."

To her surprise his face crumpled and he flung himself at her feet, and grasping her mantle pulled it over his head and burst into tears.

"O Aspasia! Aspasia!" he sobbed. "Be kind but a moment!"

So great was her disgust she would have spurned him with her foot, but his knee had caught in his own mantle, and pulling it aside revealed a dagger in the girdle of his tunic. She bent down and plucked it out and held it behind her.

"Oh, get up, Thoron," she said wearily. "A woman despises the tears of a man."

"I have suffered the tortures of nethermost Hades! And you have no pity! You are a woman of ice and snow. What does Pericles want of you?"

Her smile would have maddened Thoron, but his face was still buried in the mantle.

"Then why should you think you love me?" she asked. "A woman of ice and snow?"

He supported himself on an elbow and raised a distorted face.

"Why did you tell me you would marry me, Aspasia? Why could not you have let me go at once?"

"Look back—and ask yourself what difference that would have made. You were ready to drink hemlock. And I never promised to marry you."

"You led me on—you made me think—"

"It was partly good-nature." And then she added deliberately: "And I had use for you. You gave me valuable information, and I was enabled to refute the arguments of Pericles' enemies and win them over."

If her purpose were to turn his grief to wrath she succeeded.

He leaped to his feet, his face contorted with rage. With one hand he tore off his mantle and the other flew to his girdle. She laughed and showed him the dagger.

"It shall be put to other use," she said. "If you touch me I'll not hesitate to thrust it in to the hilt."

"You are perfidious," he gasped. "Cruel—without pity—"

"No, Thoron, merely a woman in love with another man. No cruelty can exceed such, I fancy."

But although she could not resist taunting him, she wondered just how sure and swift her wrist would be if he attacked her. She had never held a dagger in her hand before. Nor had she the least desire to shed blood. She only wanted to be rid of him. But if he touched her sacred body she would stab him without compunction.

He yelped like the young puppy he was and leaped at her. She stepped quickly out of his path and he stumbled. Before he could recover himself both heard the sound of running feet.

Some one else had seen her cross the meadow and Thoron as well. A second later her ever-watchful Xanthias burst into the grove.

Thoron sprang at him with a roar of rage, and the two men wrestled and endeavored to throw each other down. Xanthias if no longer young was still very strong. He remembered he had been born a freeman and fought this Eupatrid with a flooding sense of equality that almost made him laugh aloud.

Both men had witnessed the Pankration and practiced with friends. After they had wrestled for some moments without overcoming each other they drew back and stretched out their arms with fingers curved like claws. For a second they stood poised and then rushed in. They alternated the swinging downward stroke when possible with a blow on the top of the head.

Although both were novices, for the Pankration was the art of professionals, Xanthias in the end would be no match for Thoron, a product of the gymnasium and a winner of foot-races; with a wind as long as his muscular arms, and in the full tide of manhood. Aspasia looked on with terror as she saw the blows of Xanthias weakening. If Thoron got him under he would not hesitate to kill him. She had few better friends than Xanthias, ever ready as now to die for her; he had been her personal attendant since childhood and she was sincerely fond of him. Not for her should he lose his life, nor even suffer the ignominy of defeat. And she had her own safety to consider.

Thoron's back was toward her. She approached warily, for he might whirl about at any moment. Moreover it was difficult to aim at a jerking body. She watched intently. He drew back and squared himself, swinging his right arm down and backward for the stroke. Xanthias was in the same position, the fingers of both men curved as if they would tear out the entrails of the other. Before Thoron could swing his arm inward Aspasia lifted herself on her toes, plunged the dagger into his shoulder and jerked it out. The blood spurted and Thoron dropped his useless arm and staggered back against a tree, cursing dazedly.

"Run, Xanthias!" she cried. "Get slaves and a litter and carry him to his house."

Xanthias glared at his foe. "But, Mistress—"

"Run! Waste no time. I would not have him bleed to death."

When Xanthias had gone she said peremptorily: "Lie down." Thoron slowly collapsed to the ground, and to her relief fainted.

She washed the dagger hastily, cut a long strip from her tunic, and bound the wound as well as she could. But it was still bleeding when Xanthias returned with a litter and two slaves. He entered the grove alone.

"Put down your veil and hide in the temple," he commanded, and without the usual formalities of speech. "I told them I had found him here wounded and that a lady in passing gave him succor. Zeus knows what they believe but I threatened them with death if they gossipped."

Aspasia disappeared and the slaves carried away the still unconscious Thoron. Xanthias watched them out of sight and then summoned Aspasia.

"Come now, O Mistress," he said. "Do you return to the theatre?"

"No, I go to the house."

"Where you should have gone in the first place," he grumbled. "What will you do next? Men say you are the greatest of

women and they swarm about you like flies about honey,
fearful of losing a word; but to me you are no wiser than when
you cried because you couldn't swing right over the top of the
aula, and made the dignified Axiochus—may the dark brother
of Zeus be kind to his shade—get down on the floor and play
with you. And now you are married and no better! It is not
for the wife of Pericles to roam the country alone. If you were
tired of the theatre you should have gone straight to the house."

Aspasia accepted the scolding meekly. That he uttered sound
truths she would be the last to deny. But reaction left her a
prey to uneasiness.

"If Pericles should hear of this!" she exclaimed.

"I have told you those slaves will keep their mouths shut.
There is no one else to fear: that young fool will talk as little."

"Do you think he will die?" she asked anxiously.

He exclaimed with impatience. "Men do not die of a dagger
driven in by a woman. And I sent at once for a doctor."

"You think of everything, dear Xanthias," she said gratefully,
"and it is only just that I reward you, for Zeus knows what you
saved me from to-day. I shall give you your freedom."

"Oh—*Mistress!*" He threw back his head and raised his
arms to the sky. "I felt a man when I fought Thoron and now
I am never to feel a slave again!" He knelt, crushing the wild
flowers with his brawny knees, and kissed the embroidered hem
of her mantle. "I accept my freedom, O daughter of Axiochus,"
he said with dignity as he rose to his feet, "but I shall never
leave you. My people were all massacred when I was taken,
or sold into slavery. I have nowhere to go, and I have been
more fortunate than many, for you have made me happy in
serving you."

"But I would give you money, and you could open a jewel
or scent shop in the Agora or in one of those lively little streets
near by."

"Unless you drive me forth, Mistress, I shall still serve you.
I once promised your father I would never try to escape, but
watch over you always. And I am no longer young. It is much
to have a good home and be content. Let me remain, dear
Mistress."

Poor thing! she thought. And would Thoron be half as much a man if he had served for many years as some woman's attendant in Persia? She said aloud: "Very well. I should not know what to do without you. But go on the first of every month to Euangelos for your wages. I will tell him to attend to what formalities are necessary."

XI

Sophocles won the first prize and Pausanias his tripod. This was cause for rejoicing in their circle, and Pericles gave a banquet in honor of the event. But secretly he celebrated the singular amiability of the comic poets. Cratinus, Telekleides, Hermippus, and three others of their class had given a play each and not a reference had been made to Aspasia or himself. Whether the dramas had been written before his marriage and offered no opportunity for malicious interpolations, or whether the poets too were affected by the general atmosphere of goodwill and light-heartedness, or were out of sympathy for the moment with a defeated party, he neither knew nor cared. There were no obscene squibs flying about Athens to be rolled under the tongue of mistress and slave and quoted with joy in the market-place; the woman he loved was still unsmirched by vile tongues. He feared nothing else; he could protect her from other ills, but before the comic poets he was helpless unless he curbed freedom of speech; an undemocratic measure he was not yet prepared to take.

The guests invited to the banquet included besides those in whose honor it was given, his usual group of intimate friends: Anaxagoras, Damon, Zeno, Pheidias, Menippus (a Strategos off and on), young Thucydides; and, in addition, Polygnotus, Ion of Chios, Herodotus, Hippodamus, Philippos, whose little son Aristophanes sometimes came to play with the children and add to the tumult of the inner court, Ariphon, and his brother-in-law Simonides: his house guests had gone. Aspasia had suggested Socrates but Pericles had made a wry face.

"Don't ask me that, dear head, if you love me!" he exclaimed. "Socrates' name may be renowned through the ages and my ashes will rejoice, for I wish him well; but I'll not look at him alive when I can avoid it. And at a symposium it is every man's right to talk. I give one rarely and would have it successful, not look round upon strained faces and listen to deep sighs."

So Aspasia had said no more, but she was deeply relieved when Socrates came to tell her that he was leaving for Thebes next day to visit the Pythagorean Philolus. She quarrelled with him incessantly, when both were in no humor for high discourse, but she respected him too sincerely not to spare his sensitive nature where she could.

She was to have two guests of her own, Agariste and Zosmë; and to this she was not forced to ask her husband's consent. He would give no symposia without her and told her to ask whom she chose. Her duties ended with the dispatch of Xanthias to inform the ladies of the singular honor conferred upon them. Euangelos himself had little to do, for a caterer supplied the food for banquets and brought his own waiters. He engaged a flute girl to start the symposium, inspected the dishes and goblets, ordered garlands in the market-place, and sent to the country-place on the Euripus for fresh wine.

The andron was probably the most beautiful room of any house in Athens. The roof was supported by Ionic pillars, and Polygnotus and his students had painted the walls with scenes from the *Iliad* for Xanthippus. On a pedestal against the east wall was an amphora three feet high commemorating the Sacred War, a gift from the potters and vase-painters on the day after Pericles' marriage to Aspasia. On each of the longer sides of the room were shelves for a collection of rare ceramics, vases and statuettes of bronze gold and silver, a bowl of ancient Kamares ware from Crete, painted scarlet and white, as well as spoils from the tent of Xerxes and from Mycale, that gave the place something the air of a museum. The couches were carved and gilded, and Aspasia had induced Euangelos to supply them with cushions. There would be chairs for the ladies, for althoug Pericles would have Aspasia at his banquets even though Athen rocked to its foundations, he was not yet converted to the do trine of the complete equality of woman! Aspasia was uniqu and he respected his sister and liked Zosmë, but he had th true Athenian's contempt for women in general. Aspasia was alone with him too little to waste precious hours in talk of other women, but this press of work must decrease before long, and when the time came for uninterrupted afternoons and evenings she had every intention of delicately readjusting his point of view. She recalled the advice of Hesiod: Add little to little.

But Zosmë gave thanks for his calm acceptance of custom in the matter of chairs, for she had recently put on stays—a linen bandage wound tightly about her by her handmaid, the while she held her breath.

"I feel like an Egyptian mummy or an infant in swaddling clothes," she confided to Aspasia. "But by the Holy Twins I'll not look like the prow of a ship!" When Aspasia had suggested self-denial in sweets she shook her head. "All the delights of life for me. I'll not forego one of them and sweets and rich sauces are not the least. And I may take off this thing at night. . . . By the way, I am told the men always wear white at banquets, so let us wear colors. We'll not look as pure and sweet, but will be doubly grateful to the eye."

She dressed her hair on the night of the banquet in the high archaic style of statues recovered during excavations in the older part of Athens, and selected a yellow chiton embroidered on the front and about the edge of the square neck and long sleeves with the fleur de lys pattern of ancient Crete. It was seldom that she opened her jewel casket in Athens, but to-night, although she was late and had cause to be in an exceeding bad temper, she put on a diadem sparkling with Eastern stones, and confined her tunic with a magnificent metal girdle her father had brought from Egypt, supposedly ravished from a tomb.

Aspasia wore a full flowing violet tunic, also cut into a square at the neck and with sleeves reaching to the hands. Her embroideries were always of the classic key pattern and on this chiton the threads were of silver and purple. Thera had twisted her copper locks into the thick pointed knot that most became her and her only ornament was a small diadem chased by a Cretan goldsmith and left in Ionia a thousand years since.

Agariste stalked in arrayed in a bright green tunic unembroidered and unadorned and which became her swarthy skin not at all. But she was superior to vanity.

"You know I don't approve of this," she said as they stood in the pastas awaiting the guests. "When once you begin to violate social customs only the gods know what will come next. It is not seemly that Eupatrids should entertain like Metics. No doubt every husband in Athens to-night is explaining to his tearful wife all the reasons for keeping women in their own quarters; something he has never had to do before! First thing we know they will be running round the streets and trying to argue with men in the Agora. You have much to answer for, Aspasia."

"There is nothing I'd like better than to see women in the Agora and at their husbands' banquets," said Aspasia coolly. "I hope some of them will find the courage to follow my example."

Agariste shook her head. "I was only joking. Innovations will not go beyond this house, although no doubt the poor husbands will grow weary of the sound of your name. Many women have spirit enough to row, although they dare go no further. Divorces are too easily got—by men."

"Well, discontent is the alpha of revolution, and who knows? Here they come."

As the guests entered the aula slaves removed their sandals and bathed their feet. Pericles came from his office and greeted them. Zosmë, spared formalities, made her way swiftly to the pastas.

"I thought I'd not be able to come at all," she exclaimed. "Really, Aspasia, you must give Alcibiades a sound spanking. He and that little wretch, Aristophanes—who'll come to a bad end, I know—came to play with Archeptolemus to-day and he is black and blue. They played they were torturing a slave to get evidence against his master, and they pinched him all over and nearly pulled his arms out of their sockets. Phila came on the scene in time or I believe they would have killed him."

Aspasia laughed merrily. "Archeptolemus should learn to attack first. That is the only way to manage Alcibiades. You've made a girl of that boy with your petting and coddling.

"Oh, you may laugh!" said Zosmë indignantly. "But wait until you have a child of your own."

"Oh, no!" The light fled from Aspasia's face, and Agariste exclaimed harshly:

"I should hope not! It is bad enough as it is." She never minced words and spoke her mind on all occasions.

"Some things can't be helped," said Zosmë with a shrug, "and that is generally one of them. But no long faces to-night. Here they come—and how terribly dignified they look! One would think each was about to pose for Pheidias and had already ordered the pedestal."

"I fear you have no reverence, Zosmë," said Agariste severely. "These are the first men of Athens."

"Oh, dear Agariste, you are married yourself, why talk of reverencing men? Does Simonides never go down on his knees and hunt under the bed for his sandals, which he has kicked off the night before? And cursing by all the gods meanwhile? Even you, Aspasia, dare you say you reverence Pericles?"

"Oh, no!" Aspasia was smiling gaily once more. "Not reverence! Nothing as dull as that!"

"Well, you've got him under your thumb," said Agariste crossly. "Pericles, of all men!"

"We are both wrong," said Zosmë lightly. "They are really one. The miracle has happened in Athens."

XII

There was little conversation during the banquet. It was etiquette to enjoy the food delicately and reserve mental effort for the symposium. The night was warm and the doors were open. There was no fire on the central hearth, before which Agariste, Aspasia, and Zosmë sat in three armchairs. The couches were arranged as if on three sides of a square, two men on each and served from small tables. Pericles reclined opposite the ladies, Sophocles beside him. Zosmë's bright critical eyes surveyed this geometrical yet luxurious scene and she kept up a running fire of criticism.

"What bony legs Pausanias has, and he's hitched his mantle up, and his chiton's too short. He should marry again. Pheidias

ought to remodel himself. His arms are much too long. You
old Nous looks as if he were lying on the wrong bone, but most
of them recline gracefully enough. The gods are good to permit
us to sit up when we eat. I've always wondered that men's
food goes down the right way. Don't scowl at me so, Agariste."

"I repeat, you have no reverence for men, heroes, nor gods,
and don't make me the silly answer you did just now. You are
in the company of the most illustrious men of Athens and you
can only make sport of them. The levity of Ionians passes understanding."

"It does, dear Agariste! But I'll pass on to the food. These
caterers' sauces do not compare with those of my cook or yours.
You talk about freedom in Athens and you are all afraid of your
cooks. They refuse extra work and you are obliged to call in
caterers for your banquets. I've had three cooks since I came
to Athens, each haughtier than the last."

"I see no fault with this dish," said Agariste, who had helped
herself plentifully to young pig stewed in olive oil and served
with crisp lettuce. "I repeat you are too critical of all things
Athenian."

Aspasia smiled. "Zosmë has merely taken her cue, for Athenians must criticize everything."

"Well, I'll never turn into an Athenian, although I confess I
like Athens well enough. Indeed I would I could remain here,
for I look forward with no joy to that wild coast where my
husband is to build Thurii. A wilderness, no doubt."

"Not at all," said Agariste. "And Croton is near by. There
are good bazaars there. Nor is it far by galley to Syracuse.
That is a great and too luxurious city. I have visited it. My
husband was in the train of Cleander when he went as ambassador, and I let no man leave me behind; although I made him
bring me home before the year was out. We sailed up the coast,
for it was also Cleander's mission to inspect the colonies. The
inhabitants of Italia, of course, are barbarians, but the coast is
Greek. Why do you not eat, Aspasia?"

"I dined sufficiently on the wild fowl from Thebes. If you notice, the men are not eating much."

"No, they're afraid they'd talk less if they did." She added hastily: "They really think more of their heads than their stomachs, and I doubt if that can be said of any other race."

"Perhaps they make up for it at home," said Zosmë sagely. "They don't have to talk to their wives and go to bed early."

"Oh, an Athenian will talk to anybody," replied Agariste, smiling in spite of herself. "But I do the talking in my house."

"I'll wager!" murmured Zosmë. "Are you like your mother, Agariste? It is said she dreamed she had given birth to a lion the night before she was delivered of Pericles."

"That is quite true but she was nothing like me. She was very beautiful, and though intelligent, as feminine as Aspasia. She too was very fair and not unlike Aspasia in general appearance. I resemble my father, the great Xanthippus," she added proudly, "and it was a terrible mistake that I was born a woman. I should have led armies to war."

"And yet you have no sympathy for women!" exclaimed Aspasia. "It seems quite natural to you they should be kept in subjection."

"Certainly, and because they are women and nothing more. Suppose I were given the command of Athens to-morrow? How many Generals of my own sex could I find?"

"I for one. Zosmë for another. And many more if they were given the chance."

Agariste frowned. "I do not like to hear you say such things, Aspasia. Our civilization is perfect as it is. The gods have ordained that men shall rule. And a clever woman can always manage her husband and get what she wants. Her first duty is to bear sons to serve the State. I, who am called masculine, have borne four. And in my own household I am as supreme as Pericles in the State. My sons obey me, and will until each leaves the house to take a bride to his own."

"Did you expose the girls?" asked Zosmë wickedly.

"No, for I had none. If I was mistakenly a woman myself, at least I was spared that final indignity. And if Sparta ever invades Athens I'll throw tiles from the roof."

But she helped herself liberally to sweets.

The tables were removed and others bearing wine-cups brought in. Slaves placed garlands on the heads of the guests.

Aspasia smiled over at Pericles, who liked nothing less than wreathing himself with flowers. A flute girl entered, but had received peremptory orders from Euangelos. Instead of mingling with the guests she stood by the hearth and produced her sweet sounds while all sang the hymn of thanksgiving to the gods, then disappeared.

Pericles poured the libation, the wine was passed round in an immense silver krater, and the serious business of the evening began.

"Will it be frightfully intellectual?" whispered Zosmë to Aspasia. "I feel sleepy already, and I would I could take off this band."

"I doubt if they have come with set speeches. And at least Socrates is not here!"

"For which the gods be thanked." And she made herself as comfortable as might be in her marble chair.

XIII

There was silence for a moment, for even his more intimate friends stood somewhat in awe of Pericles. They exhaled a quiet sigh of relief when he opened the symposium on a comparatively light note.

"Tell me, Sophocles," he said, "is it true that when you tragic poets get in a tight place you invoke the aid of the gods—believing they hover ever about you?"

Sophocles gave his deep mellow laugh. "I hesitate to reveal the secrets of the drama before our young friend Thucydides, for I have always the impression he is taking mental notes and will betray us to posterity. He is said to have a prodigious memory."

Thucydides, challenged, replied coldly: "I take no interest in the drama, O Sophocles, and was probably the only man in Athens who did not attend the theatre this year. Your secrets are safe with me."

Pericles frowned, but Sophocles answered serenely, "My apprehensions allayed, I will answer your question, dear host. It is true that my inspiration sometimes fails me, and then I banish all thought from my mind and pray to the gods for help

Whether they are near and answer my prayer or whether that perfect detachment releases the reluctant forces of my mind, who can tell?"

"But you believe in the gods, Sophocles?" asked Herodotus anxiously.

"Certainly, dear friend. I choose to believe in them. Without gods and heroes what would become of the drama? And even brief mental association with the immortals gives elevation to the mind and majesty of thought. Not for a moment would I renounce my belief in the gods."

"You argue like the sophists," said Thucydides.

"No, for the sophists believe in nothing and I believe in myself!"

"And in the gods?"

"In the gods, for are they not made in the image of man, and is not the excellence of man indisputable?"

"Then you believe that when invoking the help of the gods you are really invoking yourself?"

"He invokes the god in his mind we call genius," said Pericles. "Surely that is enough."

"Then you believe that your god goes to sleep and needs must that the other gods awaken him," persisted Thucydides, who despised every man present but Pericles.

"No doubt his brethren are disturbed when they see him napping," said Sophocles smiling. "The gods are rarely jealous of one another, but darkly so of their reputation among mortals."

"Take care they are not jealous of you, O Sophocles, for when heedless men are calling you divine and inspired it is time to be fearful."

Sophocles drained a cup of wine. "I have had my hour," he said. "Let come what will."

"How can you endure that young cub, Aspasia?" asked Zosmë. "It is a wonder you have not boxed his ears before this."

"I don't like him well enough! But Pericles takes pleasure in his conversation, and as his ambition is to write history I am quite willing that Pericles should be his hero."

"He lacks the suavity of the Athenian because he spent his

boyhood in Thrace," said Agariste. "But he is a young man of much virtue, and studies, I am told, with Prodicus."

"O Hera!" exclaimed Zosmë. "That accounts for his flavor of Socrates. Shall we have dialectics after all?"

"I think not," Aspasia reassured her. "There are too many to suppress him."

Ion of Chios was speaking.

"Sophocles will always jest in private—and why not, since his destiny is to write tragedies? Magnes is a solemn fellow and dull in conversation. A comic poet's brain is naturally exhausted after grinding out his jokes; and, likewise, great tragic dramatists like Sophocles must have relief. But he really believes in the gods. Of that I do not permit myself to doubt. I dislike intensely the so-called modernism of Euripides and Socrates, and wish, O illustrious Aspasia, that you were less indulgent to such men."

"Modernism consorts with democracy, O Ion," said Aspasia drily.

"If the gods believed that democracy threatened their supremacy in the hearts and lives of men, Aspasia, they never would have permitted it to germinate," said Phillipus. "And it is but one more blessing for which we thank them daily."

"Assuming they exist. It is no longer a secret among his friends that Socrates finds his reason directing him toward belief in a deity who bears little resemblance to Zeus—and reigns supreme and alone."

"How uninteresting!" cried Pheidias. "What would life—and sculpture—be without gods? One would think Socrates had been brought up on a lonely farm far from cities. Those poor ignorant creatures pray and sacrifice to what they call 'God,' and know nothing of our brilliant and beautiful galaxy. What does he call this remote and mysterious being who reigns alone and would deprive us of all sense of intimacy?"

"He is too modest to give a name to what he has but half conceived. But be sure it is not Zeus."

"And does he deny the existence of the other gods?" demanded Herodotus, whose jaw had fallen.

"Possibly not. He alludes to them frequently. Perhaps he

would accept them as an inferior hierarchy—magistrates to administer the laws! Even a great mind like Socrates' must fumble for a time before arriving at great truths. So far, I think, he meditates upon a supreme being about whom too many legends have grown up—legends born in the dark ages and continued out of careless habit."

"It will be a sad day for the imagination of poets when the gods are banished from human belief," said Sophocles more soberly than he had yet spoken. "We rise to grandeur only when we consort briefly with immortals, made in our own image but infinitely superior."

"Imagination would but be put to a greater test, O Sophocles; and who more fitted to accept the challenge?"

The controversy raged politely for an hour and entered the realm of the abstract. Pericles, seeing that the symposium was safe in Aspasia's hands, and tired after a long day of hard work, went to sleep. Anaxagoras grew restless. He took no interest whatever in the gods and little more in poets and modern philosophy. Aspasia deftly engineered the talk round to mind, and he sat up alertly on his elbow.

"Mind, or soul," he said in his tired elderly voice, "is the ordering or containing principle of all things. Mind has absolute power, and mixes with nothing, and orders all things, and passes through all things."

"And what of the body?" asked Aspasia, while the others filled their cups. "Do you believe, O Nous, that it is the grave of the soul, which is buried in its present existence?"

"Soul is mind, Aspasia, and the mind is free, as I have just demonstrated. The body is the instrument of perception. It returns to its elements but mind persists for ever."

"Socrates rejects the Pythagorean doctrine that each of us has lived many times and will live as many more. He believes that only the essence of mind is indestructible."

"I have no patience with these modern philosophers!" said Polygnotus indignantly. And they were off again. Zosmë, who had concealed her yawns behind her fan of peacock feathers, and feared to fall from her chair if she slept, slipped out, summoned her slaves, and went home.

Aspasia since her marriage had rarely left the house, for Pericles' duties began early in the morning and he took no more rambles at night. As he walked to the Piræus and back every few days, and had much business to transact in various parts of Athens, and was no longer a victim of loneliness, he was content to remain in the house during his few hours of leisure. He forbade morning walks with Xanthias, and Aspasia was obliged to take her exercise on the roof or in the peristyle, although she slipped out occasionally and visited Zosmë.

But the general approval of his marriage, the apparent indifference of the comic poets, and the amiable attitude of the women of his own class at the theatre, were not without their effect on Pericles. He understood Aspasia too instinctively not to realize what confinement meant to that free spirit, and finally told her to go abroad when she would, as long as she avoided the gathering places of men, never forgot her veil, and was followed by a woman slave as well as Xanthias.

So while Pericles was in his office or on his way to the Piræus, Aspasia climbed Mount Lycabettus to watch the sun rise, and later—she received on alternate mornings only—wandered about in the long belt of sacred olive trees beyond the walls, or explored Athens for the first time. While Xanthias and Thera exchanged condolences, she traversed street after street and wondered that she had ever thought Athens ugly. There were statues at every corner of the queer winding streets and in all open spaces; marble gateways, little fanes, sometimes in ruins and in the most unexpected places; shrines to gods and goddesses, and great temples here and there; and outside the city, on the road to the Academy or the Lyceum, long graceful colonnades for shelter.

She avoided the Sacred Way of the Outer Ceramicus, where her love of art and beauty would have been gratified in contemplation of the imposing tombs and the dignified carvings on the stelæ, but she would invite no suggestion of death. That she and Pericles must pass out of this beneficent world some day, their passion and perfect companionship done with for ever, and all that remained of their devouring intellects and radiant bodies a handful of bones in an urn, and that in the due course of nature he would go first, was a thought she strangled and flung from her when it assailed her in sudden dark moments. Once she dreamed of wandering, a shade among shades, in the dim realm of Pluto, seeking him in vain, and then running about wildly in search of the river of Lethe. But the dream made her cling to the delight of the present more tenaciously, more determined than ever to avoid every suggestion of inexorable death.

And if she could not be with him always, reason taught her to make many interests and lose herself in them for the moment. She had her morning receptions and these long rambles in and out of Athens.

She became a familiar figure in the Inner Ceramicus, where she often lingered to watch the potters and vase-painters at work. They knew who she was but were far too polite to betray themselves and embarrass her. While Xanthias scowled they would dust off a bench that she might sit and watch them fire the jars, or block out in the natural red color of the clay, against the black pigment, the scenes domestic and historic they were unconsciously immortalizing.

She looked on as metal-workers and jewellers behind their gay little shops strove as eagerly as Pheidias for perfection, and bought freely; for Pericles, so rigid in his own expenditures, had told Euangelos to keep her money chest full.

Occasionally she invited Paralus to accompany her; Xanthippus was a vain selfish boy and Clinias both shallow and eccentric; and although Alcibiades was irresistible, after one experience she never took him out again. He climbed six statues, broke a valuable vase, and got into three fights with boys in the streets. But Paralus was a lovable well-behaved child and his father's favorite, and she knew that her attentions to him gave Pericles pleasure. It also amused her to instruct him, and he often returned from these expeditions so puffed up with pride that he was nearly demolished by Alcibiades. That young tyrant was not only tall and strong for his age but his personality overwhelmed the older boys.

But she sometimes stumbled upon things that were intended neither for worshippers of beauty nor as food for the mind. She and her attendants were passing one day a beautiful temple in a grove of olive trees, whose delicate leaves draped the marble like silver lace studded with dark beads, when she heard the deep terrible groaning of a man in mortal agony.

"Xanthias!" she cried. "Run quickly! Some one has been hurt—"

"Come away, Mistress. This is no place for you—"

"There it is again— Why—what—"

A second horrid groan had been followed by a man's peremptory interrogative voice.

"It is a slave on the rack, Mistress. His master has been arrested for murder, and they are putting his slave to the question as there is no other way to get at the truth. It is the custom, Mistress. Come away."

"O Hera! Of course I had heard of such things but I did not believe they existed to-day. Why, the Athenians are civilized and humane! Why, this is not only brutal but stupid, for it is a blot on the fair name of Athens! It is as if Pheidias painted one of his gods with the skin of a snake or a rat. I'll go within and ask them to spare this poor wretch—"

But Xanthias stood in front of her. "No, Mistress," he said sternly. "You would only bring ridicule and trouble on Pericles. He is too wise to interfere with the workings of the law. Such an act would be like removing a stone from an arch—"

"Oh, very well—" And Aspasia ran from that temple of torture with her hands against her ears. O Zeus! she thought. Will the world ever really be civilized? And they call Persians Barbarians.

A few days later she induced Constantia to forego siesta and roam with her in the Agora, and that was the beginning of a new phase. Constantia brought her friends and they brought others—all that could elude their husbands. Aspasia took an impish delight at first in sowing these seeds of rebellion, but after the novelty of playing about in freedom was over they showed a disposition to sit at her feet and be instructed; and

as she had asked them more than once why they did not make
some effort to overcome their ignorance and companion their
husbands, she could do no less than take the part for which
she was well fitted. They sat about her in one or other of the
porticoes while she taught them to read or to improve on what
little knowledge they had. She read and lectured to them and
lent them books to relieve their long heavy hours of solitude.

Xanthias and certain men slaves, educated themselves, stood
respectfully in the background and concealed their amused
tolerance.

"Do you think your course is wise, O Mistress?" he asked
her one day as she lingered in the Agora after the others had
gone; Thera, overcome, was asleep in the King Archon's Stoa.
"After all," contemptuously, "they are but women and more of
slaves than I was, for the streets were open to me at any hour.
You will make them discontented and both they and their husbands will suffer. Have you told Pericles son of Xanthippus
of these extraordinary doings?"

"Oh, yes, and he only laughed. He wishes me to fill my time
as best I may since he cannot always be with me—and knows,
alas! that nothing will alter the men. And discontent is divine,
Xanthias. I cannot endure the smugness of women who are
discontented only if their husbands love hetæræ or youths. But
when discontent leads to a desire for knowledge they cannot
fail to experience a certain happiness in realizing they are no
longer mere animals fit for nothing but breeding more men. To
feel the mind open a little more day by day, press forward no
matter how slowly toward light and truth—that is ecstasy in
itself! Have I not experienced that immeasurable delight since
I was a young girl among all those wise men in my father's
house? And here in Athens among men far wiser and greater?
There are few sensations to compare with it. And it will give
them a deep and perhaps sinister satisfaction to look forward to
the day when they will be the inferiors of their husbands in
naught but the law of Athens. Women stand in need of many
compensations, Xanthias, and it shall be my part to light their
path. I have already persuaded them to teach their girls, since
they cannot send them to school."

"O Poseidon!" exclaimed the scandalized Xanthias. "They'll go to the altar knowing more than their husbands, and that is a fine prospect for happiness! The women may cultivate diplomacy, but young girls are vain and arrogant to begin with, and if they set themselves up to know more than the man they have never seen before betrothal they'll get a sound whipping before the month is out."

"Well, I hope they'll whip back. A good many of these young men would be the better for having their pretty faces scratched, to say nothing of an agonizing pain in the shin. It is they who are full of arrogance and conceit, especially the 'beauties'—who must marry in time. A little discipline in the house won't hurt them."

"I am sure you have never said that to Pericles son of Xanthippus! But we must go now, Mistress. It is time for the dicasts to return. If men saw you here be sure the Strategos would not laugh."

xv

Aspasia was sitting in her bedroom gazing with fixed unseeing eyes into the court—quiet for nearly two months now, as the children were at Pericles' farm on the Euripus. She had been much alone during these summer months, for Constantia and her other new friends were in the country, Zosmë at Phaleron. Pericles had dutifully tried to persuade her to go with the boys, but she had refused to leave him, and he made no secret of his content. Athens in spite of stifling heat and lanes used as sewers was not an unhealthy city, for the fresh Etesian wind blew through it every afternoon; malaria at that time was unknown in Greece.

Pericles ordered out his chariot with its fleet blooded horses of the old Alcmæonid stock and took her with him to Piræus, where she spent the intervening time with Galatea; now the mother of twin boys and quite happy in her sumptuous apartment of the large and ornate mansion on Munychia.

In the evening they strolled between the Long Walls, often joined by such of their friends as had braved the heat of Athens. It was a favorite evening promenade, and if she was the only woman to be seen among the saunterers, at that time all that she and Pericles did was right. And the nights were enchanting, for they slept in a tent on the roof. On the whole, in spite of the heat and the cessation of her morning levees, and long unoccupied hours in the afternoon, it had been the most satisfactory period of her life with Pericles, for she had been more constantly with him.

All had been well until a few days since!

She hardly knew in what moment the fact that she was to have a child had penetrated her reluctant mind. But facts were made to be faced and she faced one of the most momentous of her life to-day. She had spoken with great assurance to Zosmë in that far-off time when all problems were calmly worked out in the cold light of reason; but in those days she had barely guessed at the intense pride of Pericles, who would welcome no bastard in his house.

What should she do? Abortions were common enough in Athens. Women after their husbands had begun to grumble about the size of the family submitted to them rather than have their babies exposed. Large families were no longer the fashion. Prices mounted with the ever-increasing prosperity of the State, and with an expensive household men had less to spend on their pleasures and leave to their sons.

But she shrank from the idea. Not only did she fear the possible effect on her health and beauty, but secretly she welcomed the thought of bearing a child. With her passion for perfection, for the complete and harmonious development of every part of her being, she must know all things, experience all things; and, barren, she would still be more ignorant of one phase of life than slave women.

Her set features were crossed by a faint satirical smile as she recalled the time when she had thought her life complete and took a serene pride in her unique gifts and position in Hellas. But she had lived with Pericles since! Her intellect and her great accomplishments were but a part of the whole, no longer dominant.

And to give birth to a child, loved because it was the child of Pericles, would crumble the last blind wall in her being. She might grow in mental and moral virtue as long as she lived, experience deeper happiness—were that possible—but in woman's enlightenment she would have achieved completion.

To the education of suffering she gave no thought. It was no part of the Greek ideal to suffer. That was reserved to coincide with the morbidity and anxious self-examinations of a later era.

To give birth to the son of Pericles! To be rounded and complete!

But what joy for her if there could be no share in it for him? What a cruel blow for Fate to deal a proud man but now ceasing to remember that the woman he loved with all the accumulated ardor of his being was not his legal wife! What a mockery that he should have had two sons by a woman to whom he had been too indifferent for hate, and any born to the wife of his love must be bastards in law. His own law! What dark shadow might it not throw over a happiness the gods must have envied?

She shrank with terror from the thought of telling him, and remembered with resentment the delight of Zosmë and Hippodamus when that brat Archeptolemus announced himself. If she had been able to give Pericles a legitimate son his delight and hers would have exceeded theirs as immeasurably as he and she were capable of depths and heights undreamed of by common mortals.

What irony! What tragedy!

And for a moment she hated the child who might dim the splendor of her life.

Thera entered with a plate of the first grapes of the season; golden grapes kissed brown on one side by the sun; each a globe of nectar, and such as spring from the soil of Attica only, under the Attic sun.

"Xanthias went out to a farm in the country to get them, O Mistress," said the girl looking at her anxiously. "He was nearly overcome by the heat, but is quite happy. Are you not well, Mistress? I fear this heat of Athens for you. Could we not go to the farm for a few days?"

"Later perhaps, when the Strategos has more time. And I

am quite well. Thank Xanthias for me. I have looked forward to the first grapes—the fruit of the gods. One eats the others only for health."

Thera lingered, shaking up the cushions and rearranging the bottles and jars on the dressing-table.

"If you would lie down and let me fan you, dear Mistress."

Aspasia shook her head impatiently. "Go and amuse yourself—and ask Marcus to tell the Master I would speak with him as soon as he comes in."

Thera smiled slyly. "He will come at once without any message, O Mistress! But some one might seek to detain him. He will be glad of the excuse." And she flitted out of the room and down the aula to tease old Marcus, a favorite pastime of the younger slaves.

Aspasia, to create a draught, had opened the door of her dressing-room and the one leading thence into the aula. In a few moments she heard his light step in the nearest colonnade. She rose hastily, overturning her chair, and instinctively placed her back to the light. It was the first time she had not run forward to greet him.

As he entered he flung his helmet and mantle on a chair.

"Zeus, it is hot!" he exclaimed. "Thank the gods I am not forced to go out again to-day. Marcus told me—" And then he became aware of an atmosphere of tension and the curious stillness of his wife. "Aspasia—has anything—"

He crossed the room in a stride and would have caught her in his arms but she pushed him away from her and stared at him silently, her eyes hard and defiant in her haggard face.

"What—" And then he understood.

His form became so rigid and his eyelids drooped so heavily that she was beset with a new terror. Would he send her from him and expose the child? Far better the other recourse than that.

But although selflessness was no part of the Greek ideal, love must have affected men and women in much the same fashion since the birth of intelligence promoted selection. The tensity of his muscles relaxed and he drew her down beside him on the sofa.

"It is fate," he said heavily. "Fate and the vaulting pride that made me lend a willing ear to those who were ever asserting that the old sanctities of tribal life were being violated by mixed marriages. And it is true, Aspasia, that Cleisthenes made a mistake in admitting so many foreigners to citizenship. I, with others, believed that for Athens to maintain her ascendancy she must keep her blood pure—for it is the best blood in Hellas. Oh, would that Axiochus had kept his promise and brought you earlier to Athens! But it was not to be, and our child—of all children in the world!—must be a—" He recoiled from the word and went on hurriedly. "Let the gods laugh. We will give them no further amusement. I cannot revoke that law, but if it should be a boy there may come a propitious moment when I can ask the dicastery to legitimize him. It must be some years hence, for it is no part of my policy to invite ridicule; but there is always a moment of Fate and I have allowed none to pass me so far. So be happy in the thought of our child, dear girl."

For the first time since childhood Aspasia burst into passionate weeping, and he forgot calamity in his overmastering desire to restore her to tranquillity and happiness.

So the cloud passed, and mercifully neither had a premonition of the dark circumstances in which that boon of legitimacy for his son would be granted to Pericles.

XVI

Old Marcus, sighing and shaking his head, opened the door in the early morning and bound an olive branch to one of the pillars. He peered up and down the gray street hoping for a sight of a familiar face, for doorkeepers in the same neighborhood were generally on terms of intimacy. Marcus kept the house slaves at a proper distance but he longed for a few moments of gossip this morning.

Presently he saw a door open almost opposite. An old slave emerged carrying a pail of water, which he emptied unceremoniously over the Hermes, and was about to polish the knocker when he heard a sharp "Hist!" No slave needed a second invitation to drop his work and in an instant he was standing before the house of Pericles. Marcus pointed to the olive branch.

"O Rock of Athens, it is true, then!" gasped the other. "I heard the rumor, but it has been kept very secret. And how does the great Pericles like the idea of a bastard son in his house?"

Marcus shrugged his shoulders. "Who can tell what the Strategos thinks? But I can tell you this—he walked about the outer peristyle all night. We were all gathered in the inner court waiting for the end. He came and went through the dressing-room. He is with her now. I saw him go in when the midwife gave him permission, but his face told nothing, although no doubt he hoped it would be a girl. Girls don't matter. But a son—born to Pericles son of Xanthippus—who cannot be enrolled in the phratry of the great houses of Bouzyges and Alcmæonid—the two greatest families in Athens! A sad day! A sad day!"

"I wonder he did not hide her at the farm until it was over. The child could have been left there if he didn't wish to have it exposed. Then none would have been the wiser."

Marcus shook his head. "The Strategos is too proud for that, Philo. Nor would he have separated himself from the Mistress. He would not have her out of his sight if he could help it—he is in her room almost as soon as he is through these doors."

"I overheard my Mistress say to the Master that if it was true there would be one person who would have her say, and that was Agariste sister of Pericles."

"Yes, she strode in here one day looking like Hera in a rage with Zeus, but Aspasia can wheedle anybody, and now she has sent the Spartan nurse who brought up her own boys, to tend the child. She is very fond of the Mistress, unlike as they are— but who is not? Thera lay before the door howling until the midwife sent her away, and Xanthias ran out into the country and has not returned yet. No doubt he will be the child's pedægogus, for he could teach even Alcibiades manners. Thank the gods the children are in the country. It will be enough to have a baby squalling without that Alcibiades yelling from morning till night. The Master packed them off earlier than usual."

"And will he have all the ceremonies, do you think, for an illegal child?"

"Did he not have a great wedding to marry an illegal wife? He is too proud to do anything by halves. Nor would he hurt Aspasia's feelings. She'd never forgive him, and he'd not risk that."

"But to acknowledge this child of a foreign woman—publicly acknowledge it? Surely the great Aspasia would understand— she who is said to have the mind of a man!"

Old Marcus applied the point of his thumb to his nose and twiddled his rheumatic fingers. "Women are all alike when it comes to babies and men. There are times when mind goes to sleep. And this one is full of caprice and has a temper of her own. Pericles had enough of rows with Olympias. He'd give Aspasia the moon. And she returns him full measure; I'll admit that. It's a strange marriage for Athens!"

Old Philo shook his head. "It may last—in the house. But mark my words, the comic poets will get at them sooner or later. It is not considered intellectual in Athens to love women, and many have condoned this marriage so far only because Aspasia has a man's virtues and is as learned as the sophists. Many believed it was an intellectual friendship that made them marry so that she could live in his house and hold discourse whenever the great Strategos had time for talk. But now that she's gone and had a baby like any woman who can't read her letters, there'll be less excuse made for that marriage. Pericles would have been wise to hide her away."

"Perhaps." Marcus looked worried. "If there is ridicule and ill-flavored gossip it could be kept from her, but not from the Master. And powerful as he is he would be helpless there. He is a proud man and would smart! She is a great lady, and like a goddess to look at, and kind to the slaves, but I wish she had stayed in Miletus."

XVII

But Aspasia was happy in freedom from pain, in the accomplishment of experience and in the devotion of her husband. As yet she was unable to feel an overwhelming interest in the hairless red whimpering bundle exhibited to her at intervals by the nurse. A healthy young countrywoman had been brought from the farm to nurse it. To her own performance of this maternal privilege Pericles would not listen for a moment. Aspasia was his, but incidentally the mother of this unwelcome child.

"And the very gods would laugh at the sight of Aspasia suckling an infant," he said impatiently to Agariste. "She might have had a child if she wanted it but I wish she need not have had it in the manner of other women."

Agariste smiled drily. "If you would have her a goddess, O Pericles, a niche in your house would be the proper place for her not a couch. But Hera and Demeter, to say nothing of lesser goddesses, have had children in the natural course of things, so why not Aspasia? Every woman wants a child if only to show what she can do. But she has the best of it so far, for you must conduct the ceremonies."

Pericles groaned. "May Pluto torment the shade of him who invented them!"

On the fifth day the nurse with the new-born child in her arms ran round the circular hearth followed by the other slaves, thus placing the infant under the protection of the family gods. The ceremony was witnessed by the men and women of the two clans, entertained later at a dinner of shell fish.

On the seventh day the members of the houses of Bouzyges and Alcmænoid, with Hippodamus and Zosmë, Galatea and her husband somewhat meagrely representing Aspasia, gathered once more in the andron, and Pericles formally acknowledged the child as his son and made the usual promises to bring him up and educate him properly.

The great festival occurred on the tenth day, when Pericles was obliged to assume his priestly robes, sacrifice at the altar, and name his new son; present in his shoe-shaped cradle at the toe of his nurse. The guests presented their gifts and a feast followed.

Pericles made the sacrifice and gave the child his own name with an air of majestic pride. He was determined that these watchful eyes should detect no shade of difference in his demeanor from those two former occasions when he had solemnly named the legal and welcome sons born to his house. Pericles the Younger was treated with the same pomp and imposing ritual as that observed for his father when the proud Xanthippus had burnt sacrifice for the son whom the omen of his wife's dream predestined to greatness.

But no man was ever more thankful than he when it was all over. The child was there and should have the same care as his legitimate sons, but it was a nurse's duty to keep a noisy infant out of sight and hearing.

As the doctor was insistent he consented to send Aspasia to the country for the summer months, and with less reluctance as he would be able to go there himself every few days. Things were running smoothly. The prosperity of the State was increasing steadily, the people were busy and contented, and the Oligarchs had not lifted their heads. The metal-workers and jewellers had sent presents to the child, and as far as he could judge there was no resentment felt at the addition of this left-handed son to his household. Even the family had behaved well, and Agariste, who had told Aspasia she would forgive her if she proved herself capable of bringing forth a son, was in and out every day. Privately she wished the midwife had strangled the infant in delivery and wondered the doctor had not thought to suggest it.

But she was a kind-hearted woman, in spite of peculiarities eminently Greek, and sat by the hour fanning Aspasia and regaling her with her own experiences in child-bed, the infant troubles of her brood, and the gossip of Athens. When Pericles entered she tactfully withdrew.

Aspasia, as soon as she was able to travel went by sea to the large estate modestly called "the farm" that Pericles had inherited from his fathers. It lay south of the town of Oropus and opposite the island of Eubœa. The country here was very

different from the parched Attic plain, for the soil was richer
and there were woods of ilexes, fir trees, and pines. The country
was rolling, the slopes covered with vineyards and olive trees,
some of the latter so big and gnarled they might have been
planted during the reign of Codrus. There were several little
villages, for the farm was a hive of activity, producing everything needed for the household in Athens and much for the
market. Pericles had also a farm on Eubœa for horse-breeding,
a large source of revenue.

The house, embowered in fig trees, was built about one
immense court and as simply furnished as any in the villages,
but a fountain splashed with abundant water and there was a
covered portico across the front where the family could sit and
watch the lofty azure mountains of Eubœa; the highest point
of the four ranges, Mount Dirphys, glittering summer and
winter with snow. The rich blue waters of the Euripus separated the mainland from the many harbors of the great island,
and Aspasia knew that in one of those harbors Pericles had
landed to subdue the insurrection. Farther north, just over the
frontier of Bœotia, was Aulis, where Agamemnon had offered
Iphigenia on the altar of Artemis when his fleet of a thousand
ships lay becalmed.

Agariste, Zosmë, and the lively Constantia visited her, and
Pericles came frequently; the boys spent the day in the woods
or on the hills far from the house—and the swift currents of
the Euripus. The baby was healthy and good-natured, and as
it lay in its shoe-shaped basket on the table clutching a rattle,
Aspasia contemplated it with awe. She hardly dared touch it,
certainly not in the presence of the grim Spartan nurse nor the
jealous foster-mother. But although it was not in her to achieve
the baby talk that flowed with such surprising spontaneity
from her friends, she smiled at it tenderly and occasionally
tickled it under the chin. Her pride in it was certainly maternal, for it already gave evidence of future good looks; what
hair it possessed had a golden tinge and its eyes had deepened
from blue to black.

But she thought of it less than of regaining her strength, and
sat for hours gazing through the clear radiant air at the blue

mountains of Eubœa. It was at all times cooler here than in Athens, and it was not long before she began to take short walks and then longer; before a month was out she was rising with the sun and exploring the estate, followed as ever by Xanthias. It was difficult at such times to remember that she had given birth to a child or was aught but as she had been for so many years. She conceived long arguments with Socrates, to his utter undoing, and discourses for her morning levees. But although she enjoyed the country with its fresh greens and sweet smells, she longed impatiently for the time when she could be in Athens again and hours not days would intervene between her associations with Pericles.

XVIII

When visiting his estate Pericles drove to Marathon in the early afternoon and took a galley thence to a small cove at the foot of the garden. Aspasia sat waiting for him one night and the hour was later than usual. She feared the tide had turned and he would not be able to arrive before morning; this disaster had happened twice before. Even the stout arms and backs of seamen could make little headway against that swift current.

The bright moon was at the full, the nightingales were singing. She sprang from her seat and walked up and down the portico and the pathway leading to the water. The nights were growing cooler, and she drew her mantle about her more closely. She stood for a moment on the little bluff above the cove listening intently, but the light breeze brought no sound of oars cutting the water with their steady long strokes. And then she heard a strange noise far behind her and turned with a faint cry of alarm. Flames were shooting upward from a distant hill.

"Do not be frightened, Mistress." Xanthias emerged from a grove of pines between the house and the shore. "It is the first revel of the vintage. They are dancing round a bonfire."

"I thought it was a volcano in eruption! And I did not know you were here. You should be in bed. It is very late."

"I never go to bed, Mistress, when you wait up for the Master."

"But that is nonsense. There is no danger here."

"I cannot be sure of that. You are beautiful and there are rough men on this farm. And the estate of Thoron's father is not far."

"Oh, *Thoron!* I had forgotten he lived. He'd not dare venture here."

"Perhaps not, O Mistress. But while you are without the house I do not remain within it."

"Did Thoron remain in Athens after his—mishap? I heard nothing of him."

"When his wound healed he went to his father's estate, but he returns often by night to revel with his friends in a part of the city which you have never visited, O Mistress."

"Then no doubt he has forgotten me long since. And all your rough men must be at that bonfire—after the Master has gone back to Athens you will take me over there. I have always wished to witness a Dionysiac revel."

"I am your servant at your orders, Mistress, but that is an order the Master must give; and I think he will not. Obscene revels are not for the eyes of Aspasia wife of Pericles."

"Nonsense! Is it not to the worship of Dionysus that we owe the dithyramb and the comedy? I would see it!" Aspasia stamped her foot. "I am no longer a girl. And I am no ordinary wife to ask permissions of her husband. It is understood that I do as I will—with very slight restrictions in Athens. And those restrictions I would have placed on myself."

"The Master has put his foot down more than once, O Mistress. You have more liberty than most wives, but you are not in Miletus. It would not be wise to invite the wrath of Pericles, and as you are happy now, why tempt the gods?"

"Pericles would never be angry with me—where can he be?"

She forgot the vintage and ran once more to the bluff. "Has the tide turned, do you know?"

"The tide has not turned, Mistress, but there is much to detain the Strategos in Athens."

"If he had been unable to come he would have sent a messenger."

"He may have been detained at the last minute. Messengers and agents are always coming in from the colonies, and sometimes the business won't wait— Listen! My ears are very sharp but yours are younger—do you hear nothing?"

"Oh, yes! yes! I hear!"

"Tell me when you see the helmet of the Strategos and I will go within, but not before."

"The sound is still faint but it is unmistakably oars."

She stepped to the edge of the bluff and tented a hand over her eyes. The soft rhythmic splash grew louder, and far down the straits she saw a long dark shadow gliding swiftly over the smooth water. As it approached, a man's tall figure, helmeted, rose from the deck and stood at the prow. Her form was clearly outlined against the little temple behind her and he waved his hand.

"It is he, Xanthias!" And she ran down to the shore. Her faithful guardian, satisfied that it was the Strategos and no impostor, went to his rest.

Pericles leaped to the beach before the men had time to ship oars, but he and Aspasia did not speak until they had passed out of sight.

"Why are you so late?" she demanded, as they lingered in the grove. "I have been terribly worried."

"A messenger caught me as I was halfway to Marathon and I was obliged to return to Athens and talk with Menippus, who has just returned from Samos."

"Is there bad news?" she asked anxiously. "Anything that will take you away?"

"It is only a rumor and may mean nothing. But we will not talk of it now. To-morrow I will tell you what little I know, for do I not talk over all things with you? But after six interminable days, not to-night!"

She resumed the subject next morning as they were walking along the shore. The sun was already dazzling and she held a parasol over her head. Pericles had laid aside his helmet for the broad hat he wore in the country. No decorous mantles were imperative here, and their full linen tunics were pulled over the girdles to give greater freedom in walking. They were followed by a troop of dogs, several of them descendants of that devoted beast who followed Xanthippus in his flight before the Persians, and, forgotten in the hasty embarkation, swam the gulf to Salamis to die of exhaustion at his master's feet.

Pericles looked over his broad acres with pride and content, forgetting affairs of state and recalling his thoughtless happy childhood in these woods and orchards—until that wild night when he had been snatched from his bed by his nurse and hurried down to the galley waiting to convey the family to Salamis to join the great General; overborne for the moment.

The Persians had destroyed the vineyards and burnt the house, but they had left the olive orchards, for the stout resistance of those tough old trees would have delayed their progress. He had visited the estate every summer after the return of the family from exile until his marriage with Olympias; as she chose to spend her summers there he had not seen it again until these last months with Aspasia, when he forgot all intervening years. But her question recalled him from his pleasant musings.

"Menippus arrived unexpectedly yesterday from Samos," he replied. "As you know, Samos, like Chios and Lesbos, is an ally, not a subject state. Therefore I have planted no colony there, nor even an agent, and during this long interval of peace with the Barbarian there has been little official communication between us—save once a year when they bring the tribute money to Athens. But Menippus, who visited friends there, brought the unwelcome news that trouble is brewing between Samos and Miletus."

"Miletus?" cried Aspasia in alarm. "No harm will come to her, I hope."

"We certainly shall let no harm come to a state so important to Athens as Miletus—even were that all. The trouble that seems to be pending is this: Samos has territory on the mainland and wishes to annex Priene, which of course would add to her wealth and importance. To this Miletus would never consent—but so far seems to have no inkling of the designs of Samos. Nor is this rumored intention of the Oligarchs public in Samos itself. Menippus heard it from a watchful member of the democratic minority, that would oppose aggression of any sort. But when Oligarchs are in power one never knows what they will do next. They are invariably both arrogant and short-sighted. I sent for the best diplomatist we have— Cleander—and told him to go there and take soundings, using whatever pretense for his visit he may think best. If they suspect I am alert, so much the better; they may think twice before challenging the Athenian navy."

"Unless they have some understanding with Sardis. It was said in Miletus that the satrap there, Pissuthnes, was ready to stir up trouble at any moment."

Pericles kicked a stone out of his path. "No doubt! And that might involve Persia herself. There is no telling what any stupid act may lead to. And I want no more wars. Athens must have a long era of peace. Let us talk no more about it. Rumors like that are born and die every year. Until I hear from the Captain of the garrison in Miletus or have an unfavorable report from Cleander, I shall dismiss this one from my mind."

They struck inland through a vineyard where men were gathering the grapes for the wine press. Aspasia told him of her desire to witness the night revels, and his exclamation would have gratified Xanthias.

"The men behave well enough," he said, "for the true season of the Dionysiac revels is at the end of winter. It is the women who indulge in unseemly conduct when the first grapes are trod. They go up into that wild pass over there in the mountains and the gods alone know what they do. No man has ever ventured to spy on them, for they would probably scratch his eyes out if he did."

"Do you mean to tell me they really go mad, as in the dark ages when the wild women of Thebes, including his own mother, tore Pentheus limb from limb? . . . Euripides says he will write a play about it one day. Or even goats and sheep, and get drunk on their blood!"

"Oh, no, we are too civilized for that! Such abominations have disappeared even from Thebes and prevail nowadays nowhere but in Thrace. The countrywomen of the more progressive states—more particularly here in Attica—have imbibed something from civilization, although they may never visit a city in the long course of their lives. But they keep up the tradition, drape themselves in fawnskins, twist ivy in their hair, work themselves into frenzy and make beasts of themselves. No spectacle for a decent woman."

"I shall witness it, O Pericles!" Aspasia turned her laughing eyes on the startled face of the man whose word was law in Athens.

"Aspasia! I forbid it!" he added sternly. "Understand that once for all."

She shook her head vigorously. "Oh, no, Pericles, don't talk to me like a commonplace Athenian husband. If I submitted in Athens it was because I knew as well as you did that extreme circumspection was necessary until we were sure our marriage was fully condoned. But now it is different and here there is no one to criticize. Constantia comes day after to-morrow and we'll disguise ourselves and dress up like those women. They'll never guess we're not two of them, for no doubt they're drunk with wine before they go to the defile. I must see everything that appeals to my curiosity, Pericles—and you should be gratified that I do not ask to go to the Dionysus for the comedies!"

Pericles, who had been regarding her speculatively, laughed. "And if I withheld my permission you would go anyway, I suppose?"

She nodded, her eyes sparkling.

"You would make another Hippodamus of me?" he asked, smiling.

"Oh, no! I'll never try subtlety with you. I know better! No more than I could ever deceive you. Have I not been quite frank?"

"You have, indeed!" He added more seriously in a moment: "I would no more treat you like an ordinary wife than I could have loved you if you had been an ordinary woman. I would have you feel as free as I am myself. I don't like the idea of you witnessing such things, but I fear more what they might do to you if they penetrated your disguise."

"Xanthias and four slaves can follow with stout whips. It will not be difficult for them to hide and still be near."

"But don't call them out unless there is real menace. I want no revolution on my property! If my slaves whipped those women there is no telling what might happen. These farmers are freemen and have a vote in the Ecclesia."

"I'll be discretion itself—for you consent! *Dear* Pericles!"

He shrugged. "Did you ask it? Perhaps my hearing is grown defective. But there shall be no quarrels between us over trifles, Aspasia. And you *must* be discreet, for if it got out it would make a scandal in Athens." He stooped and twisted two bunches of grapes from a vine with one turn of his strong wrist. "Let us go into that grove and eat them," he said. "The sun grows hot."

XIX

The horrified Xanthias was dispatched to Athens to buy a short black wig, and on the night after Pericles' departure Aspasia and Constantia would not have been recognized by their husbands. They had stained all visible parts brown, destroyed two chitons and two pairs of sandals with dirt and wine-lees, and a slave had procured fawnskins from one of the villages. Their heads were wreathed with ivy and they carried staffs trailing leaves of that dignified plant sometimes put to strange uses.

Constantia gasped when the transformation was complete. "Aspasia! You are almost ugly and look years older! Luckily these countrywomen often have regular features, and your eyes look black at night. If Pericles saw you on the streets of Athens he'd have you arrested for a dirty trollop. I hope I look as disreputable."

"You do! You do!" Aspasia danced about the room in glee, shaking her short black curls. "And I never dreamed that a disguise could strike in. I feel as disreputable as I look. Poor Xanthias!"

"It will take you a lifetime to regain his respect, but who cares? And I shall do every single thing those women do up there in the defile. Athens might be in Persia!"

Aspasia had a moment of caution. "Let us see what they do first. But come. We must get there before the moon rises, or some one will see us crossing the fields."

"Great Zeus on Olympus!" Xanthias was awaiting them in the outer portico, while four stout slaves stood at a respectful distance. "I hope, Mistress, if you get into trouble I shall be able to recognize you among the other wenches. Be sure to call my name and wave that staff above your head."

"I will, Xanthias, but they'll never guess I'm not one of them."

"No, Mistress, even the all-seeing gods would never take you for a lady. Shade of Axiochus! Will you not think again, O wife of Pericles?"

Aspasia laughed and ran on ahead with Constantia. It was two miles to the wild gorge in the mountains which the women claimed for their own at this season and Xanthias had ascertained that they entered it an hour after dusk and reached the height of their revels at midnight. As they climbed swiftly and silently they saw the glare of a fire and strange sounds drifted down to them.

The noise had been steadily increasing in volume when Xanthias, who had pressed on ahead, stopped at a turn in the path and held up a warning hand; then he plunged into a thicket and they followed him.

"Take off your sandals; these women are unshod," he whispered, and crept forward. In a moment he beckoned and they gazed down on a scene that looked innocent enough.

On a small plateau a few feet below them some twenty women were dancing round a bonfire. Their hands were joined, their faces rapt, their ivy-wreathed hair given to the breeze. They were chanting a song whose words were unintelligible, but were evidently addressed to Dionysus, whose image, crowned with grapes and vine leaves, stood beside the fire. Suddenly the circle broke and the women whirled in couples. Aspasia and Constantia saw their opportunity and slipped among them and danced together. When the circle formed again the slight increase in numbers passed unnoticed.

But a closer view convinced the intruders that the dance was not as innocent as it had looked from above, for the women's eyes were wild and their lips foaming. They also caught certain words of the song which were anything but prophylactic. But the wild tune was simple to trained ears and their own words in the increasing frenzy were mere plausible sounds.

Once more the women whirled in couples, once more joined hands and tore about the bonfire. Then abruptly they rushed to a pile of torches and thrust them into the flames. Aspasia and Constantia did likewise, and when the others ran up the glen followed as fleetly. One of the women held the image of Dionysus high above her head as if for a beacon. The moon was rising but his beams were obscured by the leaping glare of the torches.

"Aspasia!" whispered Constantia, "wasn't that dance glorious? My feet hurt but I feel as if my blood were running a race."

"I felt as mad as they looked," replied the star of intellectual Hellas. "What do you suppose they will do next?"

"Zeus knows, but they are quite mad. Do you think Xanthias and the others are close behind us?"

"Trust Xanthias. What fearful yells! And they are stopping at last. My feet feel as if they had been pounded in a mortar."

The women had ranged themselves in a line, and Aspasia and Constantia fell into place and eclipsed themselves as much as possible. Dionysus had been propped against a rock, and with his wreath of grapes hanging over one eye and a disinclination of his body to retain the perpendicular, looked as orgiastic as the Bacchantes.

The women's bodies were no longer moving rhythmically but in spasmodic jerks; they tore off their ivy wreaths and flung them at the feet of the god, then lifted their palms and shrieked an invocation. This religious rite lasted but a moment. With one accord they flung themselves upon Dionysus; and after a moment's tiptoeing the ladies from Athens turned their distended eyes in another direction.

"Zeus and Athenè!" whispered Constantia. "This is a little too much."

But the worst was to come.

Three young goats, attracted no doubt by the noise, and bewildered by the light, appeared on a ledge and one of the women caught sight of them. With a hoarse shriek that ran through the gorge she sprang from the mass of tangled bodies, and all heads shot up. There was no escape for the goats. In a moment those maniacal women were upon them, and above their hoarse horrid grunting could be heard the sickening sound of limb rent from limb. Blood flew in all directions, and a flying head almost hit Aspasia in the face. Constantia retired behind a bush and was bereft of her dinner.

"Oh, Aspasia!" she gasped. "Haven't you had enough?"

But Aspasia shook her head. Excitement had died out of her and even disgust. She was a cold critical intellect once more and merely interested to observe what these obsessed women would do next.

She had not long to wait. The women, their clothes nearly torn off by this time and their eyes glittering ferociously, rent the flesh of the goats with their teeth, then rushed at one another and whirled together until they fell, a mass of writhing bodies.

"What in Zeus' name—" Constantia's eyes and mouth were wide open.

"Holy Apollo!" exclaimed Aspasia. "I think we've had enough! Let us go."

They stumbled down the defile, Xanthias and his men creeping silently above them. When they reached the thicket where they had left their sandals he grimly adjusted them but refrained from speech until they had left the mountain and were hurrying through a vineyard.

"And did you find joy in feeling like a Bacchante, O Mistress?" he asked with sarcasm. "Have you had the fine time you expected in forgetting for a night that you were the great Aspasia daughter of Axiochus and wife of Pericles?"

"No, I did not enjoy myself," she said tartly. "And I shall

not question hereafter that Athenian maxim: nothing too much! But I'll not regret it," she added defiantly, "for at least I have taken part in what probably no one before has ever witnessed. But, Zeus! Pericles said those women were civilized!"

"Yes, as civilized as men on the battlefield when they smell blood. And for the gods' sake don't tell him you've looked on at such an orgy. Even I did not believe such things were done nearer than Thrace."

"No, I'll never tell him of anything but the dance—but oh, my feet hurt! Do you think you could carry me, Xanthias?"

He lifted her in his arms as he so often had done when she was a child; and she was as innocently asleep when he laid her on her bed as young Pericles in the nursery.

XX

The next two years passed in peace, happiness and security. The beautiful temple of Athenè—not for long years to be called the Parthenon—rose rapidly on the Acropolis, as white as the snow that fell on Mount Parnes in winter. Mnesicles was at work on his designs for the Propylæa, which was to rise in majestic beauty on the western summit of the rock.

Socrates' fame waxed ever and his followers among the more serious young men increased steadily. They recognized that he could teach them as much as the sophists; although he scorned the term as well as the large fees those men of business exacted; and, unlike them, elevate not deteriorate the character. In the benign atmosphere of peace and plenty that encompassed Athens they experienced to the full the desire for perfection and eagerly followed this moral teacher with a set of principles in his endless quest of truth. The Greek virtues, knowledge, temperance, justice, prudence, courage, made up the sum of their aspirations, although the last was every Athenian's birthright. They exercised even more ardently in the gymnasium and the stadium that they might be thoroughly fit for war should it come; and in spite of their enjoyment of the present would have welcomed at any moment the greatest game of all for brave and adventurous young men. But meanwhile they strove as ardently to acquire the "pure and garnished mind" Socrates demanded of them and he rewarded them occasionally by taking them to the house of Pericles to engage in dialectics with Aspasia.

Anaxagoras held his classes in the olive groves of Academe, but there was a time when he disappeared from public view, and Aspasia, grown uneasy, asked her husband to seek him out. Pericles made inquiries and discovered that Anaxagoras, too absorbed in philosophy, had allowed his little estate in Clazomenæ to go to ruin, and, a pauper, was plunged into such despondency that he was determined to starve himself to death: he scorned to take money from his pupils. Pericles wasted no time tracking him down and came upon him seated on a stone beside the Ilissus, his head buried in his mantle.

He was shocked and alarmed at the wasted appearance of the old man's body and the relaxed attitude of illness and despair. But he asked sternly: "What does this mean, Anaxagoras? You should be in bed, not here. You look as if about to expire."

"And for that I hope, O Pericles," came a faint muffled voice from the mantle. "I have come here to die, for I am now but a useless cumberer of the earth. But as I am old what does it matter?"

"You are not yet sixty—and it matters much to your friends. What of Aspasia and me? Do you think life would be the same to us without you?"

Anaxagoras was mute.

Pericles sat down beside him and put his hand on a suddenly alert shoulder. "You must live for us, Anaxagoras. Promise me that you will."

Anaxagoras removed his mantle from his head and looked at his old pupil with an expression of shrewd humor in his sunken eyes. "Pericles," he said, "those that want to use a lamp must supply it with oil."

Pericles laughed and gave him a gentle shake. "The oil shall be provided each month by Euangelos! But I do not forgive you for not coming to me at once."

"You carry too many burdens, already, Pericles. Nor would I beg of Aspasia, who has looked up to me for so many years."

"Well, be careful she does not hear of this or like as not she would box your ears—a chastisement you richly deserve. But I'll tell her you went into the country to write a book and took no count of the time. Would you care to live in my house?"

The philosopher shook his head. "There are too many children there and my old ears are still very sharp. Get back my little house from a rapacious landlord and I shall be well content."

"You shall have all that you wish. And now I must return to the city. Can you walk?"

"Send a litter for me, Pericles. Tell your slaves you found me exhausted after too long a walk for my years—and you might also send bread and wine."

"You are an old fool, Nous, to reduce yourself to such a plight; but Athens cannot spare you, nor can I. The slaves will be here with a litter in half an hour and they'll bring you food as well."

He lifted him unceremoniously and propped him against a tree. "Now fix your thoughts on that cicada and try to discover how it is that so small a creature can make such a racket. And don't go to sleep."

The philosopher's eyes twinkled. "It is the thought of good barley bread and wine that will keep me awake. And you might add a cheese-cake. Hasten, dear Pericles."

The schools of Damon and Zeno flourished also and more young men of distant parts came to Athens to learn of them, others to enter the studios of Pheidias and Polygnotus or to study architecture with the masters. Athens was become the University of Hellas, and one more dream of Pericles realized.

The Piræus was now a beautiful white city with imposing docks, and arsenal, a theatre and temples, wide streets and splendid squares, the Agora called after its proud architect. Several wealthy citizens of Athens, allured by the spaces of the new city as well as the sea breezes, had built mansions in or near it, although they spent the greater part of the day in the capital; and not only for its mental attractions: Piræus was as noisy and crowded as ever.

Hippodamus had gone to Italy to build Thurii and taken Zosmë with him. Herodotus, fascinated by what he heard of the new city, had followed, and word came back to his disconsolate friend Sophocles that he intended to finish his history there and had enrolled himself a member of one of the Ten Tribes, established after the model of Athens. Here, at least, he could be a citizen. Cleandridas, who had been a wanderer since he had deserted the Spartan army, had also turned up in Thurii and promised to be a useful citizen, and general if need be. The dwelling houses had been built first and the colonists were writing home boastfully of the beauty of their new city. All other colonies were flourishing and at peace with themselves. Nothing more had been heard of aggressions by Samos.

XXI

The inner aula was quiet for hours at a time, for Alcibiades went to school, and his old but firm pedægogus was making headway in teaching him decorum. But although he made less noise and needed rather more provocation to fight, he still ruled the other boys and would brook no question of his supremacy.

Pericles Y was tottering about the court and his beauty and quaintly imperious manner—copied from his idol Alcibiades, who was unaccountably fond of him—won a measure of amused tolerance from his father. But the paternal affection of Pericles was given to Paralus, for he had lost his pride in Xanthippus and all love for him. The boy was cowardly, shallow, mean, and defiant, and the fact that this son who had inherited nothing of himself must one day be the head of a great family was the only flaw in his content. But he was always able to forget what he did not choose to remember, and Xanthippus kept out of his way. He hated his father not only for his cold disdain but for the simplicity of fare the children were forced to endure; the eldest born had a greedy love of sweets.

Aspasia had won Pericles over to her plan for shedding some measure of light into the monotonous lives of the women of Athens, and such husbands as entertained a real respect and affection for their wives brought them to her morning receptions. Of these was Rhea, wife of Menippus, a handsome young woman and almost as lively as Constantia—never absent herself. Pericles was more in the house than formerly but he always spent the hour after siesta—rarely indulged in by him—receiving many men in his office, and at that time Aspasia gave the women instruction in the pastas or one of the porticoes, for they could linger here longer than in the Agora.

The evenings were passed in conversation with their more intimate friends, who frequently dined with them.

Agariste disapproved of everything but attended the morning levees, finding a subtle feminine satisfaction, which she would have scorned to admit, in this new phase of freedom, and, driven by curiosity, sometimes looked in on the classes. But she spent more time in the inner court, for she was fascinated by her new nephew. "Xanthippus will come to a bad end," she said more than once to Aspasia. "And Paralus, if a sweet and kingly looking boy, has little sense, although his doting father won't see it. But this child is the true son of Pericles and grandson of Xanthippus. I could curse the gods that he is not the eldest and legitimate."

But Aspasia was able to smile at Agariste's ruthless candor. She would admit no flaw in her life, and as the State was now running as smoothly as a millwheel unclogged by moss she and Pericles were often together for long uninterrupted afternoons. The subjects they found of mutual interest to discuss were inexhaustible, and she became more and more his confidante, sometimes his adviser. Moreover she was a woman of a thousand moods and he found her equally captivating in each; the ardor of his love never flickered. It was, as old Marcus had said, a strange marriage for Athens.

And then the first blow fell.

Aspasia was sitting one afternoon in Pheidias' studio in the Altis waiting for Pericles who had business with his harbor master in Piræus. She was watching the sculptor adjust the ivory plates on the colossal wooden figure of the goddess when Pericles entered abruptly. She knew by his narrowed eyes that something was wrong. But he barely glanced at her and said with unaccustomed sternness to Pheidias:

"Have you had those plates weighed? I thought not! Be good enough to do so at once; and the gold is even more important. Will you come, Aspasia?"

She walked swiftly through the streets beside him, for once not daring to ask a question, and beset by fear. His face had never looked more like a mask.

He did not utter a word until he had closed the door of the thalamos behind them and then he flung his helmet on a chair, caught her by the shoulders, and shook her almost roughly.

"O Zeus!" he exclaimed, "I must leave you!"

And then he turned as if he could not bear to look at her and strode up and down the room. She dropped to the sofa and pressed her hands hard against the cushions.

"It is war, I suppose." Her voice was faint but she strove to keep it steady. She was the wife of a soldier as well as of a citizen and a virtual ruler, and peace was an anomaly in Hellas; to be enjoyed while it lasted but never to be regarded as amaranthine. She had known from the beginning that an hour would come when she must summon all the resources of her character. Failure to live up to her standards and his would mean disaster for both.

"Is it Samos?" she asked.

"Yes. She has taken Priene and defeated the Milesian army. She is resting on her laurels for the moment, but there is no doubt that if Athens does not interfere she will eventually march on Miletus and if victorious again either occupy or sack it. Miletus has sent a call for help, and we may not ignore it, for all this means far more to us than it does to her. I have dispatched Cleander to demand that the dispute be referred to Athens, but there is no doubt of the answer from a State flushed with victory. And Samos has had her eye on the mainland too long. I shall follow day after tomorrow with forty triremes, and have called the Ecclesia for

to-morrow morning, as I must go through the formality of
putting it to the vote."

"Must you go yourself?"

"Samos must be subdued promptly or worse will follow.
I can trust no one but myself."

"Couldn't I follow and stay in Miletus? We could meet
oc—"

"Zeus, no! I must know you are safe here. Besides I may
not be gone two months. The more quickly I strike the more
quickly will it be over."

"The virtue of courage shall be mine! But two months are
an eternity—and—you might be—"

"Killed? Drive that thought from your mind, Aspasia.
When a man has survived many battles on land he does not
look for death at sea where he knows every strategic ma-
nœuvre. . . . So far there is no rumor of Persia taking advantage of this threat to the Maritime Empire; nor will she
move at present. But a triumphant Samos and a shattered
Miletus would be a terrible blow to the Empire, and that of
Athens must be swift and sure."

He continued to stride up and down the room with drawn
brows, for his face was never a mask when alone with her.
"I have expected this for two years, for Menippus was well
informed, and the thought has crossed my mind that Samos
delayed her purpose until she could come to an understanding
with Sparta. But Sparta is ever on the safe side and always
prone to delay and wait on oracles or omens—as when she left
us to fight the Persians alone at Marathon. I have friends in
Sparta and have already sent a communication to one of
them. The priests there are even more corruptible than at
Delphi. Superstition has its uses! But I never trust to any one
resource and shall increase the forces on the Megarid frontier."

He sat down beside her and took her in his arms. "I shall
leave the best part of myself behind," he said, "and I cannot
return quickly enough. But I go myself that a longer separation
may be avoided. Some day we must fight Sparta, but the
stronger I make the Empire meanwhile the longer that may be
deferred; and the glory of Athens increase, the more uninterrupted our life together."

XXII

He brought Samos to her knees in even a shorter time than he had anticipated. When the Athenian fleet sailed into her harbor she submitted without a show of arms. Pericles entered the city at the head of his troops and immediately called the Government to account. He exacted a fine of eighty talents, deposed the Oligarchs, changed the constitution to a democracy, and put an Athenian garrison in command. He then took fifty men and fifty boys as hostages and sent them to the Athenian colony on Lemnos. In less than two-thirds of a month he had reduced a powerful State, once the ruler of all the eastern Ægean, into a mere subject of Athens. He was the more implacable as both government and hostages had attempted to bribe him, and Pissuthnes, Persian satrap at Sardis, sent him an offer of ten thousand gold pieces to spare the city to the Oligarchs.

Pericles returned to his life of affairs in a vociferously grateful Athens and to the companionship of Aspasia—in whom a dispatch sent shortly after his arrival in Samos had quieted apprehension; she had endured the brief separation with little call on heroism, but much on a patience never one of her notable characteristics.

But during the few months that intervened between the first and second revolts of Samos there was a change in the benign atmosphere of Athens. The Demos was proud of the magnificent abilities of its chosen ruler and with him to a man in his policy to strike with swift ruthlessness at the first symptom of danger to the Empire. But among his own class the belief grew and spread that he had gone to the relief of Miletus to please Aspasia. They felt they had condoned that marriage too long; moreover it had been commented upon for some time that no man, not even his relatives, could get a word alone with Pericles except on business. There had been a time when he had occasionally discussed affairs of state with men of great political acumen, but it was known in these days that he consulted no one but Aspasia; and although they were forced to admit that her political acumen was second to no man's they resented her power over the First Citizen none the less for that. And a bastard son in the house of Pericles! Acknowledged with ceremonies! Any decent woman would have had it exposed. One would think they were living in the days of Theseus and she had sent philtres to all Athens and kept it half asleep.

And if the Oligarchs were negligible as a party their social power was in no way diminished and many of them were intimate with the comic poets.

These gentlemen also discovered that their unaccountable amiability had suddenly deserted them. They feared neither Pericles nor Zeus, and, taking stock, concluded they had been made fools of like other men by the beauty and charm of this foreign woman, and had overlooked the fact that great and singular talents in a mere female were an insult to their own sex. Like others they had believed that the marriage of those two was an intellectual partnership, but it was well known by this time that it was the most passionate love affair between a man and a woman in all history. After all, Helen had been abducted and Paris a fool.

And this again was an insult to their standards. They regarded such love as unintelligent and unnatural; and, moreover, a dangerous example. This Milesian was an intruder who not only had ensnared the most conspicuous man of his day, but with her high-handed independence was setting an example that might lead to a general desire for freedom—and marital devotion!—among the well-trained women of Athens. The Greater Dionysia was upon them and their comedies had been submitted to the archon, but interpolations could be made at the last moment.

And some one else was at work. Thoron now hated Aspasia more than he had ever hated Pericles—who had given a careless consent to his return to Athens. The scar on his shoulder was a perpetual reminder that he had been ignominiously vanquished by a woman—who had forced him to fight a slave! He no longer cared whether she loved Pericles or not, his only desire was to see that white contemptuous goddess besmirched. He wished he were a comic poet, but at least he could cultivate those unscrupulous powers. He avoided Socrates and lived only for dissipation and revenge.

Those Oligarchs who had accepted the decree of Fate ceased to go to the house of Pericles. They would not continue to pay court to a woman whose downfall they were determined to compass, and they saw no hope of preferment from Pericles. Only Glaucon and Menippus continued to take their wives to the morning levees, and the classes diminished; the women had won their husbands' reluctant consent to this innovation, but dared not defy them when it was abruptly withdrawn.

XXIII

"I believe the men are in a panic," said the indignant Agariste to Aspasia one afternoon as they sat in the thalamos. "Do you know what is at the bottom of all this? Know the reason why the women of Athens are kept in seclusion and ignorance? I wouldn't tell you before but I will now. I got it from my mother, who got it from hers. It is Sparta that is responsible, although even the men do not realize it to-day. The Spartan women are in most things as free as the men and mingle with them everywhere except in the barracks. And what is the result? They haven't the behavior of goats and snap their fingers at masculine authority in the house, recognizing no power but that of the State. They may have more character than Athenian women but are appalling creatures nevertheless. A Spartan ambassador brought his wife here with him once and they stayed in my house. She took her gymnastic exercises naked in the aula and had an affair with my steward. Can you wonder— Oh, you may laugh! You Ionian!"

For Aspasia, convulsed, had thrown herself face downward on the cushions. She sat up in a moment and brushed the tears from her eyes.

"And do these poor gentlemen of Athens really fear I'll turn their wives into Spartans!" she demanded when she could get her breath. "By teaching them to read and write—by enabling them to talk to their husbands of something besides how much wool they have spun or how often the cook has insulted them since morning? Athenians are supposed to be the most intelligent men in the world—surely they must know it would take two lifetimes to put real independence into these women."

"They would if they chose to reason but they don't. They prefer to think you are a danger to their power in the house. But what really is the matter with them is that they are suffering a reaction from too much amiability. They will go into the Agora or out to the Lyceum and talk lofty sentiments and philosophy off the top of their brains but the human part underneath is seething with vexation and spite. Pericles is too powerful and you are too intellectual for a woman—and powerful in your own way. And some of the wives are said to have given trouble in the house. There is a rumor that Œnone slapped the face of Xyppus when he told her to do more spinning and less talking. I can't say how true that is but at all events she comes here no more."

Aspasia shrugged. "Neither do any of the others except Rhea and Constantia, but they have reasonable husbands. And Ariphon has promised to send Phyrra."

"Oh, Ariphon will always stand by Pericles. He's not a man of ability, but he'd send the girl here if only to show that he's a man of independent spirit and believes in his brother. I would the rest of the two families were as faithful, but they have all gone over to the enemy. I fear there is trouble ahead."

"Well, what can they do?" asked Aspasia impatiently. "They cannot take Pericles from me and I am concerned with nothing else. I feel sorry for those women and shall miss them, but heaven knows my time is quite occupied without them."

Agariste had made herself comfortable in Pericles' armchair. The day was warm and she hitched up her chiton and stretched out her long masculine-looking legs to catch the breeze from the court. For a moment she did not look at Aspasia. "There are the comic poets," she said, darkly.

Aspasia turned pale. "Oh—surely Pericles is too powerful now—they wouldn't dare!"

"Wouldn't they? They'd pull the beard of Zeus if they could get at him. And they, too, are suffering from reaction. It is not in human nature to view power and happiness with equanimity for long—nor to be uninterruptedly amiable. It affects the spleen. Look at children. Look at Alcibiades. If he behaves himself to-day he must beat some one to-morrow. Emotions and impulses seem to move in a circle. The trouble with Pericles is he's too lenient. He can do what he will with the Demos and he should pass a law to curb free speech in the Dionysus. It is ridiculous that those mongrel comic poets should have the dignity and reputation of the great at their mercy."

"Have you heard anything?" asked Aspasia anxiously.

"There are rumors," said Agariste evasively. "Only that. But I know human nature and I know those little beasts. Cratinus has always been Pericles' bitter enemy, for he loves the Oligarchs and resents that an Eupatrid should have gone over to the Demos—and then rule it with a rod of iron. It was he who wrote in his *Chirones*:

> *From Kronos old, and Faction,*
> *Is sprung a tyrant dread,*
> *And all Olympus calls him*
> *The man-compelling head."*

"Very feeble," commented Aspasia. "And as ill-expressed as anything may be in Attic Greek."

"True. But when a good actor in a comic mask and in a tone of inimitable drollery drawls it out he makes the Dionysus rock. Oh, I dread the coming Dionysia! I hope you will not go to the tragedies, Aspasia. Many of the women who have never come here are as bad as their husbands, and I have a suspicion it is Olympias who has stirred them up. She hates Pericles more than ever because he sent Cleander abroad twice."

"No. I'll not go—if it is as bad as you say. I'll not have Pericles insulted through me. I can spare him that at least."

"Zeus be thanked! One never knows what you will do— ah! Here comes your little god! He grows stronger and more beautiful day by day."

Pericles Y was running unsteadily toward them, holding up

his chiton in front while with the other hand he dragged a small wagon; Alcibiades had taught him to scorn dolls.

As he stumbled over the threshold Agariste caught him up in her arms, kissed him loudly, then sat him on Aspasia's lap.

"You two always make a picture," she said. And she settled herself back in her chair to enjoy it.

Aspasia wore a white linen tunic and her hair hung over each shoulder in two long copper braids. As she fondled the child, really beautiful now with his large lively black eyes and mass of golden curls, she had never looked more lovely, and Agariste wished that great painters like Polygnotus deigned to paint women. She was bored to death with goddesses and would have liked to see in her house a breathing picture of an exquisite woman and her child.

"And curse the comic poets," she muttered. "If I were a man I'd go out and beat them until they whined they'd behave themselves."

"What are you saying?" asked Aspasia, who had been tickling the baby and enjoying his gurgles.

"Nothing. Where is Pericles?"

"In his office, I think. He was to see one of our richest men —I forget his name—whom the Council has taxed to equip a trireme."

Agariste jumped up without a word and strode out. She had never ventured to interrupt Pericles during his business hours before, but she knocked on that forbidden door to-day without a qualm.

Pericles was alone, but he looked up as she entered with no enthusiasm of welcome. "What is it, Agariste?" he asked coldly. "You know that I do not receive my family here—"

"I know all your habits by this time, O mighty Brother, but I have come to have a talk with you. And if you throw me out there'll be a scandal, for Marcus is at the door gossiping with the old man opposite."

Pericles pushed aside the accounts he had been balancing. "Very well. What is it? Sit down if you will."

"If I had been born a man and had risen to your power in the State," began Agariste in her most aggressive tones, " don't suppose Aspasia would have looked at me, but I'd have done something to protect her nevertheless—"

"Protect? What do you mean?" He looked both startled and angry.

"I mean those ill-begotten comic poets are threshing their filthy brains and that Aspasia is to be the victim at the coming Dionysia."

All expression left Pericles' face and he sat like a man of stone. "Are you sure of this?" he asked.

"Simonides brought the news home and I have heard it from others. There is a social revolution going on, Pericles, and as far as the women are concerned Olympias is at the head of it. If Cleander finds it out I hope he'll beat her."

Pericles pushed back his chair and walked up and down the room, his hands clasped tightly behind him. "I have been expecting this," he said. "It was all too good to last."

"And they'll be the worse for being complaisant so long. You are all-powerful. *Do* something."

Pericles shook his head. "I shall not curb free speech—which I have extolled and encouraged as one of the privileges of democracy—because I fear what the comic poets may say about my wife. Aspasia knew what to expect when she married me. We talked that over as well as many other things. She is a woman of strong character and well able to stand the blows of fate. She would be the last to demand that I put us both in a ridiculous position. My only excuse for curbing the malignancy of the comic poets would be if their utterances in any way endangered the State, and it has not come to that yet."

"O thunder of Zeus!" exclaimed Agariste. "You make me feel as if I had eaten olive oil mixed with honey! When a ruler is also a husband there are times when the State should take second place."

Pericles smiled for the first time. "That was not the daughter of Xanthippus who spoke, but a mere woman—Agariste who has always asserted she has a man's virtues although forced to bow to an unjust decree of Fate and bear children! Your affection for Aspasia has made you soft."

"So it has! And what of yourself? Hasn't she made you

over? Are you the cold-blooded Olympian you were before?—in the house? You worship the very air she breathes and you won't lift a finger to protect her."

"That is enough, Agariste," he said harshly. "Much as I love her my duty to the State comes first. It is not Pericles who will strike the first blow at democracy—and give the Oligarchs an entering wedge if free speech were suppressed for a purely personal reason. Now I must ask you to go. I have work still to do."

He opened the door, and Agariste, with tears in her hard eyes, went out.

But he sat down heavily and did no more work.

XXIV

The plays of Cratinus, Telekleides, Crates and Hermippus, among others, had been accepted by the First Archon for competition at the Dionysia. Pericles as First Citizen was obliged to attend the tragedies, but he was conspicuously absent from the comedies. This was regarded as the insult he intended it to be, for the comic poets did not suspect that he had an inkling of their purpose.

Thoron had sat at the elbow of the flattered Cratinus and made certain suggestions eagerly adopted by a man who was not in a position to know what went on behind the jealously guarded doors of the Eupatridæ.

"Why do you suppose the prettiest women in Athens were enticed to the house of Pericles?" demanded Thoron. "Aspasia knows that her power over him is waning and she keeps her position in his house by pandering to his sensuality. If he put her out she'd have to set up for herself and be classed openly with the hetæræ. She's too subtle and ambitious for that."

"But I thought he was besottedly in love with her." Cratinus had the sharpest brains in Athens, and even to his bitter spite this tidbit seemed a trifle dubious.

"He was, Cratinus, or he would never have married her with his entire clan in attendance. He'd merely have taken her from the house of Hippodamus and put her in another—not his own

But three years are a long time for a man like that to love one woman. I know of what I speak, Cratinus, for I have it from her handmaid who is intimate with my mother's favorite slave. When she held those classes one of the women was always missing—while Pericles was supposed to be in his office! But Rhea, wife of his intimate friend Menippus, is his favorite—another instance of his depravity, for Menippus trusts him utterly. But it were best to say nothing about that, for Menippus is an Eupatrid if not an Oligarch, and does no one harm—although he has a fiery temper. But what I tell you is true, Cratinus. Who should know better than I?"

"True, O Thoron. And I thank you for the hints, for I had not thought of anything but some lewd comparison between her and Omphale or Helen."

And Thoron, well satisfied, went on to Hermippus, to whom he imparted the valuable information that Aspasia selected her slave girls for their beauty and the men who visited her were welcome to their favors.

Neither Pericles nor Aspasia gave the other a hint of their conversations with Agariste. She did not wish to worry him and he hoped that if the worst happened it would be long before she had news of it. His instructions to his sister were brief and definite.

But he asked Pheidias, the friend whom he trusted most, to attend the comedies and report to him in the evening. When he was announced Pericles left Aspasia and the guests who were dining with them and went to his office where he had told Pheidias to await him.

The great sculptor was white and trembling. "Oh, Pericles!" he cried. "I never before felt the desire to kill, but if you say the word—"

"What did they say?" demanded Pericles.

"I'll not repeat their obscenities even to you. Don't look as if you would strangle me, Pericles. I will not! If others have the courage, let them. They'll never pass my lips."

"How were they received? Did the audience applaud with the usual enthusiasm inspired by obscenities?"

"The Oligarchs, led by that young rascal Thoron, shouted themselves hoarse, and the hetæræ of course were delighted. But—thank Zeus—the people showed their disapproval by remaining silent."

"*Aspasia!*" muttered Pericles. "*Aspasia!*"

Pheidias threw his mantle over his head and wept. "I am not ashamed of these tears, Pericles, for I love her almost as much as you do. I would that she could have been the model for my Athenè. How I longed to defy tradition! But they would have cast me into prison for impiety, and you too would suffer—"

"You must tell me the gist of what they said," interrupted Pericles with cold fury. "I care nothing for their phrases, but I must know their accusations. Did they dare insinuate that she had lovers?"

"No, they stopped short of that. Cratinus said in so many words—and with cursed wit—that she pretended to have classes in order to pander to your vices; Hermippus, that her pretty slave girls were for other men."

"Great Zeus! What else?"

"That you would not have risked the lives of many Athenians to go to the relief of Miletus but for her. That if we are ever plunged into a real war—and all Athens into mourning—it will be her fault—her revenge on the men for forbidding their wives to come to her house."

"Ah!" exclaimed Pericles, and there was an ominous glitter in his eyes. "Ah! If war threatens again I have the excuse."

"What does that mean, Pericles?"

"I mean that if the comic poets by their lies endanger my power, and therefore the State, I shall suppress them at the proper time. Now, compose yourself and come with me to the andron. I told our friends I expected you on business; and you must not let them know that you have been to the comedies."

"I cannot turn my face into a mask as you can, Pericles, but if they mark agitation on it I'll tell them I had a disaster in the studio."

"Aspasia's wits are very sharp. Be careful."

Sophocles, Anaxagoras, Menippus and Ariphon were discussing the morning performance and quoting what they could remember to Aspasia. Thucydides also was present but took no part in the conversation, for as usual he had ignored the Dionysus. Sophocles had not competed this year, but had attended to witness the effort of his younger rival Euripides— one long play instead of three short ones.

"And do you think Euripides will win the first prize?" asked Aspasia, eagerly; she had forgotten apprehension for the moment. "It was a great disappointment to me that I was unable to attend this morning, but at least he read it to me, and it would give me the greatest pleasure if he were crowned by the judges—and you too, Sophocles, I know, for you are the most generous of men."

Sophocles, who was reclining at ease, drained his cup. "Certainly, Aspasia, although he is so advanced in his theories and beliefs—we have you to thank for that, Nous—he is beginning to make me feel old-fashioned. He is a little too fond of merely human passions and everyday people for my taste, but his gifts are great and in my enjoyment of their expression I forget my prejudices. I hope indeed he will win the prize. There was a mighty enthusiasm this morning."

"Pericles, Aspasia, and Euripides are my proudest achievements," said Anaxagoras complacently. "And I discern much of my teachings in the tragedies my pupil has so far presented."

"But you have a rival, O Nous! He grows more intimate with Socrates every day, and I can see his mark in those plays as well as yours."

Anaxagoras frowned. "Socrates is a young upstart; although I admit that his influence so far is for good. But I shall talk to Euripides and warn him against too great an intimacy with that young man, lest he become didactic and therefore a bore. It is the duty of tragic poets to be moral teachers, but if they go too far, or become too modern, they will violate the traditions of the theatre and cease to win approbation."

"True, O Thinker!" cried Sophocles. "And there lies my hope of continuing to please."

XXV

Pericles and the sculptor entered and the company was immediately diverted.

"Did you go to the comedies, Pheidias?" demanded Menippus. "For one reason or another none of us was able to attend."

Pheidias frowned and flushed. "I abhor the comedies!" he exclaimed violently. "They grow more disgusting year by year, and in my opinion are little redeemed by their wit. What is more I am too busy in my studio to waste time on them."

"O virtuous Pheidias!" cried Sophocles. "Your throat must be parched after that heresy. Pericles, clap your hands that he may quench his thirst."

Pheidias drank eagerly, and then, still too irritated to recline, turned to Aspasia. "Did you go to the Dionysus this morning, dear goddess? I hear that Euripides is sure to win the first prize."

"You bring me pleasant news, dear Pheidias. I feared you had brought ill." She gave him a keen glance. "Did you go to the comedies?" she asked.

He turned pale and his hand shook. "Have I not just said what I think of the comedies?"

"I did not believe for a moment that Pericles had business with you at this hour. And I knew as soon as he entered that you had brought him bad news of some kind."

Pheidias, who was standing in front of Aspasia's chair, glanced over at Pericles, extended in graceful relaxation and talking to Thucydides. "His face tells nothing to any one," he said naïfly. "No man can—"

"His face is never a mask to me! What did those poets say about me, Pheidias? That I was too ambitious? Too learned for a woman? That I monopolize too much of the society of Pericles? That he should not have married a foreign woman, with so many beautiful and charming Athenian ladies to choose from? That I should not have been married with ceremonies? Tell me, dear Pheidias."

Pheidias stared at her in amazement and pity. It was evident she knew little of the resources of comic poets! But he saw his opportunity and grasped it eagerly. "Yes, if you *will* know. They attacked you quite bitterly not only for having won Pericles for husband but all the great men of Athens for admirers and friends. Pericles was angry they should dare mention you at all, but of course you could not avoid rousing envy and jealousy. I told him that and he agreed, but was none the less annoyed. Why did you suspect they would attack you since they had not done so before?"

"Agariste told me she had heard rumors, for Athens no longer speaks roses of me, and of course the comic poets will be on the popular side. They are always hoping to be invited to the houses of the Eupatridæ. But they really could not hurt me. I feared they might do Pericles some harm. Did they attack him?"

"Merely a thorn prick. I've forgotten what it was. Agariste might have held her long tongue."

"Oh, no, she wished to prepare me for the worst. But I said nothing to Pericles and I shall not tell him I know of their hateful attentions."

"That is right, Aspasia! It is not a subject he would care to discuss with you."

Old Marcus put his head into the room. "A messenger from Miletus, O Master. He ran all the way from Piræus."

Pericles rose to his feet, his eyes for a second dilating. "From *Miletus?*" He added at once: "Send him here."

"What can it be!" Aspasia had grasped the arms of her chair.

"We shall know in a moment," said Pericles. "But it must be serious or he would have waited until he could have sent for a horse."

The other men had risen and there was apprehension on every face.

The messenger entered, breathless and covered with dust. He carried a roll of parchment. "From the Captain of the

Athenian garrison, O Pericles son of Xanthippus," he murmured, his voice nearly spent.

Pericles clapped his hands and a servant entered. "Take this man to the kitchen and give him food and wine, and then a bed. And do not come in to remove the tables until you are summoned."

The men disappeared and he unrolled the official communication. He read it rapidly, every eye on his face, and there was not a sound in the room but the crackling of the parchment. When he had finished he crushed it in his hand and raised heavy frowning eyes.

"Samos has revolted again," he said. "Certain Oligarchs left the island surreptitiously and went to Sardis. Pissuthnes placed a regiment at their disposal. With this force they returned to Samos and overcame the Athenian garrison, which they sent as hostage to Sardis. They expelled the members of the democratic party, restored the old constitution, and rescued the hostages from Lemnos. The Samian fleet is being made ready to besiege Miletus. Their hope is that if they reduce it before the arrival of the Athenian navy they will persuade all Asiatic Hellas to revolt. They look for the secession of Byzantium at once, and are said to have invoked the aid of Sparta."

"O Zeus on Olympus!" exclaimed Menippus. "The last revolt was as nothing to this. It may mean war with Persia."

"And the Empire undone!" cried Ariphon.

"They kept their plans secret enough," said Pericles, grimly. "Not a word has reached me before this, although I directed the Captain of the garrison in Samos to advise me at the first sign of unrest. It is evident they did not strike the first blow until their plan was perfected; everything must have been done simultaneously. No doubt as the Oligarchs were landing on Samos with their troops another force was rescuing the hostages from Lemnos." He turned to Sophocles. "You are a Strategos this year. Go at once and make your preparations. I shall send swift galleys to-night to call in the fleet."

Sophocles, who was calmer than any one present except Pericles, shrugged his broad shoulders. "I shall make an indifferent General," he said, "and do not yet understand why a mere tragic poet should be elected because he has won prizes in the Dionysus. But I know how to obey orders, O Pericles, and I'll do my best.'"

He nodded to his friend and paused a moment before Aspasia, who was whiter than her tunic and stood like a statue defying Fate. "Trust Pericles," he whispered. "Remember the power of his arm and the lightning resources of his mind. This will be but another brief holiday on the water and more talents for the treasury."

"Oh, no, dear Sophocles, this is war! And Pericles knows it. It will be long before he returns to Athens. But do not fear for me. The part of women in war is lamentable but must be endured nevertheless."

Pericles was giving orders to Ariphon. "Go rouse the criers and bid them summon the Ecclesia for to-morrow at daybreak," he said, and then turned to Menippus. "I am grateful that you are a Strategos this year and may go with me. See that the transports are ready for the troops to-morrow afternoon. And tell Nicias to assemble the troops. Those that I do not take with me must be sent to the Megarid frontier."

Menippus hurried out in the wake of Ariphon, and Pericles addressed Thucydides. "You will, I know, do what you can to help me to-night, for there is not a moment to lose. Send Phormio to me here. Find out who is Chairman of the Council for to-day and tell him to convene it at once and let me know when it is assembled."

"That is little to ask, O Pericles," said Thucydides eagerly, "and there is nothing I would not do for you. But—"

"Well, what is it?" asked Pericles impatiently.

"Take me with you, Strategos. I have seen nothing of war, and I would see you in action."

"There is no position I can give you—but, yes, you may go. A man like you can be made of use. Now hasten. If those men are asleep rout them out. If at symposia track them down."

"What orders for me, Pericles?" asked Pheidias. "Would that I could go with you!"

"Thank the gods, you cannot. You have a great work here to perform, and see that you forget Athens is at war. That is your part. Go now."

As he left, somewhat crestfallen, Anaxagoras said plaintively: "And am I too old to do anything, Pericles? Is there no task for me while Athens is at war?"

"Yes. Instil obedience to the State into your pupils—and fear of the Oligarchs should they plot against us while they are gone. And bid them instil both into others. That is as important an order as I have given to-night."

And Anaxagoras, well pleased, looked askance at Aspasia and went out.

Pericles did not look at her and said harshly: "Not a word with you now! I must not turn my thoughts for a moment from the important duties I have to perform to-night. Go to the thalamos and try to sleep. I'll be with you before morning."

He left the room on the last word. Aspasia sank into her chair and sat staring before her for many moments. Finally she rose, shrugged her shoulders, lifted her head defiantly, and went to her room. I too have my orders, she thought with some bitterness. And like others I must obey and look as if I rejoiced in them—and that nothing matters but the safety of the Empire!

XXVI

The rumor of war flew over Athens that night, and while it was still dark men began to mount the Pnyx. As the sun rose one of the fifty Presidents of the Council of Five Hundred, chosen for this occasion by lot the night before after Pericles' brief appearance in the Chamber, opened the ceremonies at once. A sucking pig was sacrificed and its blood sprinkled. While incense was burning a solemn prayer was offered to Athenè, and the usual curse pronounced on all who deceived the people for bribes.

The President then rose and in a silence that was oppressive and almost breathless announced that Samos had declared war on the Empire through Miletus. Pericles had summoned the

Council in the night and laid before it two measures for con-
sideration. They had accepted his wise advice as ever and now
brought those measures before the great and all-powerful Demos
to vote upon. The first was that the Athenian navy go to the
relief of Miletus and reduce Samos before the other tributaries
had time to revolt and involve all Hellas in war with Persia
once more. The second was that while the Empire was in
danger the comic poets should be permitted to write nothing
that would lower the dignity of the State. Any scurrilous and
laughter-provoking attacks on its Generals, magistrates, and
other officials or their families during this anxious and possibly
terrible period, would not only endanger authority but encourage
enemies nearer home. But before these measures were put to
the vote they were to listen for a few moments to the great
Strategos himself.

During the brief interval before Pericles arrived there was an
excited murmur among the Demos. They had expected to vote
upon war, but were taken aback by this extraordinary suggestion that in a jealously preserved democracy tongues might not
wag as they willed and stili be blunted. They had disapproved
the insults of the preceding morning, and although they relished
the wit refused to applaud, out of loyalty to Pericles. Nor had
they believed them for a moment. But it never would have
occurred to them to call the poets to account.

There were no Oligarchs present. They knew better than to
lift their futile voices and invite humiliation.

Silence fell once more as Pericles appeared among them and
mounted the Bema; and then they burst into a storm of greeting. On him their hopes rested. Without him they might be
reduced to a mere City State, the prey of Sparta or Persia.
They were impassioned, even bitter, advocates of democracy,
but as yet too young in their liberties not to welcome as guide
of their destinies a leader in whom they had an overwhelming
confidence. They even accepted his scoldings meekly and admired him the more.

Pericles stood for a moment without speaking, his white
helmeted figure an imposing picture against the dark wall of
the Bema. When he began abruptly his voice was even more

authoritative than usual and as harsh as that golden organ ever could be. Too deep a politician to take advantage of his power over the Demos by assuming he could do as he chose without the formality of their vote, it was long nevertheless since he had besought their approval for any of his policies; he gave them to understand they were to do as he thought best.

"Men of Athens, you know why you are summoned this morning. War on Miletus means war on the Empire. Your vote is required that I may sail this afternoon with sixty triremes— and more to follow if necessary. It is the purpose of Samos to involve all Eastern Hellas, and there is no doubt that she has the moral support of Persia. We depend upon her quick subjection to strike fear into our old cruel enemy.

"But this will be a longer war than the last; for Samos has already received the help of Sardis in men and money, and manned her fleet. For that reason you have been asked to pass a law that will curb the comic poets while I am absent. They are my enemies and yours and long for the return of the Oligarchs to power. They are indifferent to the humiliation of the State in peace or war if they may gratify their spite and our enemies here in Athens. Words have a mighty power, and none must be publicly expressed that may injure the authority of the State while her men are fighting and dying for it. I leave the dignity and the authority of the State in your hands, and I hold you responsible until I return. Now, cast your pebbles, Men of Athens."

But the shout that resounded through the city as he stepped down from the Bema made voting an absurd anti-climax, and as he left the Pnyx they cheered him until he was out of sight. When the urns were brought forth they voted as one man for the restrictions on the comic poets. Nor did they permit that law to fall into disuse for several years after the war was over.

His parting with Aspasia was brief, for he was in his office or Piræus until mid-afternoon, and when he returned to the house for a few moments to change into his leather uniform he could hardly shake off the weeping Paralus; nor Alcibiades, who never wept save with rage, but clamored to be taken to Samos.

"I can spy on the enemy!" he cried, his magnificent eyes blazing as he clung to Pericles' arm. "I can swim between the tlilemes with messages. I can—"

"You will have enough of war when you are a man, Alcibiades," said his guardian with a faint smile. "I must do nothing of which your father who left you to my care would disapprove." And then as the boy looked half-persuaded at the mention of his father's name but still unhappy, he added with inspiration: "And I leave Aspasia to your keeping, for she will need comfort and protection. Promise that you will let no harm come to her until my return."

Alcibiades' eyes flashed with resolution and pride. "Oh, yes, I plomise that, Pellicles son of Xantippus! I shall guald her flom all enemies, and sleep on her thleshold if Athens is invaded. If Xantippus laughs I'll beat him as I nev'l have beaten him yet."

"You send me to my difficult task with an easy mind, dear Alcibiades, and you and the other boys may go with Aspasia to the roof of Hagnias in the Piræus and witness the fleet sail from the harbor."

Paralus forgot his tears and shouted with Alcibiades as they raced each other to carry this news to their own court, and Pericles went in to Aspasia.

XXVII

Pericles rode out of Athens at the head of his troops, the entire population with certain notable exceptions, cheering him from the streets, the roofs, and the broad surfaces of the Long Walls. There was gnashing of teeth in another part of Athens but who heard it? The comic poets knew that if they harangued a crowd on the subject of "Tyrants" and "the blow to democracy by the enforcement of silence on brave tongues," they would be answered with yells of derision and possibly beaten. Pericles was as mighty as Zeus, and they but worms. They prayed to the gods for his defeat by the enemy.

Aspasia, surrounded by the boys, Agariste, the excited Galatea and her increasing brood, stood on the roof of Hagnias—who had rented a house on one of the broad streets of the beautiful

new city—and heard nothing of the chatter about her. She was
concerned only to look calm and proud, and she feared to speak
lest her voice betray her.

But as she heard the cheering and saw the helmet of Pericles
between the Long Walls something of the exaltation of that
great hour passed into her and dried the tears of her spirit.
Every man of those shouting thousands rested all his hopes on
Pericles. The fate of the State and the Empire was in his
hands and it was a terrible and glorious trust. As he emerged
from the Walls and entered the city she looked at him almost
impersonally, forgot that this omnipotent being had been her
husband and lover. He was a great ruler and warrior, the
statesman and permanent General the people had raised to a
dizzy height above his fellow-men, and he belonged to Athens
and the Empire not to her.

"Does he not look like an Emperor?" cried Galatea. "No
wonder the people believe in and worship him."

"I too will be a gleat gen'l like him some day," said Alcibiades enviously. "And go to wal with my tloops, and the
people shouting my name as to-day they shout 'Pellicles.' "

Xanthippus sneered. "You will never be anything but a bad
lisping boy," he said loftily. "And *I* should feel like a fool on
that horse with a vast screeching crowd taken leave of its
senses."

He was promptly knocked down and the usual scrimmage
would have ensued, but Hagnias, a young man of character,
separated them, gave each a cuff on the ear and directed them
to go to opposite ends of the roof. But Alcibiades ran back to
Aspasia.

"Pellicles said I must take cal of you," he said in his grandest
manner. "And he must see me beside you and not think I have
f'lgotten."

His voice could hardly be heard above the din, for all the
Metics, the Athenian residents of Piræus, and even the slaves,
were in the streets and squares, many swarming up the columns
of temples to get a better view.

She smiled and put her arm over his shoulders, and he was

proud to clasp his own about her waist without standing on his toes.

"I am to be y'l husband and the fath'l of little Pellicles," he said proudly. "And I shall sleep in the thalamos, and I shall spank that child if he gets into the swing again by himself—" And then he felt the arm about his shoulders tremble.

"He will pass in a moment," she whispered.

Agariste, who had been watching her intently, approached and bent her lips to her sister-in-law's ear. "Think what a different sight it would have been," she shouted, "if Thucydides had triumphed and Pericles were on his way to exile. If this mob were hooting instead of cheering. This should be the proudest moment of your life, Aspasia."

"It is, dear Agariste! And I shall not break down and weep, if that is what you fear. If I cannot smile I shall preserve my dignity as the wife of Pericles First Citizen of Athens."

"If my wife weeps when I go to wal I'll beat her," announced Alcibiades, whose ears were ever alert for what was not intended for their hearing. "And Aspasia would not weep in public." He scowled at Agariste. "She is the gleatest lady in Athens, for is she not the wife of Pellicles?"

"Who said she would weep?" demanded Agariste tartly. "You are a bad little boy, and Aspasia spoils you. You should have learned before this not to speak before you are spoken to."

Alcibiades made a face at her, which was fortunately unobserved, as her eyes were once more on her brother. How many times had she watched him ride out of Athens at the head of his troops, and their father before him! What was life but war?

Pericles looked like a statue on horseback and had not cast a glance at his cheering people nor permitted a ripple to cross the immobility of his features. But as he passed the house of Hagnias he lifted his face for a moment and his eyes met Aspasia's. Alcibiades tore off his mantle and waved it, shouting frantically. But Pericles did not look up again. With that last glance he had dismissed his wife from his mind; although it increased his confidence to remember that he left behind him in Athens a clever and valuable friend named Aspasia, who would guard his interests, communicate with his secret friends in

Sparta, and send him such news as it was imperative he should know.

They watched the troops embark, the tall stately triremes move slowly down the harbor and pause each in turn at the quay called Chona, where the fifty Presidents of the Council of Five Hundred sat in state. There was no time to be lost in inspection to-day and the dignitaries were content with a show of deference and took the word of the captains that all was in order. One by one the ships passed between the great towers that defended the artificially narrow mouth of the harbor, unfurled their sails, and stood out to sea. The populace had now run to the hills to watch the imposing fleet, still in single file, skim the blue water as lightly as proud and confident birds, and once more cheered themselves hoarse.

The fleet sailed down the Bay of Phaleron, rounded the point of Sunion, and was lost to sight. It would be many days before they saw it again or had news of its fate.

XXVIII

Athens pursued her light-hearted way, confident the war would soon be over. Pericles was in command and the treasury full. She was rich enough to stand a long war and not count the cost. Even Corinth and Corcyra were paupers in contrast to Athens.

They were astute enough to guess that Samos had made no resistance the first time because she counted on bribing Pericles, and although she would now put up a fight, any state so stupid as to make such a mistake with a man like that must commit other blunders which would soon deliver her into his hands.

They were undisturbed when they learned that halfway across the Ægean the Strategos had received word that the Samian General Stesagoras had sailed southward to ask the assistance of Phœnicia, and had then dispatched Sophocles to demand twenty-five triremes from Chios and Lesbos. He had also detached sixteen of his ships and sent them to the southern coast of Caria, and a swift galley to Athens with orders to send forty additional triremes to join the fleet at once.

But before they could be made ready the news came that

with the forty-four ships at his command he had defeated the Samian fleet of seventy after a severely contested engagement, then landed his troops on the island and routed the army. Samos was now entrenched within the massive walls built by the tyrant Polycrates before the Persian War.

There would be a siege, of course, but no doubt the Samians would be glad to make terms before long, and nothing more had been heard of Persian-Phœnician relief. Nor did the watchers in the towers on the Megarid frontier see the glitter of a spear on the horizon.

Aspasia's morning levees, which had always varied greatly in attendance, were now crowded by all who had ever been made welcome, for they knew that small galleys came and went between the fleet and Athens, and that she must be in communication with Pericles. Not for tender reasons; they would have dismissed the thought with scorn and rightly; but they knew she was his political confidante and that he must send her news as well as instructions.

What she had she gave them, under orders from Pericles, quite frankly. She told them of his conviction that he would yet be forced to meet a fleet from Persia and Phœnicia, and his belief that the siege would be a long one. The walls of Samos were uncommonly sound even for that era of walled and fortified cities; not only of great height and width but surrounded by a deep fosse. It was possible that only starvation would bring them to terms, for the ram and other newly-invented engines of assault had not proved effective. He was building a wall on the land side of Samos, not only to shut off all supplies or relief from that quarter but to keep his men employed.

"It will be a long war," said Socrates to Aspasia one day as they sat alone in the pastas, "and it may be a year or more before you see Pericles again."

He watched her keenly, but she looked calm and proud, and he sighed as he realized once more that she never would admit him to deep intimacy. He still loved her hopelessly but it would have given him some satisfaction to console her even for the absence of Pericles.

"I think it will be," she said. "But if Persia and Sparta keep up their neutrality it is only a question of months."

"Would that news travelled more swiftly! You must have moments of grave anxiety, dear Aspasia."

"I have trained myself to patience," she said coldly. "It is a lesson all women must learn, still more when one is the wife of the head of the State, who must also lead his armies to war. And at least I am of use to him here."

"Have you heard aught of Sparta?"

"Nothing of importance, but I fear that ominous quiet. It is possible she is only waiting for more triremes to be ordered out. With no ships to ravage her coast, and our inferior army, she might strike at any moment. Is there any sign of uneasiness in Athens?"

"Not as yet, but as you know her patience is not inexhaustible! And she may plunge in a moment from hope into despair. Athens well knows that the fate of the Empire may be at stake, but so far only Byzantium has followed the example of Samos, and she has sent no assistance, nor induced other cities on the Pontus to revolt. Nor can Persia have forgotten the lesson she received at Salamis. Athens believes that unless other Ionian states secede Persia will send no real assistance."

"Pericles writes that cities in Caria are disaffected, but as long as Miletus is safe, and the Athenian navy off the coast, they will dare make no move. But if Miletus had fallen they would have joined Samos, for they were always jealous of the supremacy of my city."

"You have great courage, Aspasia. I believe the women of Athens are more fearful than the men, and more than one household is already in mourning. Even victories cannot be won without sacrificing brave men. I know that you would fail in nothing, for no man among us is more evenly developed in virtue, but I wish you could have been spared this test of courage."

"Oh, no, you do not, Socrates!" Aspasia smiled for the first time. "You would have me incomplete in nothing. I, myself— yes! I should like to take my courage for granted and live my life through without war, for I am not like the women of Sparta who rejoice in it. But Fate is Fate, and at least I am glad not to find myself wanting. Nor do I fear for Pericles, for I know that his work is not done."

Socrates shook his head at her solemnly. "There spoke woman not reason. Great men ere this——" And then as he saw the flash in her eyes he added hastily, "But I would quiet your apprehensions not excite them, so let us talk of other things. I would meet that remarkable boy, Alcibiades. I saw him yesterday in the street, and what he did, as well as his astounding beauty, interested me deeply. He and several other boys were playing knucklebones before the house when a cart approached and the driver shouted to the boys to get out of the way. All ran but Alcibiades, who peremptorily ordered the carter to stop where he was until the game was finished. The astonished creature whipped up his horse and drove forward, and for a moment I was terrified, for that boy flung himself down in the road and defied the man to drive over him. All the other boys and bystanders were screaming, and while the carter hesitated old Zopyrus ran out of the house and attempted to drag Alcibiades to safety but was kicked in the stomach. The boy triumphed, for the carter backed out, and he called to the other boys to come and finish the game. However, the pedægogus won in the end, for as soon as Alcibiades' back was turned he deftly approached from behind, pinioned his arms, and marched him into the house. I liked as well as anything the dignified manner in which that high-spirited boy succumbed when he saw that further resistance was useless."

Aspasia laughed. "Zopyrus is forced to exercise ingenuity, but on the whole has improved Alcibiades in deportment if not in virtue. And school has done much for him. He gives trouble of course but learns with no effort and already recites pages of Homer without prompting."

"Has he a brilliant mind?" asked Socrates eagerly.

"Extraordinarily. But he has great faults of character, and only the gods know what he will be as a man. I fear the time when he will reign as a beauty."

"I would I could have the training of that boy! Do you think Pericles would place him in my hands?"

Aspasia shook her head. "Pericles, whose knowledge and wisdom are so great, knows nothing of children, and thinks that his old pedægogus is the right mentor for Alcibiades. He says the boy is just such another as he was at that age; and what man to-day is more master of himself than Pericles? But I think he is deceived by a superficial resemblance, and I would you could have the care of him, Socrates."

"But permit me to meet him whenever I come to your house that I may win his affection, and then when he is older he will come to me of his own wish. Send for him now, dear Aspasia."

"Very well. I like that idea. But do not be discouraged if he is naughty at first."

XXIX

She went to the thalamos and sent for Alcibiades, who came running.

"What is it, dea' Aspasia?" he demanded as he burst into the room. "Have you a cake f' me, ol shall I sleep in the bed of Pellicles to-night? I have been good f' a whole day."

"Yes, you may sleep in here to-night if—" She looked at him uneasily. Like Pericles, he hated ugliness, and she doubted the power of intellectual charm over a boy of ten. And how he would act in any given circumstances was always a problem. "You have heard of Socrates?" she asked.

"Oh, yes. The ugliest man in Athens."

"And is that all you know of the great Socrates?" she said severely.

"He has classes and asks many questions—but so does my schoolmast'l."

Aspasia opened a box and handed him a cake. He nibbled it daintily, one of his many charms being that he never appeared greedy, however his palate may have hankered.

"Listen, Alcibiades. When you and I are forgotten, or remembered only as the wife and ward of Pericles, Socrates will be a beacon for all men of virtue. His mind is a torch that will illuminate the way of other great men in time to come and keep the light of truth ever before them. And none who listen to him to-day remember his ugly face. They see only the great soul within."

"Then why doesn't Pellicles like him? How is it, Aspasia, that he nev'l dines in this house except when Pellicles is absent?"

"There is no man for whom Pericles has a higher respect. But you know that he has few intimate friends and cares to have no others about him. But I am not more sure than he that Socrates' name will be written large on the parchments of posterity. And I did not send for you to-day to give you a cake, Alcibiades, but to tell you that this great man has paid you a high compliment. He wishes to meet you."

Alcibiades, far from being impressed, made a face. "I do not like to look at him," he said stubbornly. "It is the duty of all Athenians to be beautiful. Even Xantippus and Pal'us have beauty, and for that I tolelate them. But I do not believe that an ugly man may have vu—v'l—I cannot say that word, Aspasia."

"Virtue. And yet you know that Xanthippus and Clinias although handsome, have little or no virtue. And you have no faith in my judgment! You do not believe me when I tell you that Socrates has more virtue than any man in Athens. And that young men of great beauty sit at his feet."

"I always b'lieve you, Aspasia, for you nev'l lie to me and I know you are velly wise." He hesitated, reluctant to yield a point, then added: "What do you s'pose made him so ugly?"

Aspasia had an inspiration. "It is possible that when he was a boy he had a shocking accident. Suppose a horse had stepped on your face, dear Alcibiades, would you be beautiful to-day?"

Alcibiades turned pale and shivered. "I—Oh—if aught destloyed my beauty I should dlink hemlock!"

"Then you would not have the great soul of a Socrates, who bears his heavy burden without a murmur."

"But he need not go abload unsandalled and in a hollible Spartan smock, not fit f' a slave; and with his bea'd and hal unwashed and uncombed." He added hastily, for he hoped a certain escapade was unknown to his Aspasia: "Zopyrus points out the gleat men to me between the house and school."

"So even Zopyrus knows of his greatness! And Socrates is

always carefully dressed when he comes to the house of Pericles, although nothing can divorce him from his Spartan cloak.
Now, will you be a good boy and come to the pastas and meet
him?"

Alcibiades gave a sigh of resignation. "I will go to please
you, Aspasia, for I know that if I do not you will not let me
sleep in Pellicles' bed to-night and plotect you."

"That would be unkind to me also. And you will promise
me not to let him see you think him ugly?"

Alcibiades drew himself up. "I shall not f'lget that I am
the son of Clinias and the descendant of Nestol and Ajax," he
said haughtily. "And that I am leceiving a gentleman in the
house of my gualdian Pellicles son of Xantippus."

"Ah! I knew I could rely upon you if I found you in the right
temper. Now, finish your cake and we will go to the pastas."

xxx

It had never occurred to Aspasia that Socrates had any fascination but that which drew other superior minds to his own,
and she sat in amused silence as Alcibiades gradually relaxed
his polite aloofness and drew closer to that grotesque figure
until he stood with sparkling eyes at his knee. Socrates, it
would seem, knew how to charm boys as well as men and he
had the tact to make no allusion to the scene in the street.

He began as he would if talking with another man met for
the first time, and his musical kind voice alone made strangers
forget his face. They discussed the war for a while and then
Socrates said abruptly:

"Are you not very tall for your age, Alcibiades? I am astonished to hear that you are only ten years old."

The boy glowed with pride. "Yes, O Soclates, I am almost
as tall as Xantippus who is folteen. I can knock him down and
beat him and so I could when I was only five."

Socrates regarded him with admiration. "If Aspasia had not
told me I should have taken you for thirteen at least. But can
you get your way with Xanthippus only by beating him?
Surely a boy of your intelligence should be able to exert moral
force by this time."

"You cannot exult molal fo'ce, O Soclates, ov'l people of no sense. Xantippus is a fool."

"A profound truth for a boy of your age to utter! But from such you could hold yourself aloof in disdain. I believe that would inflict more pain than a beating."

Alcibiades was always willing to ponder a new idea. In a moment he drew apart, lifted his head until it seemed as if his neck must crack, curled his lip, and lowered his eyelids. "Do you mean like this, O Soclates?"

Aspasia turned her face aside, but Socrates concealed his amusement. "A little less graphic, dear Alcibiades. I would have you cultivate the lofty spirit and calm indifference of Pericles. Have you heard the story of the man who followed him about the Agora one day when your guardian was obliged to transact some business there? This man never ceased from abusing him, calling him every name he could think of, and then followed him all the way to this house, still shouting. Pericles never noticed him and when he arrived at his door—it was a dark evening in winter—told Marcus to summon a slave with a torch to light the man home. As the creature was shivering he took off his mantle and bade him wrap himself in it. Pericles is the most powerful man in Hellas to-day, Alcibiades, and that majestic repose is one secret of his power."

Alcibiades listened to this tale with both eagerness and apprehension. When Socrates finished he shook his head. "I can nev'l be like that! If I had been Pellicles I should have snatched some old man's cane and beaten that wletch."

"And so no doubt would Pericles at your age, for he is a man of great passions held sternly in control."

"When did he begin?" demanded Alcibiades, who always asked inconvenient questions.

"Before I was born, no doubt, so I cannot tell you that. But as long as I have seen him in both public and private, he has always had that same power over himself that he has over other men."

"I like to knock down boys old'l than myself. It gives me gleat pleasure. Couldn't I do it until I'm fifteen?"

"The longer you put off the exercise of self-control and in-

dulge in the pleasure of inflicting pain, the more difficult will it
be for you to change your ways." And then, fearful of the effect
of too strong a dose of moral persuasion at one time, he broke
off and exclaimed, "It is a pity you are not old enough to be
with Pericles at Samos and use your courage on the enemy."

"Oh, yes!" Alcibiades' eyes flashed and he drew near once
more. "I'll be a gleat flighter when I'm glown, and then no one
will scold me. Please nev'l scold me, Soclates, for I have
enough of that flom my pedægogus and my schoolmast'l."

"I shall never scold you, Alcibiades, for I have not the right,
nor is it my disposition, and if you and Aspasia will consent I
shall ask for you sometimes when I come to the house."

"You shall always be welcome, Soclates," said Alcibiades
grandly, and ill concealing his flattered vanity. "And you shall
teach me that word I cannot plonounce."

And so began an historical friendship that was of much influence for good in the life of Alcibiades, and might have been
still more productive had not the world done its successful best
to spoil him.

XXXI

Aspasia invited the boys to dine in the andron that evening
and they reclined in state about her chair, each with a small
table of his own. This was always an occasion for rejoicing,
for they were kept on simple fare by Pericles' orders, and as
Aspasia's guests they were sure of birds and sweets. As a rule
they behaved admirably, not only because they had been taught
good breeding by their pedægogæ, but they were well aware that
if Aspasia was kind she could also be as stern as Pericles.

But to-night discord reigned.

Alcibiades, fresh from the admirable suggestions of Socrates,
merely raised an eyebrow when Xanthippus addressed him, and
endeavored to look as much like Pericles as possible. When
he spoke it was with an air of lofty indifference and he treated
even Aspasia with condescension. The other boys, even Paralus, goaded by this unaccustomed behavior, grew more and more
excited. They laughed at him uproariously, called him bad
names, and mimicked his lisp. Aspasia endeavored in vain to

keep the peace. For once they would not listen to her; they were in that boys' world which is a dark continent best avoided by elders. Even her threat of "no sweets" fell on deaf ears.

And then the expected happened. Alcibiades' Olympianism suddenly deserted him and he hurled a plate of salad at Xanthippus. The eldest born was unhurt, but with salad in his eyes and hair and his best himation ruined, he emitted such a roar that the attendants rushed in. Aspasia arose in wrath.

"Leave the andron—all of you! Not one of you shall have another mouthful to-night. And you, Alcibiades, do not presume to come to the thalamos. Go to your room at once."

But Alcibiades was too angry to ask forgiveness, and in far too youthful a mood to care whether his goddess were protected or not. As Aspasia, shortly after the boys were herded from the room, recognized the voice of Clinias raised in a bitter yell of protest, she inferred that he was the first to incur fistic vengeance.

She shrugged her shoulders, and as her own appetite was spoiled left the andron to go to her lonely room; a recurring experience she never ceased to dread. She filled her time, and obeyed the curt orders scratched on a tablet that came now and then from Pericles, and had been of genuine service, but the days were long and the nights intolerable.

As she lingered in the pastas Thera entered. "O Mistress," she whispered mysteriously, "Xanthias would speak with you at once."

Aspasia forgot her longings in the prospect of action. She went rapidly to the inner court, where Xanthias stood at her door.

"The man from Sparta," he said briefly. "He awaits us in the Outer Ceramicus."

Aspasia put on a dark mantle and veiled her face. She took a bag of money from the chest in the corner, handed it to Xanthias, and they hurried forth. Shops and houses were closed. Only dogs were abroad, nosing among the abundant refuse. They met not even a late wanderer and left the city by the Dipylon Gate. The gatekeeper, generously rewarded, merely lifted his shoulders. Some woman stealing out to meet her lover in the groves of Academe. Xanthias had drawn his mantle over his face for he was well known in Athens.

"Why does he ask me to meet him in the Outer Ceramicus?" she asked with a shiver as they passed beyond the walls. "Why not as before in one of the colonnades leading to Academe?"

"I cannot tell, Mistress. A boy came with the message and then ran away. But perhaps he fears he was seen the last time, and no one comes here at night."

"That I believe!"

The low rocky hills covered with tombs, monuments and stelæ, rose above them, a dark ominous mass in the starlight. A breeze stirred the cypresses, but their gentle sighing was the only sound. No nightingale made his home here. Aspasia shivered again. She had hoped never to see the Outer Ceramicus save at a distance, and certainly not to pay it her first visit on a dark night.

"Where can he be?" she exclaimed impatiently. "My teeth will chatter in a moment. This place reeks of death."

"Naturally, Mistress. We are to meet him by the tomb of—"

But at this moment a man stood before them, and Aspasia recognized the faithful friend of Pericles who had come from Sparta twice before; a fact she had omitted to mention to Socrates.

"What news?" she demanded.

"Good news this time, O wife of Pericles. I feared until five days ago it would be as bad as the last. The ephors were still deliberating with the representatives from other states, and one after the other being won over to the plan of invading Attica before the return of the only man they fear. And Samos has sent call after call. But the Spartans are always long in making up their minds and while they were still undecided an embassy from Corinth arrived and dissuaded them. The ambassador reminded them of the unwisdom of taking the part of an ally or subject state in revolt, for those in the Peloponnesian Confederacy are none too satisfied under the yoke of Sparta and Corinth. It would be perhaps a fatal example, and Megara might appeal to Athens, offering her old allegiance if her bad behavior in the past were forgotten—an olive branch likely to be accepted if Sparta moved on Athens. What Corinth said had much wisdom in it and the ephors should have thought of that for themselves. But Corinth has the sharper wits. The gods only know what may happen in the future, O wife of Pericles, for Sparta is determined to regain her old dominion in Hellas. But Athens is safe for the present."

Aspasia drew a deep sigh of relief and forgot that city of the dead about her. "I shall have good news at last to write to the Strategos! And you know he will never forget the great service you have rendered him. What of the priests?"

"They have kept faith, although one may not trust them too far. If they thought the time was ripe for war and the conquest of Athens no bribe would affect them, for they know of the great treasure on the Acropolis. But they have done their part in persuading the ephors to delay—through oracles of course—and have been eager for their rewards."

"Do you need more—Xanthias has brought a bag of gold."

"There is no further need for bribery, and enough has gone into that greedy maw. The ephors have made up their minds at last, and it takes as long to unmake as to make. I will go now, O wife of Pericles, for it may take me all night to slip between the guards on the frontier and I must be on Megarid soil before dawn. It is well I have a friend there, who, like myself, is a friend of Athens." And he was gone.

XXXII

It was good news that went by galley to Pericles that night, and by dropping hints among her guests next morning, Aspasia could assure herself that the designs of Sparta and the dissuasions of Corinth would spread swiftly through Athens and increase her content. One more hope of the Oligarchs quenched.

But a day or two later that content was rudely shattered. A herald arrived, dispatched not by Pericles but by one of his Generals now hovering off the coast south of Miletus.

Pericles, while the wall building between Samos and the mainland was hardly begun, had received positive information that the Phœnician fleet was near Rhodes, and had sailed with sixty triremes to meet it. On the following night the Samians led by that distinguished philosopher-statesman-general Melissus had executed a bold stroke. There were but forty Athenian ships on guard, not all of them ready for action, for many of the men were in the naval camp; Sophocles had not yet returned with the contribution from Lesbos and Chios. Melissus made a sudden sally with his own ships and overcame the Athenian triremes in the harbor as well as those others manned none too speedily. Two ships had been captured but the rest had escaped after a brief engagement.

When this news came to Athens, that Samos was master of the situation and that nothing had been heard of Pericles, who might himself have been defeated by the Phœnician fleet, the city was plunged into a terrible depression. Gloom reigned in the Agora and in all places where men gathered; and in every household, save those where the news of the downfall of Pericles would be welcomed in any circumstances.

For his policies as well as the fate of the Empire were at stake and if he returned to Athens with the remnant of a fleet, after the loss of Samos and an ignominious defeat by Persia or Phœnicia, his downfall was inevitable; it was more than possible that his execution could be accomplished. Strategoi had been given the cup before this for blasting the hopes of the people.

But Aspasia was determined not to permit her faith in the star or the genius of Pericles to waver, and although fewer came to her house during these dark days she managed to infuse the faithful with her own confidence. If she slept little and spent her nights pacing the roof it was not through fear of what might be the outcome of the war but because nerves are not always governed by reason. She also considered what his enemies might accomplish were this ill-starred interval in his dominance of too long a duration. Shaken faith in a leader of men had ofttimes a demoralizing and far-reaching effect. But, as she had once told Elpinike, it was impossible to live with Pericles and not believe him to be a favorite of the gods; or, as she would have expressed it more reasonably to herself, not to believe in the resources of a mind and character born to rule. His star might set in due time—but not yet! Of that, as she raised her eyes to the stars above her, she was as firmly convinced as that he was alive and well at that moment.

But it was a harrowing period for Athens, who looked forward to another Persian invasion—with but two hundred triremes indifferently generalled to meet it—and Sparta, misgivings banished, coming up behind! They could not hope for another Salamis, and they had no confidence in any General but Pericles. If he was gone they might as well resign themselves to their fate.

Even the boys were affected and stood about the inner court neither fighting nor playing. Alcibiades for once in his life was completely subdued and followed Aspasia about like a wistful puppy. Socrates, profoundly disturbed himself—what hope for philosophy under the Persian yoke?—came daily to the house and raised the boy's spirits somewhat by recounting incidents of past wars when all hope had been abandoned until the moment of victory. He had no love for Pericles but it was impossible not to have faith in his resource if he were still alive.

And then one day as Aspasia was standing on the roof scanning the horizon she saw a galley racing down the bay of Phaleron toward Piræus. That could mean one thing only: news from the fleet—and she never doubted the nature of that news.

She ran down the stairs and sent for Xanthias and told him of the galley. "Run quickly and intercept the messenger!" she commanded. "He may take the letters to the Council first, and I cannot wait for mine!"

It was an hour before Xanthias returned, but during the interval she heard shouting between the Long Walls, as if many men had left the Piræus to run with the messenger to Athens. Men did not shout at bad news!

Xanthias burst in upon her waving a small roll of papyrus. "Good news, Mistress!" he cried. "They are carrying the herald on their shoulders. The Strategos returned after fourteen days—without meeting the hostile fleet—and drove the

Samians back behind their walls. He is in command of the situation again. How could they ever have doubted him?"

But Aspasia had run into the thalamos and unrolled her letter. Pericles had outlined the main facts briefly, as he had for the Council, but to her he added that although for some unknown reason the Phœnician fleet had so far deceived Samos with false hopes, it might appear at any moment; and in any case the siege would be a long one: the Samians had carried over from the mainland a large quantity of supplies. As he could trust no one but himself he should remain where he was until Samos had surrendered; giving battle to the Phœnician fleet off the Carian coast when it appeared, and had sent for a hundred triremes. He expressed his gratitude briefly for the news from Sparta—the messenger had taken refuge on Patmos—and bade her keep hope in all who came to the house during the months before Samos succumbed. There would be no more supplies from the continent for the beleaguered city, for his men were already at work on a triple wall, not only between Samos and the mainland but all round the island. There would be watch-towers on those walls and no relief of any sort would creep in. It was for her to circulate this information in her own way. And then for the first time he added a word of endearment and sent his love to the children.

Aspasia grew warm from sole to crown as she gazed at that hastily scratched "dear head." Whole pages of passionate phrases would not have meant more to her, and she knew that her breathing image must have invaded his mind suddenly and potently to have turned him for even a brief moment from Strategos to lover. Women were for peace, not for war. Perhaps he had been writing by the light of a lantern alone on deck, and the stars and the silence had relaxed his carefully guarded mind as he finished his task.

And then, no doubt, the messenger dispatched, he had wrapped himself in his mantle and lain down on the hard deck with his face toward Samos!

She heard the voice of the crier running through the streets announcing the good news, and went to the house entrance and stood there unveiled looking calm and happy; although it was

hard to maintain dignity with four hysterical boys hurling themselves at her and Pericles Y trying to climb up her back. The
streets and open spaces of the city were filled with men shouting "Pericles," men almost as hysterical as the children. A
crowd gathered before the house and felt that joy had reached
its climax in this unusual glimpse of the famous wife of their
General. She was paler and thinner than they had pictured
her, but that was to be expected, and by the gods she was beautiful! It was some moments before she realized their attentions
and then she smiled and hastily retreated, Pericles Y trotting
after her.

An hour later her friends and many more of her acquaintance
poured in to congratulate her and protest that their faith, like
hers, had never wavered for a moment.

XXXIII

Athens, although exalted, took a mild revenge on the other
Generals when the Ecclesia met to vote on the usual yearly
changes. Pericles, as ever, was reëlected and with acclaim, but
the rest were dropped and others sent out in their place. Phormio, who had already erected trophies, was chosen as well as
three others who also inspired confidence: Hagnon, Tlepolemus,
Anticles. Thucydides, in spite of his youth, was elected, for
Pericles, in his report to the Council, had recommended him for
services both gallant and brilliant.

The retiring Generals were visited with no further punishment, for the Athenians had not practiced the virtues of justice
and moderation in vain, and were not inclined to severity unless
untoward events had released primitive human nature. In this
case the loss of life had been insignificant and the captured
triremes recovered. Sophocles returned to write *Œdipus Tyran-
nus,* and Menippus to his wife and his pleasant life in Athens.

News came to the city of Pericles' methods of keeping his men
in good humor. He would permit no attempts to scale the walls,
for he always set his face against unnecessary loss of life.
If the Samians made a sally they must of course be repulsed,
but his determination to starve them out was not to be shaken
by men clamoring for action. Many of the soldiers were at

work on the walls, and he gave all days of feasting and amuse-ment. Jugglers, acrobats, dancing girls, and musicians were brought over from Miletus at regular intervals, and occasionally the men were permitted to spend a day in that city of many resources.

But as the months dragged on Athens lost her gaiety, and if she did not descend into the deeps as she had during that terrible interval, she was apprehensive and irritable. She did not question the wisdom of Pericles, and applauded his caution and humanity, but the menace of the Phœnician fleet was ever before her, and when a galley came in with letters to the Council crowds surrounded the Bouleuterion waiting for news. The fleet never appeared nor was heard of again, but rumors were almost as bad as facts in that period of extreme nervous tension. Until Samos had capitulated the Athenians felt they could not draw a long breath. The only thing that gave them comfort was the certainty that with Pericles and two hundred and fifteen triremes in the eastern Ægean no other states would revolt.

In Aspasia apprehensions were finally allayed by a letter from Pericles in which he told her that he no longer looked forward to any invasion of the Ægean by either Phœnicia or Persia. He had received reliable information that they had given up all hope of revolt by other Greek States in Asia or the islands; Byzantium was still without disciples in the north, nor had she sent a galley to the assistance of Samos. Pissuthnes would have violated without hesitation the Treaty of Callias, whereby the Persians were forbidden to send a fleet west of the Chelidonian promontory, if he could have done so with the full prospect of success; but if he had secretly attempted to persuade other states to revolt he had failed, and had no intention of risking disaster by pitting his strength unaided against the Athenian navy.

The failure of the Lacedæmonian Confederacy to come to the rescue of Samos had been accepted as a warning by Pissuthnes that the time had not come for war on Athens. He knew as well as Pericles himself that the policy of Corinth in counselling non-interference was due to the fact that she had too many exposed colonies to risk, not only on the coast of Epirus but in Thrace. Her own navy was too insignificant to protect them against the Athenian, and unless the latter were sunk or captured off the Asiatic coast she would see to the neutrality of the Peloponnese. Neither would move until the other moved first!

All this Aspasia was to disseminate at her morning levees. His reports to the Council were brief and perfunctory.

Pericles pursued his usual deep policy in making his house the bureau for such news as there was. While recognizing the Council he never took it into his confidence, and the further he held himself aloof the more was it impressed. Athens in general was even more deeply impressed by the fact that his wife was left in the position of a valued minister, alone in his confidence and in the conduct of his affair. If there were many who resented this policy (and the comic poets cursed their handicap), others visualized Aspasia on a loftier pedestal than ever and went constantly to her house. Nor were the conversations as time went on invariably political. The old philosophical discussions were renewed, and although Aspasia was in no mood for dialectical battles herself she knew how to implicate Socrates with ambitious aspirants to that art.

But if apprehensions were routed time lagged none the less, and she experienced a sensation of relief when Phyrra daughter of Ariphon involved her in a love affair.

Constantia, Rhea, and Phyrra were still her only scholars. Although the men for the most part rejected the accusations of the comic poets with scorn and went themselves to her house, they dared not yield to the entreaties of their wives, for further scandal would inevitably ensue. Olympias and her powerful friends among the Oligarchs never ceased to protest their belief in the worst that had been said, and the male gossips kept the stories alive in the market-place. Glaucon had seriously considered forbidding his wife to continue her visits, but after one interview with Constantia did not bring up the subject again. Menippus, who knew nothing of Thoron's libels, was too loyal to Pericles to indulge in even a minor defection.

As Ariphon doted on Phyrra, the eldest of his children and the only girl, he had not pressed her to marry; the more particularly as her mother was dead and she was the capable mistress of his house. She was now seventeen, a tall graceful and quite beautiful girl, with a skin almost as white as Aspasia's, dark eyes, and brown curls which she wore in a projecting sheaf at the back of her head and bound with a fillet. She was a clever scholar and eager to learn, and often remained after the others had gone to read from Aspasia's library, curled up in a corner of a sofa in the pastas.

One day Aspasia was walking listlessly up and down the portico of the outer court when she heard the sound of running feet behind her. She turned to meet excited eyes above burning cheeks.

"Oh, Aspasia!" stammered the girl. "I do want to speak with you of something—but you have so much to think of—why should I?—but you are always so kind—"

"What is it, Phyrra?" She fancied she recognized the symptoms.

Phyrra took her arm. "Were you ever in love when you were a young girl, dear Aspasia?" she asked, dropping her eyelashes.

"No," replied Aspasia drily, "but I knew many that were."

"I am in love," announced Phyrra proudly.

"That is interesting—in Athens. It is not often a girl has an opportunity to fall in love before marriage. Where did you meet him?"

"Alas, I have never met him—but at the last Panathenea, when I sat in the ship, I saw him! He was in the escort of cavalry and looked like Apollo on horseback. But, alas! he did not see me."

"Who is this Apollo?"

"Acestorides the son of Diophantes."

"The 'beauty'!" Aspasia recalled that first visit to the Agora and her indignation. She had not thought of him since

"Oh, not now, Aspasia. He is too old—more than twenty— and it is said he was cold to his admirers. His reputation is unsullied. Thasson the son of Phocion, whom he has chosen for his friend, is eight or nine years older and a man of the highest virtue; he teaches him only what is good and noble Many girls and young wives saw him that day and have talked of little else, but you have taught me to think of other things besides falling in love, and for that reason I know my own mind and would marry him."

"I do not follow your logic—but have you spoken to your father?"

"Yes, and he consented to speak to Diophantes, but met with repulse. Acestorides is too young for marriage, he says, and would care for nothing less. He is happy with Thasson and interested only in philosophy. He avoids riotous symposia and the hetæræ. Like Thasson he listens to Socrates, Prodicus, and Zeno. Oh, Aspasia, you must aid me!"

"But what can I do, dear Phyrra? I do not know this young man, and even if I did I could not ask him to meet you here. It would be all over Athens in a day, and Agariste would probably beat me. As for your father—"

"All that you do is right in his eyes, and he wishes me to be happy. Besides, I threatened—"

"Not to hang yourself with your girdle, I hope!"

Phyrra stared. "Oh, no, Aspasia. I love life, even without Acestorides, too much for that. But I threatened never to speak to him again if he refused in any way to help me to marry this man. I have not even wept, for I shall not spoil my eyes, but I know that father would weep if I kept my word."

Aspasia looked at the girl reflectively. There was character in her face and perhaps a hint of hardness that might deepen with the years. Well, so much the better, especially if she married a younger husband than common. She would like to see an Athenian trained by his wife!

But she asked: "And why are you so sure you could win the affection of this Apollo if you met him? You say he loves Thasson, and it is almost unheard of for a young man of his age to marry."

"Perhaps he would not love me—but that I must know for myself. If I fail," she added proudly, "I will put him out of my mind. But I shall not give him up without an effort to win him."

"Perhaps he will not want a learned wife," said Aspasia teasingly.

"Oh, I'll not let him know that I've learned aught but reading. But when we are married I shall make myself his companion in the house. Constantia has won the regard of her husband and she is no cleverer than I."

"But what am I to do? I know neither this young man nor his friend. They have never come to the house."

"Diophantes does. When the time comes for you to speak to him he will listen to you as he would not to my father. But I must meet Acestorides meanwhile. Ask Pheidias to invite him to his studio, and then we will call there when out for a walk— as you often do, dear Aspasia. Then you will charm both with your conversation and invite them to your house. I shall say little, but I shall be unveiled."

Aspasia laughed. "I see you are like a wise General who plans his campaigns before meeting the enemy. But have you thought of the opposition you will meet with from Thasson? He is always at his side, remember, and these love affairs between young men are the more profound and lasting when they are temperate. These two, no doubt, walk for hours together in the groves of Academe discussing philosophy, or exchanging dreams of fighting side by side on the battlefield, ever bearing in mind the devotion of Achilles and Patroclus. And if not talking they are exercising together in the gymnasium. Young men who are lovers may share everything together. A girl who enters the lists for the affection of either has little to offer in exchange, small hope of success."

"I know all that, dear Aspasia. There is nothing I have not thought of. But if I have a moment of despair I think of you and Pericles. I know that I am not yet an Aspasia, and Acestorides is far from being a Pericles. But what I mean is that when a man like Pericles, who in his harmonious development has attained the highest ideal of the Greeks, loves a woman and with utter devotion, it cannot be as unnatural as people say. It must really be more natural for a young man to love a girl if he sees the seeds of equality in her, and if she is beautiful and can give him pleasure. I must have the opportunity to make Acestorides understand that I can more than take the place of Thasson. On second thoughts I shall let him know at the right moment that I am studious and have already learned much. He will also be impressed by the fact that you make a companion of me."

Aspasia laughed again, although her laugh in these days had little mirth in it. "I feel convinced that if you do have your way you will know how to manage him later! . . . Very well, I shall speak to your father and if he consents I will send for Pheidias and take him into our confidence."

XXXIV

Ariphon gave an eager consent, for although he had no desire to lose his daughter he had still less to see her unhappy. He must part with her before long in any case, for it was unthinkable that a girl of his should be unwed at eighteen.

Pheidias was more difficult to handle. He had married reluctantly and only because the law and his duty to himself and the State enjoined that tiresome relationship. He regarded women as necessary evils, nothing more. His love for Aspasia was what some fifty years hence would be known as Platonic, and if she had been a man he would have loved her even more. He accepted the strange relationship between her and Pericles, and as he loved them both rejoiced in their happiness, but he would have been far more edified if it had been the intellectual alliance the world had believed it to be when she went to his house. The advent of Pericles Y had been a severe shock to his ideals.

"You would break up a beautiful friendship," he grumbled. "And for what? That a silly girl may be gratified. What nonsense! One would think you were one of those professional matchmakers."

"Phyrra is no ordinary young girl. She knows her Homer as well as any youth who has been to school, and has read natural science and philosophy here in my house. She has quite as good a mind as Acestorides, I have no doubt. Of course he knows far more than she does, but only because he is five or six years older. He could find pleasure in teaching her all he has learned—"

"And be a laughing-stock for deserting Thasson for a girl!

Even if he did marry do you suppose he would spend his days with her in the house? If he did the very boys in the street would point their fingers at him."

"You forget that Glaucon is very fond of Constantia and Menippus of Rhea. Neither spends his days in the house; nor would Phyrra expect Acestorides to be tied to her girdle. She is reasonable and tactful."

"Neither Glaucon nor Menippus married before he was thirty, and no one knows or cares whether they are fond of their wives or not. Many men love their wives in a way, which is well enough. But both Glaucon and Menippus have their intellectual halves and are seen with them constantly. If Acestorides at his age married, all Athens would know he was in love with a girl and he would be treated with contempt." He hesitated. "Nor would it be well with you, Aspasia, if it were known you had made that match. The men have said much about fearing your influence and example—"

"Don't quote those selfish brutes to me! But for that matter, let them think it was you made the match."

"I!" Pheidias' eyes were distended with horror.

"Well, her father then. They meet accidentally at your studio —once. After that Ariphon must take the matter in hand. Or Agariste. For Pericles' sake no gossip of any sort must be born in this house. But it is essential that Acestorides see Phyrra. Now, you will do this for me, Pheidias. If you do not I'll not see you again until Pericles' return."

Pheidias turned pale at the thought. "Very well," he said with unwilling resignation. "And do I not always obey your orders, dear goddess?" Then like a true Greek he began to bargain. "I need a model for the beautiful girls in that part of my frieze that will represent the Panathenea. If this Phyrra is as beautiful as you say—and who more exacting in beauty than you?—she might sit to me. It is permitted that we use living models for all but the immortals."

"I have no doubt she would be flattered. And you might get Acestorides to your studio on the same pretext."

"Ah! You always give me ideas, Aspasia. I wonder I had not thought of it myself, for he still has great beauty of form and feature, although past his bloom. He shall lead the ephebi."

"Let me know as soon as you have made the appointment for the first sitting."

"I will—and when will you keep your promise to sit to me for the bust with which I would fain surprise Pericles?"

"I am not looking my best, dear Pheidias. My cheeks have lost their roundness—"

"But not their lovely contour. Nor your profile its pure grace. I would give Pericles this supreme pleasure immediately upon his return—and—aha!—that would be your excuse for visiting the studio should Acestorides wonder. You will have brought that young girl in place of a handmaid, and then I shall see her and ask her to sit to me!"

Aspasia hesitated. "I would not only gratify Pericles," she said in a moment, "but would fain go down to posterity under your inimitable hand. Be sure no one else shall ever model me. Lesser men have asked me to sit to them, but I have always refused. But I am very thin—"

"I repeat that your beauty is enhanced. Be sure Pericles when he returns will not find you wanting. If you don't," he added sulkily with one of his quick changes of mood, "I'll not be the one to bring misery to Thasson."

"Oh—very well. And as you have known me so long your memory will supply all I now lack. I shall expect to hear from you to-morrow."

xxxv

It was two days later that Aspasia and Phyrra, followed by Xanthias and two women slaves, were wending their way through the Sacred Grove at the foot of the Acropolis toward the studio of Pheidias. It was late in Pyanepsion and leaves were falling from the deciduous trees; only the pines were still fragrant and green. The air was chill and crisp, a change grateful to Aspasia. She had not gone to the country this year and the heat had taken its toll of her energy. Her step still lagged, and she raised her face eagerly to the sharp wind blowing down from Thrace. And she always felt at peace in the Altis, with its beautiful statues of the gods symmetrically grouped, and its graceful little temples; although no one could call it quiet in these days! There was a constant ringing of hammers on the Acropolis, pounding in mortars, and the shouts of masters and workmen. Tall fluted columns glistened in the sunlight, their frozen beauty as yet unenriched by color. Would that great temple be finished before Pericles came home?

"Why do you shiver, Aspasia?" asked Phyrra. "I do not feel cold, but perhaps you should have worn a warmer mantle."

"I am not cold. Are you nervous at the prospect of meeting a young man?"

"I am rarely nervous, dear Aspasia, but I am excited. Let us hasten or we shall not get there first. They are to find you, remember, sitting for your portrait."

It was Pheidias who was nervous, for he was anything but a man of the world. Great genius though he was, he came under the social ban of all who earned their bread by the work of their hands (what man could attain virtue who spent his life in toil?), and the only house of distinction in which he was intimately received was that of Pericles. He took this as a matter of course but was always worried when called upon to exercise social initiative. And to-day apprehensions were troubling him far more than his manners.

"I thought you would never come," he exclaimed irritably as they entered the studio. "Sit down at once—there"; waving Aspasia to a stool. "I have already modelled a head roughly that it may look as if you had sat before. I don't know how I shall explain your presence, even so. You must say something to indicate that you came to-day without an appointment."

"Compose yourself, dear Pheidias," said Aspasia drily. "I have had much experience in helping men over difficulties."

He glared at Phyrra. "Take off your veil," he said curtly. "I would see if you are worthy to be immortalized by Pheidias."

Phyrra laughed gaily, and obeyed with a tantalizing lack of speed. She extended her arms beneath the veil, raising it slowly to the height of her shoulders; then until only the upper part of her face was still covered. Finally, with a sudden whirling motion, she sent it flying to a table.

Pheidias smiled in spite of himself, then narrowed his eyes

and looked at her from head to foot. She wore a white mantle carefully draped to reveal the outlines of her graceful rounded young figure, and her face with its regular features was glowing with health and vivacity.

Pheidias shrugged his shoulders. "A good type—nothing more. All Greek women are beautiful unless they are ugly. Aspasia alone is a goddess. But you will do." He beckoned to one of his students. "Make a rough model of this head for me, Alcamenes," he said sharply, "and see that you put life into it."

He turned his back on the somewhat discomfited Phyrra and sat down opposite Aspasia. In a moment he had forgotten everything but the clay between his hands and the face opposite.

The studio of Pheidias was an immense workroom crowded with students at work on the pediments, friezes, and statues for the temple of Athenè Parthenos. The quantities of clay and marble in the room would have made it cold but for the sun streaming down through the open roof. Except for the sound of chisels the studio was very quiet, for these young men from all parts of Hellas were too intent on their work and on improving every hour of their blessed opportunity to indulge in conversation. They stole occasional glances at the two ladies, but even Phyrra was unresponsive; she had no intention of wasting her eyelashes on small fry.

There was a sound of masculine voices outside. Pheidias sprang to his feet and ran to the entrance. Aspasia feared he had lost his head and would send the young men away; but he returned in a moment, very red, and frowning portentously. He was followed by the friends, each with an arm resting lightly across the shoulder of the other.

"I am sorry," he stammered. "I have an unexpected sitting—but you are welcome—"

The two young men stared at the unveiled women. "No doubt we had best go and come another day," began Thasson; but Aspasia rose and came forward, darting a glance at Pheidias that he well understood. He performed the introductions ceremoniously, ignoring Phyrra.

"We planned a surprise for Pheidias to-day," said Aspasia in her most stately manner. "And now I know why he was so cross! But it gives me pleasure to meet you, O Thasson and Acestorides, and I have long intended to ask Socrates to bring you to the house of Pericles."

But both were of the oligarchical set, as she well knew, and although they replied with graceful courtesy they showed no undue enthusiasm at this unexpected meeting with the renowned Aspasia. But they were susceptible to beauty in any form, and neither took his eyes from her face as they assured her that her politeness was deeply appreciated.

"As we have met in this unconventional manner I think I shall venture to present you to my young niece," she said; and her face, which had worn a faintly puzzled expression, broke into a smile that had dazzled wiser heads than theirs.

Aspasia moved toward Phyrra, whose classic profile had taken on an expression of dreamy serenity. She turned with a slight start as she heard her name and rose with a young girl's awkward glance, dropping her eyelashes. Then, as Aspasia made the introduction, she lifted her large sparkling eyes and shot a winged glance straight into Acestorides', her rather thin but very pink lips curving into a slow smile.

Where do girls learn such things? thought Aspasia. But they are all alike.

Acestorides would have moved forward but Thasson detained him. "We have intruded without intention," he said coldly. "And although we have been so graciously received we will now retire."

Aspasia directed an imperious glance at Pheidias, and he said hurriedly: "Oh, not, I pray, before I have asked a great boon of Acestorides. I have been at loss for a model of sufficient beauty for my leader of cavalry. Alas, I had not dared ask this great favor of you, Acestorides, until Aspasia gave me courage by suggesting it herself. When Phyrra daughter of Ariphon consented to sit for the maidens—I felt—I hoped—"

"Oh, but I shall be greatly flattered, Pheidias!" cried the young man blushing, and even the cold intellectual face of Thasson wore a gratified smile as he turned with more warmth of manner to Aspasia and thanked her for this great mark of favor, so coveted by all the young men of Athens. He frowned again, however, as Pheidias, now determined to do his part, led both the young people to a bench and summoned another of his students.

"Will you not sit beside me, Thasson, while Pheidias is at work?" asked Aspasia, and she was unable to conceal the mischief in her eyes. "The monotony of sitting for one's bust is great and I am sure Pheidias will not mind if we talk."

"Well, do not talk to me," growled Pheidias. "And don't move your head."

Although Thasson was deeply prejudiced against Aspasia, not alone for her marriage with Pericles, but because he held her responsible for the downfall of Thoron, he secretly congratulated himself upon this unavoidable opportunity to converse with the most famous woman in Hellas.

Aspasia, if she had not recalled his name, had recognized him instantly.

"You came to the house of Hippodamus when I had recently arrived in Athens," she remarked. "Have you forgotten?"

"No, Aspasia, I have not forgotten"; and again his fine brows met in a frown. That were a subject best ignored, but this Ionian was known for her audacity. It was even whispered she had no reverence for the gods.

"Thoron has turned against me," she said sadly. "But surely it were best to repulse him? I had talked with too many men not to be convinced that Thucydides would never become the supreme demagogue of his ambition. To marry Thoron would have been to ruin him. Was it not, therefore, better to dismiss him?"

"True, O Aspasia, but his friends nevertheless regret—"

"That he ever met me? But remember, O Thasson, that he came to the house of Hippodamus of his own will and out of mere curiosity—and that if the gods made him weak no woman should be held responsible." And then she changed the subject deftly, and they were soon deep in a discussion of the Eleatic school of philosophy as expounded by Melissus, now shut up ignominiously in Samos.

Occasionally Thasson cast a glance at Acestorides, but he knew nothing of the deep wiles of women, and as the backs of

those two were toward him he was mercifully spared the sight
of Phyrra's eyelashes and dimples, Acestorides' somewhat terrified response. Once or twice the late beauty ran his hand
through his bright hair, but gave no other sign of agitation to
Aspasia's keen eyes. When the time came to go she talked with
him for a few moments, and veiled her appraisal under a smiling
kindliness of regard. He was a handsome creature, no doubt of
that, and might well have sat for a statue of Apollo. But the
high regular beauty of his features was marred by an expression
of petulance and conscious superiority, and his full drooping
mouth was weak.

He is made to be wax in some one's hands, she thought, but
will those hands be Thasson's or Phyrra's?

She asked them both to call some morning and they replied
as politely that they would, but, as all knew, with no intention
of setting foot ever in the house of Pericles. And then summon-
ing Xanthias and the women she nodded pleasantly, and Phyrra
bestowed as sweet a smile upon Thasson as upon Acestorides.

"Well?" asked Aspasia, as they walked briskly through the
Altis. "Are you satisfied? He is a pretty boy and his brow is
intellectual, but he lacks character. I fancy the conversation
of Thasson is the more interesting—"

" 'Pretty!' " exclaimed Phyrra indignantly. "No man in
Athens is as beautiful as he. I could not say all I wished with
those students so close, but we whispered, and exchanged many
glances."

"And do you feel that you have progressed?"

"Yes, for has he not seen me? If Pheidias thinks me beautiful
enough for a model, surely he must be impressed—he who perhaps has never looked at a girl before."

"No doubt. Did you talk—or whisper—of Thasson?"

"Of course. I made him think I was deeply interested in his
friend and told him how fortunate he was and how I admired all
I had heard of that noble young man."

Aspasia, for the first time in many months, burst into a ringing laugh. "Rhea, who has visited Samos and Syracuse, and
is a coquette of much experience, could not have done better.
But beware of Thasson. For at least twenty minutes he dis-

coursed upon the virtues and promise of Acestorides, and of the happiness of moulding such a mind. But you have this in your favor. In these affairs it is generally the elder only who really loves; the younger does little more than accept the devotion so richly lavished upon him. Thasson would be insensible to the charm of any woman, but that vain youth will be as susceptible to your roses as to his. But he will never pursue you—he is far too spoiled for that. It is you that will have to do the wooing. But how? What is to be your next step?"

"We agreed to meet in the studio to-morrow—"

"Pheidias will never consent—"

"Is he not having us both modelled for his frieze? He cannot turn us out—after inviting us!"

"I shall not take you again," said Aspasia firmly. "I am held to account for the ruin of that despicably weak Thoron, and if Thasson drinks hemlock I do not wish it laid at my door. I make no enemies for Pericles—with intention."

"Very well." Phyrra's voice was sulky and she tossed her head. "I'll manage for myself. Father shall take me to that studio—he'll know what to expect if he doesn't."

XXXVI

It was nearly nine months since Pericles had left Athens, and although her people had dismissed their fears of intervention by Persia, they were beginning to talk of the siege of Troy. Ten long years had the Greeks besieged that mighty stronghold, and it was said that the walls of Samos in comparison were as rock unto clay. The cost of the war was already enormous and the thrifty Athenians cursed the inventors of the battering-ram and whatever for not knowing their business. No doubt the cunning Samians found ways of getting supplies from the mainland— who knew but there were communicating caves beneath the sea? If this war went on for years the treasury would be exhausted, the citizens impoverished, and Athens no longer the wealthiest State in Europe. True, commerce was uninterrupted, and the richer the Metics grew the more would they be taxed, but so would the wealthy citizens for more and more triremes, and who would patronize the artisans and shopkeepers? The Metics had their own shops in the Piræus and took a quiet revenge on Athens for their social ostracism. As for the masons, carpenters, marble-workers, cutters, and other workmen employed on the Acropolis and elsewhere, they would soon be loafing in idleness and grim want, for there would be no money left in the treasury for the embellishment of Athens.

But before they had time to descend into the nethermost depths of gloom another messenger was running between the Long Walls followed by a shouting crowd. Samos had surrendered and the fleet would return as soon as Pericles had witnessed the razing of those famous walls, reorganized the government, and exacted a fine that should cover the costs of the war and fill another chest on the Acropolis. Athens gave herself up to a night of delirium.

Aspasia, whose bloom had returned as abruptly as if she had drained some magic philtre, received a great throng on the following morning. It was not she who said it had taken Agamemnon ten years to conquer Troy and Pericles less than one to compel the surrender of the most strongly fortified city in the modern world, but she put the idea into the muddled head of one of her admirers and it was taken up and repeated with acclaim. Pericles had erected many trophies but never would he have returned to Athens in such a blaze of glory.

But half a month passed and then many days and nothing was heard of the return of the fleet. It might be a full month before it was sighted off Sunion, for walls may not be razed in a day, nor a government reorganized. This time there would be no question of even a brief recovery for Samos, for not an arrow would be left in her quiver. Her ships would be sunk, her treasury depleted, the Oligarchs would not have a talent between them. She would be able to derive some small measure of comfort from the fact that her temple of Hera—the largest in existence—her other magnificent buildings built by Polycrates, her aqueduct and theatre, were to remain intact. Pericles was not the man to destroy beauty. They were also spared the massacre they had every reason to expect, and their relief was profound when they realized that if Pericles was a ruthless conqueror he was not a cruel one. Hostages were taken but freemen were not enslaved, and although the active Oligarchs were expelled the remaining citizens were merely warned to conform to the new government and pay the heavy yearly tribute as best they could. And after the sporadic sallies he had permitted them to take their dead within the walls.

Before he had time to send a section of his fleet to Byzantium word came that she had returned to her allegiance. He dispatched a trireme commanded by one of his Generals to exact a fine and give notice that the yearly tribute of that shamefaced city was increased. The Maritime Empire was once more a unit under his cold deliberate authority. Not in his time would heed again be given to ambitious Oligarchs.

His letters to the Council were briefer than ever and to Aspasia he did not write at all. Nor did he mention the probable date of his return. Tlepolemus, who had been wounded, was permitted to return ahead of the fleet, and satisfied the curiosity of the people. But the Athenians could hardly control their impatience, for they longed to shout themselves hoarse and watch Pericles ride in triumph through the city.

But their impatience was as nothing to Aspasia's.

She had deliberately frozen herself into a passive endurance during those long months when the end was never in sight, and after his assurance of the neutrality of Persia her restlessness had left her and she had been listless and apathetic when alone. But all her inner defenses crashed down at the first news of victory, and her impatience for his return and for him were unbearable. She suspended her afternoon classes, and refused to listen to the confidences of Phyrra, whose wooing was pursuing an intermittent course; the loves of those two immature children seemed to her of less significance than the swollen ear of Xanthippus, nearly bitten off by Alcibiades.

She was pacing up and down the outer court one night after the rest of the household were deep in slumber. A cold wind was blowing and whistling among the columns, but the blood was warm in her veins and she was wrapped in a thick white mantle that covered her head; bats were flying about in the darkness. The owls that were almost as numerous in Athens as the inhabitants were hooting on every roof; homeless dogs

howled and barked in the streets. Athens was never quiet.
"The silent watches of the night" was a poetical fancy that
never would have been conceived by the most errant imagination.

But Aspasia welcomed the storm and the discordant noises.
The peace of the country would have been intolerable. She
had never been able to endure it save when she might watch for
the galley of Pericles.

Reasonableness had flown off with patience. Why had he not
left details to his Generals and returned at once to her? Had
she still been an exile from his mind during that proud moment
of victory? Surely he must have thought of her then and the
message flashed through him that their hour of reunion was at
hand. Sometimes she almost hated him. She was married to
a superb machine that only turned into a man when he had nothing more important to consider.

She heard a faint sound and turned toward the entrance door
in alarm. Had Marcus forgotten to lock and bolt it? She had
no desire for burglars or footpads as a relief from inner tumult.

A lantern hung above the lintel and shed its light upon a
closed door and the bolt in place. The sound had not been
there, but assuredly she had heard the click of a key turning in
a lock. And then she heard a door close very quietly. The door
of Pericles' office. She was about to turn and run to the
servants' quarters when she saw a dark form, tall, helmeted,
stand under the dim ray of the lantern.

She clutched a pillar as superstition assailed her. Pericles had
been assassinated and his shade returned to his house. In another moment she would have fallen, for her legs were sinking
under her, and she felt too drained of life to scream; but a glad
note of triumph came from that shadowy figure and Pericles ran
forward and caught her before she fainted. She revived quickly.

He held her so tightly that it was some time before she could
speak, and demand where he came from—what had brought
him—

"The fleet will be here to-morrow," he said. "I came ahead
in a galley and landed at Sunion. A man brought me here in
his chariot. I must return before dawn, for I must enter with
the usual cursed formalities and pomp. I could not wait longer

to see you—Zeus only knows when I shall be permitted to come here to-morrow. But dawn is still far off." And he lifted her in his arms and carried her into the house.

XXXVII

Aspasia would not go to the Piræus to witness the majestic return of the fleet, but sent the boys with Agariste and went to her own roof. Every other roof in Athens was crowded with men, women, and children, as well as the Acropolis, Mount Lycabettus, and the walls. The day was clear and cold, but the deep blue sky was unflecked and the air had never been so light and brilliant. All nature seemed to rejoice with Athens.

The progress of Pericles through the harbor city and between the Long Walls was slow, for the people crowded about him and clung to his feet; several times he had to rein in and address them. In Athens he found that the archons had arranged a program which compelled him to ride through all the principal streets that every one might have a glimpse of his helmet at least. He lunched in the Tholos at the public table, and it was late afternoon before he was permitted to go to his house. Even then he must give a full ten minutes to the boys and his servants, standing before the door; Alcibiades and Paralus dancing with impatience. Xanthippus greeted him formally, then walked off with a swagger.

"I have taken wondleful cal of Aspasia!" cried Alcibiades. "She is alive and well and she has often said she didn't know what she should do without me."

"I am sure of that, Alcibiades. Quite as sure as I am that your conduct during my absence has been above reproach. No doubt Zopyrus has an excellent account to give me!"

Alcibiades dived into the little crowd and emerged dragging Pericles Y. "And I have been a fath'l to this child," he said eagerly. "I have spanked him, and taken a gnat out of his eye with a ling, and sometimes amused him when he clied f' nothing. Is he not beautiful?"

And he clutched the baby by the back of his chiton and flung him into the arms of his father. "It is not for Pellicles son of Xantippus to stoop too low, even to kiss his son," he said with an air; and devoutly hoped his guardian would be sufficiently diverted.

Pericles looked down into the eyes so like his own, and felt his first impulse of tenderness for this child whom he had barely tolerated, and whose absence he would not have noticed. Pericles Y was afraid of no one, and far from having been made acquainted with repulse received constant and flattering attentions from his mother, Agariste, Ariphon, and all who had access to the inner quarters. He put his arms about this tall man's neck, gave him a hasty kiss, then, with a practiced wriggle, freed himself, climbed down and ran back to his nurse. Pericles found his childish impatience as charming as his bright face and soft lips.

"Now, perhaps, you will let me go in to Aspasia?" he said to the boys. "After all, it is her due, and I am sure you will not detain me longer."

A moment later he was in the thalamos and had flung off his mantle and helmet with his usual impetuosity when alone with her.

"That is over!" he exclaimed, as he pulled her down beside him on the sofa. "But worse is to come. I must make the funeral oration over our dead six days hence. And I have ten thousand things to attend to meanwhile. Would that I had nothing and could go to the farm with you for a month."

"Why not give me the points and let me write the speech? I know that I could. I shall be glad of something to occupy my time while you are absent, and my greatest ambition is to help you."

"Ah!" he exclaimed. "That would be a relief to my mind! I am sure you could write it, so much are our minds in tune. And I memorize quickly." He meditated a moment. "A sad figure of speech occurred to me as we were sailing home so gaily, with that box of charred bones in the hold of my ship. It is something like this: 'The loss of her youth to the city is what the loss of spring would be to the year; but they have fallen in a noble cause and achieved a famous victory.' Put it in your own words, dear head. And now tell me of all that has occurred in Athens during this interminable time. I care to ask questions of no one else."

When she had half finished he rose to shut the door leading into the court, where the usual row was going on. As he turned he caught sight of a new pedestal in a corner and on it a veiled bust.

"What is that? Ah! I think I can guess." He reached it in a stride and whisked off the veil. And then he stood speechless for a moment, profoundly moved; not only at this manifest of his wife's and friend's affection but at the perfection of that exquisite work of art.

The marble was from Paros and delicately tinted. The hair was arranged in the high knot at the back that displayed to best advantage the beautiful shape of the head and its poise on the long slender throat, and was crowned with a small diadem of beaten gold. The full low brow, the pure oval, the delicate contours, the fine straight line of the profile, were reproduced with masterly fidelity, and infused with a lofty and sweet serenity. The eyes were of smoky rock crystal and Pheidias had managed to give them light and expression; the lips deeply red and alluringly curved.

"Pheidias has excelled even himself," he said, turning to Aspasia, who was watching him eagerly. "He put his soul into it, and no wonder. He told me once that he loved you almost as much as I. But not quite. If he did I should strangle him!"

He laughed and replaced the veil. "This is for my eyes alone. And when I go I take it with me. Remember that. Now, finish your chronicle."

XXXVIII

Athens gave herself up to festivity and nightly symposia for five days, but on the sixth day it went into mourning. All shops were closed and the Acropolis was as quiet as in the long years of its ruin. The Agora was deserted and all who went abroad were clad in the black himation. The wailing of women sounded through the streets as they walked behind the cypress coffins containing the bones of the dead, and the empty couch symbolical of unrecovered bodies, to the Outer Ceramicus.

They were followed by a procession of citizens and their

wives, and although all wore black out of respect for the grief of the families in mourning, many of the women carried garlands. Nor did their faces reflect the sorrow of the afflicted. Like a wedding, a funeral meant a few hours of unveiled freedom and they made the most of it.

No girls were in that slowly moving throng. Phyrra had begged her father to permit her to go with Aspasia and Agariste, but for once he was obdurate. It was enough to hang round Pheidias' studio while his daughter and Acestorides whispered and Thasson glared; he would not violate a sacred convention. The procession would pass the house and she might go to the roof with the boys if she wished.

Pericles had abolished hired mourners from Athens, denouncing the custom as a relic of barbarism, but the mothers, wives, and sisters of the dead soldiers screamed and beat their breasts until the coffins were interred.

As there was no corpse to pollute the sun and the day was cold, the funeral did not take place until the morning was well advanced; the water clock in the law courts indicated the hour of ten when Pericles mounted the tribune erected on the highest point of that mass of rocky hills, and looked down upon an audience greater than any ever gathered in the Dionysus. The tombs were almost obliterated and no chariot could have made its way through the dense masses in the Sacred Way and the spaces beyond. Aspasia and Agariste had come early, and stood near the platform. Just before Pericles' arrival his sister, detecting a strong perfume, turned her head and saw Elpinike opposite.

"Zeus!" she muttered. "What has that old mænad come for? I wonder will she dare interrupt?"

But Aspasia was concerned only with the fear that Pericles might forget one of her fine phrases. He had not looked at the speech until last night. She had made it as short as convention would permit, and ordered him to recite it to her before he left the house. When he had omitted a sentence she looked at him reproachfully, but he had laughed and reminded her that he was never at a loss for words.

She glanced indifferently at the malevolent visage of the old woman, whose snapping eyes were fixed on the platform; and then, as Pericles approached with The Nine, and chosen members of the Council of Five Hundred, her gaze swept the mass of upturned faces. There were few that were hostile, certainly none among the women, who had crowded to the front. Like Constantia and Rhea all were gazing on Pericles with eyes of admiration and awe. Indeed that entire throng with but few exceptions, and in spite of their dark mantles, wore a holiday expression. Uncertainty and fear were behind them and the future beckoned gaily. Death was something they thought on as seldom as possible. And as not only the women of the Eupatridæ but the Metics and wives of the humbler citizens carried garlands, they created a festive picture little in keeping with death. Pluto must have scowled on his dark throne below! Eight years later as she stood on that same spot and looked down upon a similar yet vastly different scene she recalled this bright morning with its atmosphere of suppressed gaiety. There were no laughter-loving eyes raised to Pericles then!

The President of the Council poured the libation and Pericles began his speech. His golden voice with its polished enunciation was always an artistic pleasure to listen to, even when abrupt and scornful, but when he infused it with sadness and sympathy it was irresistible. Aspasia saw Elpinike dash away an angry tear.

But he was far too great an artist to finish on a note of woe, and Aspasia had composed the oration according to instructions. When he had dwelt upon the bravery and virtues of the fallen, whose death had taken the spring out of the year, and had condoled with the sorrowing families, he gave his breathless audience a vivid account of the past nine months, and tears dried as they listened to details they had ardently desired. They could see the great battle with the Samian fleet, when for long hours the fate of Athens had hung in the balance, then the sharp engagement on land before the gates of the city had closed on the last of the beaten rebels. They held their breath as he related the search among the islands for the Persian or Phœnician fleet, and described the anxious nights when there was little sleep for the Generals, and at every distant splash even the rowers were alert. Then his quick race for Samos when he heard of the reverses of the ships on guard, and the brief sanguinary engagement. He told them of the long weary months of inactivity, and dwelt upon the admirable conduct of men impatient to distinguish themselves and to restore Samos to Athens. And then of the great day of surrender when the cheers could be heard in Miletus. It was a mounting pæan of triumph for Athens, for he said little of himself; and every heart present beat faster with pride and a joyful sense of security. They understood as never before that if Samos had won, the Maritime Empire would have passed into her hands, and once more she would have been "Mistress of the Ægean." On that war, verily, had depended the fate of Athens.

He returned briefly to the subject of the fallen at the end of his speech. "The citizens who have died for their country," he said, "are living still and will live forever, for they are immortal even as the gods. We do not see the gods, but we conceive them to be immortal by the respect we pay them and the blessings we receive from them; and so it is with those who die for their country."

As the occasion was a solemn one there was no cheering as he stepped down from the rostrum, but the women ran forward and flung garlands and ribbons all over him until he looked like a victorious athlete at Olympia. He had cast more than one apprehensive glance at those garlands, but there was nothing to do but submit. This was the women's only opportunity to honor the returned hero and they were entitled to their hour.

He thanked them and told them he was glad to see so many faces unstained by tears, and was making his way slowly but firmly through the throng when old Elpinike stood suddenly in his path.

"A fine exploit truly, Pericles!" she cried, and her high shrill voice carried far. "And well worthy of a crown, to lose many of our brave fellow-citizens, not fighting with Persians and Phœnicians as my brother Kimon did, but in ruining the people of a city of our own blood, and our own allies!"

This denunciation was greeted with a loud hiss, and one of the women pushed her aside, quoting rudely, "Too old art thou for rich perfumes": a remark that was afterward attributed by his enemies to Pericles, although no man was more rarely discourteous, even under greater provocation than any old woman could offer. He took no notice of her whatever. Indeed the only thought that animated him was to get away and divest himself of trappings that made him feel ridiculous. He saw a narrow opening between two tall tombs, plunged through, and was soon lost to sight.

XXXIX

"Aspasia," said Agariste, when they had shaken off their friends and were approaching the house of Pericles, "what is this I hear about Phyrra and young Acestorides? It was only yesterday that Simonides brought home the astounding news that Ariphon—who is a fool—takes her daily to the studio of Pheidias that she may meet this boy, who is loved by Thasson. I went at once to the house but did not see Ariphon—no doubt he hid when he saw me coming—and when I taxed Phyrra she flew into a rage and told me to mind my own business. I boxed her ears and she ran out of the room; so I am no wiser than I was before. Of course you are at the bottom of it, with your ridiculous ideas of letting women do as they please."

"Both Acestorides and Phyrra are sitting to Pheidias for important figures in his frieze," said Aspasia evasively. "It is natural her father should go with her—"

"You always blush when you quibble, so don't imagine you can get out of it. Tell me the whole story."

Aspasia laughed and gave a little shrug. "Very well, dear Agariste. Of course I knew you would find me out. But tell me first—did you not think Pericles made a beautiful speech?"

"Of course. Is he not a great orator? And although we have several fine orators in Athens he is different as well as greater. If I heard one of his speeches in the dark and he had pebbles in his mouth I should know it as his."

And Aspasia, delighted at this reassurance of the unity of her mind with his, told Agariste of Phyrra's importunities and the mild escapade in which she herself had taken part.

The daughter of Xanthippus was secretly rather proud of the

spirit and enterprise of her niece, but her standards were out-
raged nevertheless. "I never heard of such a thing!" she exclaimed as they sat down before the fire in the pastas. "The
girl is a regular Spartan, and you are not much better. I don't
believe for a moment she will get him away from Thasson, and
she'll be laughed at by all Athens. No other man will have her.
Have you told Pericles of this?"

"We have had no time for gossip."

"I suppose not! And I'd advise you not to tell him of your part
in it; he'd vary his love-making with a Zeus thunderclap you
wouldn't forget. However, there is no talk of you in the matter, and I betray no woman to her husband. But I would I had
been here that day she confided in you. By the dog of Egypt
I'd have put a stop to it! What did you do such a thing for,
Aspasia? Couldn't you foresee the consequences?"

"No. Can you?"

"Assuredly. She'll be an old maid and grow gaunt and yellow
at her spinning-wheel."

"I doubt it. I fancy she is one to get what she wills. And
she is beautiful. Why shouldn't she win that conceited youth,
who knows naught of the wiles of girls? I should be surprised
if she did not. After all he is a man and they see each other
daily."

"Such a thing has never been heard of in Athens, except
among Metics, who don't count—by the two goddesses here
comes Thasson now!"

Marcus was showing the young man to a bench in the peristyle, and a moment later he came forward, concern in his face.

"Shall you receive him?" whispered Agariste eagerly.

"Certainly. Why not? And I would not have you expire of
curiosity, dear Agariste, so please remain."

"He has seen you, O Mistress," said Marcus, "or I would
have sent him away. He should have seen for himself that you
did not receive this morning—and it is near the hour for
lunch—"

"Ask him to come to the pastas. No doubt he could not wait
longer to congratulate the Strategos."

Thasson walked up the long aula with a dignified composure,

but his high calm brow contracted as he saw Agariste. Her smile as she acknowledged the introduction was not unsympathetic, but as she settled herself back in her chair, he said hesitatingly:

"I would speak with you alone, O Aspasia—and I mean no discourtesy to Agariste wife of Simonides. But the affair is of some moment—"

"And I would see our little Eros eat his pease soup," said Agariste amiably, and retired; to listen behind the door of the andron.

"What is it, Thasson?" asked Aspasia, who felt kind to all the world this morning. "Would you speak with me about Acestorides and Phyrra?"

"Yes, Aspasia. I am deeply troubled and unhappy, and although I have never come to your house before and you probably know why, so great is your intelligence I feel sure you will understand when I tell you I have come to-day to beseech a favor of you. Acestorides is falling in love with that girl."

"They are both young and beautiful; what more natural?"

"Natural!" He stared at her in cold disgust. "You speak as an Ionian, Aspasia. This is Athens."

"Youth is youth everywhere, O Thasson. The young men and maids of Athens need only opportunity to fall in love like those who are more fortunately situated. And many do, as you must know, yourself."

"Only a passing fancy, born of the exchange of a glance or whisper during the Panathenea. But why bandy words, Aspasia? You know our customs and our ideals. True love can exist between intellectual and high-minded men only. It is but the meaner sort of love that a man may feel for a woman, who is without virtue; or with only those lesser virtues which are necessary in the house. I realize that I am talking to a woman, but I am also talking to Aspasia. You have the mind of a man and it was due to a strange oversight of the gods that it passed into the form of a woman. Pericles would not have loved you if you had been a mere pretty girl. You should recognize that your marriage stands alone in the history of Athens, O Aspasia, and not seek to bring misery to others by a mistaken idea that your example can be successfully followed. No, never!"

"It is true that I took her to the studio that day and did not leave at once when you and Acestorides entered. But I disclaim any further responsibility. And I have little influence over Phyrra. Nor has any one. She is a girl of strong character. Why not remonstrate with Acestorides?"

"I have, indeed! But he only blushes, and protests that he loves no one but me. And I have seen him look at that girl as he never looked at me! I, who selected him from all the youth in Athens for my friend, and would go through life at his side! For three years I have thought of no one else, and have opened that fair garden of his mind flower by flower. He is weak—with the beautiful weakness of youth—and I shudder when I think of what might have become of him if my suit had failed. His father was as happy as I when Acestorides consented to become my beloved. He has fallen completely under my influence and avoids of his own will depraved men and women. He loves study and deep reflection. Intellectually he is the most promising young man in Athens, and I would develop him into a philosopher. The ordinary marriage—which both of us must undertake in due course—would make no difference in our friendship; my character is formed, and his will be before he is thirty. But to transfer his love—at his age! —to a girl will be his ruin. If women have little virtue girls have less, and this one is full of amorous vanity—"

"Phyrra has more virtue than you think. She is studious and clever, and, I repeat, has much force of character. You could remain Acestorides' friend, and what you continued to teach him he could teach her. It is a tragedy for both men and women that there is no companionship in the house."

"I will share Acestorides with no one!" cried Thasson passionately. "What you suggest is preposterous. If he gives himself up to the most contemptible form of lust he will be a pliant wand in that girl's hands to bend at her pleasure. I can see that she has will—I do not dignify it by the name of character. Oh, Aspasia! *Think* before you countenance this iniquity!"

"Do not make me angry, Thasson! I repeat that I refuse to be held responsible. I have hardly seen Phyrra since that day at the studio. There has been much of far more importance to think of in this house, as in Athens. It is Ariphon you should seek."

"Ariphon is wax in that girl's hands. I do not hold you responsible, Aspasia. Believe me when I say that I came here to-day not to reproach you but to ask your help in my extremity. I know that Phyrra studies with you and that your influence must be great—think of the men who bow down before you! And she a mere girl! You can turn her mind from Acestorides if you will."

Aspasia felt herself in a quandary. She knew she must not make an enemy of this solemn tiresome young man—no wonder Acestorides preferred Phyrra!—but if she gave a formal promise he would hold her to account if she failed; and she might as well consider plucking a star from the firmament as diverting Phyrra from her purpose. "Why don't you take him away?" she asked. "Diophantes, no doubt, would be glad to consent, and you could travel—to Carthage—Syracuse—"

"There is no happiness out of Athens. The world comes to us—there is nothing better to seek."

"Why not make him think you have turned your affections to another? A man does not lightly lose a friend in whose companionship he has found delight for three years. It is against all tradition. Jealousy might bring him to his senses."

Thasson drew himself up. "I cannot stoop to meanness and deceit, O Aspasia wife of Pericles. Besides I should be held in contempt by all men for my fickleness—as I shall be—O Zeus! —when it is known he has left me for a girl."

"I find a great inconsistency in your attitude, Thasson. All of you would have had me marry Thoron if Thucydides had won."

"Thoron loved no one, and to have married Aspasia would have been a triumph for any young man. It would have been attributed to vanity, for although we did not approve we should have kept our counsel. But no one else has ever heard of this girl—both Acestorides and I will be shamed before all Athens.

Oh, Aspasia! Give me your aid!" And to her horror he burst into tears.

"Compose yourself, Thasson," she said severely. "Pericles has gone to the Piræus but may return at any moment. I will do what I can—and you must commit no desperate act. Promise me that."

He dried his eyes on a large linen handkerchief from Egypt. "No, Aspasia," he said with dignity. "I shall not drink hemlock nor fall on my sword, if that is what you fear. I am not one to forget my duty to the State. And I shall take your advice in part. Pheidias can have no further use for Acestorides, for he and his students work with an extraordinary rapidity. I shall ask Diophantes to send him to the country to practice on horseback and I shall go with him. There I shall hope to teach him once for all that the passion of friendship is the only ideal and that there is no such happiness in life as philosophical converse."

He rose and adjusted his mantle carefully; he was a fashionable young man, and great minds were rarely indifferent to dress. A man may not train himself to perfection of form in gymnasia and ignore its natural complement.

"I go, Aspasia," he said. " And I thank you. And meanwhile will you talk to that girl?"

"I will talk to her!"

He smiled punctiliously, and walked with the slow measured pace of the Athenian down the aula and out the door.

Agariste burst in. "I heard every word!" she exclaimed triumphantly. "I listened and I'm not ashamed to admit it. Besides, I was afraid you would need my protection if he lost his head. But what a virtuous young man! I hope he wins Acestorides back—I'll see that Phyrra is betrothed at once. But I suppose he bored you, Aspasia?"

"Yes, he bored me," she said slowly. "But—Time changes all things—I wonder will men ever find a higher ideal?"

XL

The subtle poison of success was working in the veins of Athens. She forgot her old passionate desire for peace and tranquillity, forgot those months of anxiety when she had only Samos to reduce and punish, forgot the temporary depletion of her treasury and her families in mourning. She was the proud mistress of a Great Empire and had proved herself invincible. Why should she not go out and conquer other proud cities and States—Syracuse—Carthage—Egypt? Then indeed would she be mistress of the world and her place great in history.

She was like a premature composite Alexander, swollen with pride and ambition. But luckily the swollen body lacked a head.

Great pressure was brought to bear upon Pericles, and not only by the people but by men of his own class. Many of the Oligarchs buried their grievances and came to his house and delivered themselves of resounding phrases by the hour. They were willing to see him come home in triumph once more if only he left smoking cities behind him. Besides, there was always the chance he would be killed.

Pericles listened to them politely; he knew it was better to let them talk than to suppress them peremptorily, and he always played for time. But a day came when the people clamored for his presence on the Pnyx, and he shrugged his shoulders and went.

For two hours he sat among the archons and listened to oration after oration. Eupatrid and artisan shouted themselves almost into a frenzy as they pictured Athens standing on the apex of the world, its peoples her subjects, its inestimable riches at her command. Constant cheering interrupted them. He had ordered the President not to call his name until he gave the signal, but finally he could contain himself no longer. His name was announced and he took his place on the Bema amidst the usual clamor.

He raised his hand with a gesture of command and silence fell at once.

"I have very few words to say to you," he began; and the withering scorn in his voice created a swift uneasiness. "To me you are all children and fools, and I have lost all respect for you. We have a navy of three hundred triremes and you would embark on a series of wars that would combine all the forces of the Barbarians against us, and make Sparta rejoice. We hovered upon the edge of one terrible calamity for nine months, and you are already impatient to plunge into certain disaster. You shout the name of Egypt as if it were a talisman. Are your memories so short that you have forgotten the humiliating conclusion of that ambitious enterprise? Have you forgotten Coronea when you were ignominiously beaten by a petty City State? A few years back you were desperately afraid that under an oligarchical government you would be driven into another war with Persia. Otherwise, why did you ostracize Thucydides and permit me to remain, when I have always set my face against war if it is possible to avoid it? And now you would challenge the world—which includes Persia; make no doubt of that. To be great and prosperous our condition must be one of uninterrupted peace; and you would lightly embark upon a series of wars that might last for twenty years, for war breeds war—unless, indeed, we were speedily annihilated by an immediate combination of forces.

"I advised against the little war with Bœotia and you know the result. I advised against the aggression in Egypt, where we lost more than a hundred triremes and many of our best men—young as I was at that time. I shall never give my consent to this ridiculous project to go out and fight the world—to the undoing of all I have given a lifetime to accomplish. But the power to make fools of yourselves lies with you, not with me. Embark upon ruin as quickly as you will. But the day you declare war that day I leave public life and retire to my place in the country. You will have looked your last upon me to-day. Be sure that Pericles will take no part in the downfall of Athens. I have nothing more to say to you, Men of Athens. Farewell."

And he strode from the silent Pnyx, his eyes still flashing and his face set in contempt.

"I think that is the last I shall hear of wars of aggression," he said to Aspasia, as he recounted the scene. "It is necessary to tell the Athenians from time to time they are fools; but they are not, and need only to be shown the truth to return to their senses."

And he was right. There was grumbling, and outbursts of indignation, but his words had deflated them, and the wiser heads convinced the others that he had spoken wisdom; and that prudence was the greatest virtue of a statesman.

XLI

Pericles had brought more than talents from Samos and their arrival made almost as great a sensation as his own.

Ancient Crete had been renowned for her peacocks, and in course of time her friendly relations with Samos had led to the present of a pair of those jealously guarded perambulating tapestries of Knossos and Hagia Triada. The Samians had been equally jealous and bred them century after century in the sanctuary of Hera. Visitors from all parts of the world had come to gaze at them, but the wealth of Asia would not have purchased one of those sacred birds. When Pericles commandeered twenty-four pairs the Samians mourned the loss of their exclusive proprietorship almost as much as the demolition of their walls.

The peacocks were exhibited for several days in the Agora, where they strutted proudly up and down before the eyes of admiring crowds, and then Pericles, after dividing five among Aspasia, his sister, Constantia, Phyrra, and the wife of his friend Menippus, sent the rest to Pyrilampes, a farmer-friend who had land adjoining his own and went in for bird-fancying.

All the women in Athens wanted peacocks, and several orders were sent to Pyrilampes by amiable husbands. Those whose husbands were less complaisant or too stingy, were bitterly jealous, and there was discord in the house. No hetæra would look at a man who did not provide her with a peacock, and these ladies went abroad with peacocks on leash, where before they had been content with rare breeds of dog. As there was little else to talk about after the excitement of victory had subsided, these royal birds were an absorbing topic of conversation among the women; and reports of their envy, or triumphs of acquisition and breeding, caused Pericles much amusement.

But for once his foresight failed him. Little he recked of the scandal in which those peacocks would one day involve him.

Zosmë returned with Hippodamus on their way from Thurii to Rhodes, where he was to build another great city, and when she went into raptures over the gorgeous creature sunning himself before the altar, she was made happy at once with the promise of a pair. Her precious peacock fan had come from Samos, but never had she hoped, when she had stared at those famous birds in the Sacred Grove of Hera, to possess any part of one but a few tail feathers tied with a ribbon.

"Are you not afraid those boys will pull out that beautiful tail?" she asked Aspasia. "I wonder Alcibiades has left a feather in it."

"Oh, Alcibiades is too ravished with its beauty; he would defend it with his fists, and has named it Achilles! The elder boys now spend the morning in the palæstra, and the rest of their spare time on horseback. Clinias might take a spiteful pleasure in ruining Achilles' fine appearance, or incite the baby, and for that reason I keep it out here where the children never come except when invited."

Zosmë was her guest and they were walking up and down the outer peristyle. It was evening and Pericles was giving a banquet in honor of Hippodamus. Agariste had a cold and Zosmë had begged to spend the evening in lighter converse, so the symposium was to be truly Athenian.

"They'll probably talk architecture for an hour at least," she said. "And I am sick, the gods know, of architecture. Don't you think I am really thinner? That famous old doctor, Herodicus, came from Thrace, and we women attended his lectures and gave up cakes, honey, and the midday meal. I was faithful for three months, and although I have fallen since, I am really quite abstemious and do gymnastics every morning. But the women talked of nothing else and I got sick of hearing how many inches they had taken in their bands and this and that they were denying themselves. I shall not be bored by you," she added enviously. "You are as much like a willow wand as ever, and always will be, I suppose, as you care nothing for sweets and sauces and walk miles every day—but tell me: am I not thinner than when I left?"

And Aspasia after the manner of women assured her she was a sylph. "And," she added more veraciously, "you will always be handsome, dear Zosmë. I can see that Hippodamus is as proud of you as ever."

Zosmë exhaled a deep sigh of gratification. "Yes, I keep my looks—with the help of unguents, a little alkinet, and the determination to let nothing worry me, not even exile. But I feared for you during those terrible months when Pericles was absent, and made sacrifice for you. It was a delight not to find you looking a day older, although there is a subtle change in your expression. One cannot experience many things and remain exactly the same. And now, dear Aspasia, tell me all the gossip of Athens. Just enough came to us in Thurii to make one eager for more."

"I am afraid I know less. Little happens here that is worth recounting. During the war the women were too sad or too apprehensive to gossip. They were permitted to go constantly to the temples and offer sacrifice. But perhaps you would be interested in Phyrra." And she told that tale from its light-hearted beginning to its anxious present.

"What an extraordinary story for Athens!" exclaimed Zosmë, who had listened breathlessly. "It makes me feel homesick! And that boy is still in the country and Phyrra languishing for him!"

"Not languishing. You do not know Phyrra. She is in a state of suppressed fury and heaven knows what she is planning. There is no doubt that Acestorides was falling in love with her, although he fought against it as unworthy of an Athenian and a philosopher! But he is young and human, and had it been possible to see him alone she would have made him kiss her no doubt and opened his eyes to something besides the pleasures of discourse. His father had become almost as alarmed as Thasson and willingly sent him to the country, where, between hunting and his masterful friend, he may forget her. Agariste has done her best to betroth her to Atrometus son of Sopolis, but Ariphon dares not mention the subject to Phyrra, although he is deeply disturbed. The gossip has died out, for none who breeds gossip knew the facts, and it is now understood they met accidentally once or twice in Pheidias' studio. It might be worse, but I am sorry for Phyrra. Of course she comes to me for consolation and I can do nothing to help her."

"It would seem incomprehensible that Thasson could make Acestorides forget a beautiful girl were this not Athens. Athens! . . . Tell me, Aspasia, have you never found aught to regret in your marriage with Pericles?"

"I—regret—I!" Aspasia looked at her in indignant astonishment.

"Well—I mean—of course—" The outrages of the comic poets had flown on the first wind to Thurii, but she could not be certain they had reached the ears of Aspasia, and she did not care to be the one to enlighten her. But she was consumed with curiosity nevertheless. "You see—there has been so much unpleasant gossip, and I have heard that Olympias and her friends behaved badly—"

"What is that to me? It is true that few women come here now, and I regret that, as it gave me pleasure to develop their understanding and encourage their wish to be something more than the mere property of their husbands. But whatever gossip the women may run with from house to house, it never penetrates here. I see none but Agariste, Constantia, Rhea and Phyrra, and they would neither listen to gossip about me nor repeat it. Nor do such matters ever occur to me. No life could be fairer than mine."

The gods be thanked, thought Zosmë. And if they ever permit those comic poets to turn loose again I'll not make sacrifice for a year.

XLII

"O Mistress," said a voice and they turned to see Xanthias behind them.

"What brings you here?" asked Aspasia in surprise, for the servants never came to the outer quarters except when summoned.

"It is Lagus, the steward of Ariphon, Mistress. He wished to see his master, but—after what he told me—I thought it best to see you first—"

"Has anything happened to Phyrra?"

"She has disappeared and taken her handmaid with her."

"O Zeus! What now? Come, Zosmë." And they went quickly through the thalamos to the inner court where a perturbed elderly slave was walking up and down.

He ran forward. "Is she with you, O wife of Pericles?" he asked eagerly. "I am distracted!"

"She is not here. When did she leave the house?"

"An hour since. A slave in the next house saw them stealing out the back way, but I was told only a few moments ago. I could not believe it and went over the entire house. Her old nurse went with me and found she had worn boots not sandals, had taken her comb, and worn her new embroidered chiton under a dark mantle. I also discovered that she had taken a bag of silver from the Master's Chest. But the worst is to come, O wife of Pericles. Two horses are gone from the stables. The boy who should have been there had stolen off to a winehouse, no doubt. He'll get a beating to-morrow—"

"How far is the estate of Ariphon from that of Diophantes?"

The man stared. "Not eight stadia. They are both in the north—"

She turned to Xanthias. "Go quickly and get the chariot—no, have it taken to the Archarnican Gate. They have an hour's start, but we may not be too late. Send Thera to me first. Go now," she said to Lagus. "Tell your household that Phyrra is with me. The gentlemen will not leave the andron for hours yet. If I do not return before the symposium is over Thera will tell the Master that Phyrra is ill and I have gone to her—"

"Oh, Aspasia, take me with you!" cried Zosmë. "I have not felt so excited for years."

"But the chariot is narrow and Xanthias goes with me—"

"You just said I was a sylph—for that matter Xanthias can drive us."

"Very well. We may have need of a little humor to-night!"

Ten minutes later, heavily veiled, they were following Xanthias rapidly through the deserted streets to the northern gate, Zosmë panting a little and almost running to keep up with Aspasia. She took her seat in the chariot with a sigh of relief.

"The gate-keeper told Xanthias they had gone by this road," said Aspasia. "So we are on the right track, at least."

"Does Xanthias know how to drive?" asked Zosmë anxiously, forgetting that she had suggested him. "The Alcmæonid horses are known for fleetness but I never heard they were easily driven."

"Xanthias can do anything," said Aspasia impatiently. "He has only to put his mind on it."

And as it was moonlight and cloudless and the road wide if rough, Xanthias found little trouble in guiding the horses straight to the north. No one else was likely to be abroad but themselves. They dashed along over the flat Attic plain, through forests, up and down low hills, past the bend of the mountain that hid Marathon and the Euripus, and always toward Parnes looming ahead of them. They could see the lights in the watch towers on the summit, and Aspasia pointed out the stronghold of Lypsydrium whence the Alcmæonidæ a hundred years since had made their attacks on the Tyrant Hippias son of Pisistratus.

Xanthias drew up at the gates of Ariphon's estate. "Shall we approach the house in the chariot, Mistress?" he asked. "If she heard the noise she might take alarm."

"Leave us here and go to the stables and see if the horses she took are there. Ask questions if you think best."

"I shall descend," said Zosmë hurriedly. "Not only to uncramp my muscles, but I trust those horses only when a man has the reins."

Xanthias lifted them both down and disappeared among the trees.

Zosmë stretched herself and stamped her feet. "O Zeus, these roads of Hellas!" she exclaimed. "And we must take that drive back! I feel as every bone in my body were broken. What do you suppose the girl is up to?"

"That is what we have come to find out! But I doubt if she is here."

"Where, then? Do you mean she may have gone to his estate? Even after what you told me of her—"

"She is capable of anything—that cannot be Xanthias already?"

But it was, and he said rapidly: "They came here and the daughter of Ariphon left her handmaid who was overcome. She demanded a fresh horse and when the slave in charge of the stables remonstrated and would have detained her until he could send word to her father she struck him with her whip and got her way. Where she went he does not know and as the girl was asleep on the hay—he would not permit her to go to the house—I could ask no questions—but I did ask, O Mistress, the direction to the estate of Diophantes."

Aspasia was already in the chariot. "Come, Zosmë," she said peremptorily; "unless you too prefer to sleep in the hay until our return. How far is it, Xanthias?"

"Between seven and eight stadia, Mistress, and on this road."

Zosmë, groaning, and wishing she had treated her desire for adventure with the scorn it deserved, climbed into her seat, and once more the horses were galloping along the road. It was but a few moments later that Xanthias drew up before another gate in a stone fence. He leaped to the ground, tied the horses, and lifted the ladies down. They all advanced cautiously together.

It was evident there was a wood of pine and fir trees between the road and the house, and that it possessed more than natural beauty; statues of gods stood in clearings, and at the end of a vista they could see a little temple.

"I'll wager a daric they are in there," whispered Zosmë. "What a pity to disturb them!"

They stole forward until they saw the dark mass of a house. There was not a glimmer of light anywhere, nor a sound. The household, at least, had not been disturbed. Nor was there any sign of Phyrra.

"How do you suppose she got him out—if she did," Zosmë was beginning, but Xanthias interrupted her.

"Here is her horse," he exclaimed under his breath. "Sacred Apollo, what are girls coming to!"

They peered from the shelter of the trees at the garden. Nothing moved there; there was no sound but the splash of the fountains and the murmur of the wind in the wood.

"The temple!" said Zosmë with emphasis. "I am sure they are there."

"Can you find it?" asked Aspasia of Xanthias. "I only caught a glimpse of it some time since."

"I know the direction," and once more they plunged into the wood. A few moments later they saw the temple. It stood white and empty in the moonlight.

"What a pity," sighed Zosmë. Romance had expired with the last of the lyric poets, not to flourish again for many centuries, but the Greeks had their moments of premonition. "Still, it is rather exposed!"

Xanthias lifted his hand. "I think I hear voices. Wait here."

He stole forward, was lost to sight, but not long in returning. "This way, Mistress. I did not see them, for they are concealed in a thicket, but I heard them—and I think the daughter of Ariphon has lost no time."

Aspasia outdistanced the others, and peering through the branches saw the two culprits. Phyrra was methodically rearranging her hair and Acestorides stood before her looking both ashamed and adoring. She skirted the thicket and confronted them. Acestorides looked wildly about. Phyrra screamed, then burst into a gay laugh, and caught her lover by his tunic.

"You shameless girl!" exclaimed Aspasia, although she had much ado not to laugh herself. "You should be beaten and locked up on bread and water."

Phyrra giggled and nestled against the rigid heavily breathing young philosopher. "He is mine!" she said triumphantly. "I say to that. He knows more now than he will ever learn from Thason, and he loves me. We shall be married of course, and at once."

"And you must return to Athens at once, before your father knows of this! And you, Acestorides, you return with us; your betrothal will take place two days from now. Go and get a horse."

Phyrra took him firmly by the arm. "He shall, dear Aspasia. But I go with him. Come, too, if you like."

The helpless Acestorides progressed in silence to the stables, and a horse was led cautiously to the gates. The two rode beside the chariot to the estate of Ariphon to procure fresh horses, then all started for Athens at the usual breakneck pace.

On the following day Aspasia sent for Diophantes, who listened to the story with amazement and horror. But he was a friend of Ariphon and would not see his daughter disgraced; he gave his consent to an immediate betrothal, and promised that his son should not see Thasson until after the wedding.

But Aspasia sighed as he left her. One more enemy for Pericles, she thought, for Thasson will never forgive me. But it cannot be helped. The girl is the granddaughter of Xanthippus and the niece of Agariste and Pericles. The wonder is she didn't abduct him in a galley and carry him to Crete.

BOOK III

I

THE Temple of Athenè Parthenos was finished; the white dazzling magnificence of the great Doric structure could be seen from all parts of the Attic plain. The eyes of Athenians were turned to the Acropolis at all hours in worshipful awe and a thrilling sense of possession; strangers came from distant parts to gaze at this contribution of Athenian genius to the beauty of the world, and to witness the Panathenea—the first to be held since the completion of the temple.

Girls had been at work for nine months in the Parthenon, or inner room of the new temple, on the peplos for the goddess and danced at the thought of that day of unveiled freedom in the procession; a day that came only once in four years and never to the same girls twice. Those who would take part this year, and see the robe they had embroidered during long days of happy gossip cover the mighty chryselephantine statue of the goddess, would tell of that unique experience to their grand children. Other girls would embroider other robes, but never again would there be such an occasion as this: the great temple would receive its dedication on the last day of the Panathenea and be open to the public for the first time.

Not only colonists, allies, and distinguished strangers poured into the city but vendors of all sorts from Thebes to sell their tempting wares in the streets, and in the courtyards to eager women. The finest horses had been brought in from the breeding farms, and the young men who had been selected for their beauty and riding skill to take part in the races and the procession on the last day could be seen dashing constantly about the plain.

Xanthippus and Paralus, now nineteen and eighteen, were among them, and Alcibiades was deeply envious. He was one fourteen but almost as tall as the others, and his body, since he had exercised daily in the palæstra, was as supple as a reed and as beautiful as his face. His old pedægogus never left his side when abroad, nor took his eyes from him in the palæstra, and if he disappeared for a moment was after him. His fame which was to increase with the years had already begun; men were flocking to the palæstra to watch him exercise, and all agreed that at fifteen he would be the beauty of Athens. No other boy could approach him in looks, in grace and speed, in wrestling, boxing, swimming, dancing, and leaping. He was too young for the stadium, where Paralus, to his father's delight, had distinguished himself in running and discus-throwing, but there was little doubt that when his time came he would display his genius in both gymnasium and stadium as he did every day in the palæstra.

The other boys of his age were too well versed in the tradition of an outstanding figure and too lost in admiration of the supreme gifts of this one in particular to be more than passing envious; but they sometimes resented his masterful manner and the short cut he took now and then to victory. One day when wrestling with a boy of unusual strength and skill and determined not to fall, he bit his opponent's hands, forcing him to let go. "You fight like a woman," said the boy contemptuously, but Alcibiades replied proudly: "No, like a lion." And his flatterers laughed and applauded as usual, for Alcibiades was the focus of interest for more than beauty and skill; a few years hence he would be the wealthiest young man in Athens and his own master.

"And I must take no palt in this great event," he said haughtily to Aspasia, as they sat together in the outer court and he had tired of teasing Achilles. "I, Alcibiades son of Clinias, who should go down in history as the leader of the ephebi. Why could not Pheidias have delayed the building of that temple for five yea's?" His *rs* were still an obstacle which he made an effort now and then to overcome, but he was more concerned with the break in his voice, and ready to knock any one down who laughed at him.

"But you are to take part, dear Alcibiades," said Aspasia,

who was the confidante of all his grievances. "There are to be foot-races for boys in which you are sure to excel."

"I would lead the ephebi on a magnificent horse. Who cares what boy wins the foot-lace in the festival of Panathenea?"

"I wonder—how would you like to be the boy who receives the folded peplos as it is taken into the temple?"

His eyes flashed. "You always think of something wonderful, Aspasia! I shall like that tlemendously—since I cannot lead the plocession. Can you allange that, Aspasia?"

"I will speak to Pericles. Of course the Panathenea is in the hands of the ten stewards the people elect every four years, but they consult Pericles daily."

"Pellicles does as he will—as I shall some day; and he denies you nothing. But—" He heaved a deep sigh. "It takes so long for a boy to glow into a man. Four years before I am of age and may enter the army!"

"It is tragic, I know! But to me it is more tragic that they hold this festival in midsummer and heat. We should all be in the country. Remember, I have to walk with the matrons in that procession, and pity me."

"You have never walked in a plocession before, dea' Aspasia, and I am ploud that all Athens will look on your beauty at last."

"I am not anxious to walk unveiled in public: it was easy to make myself inconspicuous on the day of the funeral four years ago. But Pericles insists that I take part in this great festival, and Pheidias would weep and storm if I did not. I shall probably get as sunburned as you are, and Thera will have to go out and buy unguents!"

The festival started on the twenty-first day of Hekatombaion and lasted for eight days. Aspasia went with Agariste to the Odeum and listened to the contests in singing, flute, and lyre playing, recitations from epic poems by the rhapsodes. The vast hall was crowded to the dome, not only with all Athenians of quality and their wives but with every official in the city and Piræus, and all visitors who had braved travel in midsummer to be present at this historic festival. They came from the colonies in Iberia, Gaul, Italia, the islands, the north, and Asia

Minor, a few from the great cities of the Barbarians. Several hundred workmen had drawn lots for their seats.

They sat through long hours without impatience or fatigue and applauded as vigorously at the end as earlier. Pericles, who had been elected athlothetes as a matter of course, had superintended the program and rehearsals. The contest, which lasted for three days, was another triumph for him; in honor of the dedication of the temple it was more ambitious than ever before, and the chorals particularly fine. He made his awards— gold crowns and bags of money—amidst applause that shook the dome. Alcibiades, sitting beside Ariphon, when he saw one of his friends win the prize for flute execution, felt a momentary regret that he had defied his music-master and refused to learn to play on that instrument. Protesting that nothing that distorted the face and made a man look like a porpoise could have any place in art he had invited a sound whipping, which he took philosophically. The music-master in despair had let him have his way.

The women went into seclusion for several days, for on the fourth day there were gymnastic exhibitions in the stadium, and on the fifth the men gathered about the course outside the city to witness the horse and chariot racing. The Pyrrhic followed: a pantomimic war dance in the stadium, in which the young men wore helmets and clashed swords and shields, their feet moving in time to the music. This was followed by footraces of men in armor, discus and spear throwing, the prizes painted jars containing olive oil, in honor of Athenè. After dark on the seventh day there was a torch race starting from the altar of Prometheus in Academe, accompanied by revelry that lasted till dawn, and shattered what peace there was in an Athens night.

But all this was a mere preliminary to the last day when the great procession took place. The young cavalry officers were in the Ceramicus by daylight, to guard the great ship on wheels whose sail was the peplos embroidered by the maidens with the battle between the giants and the Olympian gods, led by Athenè in full armor. The saffron of the background of this immense mantle was hardly to be distinguished under the rich colors of the pattern. When the girls arrived, however, they gave that proud accomplishment but a fleeting glance; their eyes, in defiance of stern admonitions, stole to the young officers on horseback, whose bright cloaks, alas! did little to illuminate their jaded faces and heavy eyes. They had slept not a wink the night before and little since the season of festival began. They were far too tired to appreciate mere girls.

They led the procession, when it finally started amidst much shouting and pushing by the officials in charge; acting as a bodyguard to the ship with its precious sail, now filled with the maidens who had wrought that lively scene, and as many of the victorious young men as could crowd in. All wore garlands and were splendidly arrayed. This ship had a double significance, for it recalled to all lovers of legend or history the expedition of Theseus to Crete with his cargo of youths and maidens, and the sail which was to have meant so much but escaped his mind.

Bulls for sacrifice—their horns richly gilded—were followed by the winners in the various contests wearing their wreaths of victory. Behind marched the dignitaries of Athens and certain old men still conspicuous for good looks, each bearing an olive branch from the Sacred Wood beyond the walls, and led by Pericles and First Archon Theodorus, whose proud privilege it was to give his name to this year of years.

The matrons carrying baskets of fruit for sacrifice were next in order and more eyes were on Aspasia than on the maidens. She had taken great pains with her costume. It was a delicate shade of green embroidered with the classic pattern in gold and a thin veil of the same color floated back from the gold diadem that crowned her head; never more proudly poised. She wore long earrings and a necklace, that brushed her instep, of green crystal beads. Beside her walked Phyrra who looked a model for all matronly virtue.

They were followed by the maidens, each bearing a basket of flowers on her head, a garland of roses or figs about her neck and attended by Metic girls whose mission it was to protect with a parasol the complexions of the proud daughters of the Eupatridæ, and to carry a campstool for their use when sun baked bodies would rest later on.

The long procession was closed by the victorious racing chariots, another regiment of horse, and every Athenian able to walk. All moved to the accompaniment of the lyre and the flute, and at every corner ambitious men of the poorer class gave exhibitions of sword-swallowing, fire-swallowing, conjuring tricks and acrobatics. All through the festival enterprising vendors had sold in movable booths sausages, barley- and honey-cakes, cheese and wine, and reaped a rich harvest.

The procession moved slowly out of the Ceramicus, through the Agora and principal streets, past the twelve gilded statues of Victory Pericles had erected in various parts of the city, and in the course of two hours reached the foot of the Acropolis on the western side. The cavalry separated, the peplos was taken down and folded, the youths and maidens descended, and the ship trundled out of the way. The slow climb began, and the column entered by the wide central gateway and progressed up the gentle slope of the summit, past the brazen statue of Athenè Promachus, the rude temporary structure that contained the ancient olivewood statue of the goddess, and the ruins of older temples, until the Acropolis was covered by so dense a crowd that if any one had fainted he would have remained on his feet; many were left to mourn their fate without the gates. A space was kept clear by the police before the eastern portal of the fane for the sacrifice, and priests in new and gorgeous robes slew the bulls at the altar while every heart was supposed to be lifted in devout adoration of Athenè, as they gazed with eager satisfied eyes at her temple.

Aspasia had often accompanied Pericles and Pheidias to the Acropolis during the last months, when the pediments, friezes, statues, and entablatures were set in place, and she never tired of roaming about that temple both lovely and magnificent, with its forty-six columns as light and graceful in effect as if they had been of frozen Attic air not mere Pentelic marble. The Athenians were slaves to no tradition, and a Doric structure with them took on an airiness and grace with which not even Ionic architecture could compete. This beautiful temple to the Virgin Goddess was unrivalled in the world and would never be equalled. Its dazzling whiteness was relieved, wherever it was possible to apply color, with blue, scarlet, and gold, and rising above the marble tiles of the sloping roof were gilded statues and urns. The frieze of Pheidias, representing the Panathenea, was within the colonnade and invisible to those at a distance, but later in the day all would have an opportunity to loiter within the portico and gaze at that masterpiece of Attic art. Meanwhile their eyes were adequately feasted, the gods knew.

"How proud I am that I am a matron of Athens and have given two sons to the State," said Phyrra. "Don't you wish you had been born in Athens, Aspasia?"

Aspasia smiled faintly. "I am proud to be an adopted daughter of Athens, and too wise to anger the gods by harboring regrets. I wish for nothing, dear Phyrra—except that it were the hour for the Etesian wind."

"Yes, Zeus knows it is hot, and some one's elbow is planted in the middle of my back. I wish those priests would hurry, and the smell of roast meat makes me hungry. Are you sure we shall be able to get through this crowd and inside, out of the heat? The temple looks three times the size of the Hephæsteum but we can't all crowd into it."

"Cling to me. Pericles has given strict orders. And it cannot be long now."

"How glad I am to be too young to put alkinet on my face," said Phyrra complacently. "It was never intended for hot weather. Some of these matrons look as if they had put it on in stripes with a feather. I see one of them glaring at you because you are still as white as milk in spite of the sun. Whom are you looking for?"

Aspasia's glance had been roving over the mass of patient heads. "I was looking for familiar faces and reflecting how few people I know in Athens after living here so many years. . . . I see Diophantes and Thasson but not Acestorides."

"He must have been in the procession wearing the wreath he won for something or other," said Phyrra indifferently. She was very tired of Acestorides, and had long since handed him over to Thasson to amuse during the day. She had two children and intended to have more; and already realized that her infatuation had been directed by the gods to this end. She was also the head of a little empire within four walls, and her masterful spirit was gratified to the full. The many slaves were her subjects, and her children should be under her sole sway until they left that roof for their own. She dominated Acestorides, and even Thasson when he came to the house did not presume to contradict her. Not for nothing was she an Alcmæonid-Bouzyges and the most promising pupil of Aspasia.

"Did you notice Xanthippus when he lifted that pretty girl down from the ship?" she asked. "His eyes never left her face. There may be another marriage between two of equal age before long."

"No, I did not notice. Who is she?" Aspasia spoke eagerly. She would have rejoiced to see Xanthippus marry and go his way. He and his father rarely spoke and it was the only shadow in the house of Pericles. When he did speak it was to grumble at the meagreness of his allowance, and he was influencing Paralus to discontent. He was as dissipated as he could be with the small amount of money at his disposal and Olympias would give him little as it was her policy to make as much trouble in that house as she could. She succeeded in persuading Xanthippus that he had Aspasia to thank for his father's "miserliness," and he treated her as rudely as he dared.

Phyrra replied: "Dianana daughter of Tisander the son of Epilykus— Ah! They are chanting the invocation at last!"

The sacrifice over and the great slabs of meat left to roast on the coals, the priests ascended the steps of the eastern portal; the officers marshalled the people into ranks, and they entered four abreast and gazed their first upon the colossal gold and ivory statue of Athenè Parthenos; crowned with a superb helmet, balancing a Nike, or winged Victory, on the palm of her right hand, shield and spear at her left. She stood on a low pedestal at the end of the great room and between the two rows of columns. The walls were painted a deep red, and the ceiling divided into square lacunæ gay with color; but no eyes took in any detail that day; all were fixed on the tremendous shining figure of the goddess and when not lost in awe reckoned its cost. The gold alone would have built a temple.

The officials packed the people against the walls and between the pillars, leaving a narrow path from the door to the statue. Aspasia, with the matrons and maidens bearing their votive offerings, stood near the table at the feet of Athenè. The cella glittered with helmets, and occasionally there was a faint clash of shields. The priests stood before their goddess with arms upraised, the air was heavy with frankincense.

Aspasia saw Alcibiades waiting with great dignity at the door. He wore a laurel wreath, for he had won the boys' foot-race. But his pride was admirably repressed, and he was endeavoring to look as lofty and aloof as Pericles, standing with the archons and members of the Areopagus.

An officer entered carrying the folded peplos, and handed it to Alcibiades, who received it on both arms. Like Pericles, he had an inherent sense of drama, and as he walked with measured pace up the narrow lane between the people, his beautiful head with its bright crest of curls held with precisely the right tilt, his classic features set in a godlike repose, not an eyelash betrayed his consciousness of the loud murmur of admiration from both women and men. During those few moments he not the chryselephantine goddess was the focus of attention and well he knew it.

He was followed by the officer who had been chosen to carry the peplos to the temple, a young matron, and two girls. He slowed his pace as he approached the goal, and reached the table exactly at the moment when their part was finished and they stepped to one side. Then he handed the peplos to the priests, and resigned himself to oblivion. Alcibiades had ever an exact sense of values.

The matrons and maidens came forward with their bloodless offerings and laid them on the table. The priests mounted a scaffold and draped the goddess, while all sang the hymn to Athenè, accompanied by the grave Dorian music.

> *Pallas Athenè, glorious goddess, now will I sing,*
> *Sea-gray eyes . . .*

The priests descended and poured the libation, and the greatest festival in the history of Athens was over. Those who had been fortunate enough to witness the final ceremonies were herded out that others might enter and gaze in rapture and wonder. Pheidias was carried home on the shoulders of his students singing songs of victory. They were elated with more than the day's triumph, for Pheidias was to go at once to Olympia and make a still more colossal chryselephantine statue of Zeus, and several would go with him. He had been nearly smothered in congratulatory arms and was the proudest man in Athens that day.

II

"Pericles," said Aspasia teasingly that evening after their friends had left them and they sat alone in the pastas, "I believe you were secretly more exultant to-day than when Samos capitulated."

"Why do you think that?" he asked smiling. "Because the world saw my wife and pronounced her the most beautiful woman in Hellas?"

"I feel vainer than ever! But you haven't answered what I meant to be a question. Representatives from the greater part of the world have done little for eight days but exclaim at the glory and magnificence of Athens. They say that all the great Barbarian cities are heavy and almost ugly in comparison. And more. They call it 'the City of Pericles.' Have you heard that?"

"Oh, yes, I have heard that." He looked absently at the wall.

Aspasia laughed mischievously. "Don't try to look like a statue to me, Pericles! You forget how well I know you. You are the proudest man in Europe, Asia, and Africa to-night. Why not admit it to me?"

Pericles rose and leaned against a shelf, hooked his thumbs in the girdle of his tunic, and looked down upon her with an expression that for him was embarrassed and almost apologetic.

"I hope I did not betray myself to the multitude," he murmured.

"Oh, no, you looked more aloof than Zeus. But I knew when we stood there at the foot of Athenè that you were full of pride.

There would have been no such day in Athens but for you, and you never erected a trophy more exultingly."

He laughed. "You would know! And you are welcome to the knowledge. You alone. Yes, I was so proud that the gods if they existed would punish me, no doubt. But I have a deeper reason to exult than even you have divined. There have been men from Sparta and Corinth here, and I am told that Perdiccas of Macedonia sent a private agent to make observations and report to him. Our possible enemies, to say nothing of our reluctant tributaries, take home the impression of something more than the artistic excellence of Athens. They believe that our treasure chests are inexhaustible, and that gives us an added security."

"Aha! Hippodamus said once that if you were the greatest of statesmen you were also the profoundest of politicians. And again you have made no mistake. One of those women who stayed with us—thank the gods they are gone—told me that her husband, Callimachus of Syracuse, remarked that Athens must have resources of which the world knew nothing; resources beyond the Delian Chest, the mines of Laurion, and her commerce. I merely smiled, and endeavored to look neither wise nor mysterious. Merely—well, rather absent. In that moment I had a dim intuition of your policy."

He looked at her with fond admiration. "I tell you everything as a rule, but there are some things I like you to discover for yourself. Yes, the impression these Peloponnesians take home with them gives us the greater security for a time. But they will envy and hate us more than ever. I do not overlook that. The future holds more than pride, beauty, and prosperity for Athens. But I have my agents in Corinth and Sparta, and although I shall keep war at bay as long as possible, I shall force it myself when I am convinced they have made up their slow minds to strike. I must drive that chariot—but that is for the future," he added, as he saw the cloud in her eyes. "We still have a few years of peace and happiness before us. And we both have the gift of making the most of the present. Now that the present is flawless, outside of this house. Have you heard of these new clubs."

"No. Why should there be new ones?"

"Reason enough for them. The clubs heretofore have been composed of the older politicians but we are now witnessing an innovation. It would seem that some of our young men, weary of peace, plenty, and philosophy, are beginning to take a lively interest in politics. They do not care to ally themselves with the Demos, and the older Oligarchs have no leaders but Nicias and Antiphon, who are too wise to counsel activity in a hopeless cause. So these young men have formed their own clubs, and meet to discuss my iniquities and the best method of dethroning the Tyrant. Thasson, the friend of Acestorides, is the founder of one, and Thoron, who, as you may remember, pursued you at one time, of another—less respectable."

"Thasson—Thoron—" Aspasia lowered her eyes and felt as if the floor were sinking under her. But Pericles for once was not looking at her.

"They are only two. Clubs have become the fashion. Young men need war, and as I shall not give it to them until it is inevitable I must expect unrest. If they do not corrupt the Demos they can do me no harm. And there is nothing the Demos desires more at present than peace—and prosperity. Only idleness breeds discontent. If these young men find relief in talk and vituperation I should be the last to deny them." But he sighed. "I would have perfect content and happiness in Athens. An impossible ideal!"

"Do you think they will attempt to assassinate you?" she asked faintly.

"Oh, no!" He smiled at her reassuringly. "That would not satisfy them! They live to see me disgraced and powerless. I forgot to tell you that the comic poets belong to these clubs; and that one of the most active members is Xanthippus. But that was to be expected. There is no hatred like that of a fool for his father."

"Couldn't you increase his allowance?"

"That he may be more dissipated than he is? The son of Pericles may not live a life of extravagance when I am ever counselling economy as a virtue. And he would hate me none the less."

"Phyrra said he looked more than favorably on one of the girls in the ship. Should you care to have him marry and leave the house?"

"I should like nothing better. But I cannot believe he is in love with any girl. He is thoroughly depraved. Who is she?"

"Dianana the daughter of Tisander."

"Ah! She will have a large dowry. That is probably the secret of her charm for Xanthippus. But if he wishes it and her father is willing they will meet with no opposition from me. His influence over Paralus is far from good and the sooner they are separated the better. Paralus won four prizes and should distinguish himself at Olympia. So far he is too interested in games for dissipation, but boys of his age are easily led. Shall we go within? You have had a tiring day and I have kept you up late."

III

But the time for rest was still afar. Before Pericles could clap his hands and summon a slave to extinguish the lamps there was a loud knock at the entrance door.

"Who can that be at this hour!" he exclaimed impatiently. "Not Xanthippus, for I suspect that when he comes home late he employs some private signal and Paralus lets him in."

Aspasia sat down suddenly, assailed by a foreboding of disaster.

Marcus, who slept in his room beside the door, emerged in his nightly condition of nudity, and his loud grumble reached the pastas. He let the bolt fall with a clatter and turning the key applied one eye to a crack and demanded the name of the visitor with his usual urbanity. Then he threw the door open and shuffled back to his room.

To their amazement they saw Pheidias, and the bright moon revealed the agitation in his face as he ran toward them.

"Thank the gods you are here!" he cried, his voice shrill from inner turmoil. "But I should have sent for you, for I am distracted. O Zeus! O Zeus!"

Pericles pushed him into a chair and summoned a slave, who returned in a moment with a goblet of wine. He was accustomed to his sculptor's attacks of nerves, and few days passed that one or other of his geniuses did not come to him to be soothed or encouraged. After Pheidias had gulped down the wine he commanded him to explain the purpose of his late visit.

Pheidias took his head in his hands and rocked to and fro.

"They are bent upon my destruction, Pericles," he wailed. "Have you heard of these new clubs?"

Aspasia, whose eyes were on Pericles, saw a curious flicker in his eyes, but he replied lightly: "We have just been speaking of them. What have they to do with you?"

"Many men are jealous of me for my great genius, Pericles, and what it has enabled me to achieve. I have known that for long, but I believed that for the sake of Athens they would do me no harm. But now they can no longer contain themselves and would see me disgraced—O Athenè protect me!"

Pericles, who was walking up and down, said impatiently: "Come to the point. I thought those clubs were political. What have they to do with artists?"

"They hate every one who is great and popular. A member of one of those clubs is a man called Glycon, who is a friend of the Oligarchs. He has bribed Menon, one of my discharged workmen, to sit in the Agora to-morrow by the altar, placing himself under the protection of the gods, while he denounces me for stealing many of the talents that were voted for the gold on my statue of Athenè—that glorious statue before whom all Athens stood spellbound to-day! You know what the Athenians are, Pericles. They cannot endure superiority and fame. Only you have been able to control their fickleness and malice. My triumph to-day—when my name was on every tongue—was too much for their endurance, and this Glycon knows it is the moment to strike. I shall be tried and convicted and cast into prison!"

Pericles, whose serenity had been but slightly ruffled, smiled, but not genially. "Oh, no, Pheidias. Nothing of that kind will happen. You forget the orders I gave to have that gold and ivory weighed and applied in such a manner that it could be removed at a moment's notice. I anticipated something of this sort, and the estimates are in the Master's Chest in the thalamos at this moment."

"Oh, Pericles!" Pheidias seized his hand and kissed it. "I had forgotten, for details of that kind do not remain in my mind, and you did not explain your purpose." And then agitation returned. "But I shall be denounced in the market-place for all men to hear, and be tried by men that hate me! Cannot you order the arrest of Glycon and Menon?"

Pericles shook his head. "I curb the liberty of no Athenian when he is within his rights. The law permits any man to denounce another, and the archons to take cognizance. Any attempted interference on my part would make matters far worse than they are."

"Pericles," said Aspasia suddenly, "are these men aiming at you through Pheidias?"

"Nothing less, Aspasia. They dare not accuse me openly, so they fling a spear at one of my most intimate friends, hoping it may hit me in passing; in other words, that if he is proved guilty I may safely be accused of connivance. But they show their usual short-sightedness, for they should have guessed I would have had that gold weighed, and removable. You are sure you were guilty of no oversight there, Pheidias?"

"Oh, no, Pericles; it can be done in an hour. But how am I to face those jurors? I have no gift of words, and you know how nervous I am. I shall look as guilty as I am innocent!"

"Leave all to me. Iolaus is the cleverest of the speech-writers. I shall send for him to-morrow and give him the facts. Then you must commit the defense to memory, and also control yourself when you appear in court. The mantle and other parts will be weighed there before them, and that alone will give you courage. The trial will be a short one and you can depart for Olympia immediately after. Now go home and go to bed."

"I shall not sleep!" moaned Pheidias. "Nothing like this has ever happened to me before. Why should the great day of my life be ruined?"

"You cannot hope to escape the common lot. The few whose gifts elevate them above the mass must expect envy and malice.

The little minds must have their compensations. But the compensations of the great are beyond their imaginings. You will forget this affliction in the joy of creating your great statue of Zeus. Now try to borrow some of the dignity of the gods you worship, Pheidias, and bear yourself like a man not a bundle of nerves—without which, however, you might not be the great genius you are."

Pheidias turned to Aspasia. "I know you do not believe in the immortals, dear goddess," he said humbly; "but it would help me to endure that terrible ordeal to-morrow if you would go to my temple and make sacrifice to Athenè. Surely, if propitiated, she would not permit her servant to be disgraced— for who has done more to add to her fame on earth than Pheidias?"

Aspasia smiled and patted his trembling hand. "I have never quite been able to make myself disbelieve in Athenè, and I shall go willingly in the morning, dear Pheidias, and offer up prayer and sacrifice in your behalf. Remain in your studio to-morrow and work on some unfinished statue, that your enemies may be daunted by your serene indifference to their attacks. Be sure they will spy on you."

Pheidias sighed profoundly. "That proud serenity which is second nature to you and Pericles is beyond my achievement, I fear, but at least I can appear busy and indifferent if any one looks in on me. And your promise has given me courage."

Pericles walked with him to the entrance door and let him out. When he returned to the pastas he smiled at Aspasia's white anxious face.

"I see you have recognized this as the first clash of the shields," he said; "but do not fear for me, dear head. When another man rises strong enough to govern the Athenians I shall fall, but not before. They cannot do without me and are well aware of the fact. The trouble is they have been contented too long and have shown too much good-will toward one another. It is time to pull some one down and assert their sense of equality. Poor Pheidias is the victim. Democracy is the highest ideal the mind of man has so far conceived, but it is full of poison. I have endeavored to seal down that poison, but it is bound to spurt up at times. And for that I am prepared."

Aspasia shook her head. "I am full of forebodings, Pericles. You are talking of the people, but what of these clubs? Those men are your active enemies and will see to the release of that poison. And the Athenians are notoriously ungrateful—and short-sighted. Look at Miltiades. The Athenians worshipped him for a time as their deliverer at Marathon. He died miserably in prison. And Aristides, whom they called 'The Just,' and admired and consulted above all men. He died so poor there was no money to pay for his funeral. Themistocles gave Athens her navy and her walls and saved the day at Salamis, and the Athenians, ready to believe the accusations of his enemies because they were tired of praising him, cast him out."

"That is all true, Aspasia, and no one knows better than I the uncertain tenure of popular rulers. Man made the gods in his own image and endowed them liberally with the human attribute of jealousy. When men rise too high above their fellows it is not the gods they must fear. I have never permitted myself to lose sight of this powerful human passion for a moment. All my foresight is devoted to checkmating it. I may fail in the end—for foresight is not infallible—but of one thing I am positive: the end is not yet. And remember that until the fall of Thucydides my enemies were plotting continually—men far cleverer and more deeply versed in every political trick than these young men. For ten years I have had unlimited power and popularity; it is time to expect reaction and trouble. But I hope and believe I shall be able to meet both dexterously for several years to come. And I always have you! Now let us go in."

IV

There was a new excitement in Athens next day when Menon, a workman with his head full of spite and his pouch full of drachmæ, sat by the altar in the Agora and in a high shrill voice accused Pheidias for four hours on end of stealing nine of the forty-four talents appropriated for the statue of the goddess. This he iterated and reiterated until the crowds surrounding him felt as if it had been hammered like so many pegs into their skulls, never to be forgotten; and were equally ready to believe that at Olympia Pheidias would further enrich himself at the public expense.

They listened eagerly to this exposure of a hitherto trusted and too-famous man. Some turned away in disgust, but not the majority. It is not in average human nature to turn the back upon sensational disclosure and forego the pleasurable ticklings induced by the revelation of a fellow-citizen's criminal weakness. The Athenians felt more virtuous than ever. The great tragedies in the Dionysus purged their minds of pity and terror and it was as if the conviction of Pheidias would purge the community of thoughts of crime for a long while to come.

But they were doomed to disappointment. The case was brought before the court four days later and the hall crowded with men eager to witness a living tragedy. The panel of five hundred jurors sat at one end of the large room, protected from the curious by a rope. A judge was chosen for the day to keep order.

Pheidias, accompanied by Pericles, appeared before this august body. He was composed and dignified and recited his defense with the air of an innocent man. The great plates of gold, the spear, shield and helmet were brought in and weighed and the original estimates presented. One unfavorable vote would have condemned him, but he was reluctantly acquitted. There were many on the jury who hated both him and Pericles, but they had the justice of the law and the honor of Athens to uphold; he was told to go in peace.

He departed the next day for Olympia after many congratulations, but that trial left its residuum of bitterness and spite. An abortive attempt was made by Draconitides, a member of Thoron's club, to force Pericles to give a stricter account of the large sums of money that as head of the Board of Generals and Director of Public Works passed yearly through his hands; an attempt defeated by Hagnon, that able General and leader of the emigrants to the new colony, Amphipolis.

One thing the clubs did accomplish at this time however was the repeal of the restrictions on the comic poets. The

Athenians were easily persuaded that the reason for that law had long since passed and they voted unanimously for the old spice in their comedies. The poets lost no time, and in the next Dionysia bombarded Pericles with ribald wit, but for the moment ignored Aspasia. The play of Hermippus caused some consternation and much gossip in Athens. It was called *The Peacocks* and the scene was an artist's studio which served as a rendezvous for a certain prominent citizen (conspicuous by his helmet) and no less than five matrons of Athens, bent upon adventure. As each lady emerged from the inner apartment and adjusted her veil she was presented with a peacock, and the remarks made by the actor dressed up as this bird, being as witty as they were indecent, gave that ribald audience a stentorian delight.

V

Xanthippus married and left the house. Paralus finished his apprenticeship at war in the garrisons and was practicing for the chariot races to be held at Olympia. Alcibiades became the beauty of Athens and impatient of restraint, showing little deference to any one but Socrates, who sometimes lectured him into a proper state of humility; but his flatterers were many and he was the undisputed leader of all youth of his class. "That is naught to Hippoclides," was his pet retort. Pericles Y grew in beauty and intelligence. Xanthias was his pedægogus and he was far better disciplined than any other boy had been in that house. Clinias was little more than the servant of his gorgeous brother.

The marble front of the Propylæa had enhanced the magnificence of the Acropolis. It was divided into five gateways, its pediments and entablatures blazing with blue, gold and scarlet. The massive doors were not yet in place and curious visitors, driven back by the workmen, could see the Ionic columns within. Its great hall and wing were to be decorated with statues of Xanthippus and other famous Athenians of recent history; of the living, notably Pericles, who was sitting to Cresilas; and of gods goddesses and ancient heroes; the interior walls painted by Polygnotus. The beautiful Ionic temple to be called the Erectheum was begun on the northern side of the Acropolis and the little fane of Nike, that gem of Attic art, rose at the southwestern extremity.

Sophocles and Euripides won first prizes in the Dionysus, and they had few rivals; wise pessimists affirmed that Attic drama was in a state of disintegration, and saw not a flicker of genius in the younger competitors. More women were permitted to attend the classes of Aspasia, and her morning levees. Socrates' reputation increased always, and restless young men found relief from plotting in improving their minds.

All was well on the surface, but Pericles had the map ever before him of what was going on underneath.

The clubs were increasing in membership, and Thoron and Hermippus, now inseparable friends, had put their heads together and admitted certain of the Demos, among them one Cleon. This able, quick-witted, ambitious son of a tanner hated Pericles and all he represented. He dreamed—and talked loudly—of a democracy that should be one in fact, not a flock of sheep at the heels of an Eupatrid. Pericles appeared more rarely than ever in the Ecclesia, and when he did it was merely to lay down the law. A king could do no more. Athenians, smothered in roses, were no better off than Spartans under their two kings and five stern ephors. He would have Athens a great free democracy, purged of Eupatridæ; and his sympathies extended to the tributaries groaning under their heavy load. If he had his way they should pay no more yearly talents into the gorged treasury of Athens, merely send ships and men in time of war. Moreover this was the age of young men and it was time they were admitted to power—a vain dream as long as Athens groaned under the tyranny of Pericles. He talked so much and with such a mighty volume of sound that he convinced himself and others of the purity of his ideals.

He expounded his views with much discretion in the Ecclesia, where his booming voice, shrewd reasoning, and coarse humor and flattery won him applause, and never mentioned Pericles by name; but in the clubs he gave full rein to his eloquence, and shrewd men like Thoron and Hermippus were quick to see his uses. They encouraged him to sow discord among other men of his class, and conceived the policy of flattering the Demos until it must in time resent the arrogance of the man who never flattered it.

Thasson would have nothing to do with him. That serious and virtuous young man was too loyal an Oligarch to consort with democracy in any form, but he had convinced himself that Aspasia was a malignant influence in Athens, and that the only way to get rid of her before she ruined the happiness of other young men was to pull down the House of Pericles about her scheming head.

He had resumed his relations with Acestorides and they were as much together as of old, but the bloom was gone from that peach. Acestorides was, as ever, eager to learn, and his mind was really exceptional, but his character seemed to the exacting Thasson even weaker than before. He feared Phyrra but he was none the less infatuated with her. Thasson's passion for that triumphant young matron was a cold and deadly hatred. He would have liked to take her up to the top of a mountain and deliver her into the embrace of a lion.

Nor had he ever approved of Pericles, and had worked industriously to accomplish his ostracism. Thucydides gone, he longed to see Antiphon First Citizen of Athens. If this could not be there would be a profound and virtuous satisfaction in accomplishing the downfall of Pericles. The Alcmæonidæ had ever been a curse, and their record should prevent any one of them from rising to power in this enlightened age. His club was not as fertile in ideas as others, and the plotting somewhat inept as they hardly knew where to begin; but at least it kept hatred alive—or, as Thasson would more righteously have expressed it, moral indignation.

Pericles was less apprehensive than interested. He could have sent them all to his new colony Amphipolis, a colony so flourishing that it promised to rival Thurii. But one object in founding it was to extend the line of loyal clerouchiæ in the north, and it were better to keep these restless spirits under his eyes. Moreover he knew that such an act would be construed by his enemies as fear for his own political safety, and no man was less likely to make a mistake of that sort. So far they had not affected his power by one unfavorable vote. His serenity was undisturbed but he kept his eye on them nevertheless.

He soon had other reasons for apprehension and was the first to see the war clouds gathering in the Peloponnesus.

They were too far away in the beginning to attract the attention of the average Athenian as anything more than a subject for conversation in the Agora. The beautiful and flourishing island of Corcyra (Corfu), already famous as the jewel of the Ionian Sea, founded as a colony some three hundred years since by Corinth, but disdainful of the mother-city, and holding herself aloof from both confederacies, had established a colony of her own on the Illyrian coast and named it Epidamnus. Following the invariable habit, trouble arose between the Oligarchs and Democrats of this now thriving state; the latter were victorious and usurped a government that had lasted for a hundred years. The exiled Oligarchs had friends among the barbarous Illyrians, who sympathized with their grievances and plundered the fertile country without the walls. The Epidamnians sent an appeal to Corcyra but were ignored.

Corcyra, although an undutiful daughter, had made one concession to tradition in the past: when founding Epidamnus she had invited the Heracleid Phalilus of Corinth to lead the emigrants. Epidamnus, snubbed by the mother-city, consulted the oracle at Delphi and received the welcome advice to appeal to Corinth. That ambitious and still important city was not slow to see the opportunity for revenge on her recalcitrant colony, and the possibility of adding to her own wealth and consequence by its subjection. She sent a band of emigrants to Epidamnus and troops to protect them. The Oligarchs carried their wrongs to Corcyra and found her in the right temper. She was infuriated at the action of Corinth and sent a fleet at once to demand the surrender of Epidamnus and the expulsion of the new settlers. The result was a great battle between the Corinthian and the Corcyrean fleets, in which the former was defeated with a loss of fifteen ships. On the same day Epidamnus capitulated.

Corinth, enraged and humiliated, immediately set her shipbuilders to work with the expressed intention of attacking Corcyra again when her navy was redoubled. As this rapid building of many triremes progressed Athens woke up and was filled with uneasiness. Corinth's hatred of the State that had created the Maritime Empire and was now rich and powerful above all others, was well known; and so was her influence over the slow-moving but no less resentful and jealous Sparta. If she was building a great navy it must be for something more than conquest of an independent state she had civilized some three hundred years back and practically ignored until now; she aimed at nothing less than outnumbering the Athenian fleet. And if she conquered Corcyra she would add that second of Hellenic navies to her own.

This unrest was augmented when it was discovered that she was bribing sailors both in Athens and the tributaries to transfer their services to the new navy. These sailors were Metics for the most part and free to go where they pleased, and they had the love of change of their class. Many responded to the tempting invitation without asking for an increase of pay from the Athenians. The subject states smiled and made no attempt to detain their own men.

Nothing else was talked of in the Agora or wherever men gathered. The clubs were more active than ever, watching and weighing every symptom of excitement and waiting impatiently for the moment when it would be safe to strike at Pericles. With that atmosphere of peace and content gone from Athens, ugly human passions, almost forgotten, would rise to the surface and be easily manipulated.

VI

"Corinth has her grievances," said Pericles to Aspasia one evening as they were walking up and down the peristyle after Menippus, Ariphon and other anxious friends had left them. "It was she who invented the trireme, and the triremes of an old colony defeated her. Shortly after we took the town of Naupactus, at the mouth of the Corinthian gulf, we invited a large number of the Messenians exiled by Sparta after their revolution to settle there: our friends and the natural enemies of all Lacedæmon. Naupactus stands like a pirates' fort between Corinth and the open sea and lives are lost in attempting to pass it. We find no difficulty in keeping Corinth out of the Ægean, and those are only two causes for the decline of her commerce. She cannot compete with Athens in articles for use and luxury demanded by Syracuse or the cities on the Italiot coast; nor has she anything of consequence to offer the Barbarians. Had she defeated Corcyra and confiscated her navy her next step would have been to incite Sparta to action. I think there is no doubt that Corcyra, alarmed as she is, will appeal to us before long; and although it may be looked upon as a breach of neutrality, I shall not hesitate to accept her as an ally. Her navy is considerable, and joined with ours would be more than a match for any other. She could wreak ruin in the west and prevent egress from the Gulf. Corinth's navy would do her little good. . . . There are occasions when it is well to play for time, but not when the enemy is moving. You must make up your mind, Aspasia, that our fair days are approaching an end."

"I am prepared for war," she said sadly. "I have known for years that it must come and have reconciled myself as best I may. And nothing can take the past from us! Will it be a long war?"

"It would be a short war if we met them in the field! Our army would not last a month against the combined forces of the Peloponnese—and Thebes is an ally of Sparta. Her hoplites are famous. Sparta will lead that army and she has the best soldiers in the world. Her generals are quite capable of disciplining those from other States. Our men are brave enough, but they are insignificant in number and impatient of discipline. I have never encouraged the Athenians to keep a large standing army because I wished Athens to be a civilized State, not another Sparta, and our navy and our walls are a sufficient protection. I shall shut up the entire population of Attica within the walls of Athens, the Long Walls and the Piræus, ravage the enemy coast with the navy, sink their ships and wear out the invaders. Even if I collected a large army from the colonies and tributaries, Athens could not feed them. Only their ships will be of use."

"And Attica will be laid waste! All those little farms and beautiful estates. And the old olive orchards and vineyards."

He sighed heavily. "Yes, I must stand on the walls and see Attica devastated and Athenians impoverished. But there is no alternative unless I open the gates to the enemy, and Athens must be saved at all costs. I believe that three years will wear them out and I can inflict much damage on their coasts and for many stadia inland. Meanwhile there will be not only crowding and sickness and misery in the city, but an unrest that will call upon all my powers to control. Cleon and his party will vociferate in the Ecclesia, and the young men who have served in the cavalry and on the frontiers will chafe at a humiliating inaction. But they must submit. Our walls are impregnable and we shall save our monuments and our civilization. But let us change the subject. I have heard nothing of Alcibiades. Has Zopyrus?"

Alcibiades had been missing for two days and there was consternation in the house.

"Zopyrus is useless and does little but wring his hands. He fears he will be sent back to the farm. Nor has Paralus been able to trace him. I have told Xanthias to make a search of all Athens and not to return without him."

"Ariphon wishes to have him cried but I have refused. If he is dead we should hear the news only a day or two sooner, and if he is hiding in the house of some admirer the discovery could not be kept secret and he would be disgraced. Alcibiades is born to make trouble for himself and others, but he must not begin life as an outcast. I shall be glad when he attains his majority and takes himself and his fortune to his father's house. He'll be even worse when he is old enough for the women to take notice of him."

"He was such an enchanting little boy in spite of his naughtiness," said Aspasia regretfully. "He is fascinating now, the gods know, and has much good in him and kindness of disposition. But he is entirely unmanageable, and he no longer confides in me freely."

Pericles laughed. "Probably not! And don't ask too many questions. Boys are entitled to their reticences, and Alcibiades is not only a lawless spirit but too full of self-esteem to confess anything to his goddess that might lower him in her regard."

"Oh, but I do wish he would return! I am terribly worried —and so is Socrates. He came here after him when he had not seen him for two days. I could not deceive him, but of course he will keep our confidence, for he worships Alcibiades and would be the last to do him harm. I doubt if he has done anything wicked, but he inspires jealousy—and hatred, for he is very arrogant. Some one may have killed him and thrown him into the Barathrum. Alcibiades! Who should have a long and brilliant career and be buried with all pomp in the Sacred Way!"

"I have no doubt that Alcibiades will have a career," said Pericles drily. "As little as I have of his health at this moment. It is my idea that he and a few of his choice followers have put their drachmæ together and are having an orgy in some wine-house. I doubt not there are other uneasy households in Athens to-night. It would be like him to crave the experience of getting thoroughly intoxicated. When he recovers be sure he will walk in with some ingenious tale."

And half an hour later while they were still in the court, there was a loud knock at the door, and Marcus, who made the household affairs his own and had worried as loudly as Zopyrus, hastened to open it.

They heard a brief conference, and then Alcibiades sauntered in, his head high although his face was somewhat drawn and his mantle by no means as carefully adjusted as usual.

He bestowed his charming smile on his elders. "I salute you, Pellicles son of Xanthippus and beloved Aspasia," he said with the graceful courtesy that never failed him. "And I ask pardon for my two days' absence from this house and sending no message. But I went for a long ride out into the country with Alistophanes, son of Philippos, and we were so deep in discussion of the ill condition of the drama that we were at his house far in the north before we realized it. We intended to return in the cool of the evening, but we wrestled and I fell

and hurt my head." He lifted his bright mop and exhibited a
slight discoloration. "I was unconscious until this afternoon,
and I leploved him hotly for not sending a message to the house
of my guardian. I was obliged to leturn in a chariot, for I
am still weak. I will go to bed at once if you will permit."
And taking care they should have no time to answer he walked
swiftly across the court and disappeared into his own room:
all the boys after they had passed their sixteenth birthday were
moved from the inner to the outer quarters, their pedægogæ
established in adjoining rooms.

"And what do you think of that work of art!" cried Aspasia.

Pericles shrugged. "I shall make no attempt to find out
the truth. But I shall deprive him of his allowance for two
months, and Xanthias shall go with him to the palæstra and
attend him on horseback. Zopyrus can look after Young
Pericles for the present. Like Paralus that child needs no
watching."

And Aspasia for the moment forgot Alcibiades and war in
a glow of pleasure. She doubted if Pericles were fonder of
Paralus to-day than of the little boy who looked more like him
year by year.

VII

The Megarid incident gave a fresh impulse to the clubs, and
Cleon for the first time attacked Pericles openly in the Ecclesia.

Megara, once a flourishing City State with her own Long
Walls, fine crops, and articles for commerce, was now reduced
to poverty by a decree that excluded her from trading in the
markets of Athens or any part of the Maritime Empire. Shut
up within herself, with nearly a thousand profitable markets
closed to her either for export or import, she felt herself to
be on the verge of dissolution. Sparta exacted no tribute from
her allies, but she left them to shift for themselves.

Megara sent an embassy to Pericles and begged him to rescind
the decree. He peremptorily refused, for he knew that any
concession to a State as importantly situated as Megara would
be construed as weakness on his part, now that war clouds
were rising thick and fast. He suspected moreover that this

supplication on the part of Megara was instigated by Corinth as a test of his courage or intentions; although the desire of the Megarians for rehabilitation was sincere enough. And such a measure if brought before the Ecclesia would probably be defeated, for hatred of that State was intense. Not only had her rebellion cleared the road for Sparta, but it had been discovered that Megarian agents had bought large quantities of war material in Athens for Corinth and were the intermediaries for bribing sailors. Furthermore ever since the secession Attic slaves had escaped into Megara, who refused to give them up. The list of grievances was too long. To confer an inestimable benefit on a State that had nothing to offer in return would be to convey the impression to the rest of the world that Athens was in her dotage.

War was inevitable and Athens must present a calm and contemptuous front, too conscious of her power to make a single concession to her enemies; least of all to a traitor ally who had once sought to take advantage of a moment of weakness.

The Megarians bewailed their lot and had many sympathizers in Athens. The clubs saw to that. Thasson, whose intellect had no space for political acumen, was righteously indignant and delivered a beautiful essay on Callous Tyrants in the Agora. Cleon shouted in the Ecclesia that Pericles had rejected an olive branch that might have averted war, and the Oligarchs, who had never believed in the designs of Sparta and Corinth, sent private messages of condolence.

The Megarians, taking what vengeance they could, encroached upon the sacred soil of Eleusis and planted a crop. This could not be overlooked and Pericles sent a herald to Sparta to complain of an act which had caused a profound irritation in Athens. The herald was murdered not far from the frontier, and at the same time two hetæræ on their way from Athens to Corinth were detained, while another, the friend of a Megarian, and anxious for a more lucrative field, escaped into Attica.

The Athenians needed no advice from Pericles to take summary vengeance on Megara. They passed a law decreeing that any Megarian found on Attic soil should be put to death, and announced that if war was declared every General when taking his oath of office should be required to swear to invade Megara once a year. Anthemokritas, the herald, was buried ceremoniously near the Dipylon Gate.

The Megarians protested their innocence; and other things which came in due course to the ears of the comic poets. The Dionysia was near, and Hermippus, a competitor on the first day, interpolated a jingle to the effect that the Megarians had stolen two harlots from the house of Aspasia in revenge for the abduction of their own Samantha; a clever distortion that the more brilliant Aristophanes made use of in his day. But the insinuation that followed those scurrilous lines was even more deadly and far-reaching in effect. War was possible but by no means certain, philosophized Hermippus. Great wars might often be traced to trivial or disgraceful events, and more than one wanton woman had been the precipitating cause. Even the great war between Hellas and Troy, mercantile though it was, might have been averted for years, possibly for ever, had Helen not tempted a foolish boy with her shameless wiles. If Megara carried her grievances to Sparta and the result was war the Athenians would know whom to thank.

Once more Agariste stormed, but Pericles wisely refused to take action. This was no time for internal quarrels, nor for the head of the State to risk a rebuff. Aspasia's position was secure and no one believed the libels, save those who hated her and were fertile in libels of their own. Some one sent her anonymously a copy of the play when published and put on sale at the bookstall in the Agora. But although she turned hot and cold and her hands shook, she concluded to treat it with the silent contempt it deserved and dismissed it from her mind. She soon had far more important and terrible matters to command her attention.

VIII

Pheidias returned in triumph to Athens. The Olympic Games had taken place at the same time that his statue of Zeus was finished and unveiled in the huge temple erected in honor of the god. Competitors and visitors came from all parts of

Hellas for this great Pan-Hellenic festival, and political grievances were buried as long as it lasted. The Peloponnesians applauded as vigorously for Paralus when he won a chariot race with the Alcmæonid horses as if he had been bred in Sparta, and there was not a dissenting voice in the acclaim that greeted the supreme effort of Pheidias. Corinthians, Spartans, Thebans, even Megarians, agreed that an Athenian had created the most sublime work of art in the history of Earth. Athens seethed with pride, and for the moment the clubs, still bent upon Pheidias' destruction in the hope of involving Pericles, were nonplussed. But they waited patiently for the reaction that follows upon too much enthusiasm, and sowed their seeds of jealousy in a fertile field.

Their moment was closer than they had dared to hope.

Thasson, who had a ponderous love of art, was alone in the temple of Athenè one day, reverently contemplating the goddess, when it occurred to him that it would be interesting to study the small figures carved on the shield. The subject was the battle between Theseus and the Amazons; and after Thasson, greatly daring, had mounted the table sacred to bloodless offerings, and was face to face with that exquisite work of art, his discerning eye was caught by a resemblance of the more or less legendary hero to some one hardly less famous but as modern as himself. He gasped and shifted his position, looking this way and that. The warrior's face was half concealed by his spear, and the helmet covered the upper part of it, but he could not be mistaken: it was Pericles son of Xanthippus! And, also in the center, was Pheidias himself, lifting a stone with both hands.

Desecration! Abomination!

He hastened from the temple and sent messengers to summon the members of his own club and that of Thoron; he recognized the uses of activities and unscrupulous dealings that he did not care to emulate himself. Some two hours later a small procession might have been seen wending its way up the western approach to the Acropolis, to disappear through one of the lesser gates of the Propylæa.

There was none with sight too astigmatic to detect the impiety. The next day Athens was profoundly shocked; and Pheidias was arrested and ordered to appear before the court six days hence.

Aspasia had never seen Pericles in such a state of perturbation as when he came home that night; he had not returned for dinner and she waited for him in the thalamos.

"What in Zeus' name possessed Pheidias to do such a thing!" he cried as he strode up and down the room. "I have been with him for two hours and he can only moan and protest that he acted on impulse and then forgot all about it! He has ruined himself—Pheidias in the height of his career! And the scandal will be abominable! I sometimes wish I could tie all these geniuses into a bundle and throw them into the Styx!"

It was Aspasia's part when Pericles let himself go to be quietly sympathetic and understanding, but to-night she was cold with horror and could only wring her hands. "Pheidias!" she whispered. "What will they do to him?"

"Zeus knows. They have executed men before this on more trivial charges, and at the least he will be cast into prison. He is too nervous to endure it and may lose his mind. What a fate for the greatest sculptor the world has ever known!—and it is doubtful if there will ever be a greater. I might resign myself if the malice were really directed at him, but it is bitter beyond enduring that he is sacrificed on the altar of their hatred for me. I fear nothing for myself, but if I must stand by and see my friends persecuted that I may be bereft of them, or implicated with them—gods! If it were not for this impending war I'd leave Athens for ever and forget that such filth as politics existed."

"Can nothing be done to save Pheidias?"

"Nothing. If I had had warning I could have got him out of the country last night. I sent for Iolaus and told him to prepare a defense and rehearse Pheidias. He shook his head, and no wonder! The figures are there for all to see—and the temple, as you may have heard, has been crowded since morning. Oh, the ingratitude of Athenians! They boast of their men of genius—and forgive them no vagaries when they are in the mood for a victim. We are little more civilized save in externals than we were a thousand years ago."

"It seems such a little thing! If he had used me as the model for Athenè and you for the Zeus I could understand it—but two inconspicuous figures on a shield! So inconspicuous they have passed unnoticed for nearly two years."

"The impiety is not all. The Greeks worship heroes little less than gods, and our Athenians' Theseus has been desecrated by the use of a living model! They fear not only the wrath of the goddess but the vengeance of his shade. Cursed superstition! Would that it had passed before my time. Human nature is hard enough to deal with and has poison in good measure, but drained of superstition reason might sit a little more securely on her throne. Poor Pheidias!"

"Then the dicasts will condemn him! But if he is imprisoned could not he be rescued?"

"Of course I have thought of that. When the excitement is over and they have forgotten him the watchers may be bribed and he can be rushed at midnight to the Piræus and sent away in a galley. But what irony! Pheidias in exile from Athens—Pheidias to whom she owes half of her glory!"

"But she may recall him. She has recalled others when her vengeance was spent."

"It is possible—if he does not pine to death meanwhile. Artists are not politicians. Will you come for a walk? I cannot sleep."

IX

There was one accusation to be brought against Pheidias that Pericles had neglected to mention to Aspasia and he devoutly hoped she would never hear it from another. Pheidias, who hated all women but Aspasia and was barely polite to his models, "had permitted his studio to be used as a place of assignation for Pericles and certain ladies of the Eupatridæ (unnamed) after the students and workmen were gone"; and although Hermippus and Thoron, who concocted this precious document for the use of the dicasts, found it beyond their ingenuity to introduce peacocks into the studio, they asserted boldly that each lady was rewarded by finding one of those fatal birds in the aula when she returned to her lawful roof. Menon had been bribed to appear once more as a witness.

Pheidias was tried before a panel of fifteen hundred jurors— and many more of his fellow-citizens! He had recovered his composure, and recited his defense without faltering, although he knew it was weak, if ingenious. The portraiture had been unintentional. Like all artists, he often found familiar faces growing under his hands, and when his imagination was infertile he used his own. As the shield would be so high and the figures so small, he had given little thought to the faces on it; his whole attention had been devoted to the intricate carving. No one was more respectful of gods and heroes than he.

As to the shameful accusations that implicated his patron and friend, Pericles son of Xanthippus, he must ask them to take his word against that of the witness; and was not the word of Pheidias of more worth than that of a discharged and spiteful workman? His patron had often visited his studio, as all the world knew, and his students, who were always coming back after working hours were over, could testify that he never met a woman there except his wife. Pericles was above suspicion, he exclaimed with the only passion that shook his calm delivery, and all Athens knew of his devotion to the great woman he had married. That charge was as ridiculous as it was abominable; and while he could understand the indignation of Athenians at his own unintentional impiety, it was beyond comprehension that honest and intelligent men could listen to the scandal conceived by mean and envious minds in the vain hope of ruining the man to whom Athens owed her security and her greatness.

It is possible that if his trial could have been delayed six months his defense would have been accepted and he would have been dismissed with a reprimand, or at most with a fine. But with six thousand dicasts, always ready for duty if called upon, trials were never delayed, and every man present, even those neither hating nor envious, was still shocked and resentful.

His life was spared but he was condemned to a long term of imprisonment.

Pericles, for obvious reasons, did not appear at the trial, but he went with him to the prison and saw to his comfort. Pheidias was shackled, but, like other prisoners, permitted to receive his friends at all hours, and was treated with kindness by the jailers. He could order his food from a caterer and send for his own bed. But he was overwhelmed by this undeserved misfortune that had come upon him almost in the hour of his supreme triumph, and his spirit was broken. Pericles promised to see him daily, but there was little more he could do. He returned home with a heavy heart.

What next? he asked himself. What next?

x

The next was not long delayed.

Pericles and Aspasia were returning home one night from a visit to Pheidias, ill and miserable in his confinement and idleness, when they met Socrates at the door of the house.

"I have waited an hour for you, O Pericles," said the philosopher, whose face bore unwonted marks of agitation. "I will go within once more as I do not wish to be overheard."

"What now?"

"I have brought you ill news and it cannot wait, for no time must be lost. I was going to seek you."

They went swiftly to the pastas. Winter was approaching and it was too cold to sit in the aula.

"We shall not be overheard?" asked Socrates anxiously.

Aspasia opened the door leading into the andron and reassured him. She was too sad to be apprehensive and assumed that Socrates had come to tell of some new escapade of Alcibiades. But apathy left her at his first words.

"Pericles, you must get Anaxagoras out of the country at once."

"Nous!" Aspasia sprang to her feet. "What danger threatens him?"

"Thoron and that fanatical priest Diopeithes are about to accuse him to the archons of impiety; of 'disallowing things divine,' of 'inculcating things above the earth.' This is another roundabout attempt to find some weak spot in your armor, Pericles, and for your sake as much as his you must not permit him to be brought to trial. You are his patron-in-law, are you not?—and would have to appear before the dicasts in his place—"

"To-night!" cried Aspasia. "To-night!"

"Certainly, to-night." Pericles also was on his feet. "Does Anaxagoras know of this?"

"Yes. I left him to come here. He is quite calm but knows his danger in the present temper of Athens. Cleon prepared the way in the Ecclesia this morning by talking of the coming vengeance of the gods on Athens for harboring unbelievers. He was too clever to mention Anaxagoras by name, but he alarmed them; and these clubs are working continually among the dicasts and archons, counselling them to seek out and punish all who anger the gods; to 'purge the city of them before it is too late.' Athenians are so apprehensive of the designs of Corinth they are willing to believe the vengeance of the gods will take the form of immediate invasions by the Peloponnesians." He hesitated and stole a glance at Aspasia, who was standing like a statue staring out into the court. His own face blanched, but if he was about to address her he changed his mind and turned once more to Pericles. "There is no time to be lost," he said.

Pericles summoned a slave and sent for Euangelos.

"Fill a bag with gold and silver," he said to the steward. "Give it to Xanthias and tell him to meet Socrates at the outer door and go with him to the house of Anaxagoras. He will give the money to our friend and conduct him to a galley manned by trustworthy men. Hagnias son of Conon will advise him. Anaxagoras will decide upon his own destination—"

"Advise him to go to Miletus," interrupted Aspasia. "He can live in my house. It is rented to a cousin, but he has no family and it is understood that it is always at my disposal."

"He spoke of Lampascus," said Socrates, "but that is far away. It will be well to sojourn for a time in Miletus. I shall advise him."

"I must see him before he goes. He is the oldest friend I have. You will take me, Pericles—"

"No! No!" exclaimed Socrates. "You would be seen, Aspasia. And—it would do you no good. Nor Pericles. Xanthias can cover his head and pass unnoticed, but you could not disguise yourself, Pericles, and it must not be suspected that you had aught to do with his escape. I shall not be suspected, for I am known to be poor and without influence."

When he had gone Pericles and Aspasia stared at each other in silence. His face was almost as white as her own.

"Who next?" she whispered. "Who next?"

But neither dared answer that question, and they left the room feeling for the first time that they were withholding from each other a vital confidence.

XI

Anaxagoras was smuggled safely out of the State, to the indignation of Athens. But Thoron and Hermippus exchanged smiles of content. They knew the effect of unappeased appetites, knew that fear of divine vengeance would be augmented by this loss of a victim. If Anaxagoras were no longer there to be laid on the altar, there was still another human offering and one of a far more sensational importance. They were making their plans with all possible speed when a diversion occurred that claimed the excited attention of the city and forced them to suspend their activities for the present.

An embassy arrived from Corcyra and asked for an audience on the Pnyx.

It was a welcome diversion for Pericles. He put all personal matters out of his mind and was once more the cold calculating statesman.

The Ecclesia was called for the following morning and it was crowded before daylight. There was often a thin attendance of this important assembly, and criers had to go about the city, and even surround the Agora on all sides but that leading up to the Pynx with a rope covered with wet red paint, in order to secure the quorum; but on great occasions the hill overflowed and many sat on the walls. Sometimes, to make more room, stools were abandoned in the road (each man brought his own), and they stood patiently for hours.

As Pericles was making his way to the house of Ariphon, who had given up his house to the embassy, he was joined by Thucydides, still his faithful satellite and much in his confidence.

"Pericles," said that sometime General, whose brow was even graver than usual, "this means the hastening of the war; is it not so?"

"There is no doubt of that, Thucydides. Athens will be called upon to make her decision within the next few days, whether she realizes it at the moment or not. I talked with the ambassador last night, and he has come from the Corcyreans to ask admission into the confederacy—the first step!"

"And you will take that! War must come and it is well you should let these Lacedæmonians know you are prepared to defy them. For of course you will grant the wish of the Corcyreans?"

"Certainly."

"I sincerely hope I shall be elected a Strategos next summer, although I would have my life spared; for it should be a great war—involving all Hellas, no doubt—and I wish to write its history. I have my tablets with me and I shall note all that is said on the Bema to-day. Do you think it will last for many years, Pericles? You have told me of your intention to gather all Attica within the walls, and wear out the enemy—but what if the Corinthian navy should escape the vigilance of Corcyra, and what if the tributary states should revolt and withhold their navies?"

"All things are possible, but I believe that if my life is spared the war will not last three years. If it is not, these extreme democrats under men like Cleon will seize possession of our Ship of State and probably founder it. I need not ask you, Thucydides if you have spoken of my plans to any one. They must be kept a profound secret. I have told them to no one but you and my wife."

"*I?* Pericles! Your intentions are as safe with me as under your own helmet. But is it safe to confide in a woman?"

"That woman is Aspasia, O Thucydides"; and a cold wind smote the young misogynist full in the face. "You have a great mind, my young friend, but the gods neglected to furnish it with tact and discrimination. I enter here."

And he turned into the house of Ariphon, leaving his abashed but unrepentant admirer to go on to the Pnyx and take his notes.

The ambassador and his suite awaited Pericles in the courtyard, and a moment later the escort of cavalry came clattering up, the proud Paralus among them; a handsome and gallant young figure, and a reasonable and amiable youth if not a brilliant one. Xanthippus was in a different regiment and if it had been designated for service to-day no doubt he would have seen fit to fall ill. He had never crossed his father's path since the day of the wedding, and longed only for his death and the division of the estate. Meanwhile he did him what harm he could by derogations and hinted scandals.

Pericles and the members of the embassy walked the short distance to the Pnyx and took the seats of honor on the right of the Bema. The President of the day made sacrifice and poured a libation. He then invited the ambassador to address the Men of Athens, decorated his helmet with a garland, and led him to the Bema.

The Corcyrean, robed in purple heavily embroidered with gold as befitted his dignity, made a short and somewhat ingenuous oration, the pith of which was that his country was in sore straits and asked to be admitted to the Delian League. He apologized profusely for ignoring it before, but Corcyra had been animated with a desire for complete independence; a sentiment she now recognized as "weakness and folly." After dealing frankly with the apprehensions of his country over the rapid increase of the enemy's navy, Corinth's avowed intentions, and her promise of help from Lacedæmon, he passed on to the "glorious opportunity" he was offering the Athenians in securing the favor of a state that had the second navy in Hellas.

"For if any one thinks," he said with slow impressiveness, "that the war in which our services may be needed will never arrive, he is mistaken. He does not know that the Lacedæmonians, fearing the growth of your Empire, are eager to take up arms, and that the Corinthians, who are your enemies, are all-powerful with them. They begin with us but they will go on to you, that we may not stand united against a common enemy; they will not miss the chance of weakening us or strengthening themselves. And it is our business to strike first; we offering and you accepting our alliance, and forestalling their designs instead of waiting to counteract them."

He then went on to point out that the Athenians would not be breaking the treaty—the Thirty Years' Peace—with the Lacedæmonians by receiving the Corcyreans as allies, for the treaty stipulated that any Hellenic city that was an ally of no one might join either league it pleased.

There was more to the same effect, much emphasis laid on the designs of Sparta and Corinth, and the advantages to be reaped by the proposed alliance; and the warning that "if Corinth got hold of our navy and you allow the two to become one, you will have to fight against the united navies of Corcyra and the Peloponnese."

As he stepped down from the Bema the Ecclesia applauded politely; they had no intention of committing themselves until after due deliberation, and the eloquence of the orator had left them firmly planted on their feet. This was no Pericles, although what he said might be wisdom. But they would listen to their own orators first.

They had little time for comment among themselves, for their attention was immediately diverted. A Scythian archer had forced his way to the side of the President, and the latter, after lending his ear, walked to the foot of the Bema and raised his hand.

"An embassy has arrived from Corinth," he said. "It paused in the road to listen to the speech of the ambassador from Corcyra, and asks that it may reply at once."

This announcement was greeted with a loud clapping of hands and several cheers from that end of the Pnyx where the Oligarchs were foregathered. They had refrained from applauding the Corcyrean.

After much pushing and shoving by the police a way was made for the Corinthian embassy, an imposing retinue with flashing helmets, and arrayed in Persian red and massive chains set with jewels: the Corinthians were renowned for their ele-

gance and extravagance. They were escorted to the flight of
seats (hastily vacated) on the left of the Bema and exchanged
inimical glances with the disturbed Corcyreans opposite.

"They must have got wind of your coming," said Pericles.
"It was to be expected they would follow and make a counter
appeal, but I had hoped to get a favorable decision from the
Ecclesia before their arrival."

"We have a spy to thank, no doubt." The tones of the somewhat pompous ambassador were uneasy. "Will they prevail,
do you think?"

"For the moment, perhaps. I shall see that the matter is
not settled to-day. I shall instruct the Council to call three
successive Ecclesias, and not speak myself until the others have
exhausted themselves—and the Athenians are tired of listening
to them."

The President meanwhile was apologizing for the necessary
delay to the haughty gentlemen from Corinth. An archer had
been sent in all haste to the market-place for a pig and a garland, for all deference must be shown to visitors so august and
so welcome. All Athenians must regret they had not had due
warning of the honor to be conferred upon them, for the embassy should have been met at the frontier and escorted into
the city with due pomp. But many citizens would be eager to
give up their houses—

The ambassador had not condescended to reply, and the
President turned with a sigh of relief to greet the pig which was
being driven protestingly toward the altar. He caught it deftly
as it attempted to escape, sacrificed it in haste, made his invocation, then placed the garland solemnly on the gorgeous helmet
of the Corinthian, and led him to the Bema.

There was nothing conciliatory in the attitude of the gentleman from Corinth; he would have it appear that he was too
full of righteous indignation and confidence in his cause. He
launched at once into a bitter attack on the Corcyreans, accusing them of the meanest of motives in applying for admission
into the Athenian Confederacy when they were in difficulties;
asserting that their reason for avoiding both leagues was the
desire to "keep their criminal courses to themselves; where

they are strong, to oppress; where they cannot be found out, to defraud; and, whatever they may contrive to appropriate, never to be shamed."

He excoriated them for their undutiful conduct to the mother-city, and related the many indignities suffered by Corinth at their hands, more particularly during the late war; and having proved to his satisfaction and to certain of his hearers that the Corcyreans were utterly contemptible, he proceeded to demonstrate to the Athenians why they had no right to receive them as allies. If the treaty permitted the admission of unenrolled cities, that provision did not apply to those who meditated injury to the other confederacy; and if the Athenians admitted Corcyra such a proceeding would be regarded as an act of war, "They have come here to ask you to be, not their allies, but their accomplices in crime. . . . You have never received any benefit from their power, but they would now be benefitted from yours, and although innocent of their crimes, you will equally be held responsible by us."

He was a better speaker than his rival, and although he reiterated his statements, he clothed them in different words each time; his method due either to pride in his command of language or to consciousness of the weakness of his cause. He had nothing to offer but threats.

When he passed on to the obligation Corinth had laid upon Athens at the time of the Samian War he felt himself on surer ground, and his tones were still more emphatic. "At the revolt of Samos, when the other Peloponnesians were divided upon the question of giving aid to the rebels, we voted in your favor and expressly maintained that every one should be allowed to chastise his own allies."

He dismissed the warlike intentions of Lacedæmonia against the Athenian Confederacy as if it were a mere bugaboo born in the desperate brain of the ambassador from Corcyra, and ended his long speech by counselling the Athenians to consult their own interests by listening to him and following his advice.

As he gathered his mantle about him and descended the steps of the Bema with a haughty and confident air, he was greeted with violent applause in one quarter and silence in all others.

His arrogance and scoldings had not made a favorable impression, and the sharp Athenians had put their fingers on the weak spots in his arguments; nor were they deceived for a moment by his protests of the pacific intentions of Sparta. He had too much the air of a would-be conqueror spreading out his mantle to conceal the inferiority in number of the forces behind him.

The President, having escorted him to his seat, went quickly over to the right of the Bema. "Will you advise me, O Pericles?" he asked. "Shall I invite—"

"Dismiss the Ecclesia and call it for to-morrow. And the next day and the next, until every man has had his say. Then send for me."

Thoron, meanwhile, had forced his way through the crowd and invited the Corinthian embassy to take possession of his house, where they would be far more comfortable than in that of the proxenus of their city. His father was dead and he was free of all restraints. Nothing suited him better than to show honor to the Corinthians when Pericles openly favored the Corcyreans. The ambassador courteously accepted, and Thoron marched them off proudly and assured them of the success of their mission.

XII

Athens was prepared to give this momentous question her undivided attention, no doubt of that; they packed the Ecclesia daily. The Oligarchs had never permitted themselves to believe in the enmity of Sparta; they commanded attention once more on the Bema, and in favor of Corinth. They were supported by the clubs, for although many of those young men would have welcomed the excitement of war, it was against their principles to follow any example set by Pericles. Moreover war would cement his power, and no doubt he would welcome it; the clubs would be broken up and he would laugh at their former hopes and designs. There was no question as to his present intentions. He had given a banquet to the Corcyreans, and although he granted an audience to the Corinthians, he had received their protestations in silence.

Antiphon, who possessed real eloquence, ridiculed the arguments of the Corcyreans, and clothed those of the Corinthians in admirable rhetoric. Thasson made a well reasoned if rather dull speech. Thoron, who had a fiery gift of words and specious argument, drew on all his resources; and Cleon told the Demos how great and all-powerful it was, how intelligent and reflective. It was a time for it to shake off the yoke of an aristocrat who despised it, and prevent a terrible war while there was yet time.

Thucydides made a brilliant speech in favor of the proposed alliance, but he was almost as cold as Thasson. Sophocles, always an imposing figure on the Bema, and adored by the Athenians for the beauty of his middle-age, his unfailing urbanity, and the joy he gave them in the Dionysus, devoted himself mainly to advising his compatriots to follow the counsel of Pericles when he was ready to give it, and reminded them of the disasters that had always ensued when they had ignored it in the past. "For more than thirty years," said Sophocles, "you have had the benefit of his guidance, and he has led you steadily on to an unexampled greatness—and always to victory when unhampered. The well-being of Athens is as precious to him as to you, and he has no personal malice to gratify. If he does not flatter you it is because he has too high an opinion of your good sense."

Menippus, Hagnon, Phornio, all spoke. They longed for war, but were careful not to commit themselves and talked only of the indignities Corcyra had suffered at the hands of Corinth, and the advantage to Athens of having the coöperation of her navy in case of trouble.

Cleon thundered again, accusing these "intimate friends of the Tyrant" of speaking at his dictation. They pined for glory and were too short-sighted to see that Athens would immediately be devoured by a united Peloponnesus.

When the large body of Athenians whom the gods had neglected to dower with the gift of eloquence were not on the Pnyx, they put their heads together and discussed the matter soberly. They might be unreasonable, and easily excited when beset by superstitious fears, but with temporal matters to decide they were generally calm, and for the most part unprejudiced; and proud of the fact. No one wanted war and it might be well to listen to the friends of Corinth, but they would hear what Pericles had to say first.

He took his place on the Bema on the afternoon of the third day, when, as he had anticipated, the Athenians were weary of much talk and somewhat muddled. His speech was a brief one. An important state who would fain become an ally had come with her hands full of gifts that it would be the policy of fools to ignore. Sooner or later there would be war with Sparta, and it would be to-morrow if Corinth, who was playing for time, had already conquered Corcyra and confiscated her navy. He riddled the attempt of Corinth to pose as the friend of the Empire in the past. She had persuaded Sparta to refrain from interference during the Samian War in her own interest solely: she had too many exposed colonies, and she knew the danger of taking the part of an ally in revolt. She had every reason to hate Athens, and no sane man would believe for a moment that her hatred abated with the years; her commerce declined steadily and her only hope lay in conquest.

"You must make up your mind, Men of Athens," he said sternly, "that war between the Empire and the Peloponnesus is bound to come. It may not come for years, for Sparta moves slowly. You well know that I would avert it altogether if I could; you know also that I never seek war; there should be none in my time were it possible to avoid it. . . . Our only fault lies in our riches and our power, and in the beauty and magnificence of our city; we invade no territory and threaten the rights of no State, and the Lacedæmonians have not a grievance against us but that inspired by envy of our greatness.

"But whether war is near or far we must be prepared to meet it when it comes, and the friendship of Corcyra with her navy, the second in Hellas, should be welcomed by all men without debate. The navy of Corinth will be sealed within the Gulf, and that of any other State is insignificant. Athens has three hundred triremes besides those she may always command from her allies and subject states; and she has wealth in her treasury that may be drawn on for years without tax on her people.

"Nor do I regard this proposed alliance as a violation of the treaty. If we send a fleet to Ionian waters at the next outbreak of war between Corinth and Corcyra the Generals shall have strict orders not to engage in the action unless our new ally is in danger of being overcome by the enemy—when we must look to our own safety. No doubt Corcyra will be able to take care of herself; and Corinth left without excuse to attack us, even were she not severely crippled. That our admission of Corcyra into the Confederacy must be regarded as an 'act of war' was a foolish threat uttered in the hope of striking terror to hearts that have rarely known terror.

"I shall not flatter you, Men of Athens, for your ears must be weary of compliments. But I ask you, when called upon to vote, to use the foresight and judgment you have so often displayed in the past."

While the greater number of the Men of Athens were applauding and cheering, Pericles told the President to order out the urns at once. Sometimes the voting was with pebbles, but to-day large jars of black and white beans were trundled forth, and each man went up to them alone that none might know his choice. There were many black beans found in the urns that night but the majority had voted in favor of the Corcyrean alliance.

That embassy departed in triumph, the Corinthians in silence and wrath. The clubs united for conference, and when a few days later the Ecclesia met to debate on minor matters, Cleon took advantage of the occasion to explode in anger and terror over the escape of Anaxagoras. War with the Peloponnesians was now inevitable and the gods had not been propitiated. There were still those in Athens who ridiculed the immortals and inculcated their disbelief in others. If they remained unpunished, Athenè, who had saved them at Salamis, would inspire the enemy to victory. The Demos left the Pnyx in a state of uncertainty and perturbation. Many went to the temples and made sacrifice.

Pericles, who was ever on the alert, met the crafty manœuvring of Cleon with a swift counter stroke. One of the masons at work on the Propylæa had fallen from a wall and injured himself so severely that he was unconscious and believed to be dying. Pericles ordered Acron to have a casual talk with one of the doctors in attendance, discover exactly what was the matter with the man, make no suggestions, and report to him at once. That evening, as the weeping relatives and inferior doctors were crowded about the unconscious figure on the pallet, the door opened and they looked up to see a tall helmeted figure in a white mantle on the threshold. In the dim light they mistook it for a god and even when they realized it was Pericles were almost as overcome. He had never looked more awe-inspiring, more aloof from common mortals.

His deep rich voice filled the room. "Children of Athens," he said, "I have come to bring you the assurance of the speedy recovery of Donax, for Athenè in her guise as Healer, appeared to me last night in a dream and informed me of the only method by which he may be restored to life and health. I have communicated the course of treatment to the State-physician Acron, and he has come with me to administer it. He will remain here to-night, and the other doctors are welcome to remain also and witness the result of divine inspiration. I bid you farewell." And he was down the street before they could recover from their astonishment and thank him.

The man promptly revived under the ministrations of the pupil of Hippocrates, and once more the Demos felt that whatever happened they were safe in the hands of Pericles, beloved of the gods. The clubs were shrewd enough to divine the trick, and wondered gloomily if it ever would be possible to get the best of him. They were quite positive that he had arranged the escape of Anaxagoras, and kept a vigilant watch on the prison where Pheidias rarely left his bed. They must defer their plans again, but ruin Pericles in the end they would if their own lives were sacrificed in its accomplishment.

Pericles gave an order to Pyrrhos to make a statue of Athenè Hygeia, to be erected on the Acropolis in commemoration of her miraculous intervention in behalf of a humble workman.

XIII

Aspasia resolutely dismissed the fear that she had barely admitted to her consciousness. The triumph of the Corcyreans proved that Pericles' power in Athens was as great as ever, and she felt he would protect her whatever befell. If it had not been for her anxiety for Pheidias she would have been happy and gay once more, for Anaxagoras was safe with his relatives in Lampascus, and, if possible, she was with Pericles more than ever; it would seem that he could not bear to have her out of his sight. But he would not permit her to leave the house and once more she took her exercise in the aula or on the roof. He visited Pheidias daily himself and Xanthias carried delicacies from the kitchen. But Aspasia was unreconciled. She feared that she never would see Pheidias again, and there was no present hope of his escape even had he been well enough to travel.

The morning receptions, which had fallen off for a time when clouds appeared to be gathering over the house of Pericles, were now fully attended by men anxious to stand well with this woman known to be all-powerful with him, and Aspasia smiled upon them impartially. Sophocles, Socrates and her other friends had never failed her.

There was little philosophy or rhetoric talked in these days, for the impending war and the preliminary skirmishes were absorbing topics. Pericles had dispatched ten triremes to Corcyra when her war with Corinth was renewed and ordered twenty more to follow a few days later. The first through blundering were drawn into the engagement, and the treaty must be regarded as broken. The Corinthians, however, were getting the best of it when they saw the second fleet on the horizon. Believing that the entire Athenian navy had come to the rescue of Corcyra they retreated in haste—and sent envoys to Sparta. Athens had now nothing to lose and Pericles took the next step.

In the northern Ægean, on the island of Pellene, Corinth had established the colony of Potidæa, almost as important a City State as Corcyra, but still dutiful. She was a tributary ally of Athens, for she needed the protection of her navy against the Persians, but consented to admit Corinthian magistrates into her government. Pericles determined that the intentions of this critically situated ally should be determined at once; and there was no time to be lost, for Perdiccus, King of Macedonia, the most fickle and treacherous of potentates, had suddenly withdrawn his friendship from Athens and was employing all his craft to incite Sparta to enter upon a war in which he might find much profit for himself. If Potidæa revolted, Perdiccus, with whom the Athenians were already in difficulties, would incite the Chalcidian cities to follow suit.

Pericles stated the danger to an alarmed Ecclesia and they voted him full powers as ever. He sent an immediate demand to Potidæa to raze her walls and give hostages for good behavior.

No state could be expected to make such a submission without protest. Potidæa sent an embassy to Athens to beg its indulgence, and make due protestations of fidelity. But Pericles was inexorable, and the embassy went on to Sparta.

There were already thirty ships and one thousand hoplites in the north, watching Perdiccus and in league with his brother and enemy Philip. Pericles sent this force orders to besiege Potidæa, now in open revolt. Corinth sent sixteen hundred hoplites and four hundred light infantry to the relief of Potidæa.

Athens was in a ferment once more. For the first time war with the Peloponnesus seemed really imminent, for it became known that Sparta had promised Potidæa that if Athens refused her indulgence she would invade Attica. Cleon shouted in the Ecclesia, and the clubs met openly in the Agora and demanded the arrest of Pericles. Pericles replied by sending another force, of two thousand citizen hoplites, to Potidæa, and the clubs were depleted. They understood his policy and felt there was no time to lose.

The Demos would not listen to the agitators, for if war must come there was no one to take the place of Pericles and they could not do without him. Cleon had sown the seeds of resentment for his high-handed methods, and their blind love for him had sensibly diminished, but they would as soon have dethroned their gods while danger threatened. They valued their lives and their city too highly to give way to anger and jealousy, and they more than half believed that he was under the protection of Pallas Athenè. Perhaps one secret of his power was that Olympian repose of which the comic poets made sport and which no one had ever seen ruffled. Other Generals had erected trophies, but they were often seen in excited discussion, and lost their tempers like other men. There was something godlike about Pericles son of Xanthippus, and, like the gods, he failed in nothing he undertook. If one resource was ineffective he promptly found another. He alone had achieved the highest ideal of the Greeks. Nevertheless their ingrained sense of equality and hatred of superiority sometimes rebelled, and if Sparta could be kept at bay, and the peaceful atmosphere of Athens restored, there might be a profound satisfaction in seeing him reduced to the common level—for a time. But for the present Pericles was Athens and Athens Pericles.

XIV

"What will the next step be?" asked the serious gentlemen as they paced the colonnade of Pericles' house. It was winter again but the day was bright and mantles heavy and warm. They never went indoors during the morning and late afternoon unless the rain fell and sometimes not then.

"I hear," said Sophocles to Phormio, who was chafing at inaction, "that the Spartan king is still hesitating in spite of his promise to Potidæa—would that he would hesitate forever!"

"You will have time no doubt to compete twice in the Dionysia before they do anything," growled Phormio. "But at least the trouble in the north will not be settled in a hurry and Pericles, thank the gods, has promised to send me when reënforcements are necessary."

"And I, thank the gods, am not likely to be elected a Strategos again. I did as well as any one could, and Pericles commended me, but if the Athenians think I am no general so much the better. I have no disinclination to fight, but I prefer to serve under Pericles. I hope I may take part in the defense of Athens, for there will be much time to write and to see my friends meanwhile. But tell me, Phormio—you are second in military wisdom to Pericles only: when do you think Sparta will move?"

"As well ask when a sleeping crocodile on the Nile will wake up—gorged and comfortable and in no immediate need of prey. But Corinth is ever at the ear of Sparta and has advocates among the ephors. Sthenelaidas, the most powerful among them, is for an immediate declaration of war, but the old king thinks there is not money enough in the treasury, and what not. They all talk interminably. Meanwhile Corinth has sent envoys to all the Peloponnesian States, save Argos and Acarnania, who hate both, warning them they will suffer the fate of Potidæa if they do not take up arms and add their arguments to hers. More talk!"

"What are Pericles' plans? Do you know? How are we to meet that great army with our insignificant forces—most of them half-trained citizens?"

"Pericles' plans are known to no one—save possibly to Aspasia. But be sure he has them matured. I can only guess—and long to get out of Athens!"

They paused before Aspasia, who was discussing with a group the prospect of long-drawn-out trouble in the north. She was enveloped in a violet mantle, and a veil of the same color protected her head; no matter what her words of wisdom her intellectual admirers never failed to notice they were talking to a beautiful woman.

"And will Pericles go to Potidæa?" asked Sophocles.

"Oh, no!" Aspasia spoke with assurance. She knew that Pericles would never leave her again if he could help it, and he had able Generals this year. "Not while he has Phormio." And she smiled at the gratified Strategos.

"Do you know how soon he will send the next reënforcements?" he asked eagerly.

"Not the date, but I know it will not be long now, for things are not going well—here he comes."

Pericles had left his office, and sauntered toward them. He paused to speak to several of his guests, but reached Aspasia's side in a few moments.

"I see by your corrugated brow, Phormio," he said smiling, "that you are in your usual state of discontent. But I bring you happiness. Ten days hence you will take two thousand hoplites to the north, and I do not doubt you will then have action enough."

Phormio refrained with difficulty from raising a war-cry. "I go at once to make my preparations!" he exclaimed. "Aspasia, I ask your permission to retire."

Pericles laughed. "Your brow is as smooth as mine! Take those citizen-hoplites out on the plain and drill them. They are raw enough!"

As Phormio was turning into the narrow entrance hall he collided with a man of mean appearance who was entering hurriedly.

"A court herald!" said Pericles. "What has he to do here?" And unconsciously he caught Aspasia's hand under her mantle.

The man walked forward and paused beside the altar, while all ceased their conversation and stared at him in wonderment.

"I have a message from the court, O Pericles son of Xanthippus," he said in a loud voice. "You are summoned to appear before the dicastery four days hence as the patron-in-law of the Milesian Aspasia, there to defend her against the following charges: disbelief in the gods, and furthering your intrigues with free-born Athenian ladies under this roof. If convicted the sentence will be death, but the law permits you to defend her and disprove those charges if you can. She will remain in this house under guard until the just decision of the court is rendered."

As these horrible words assaulted the ears of that distinguished assemblage there was a moment of frozen silence; and then several of the men, Menippus and Socrates among them, made an involuntary rush at the herald, but he escaped nimbly. The aula was filled with a roar of indignation. A few slunk away, but the rest—there happened to be no women present—crowded about Pericles and Aspasia, uttering disjointed phrases —promises of help—curses on the despicable men who had perpetrated this outrage.

She had swayed slightly for a moment, but stood erect and calm as all eyes turned toward her. Pericles had not moved a muscle of his face although all color had left it.

"It was to have been expected, my friends," he said. "And I am not unprepared."

"But she must escape—at once!" cried Socrates, whose eyes, always bulging, looked as if about to leave his head. "It can be done at midnight—"

"I shall not run away," said Aspasia, who had summoned all

her pride. "I am innocent, and Pericles will be able to prove it. Nor would you run from your enemies, Socrates."

"But you are a woman!" Socrates, ardent and brave within his grotesque exterior, longed to pick her up and flee to the coast.

"I am the wife of Pericles," said Aspasia proudly. "He will always turn his face to the enemy and so shall I."

"O Zeus!" cried Sophocles. "That such things should be in a civilized State! That such men should be permitted to live! It is they who should be thrown alive into the Barathrum."

"She shall be saved," exclaimed Menippus, "if I have to incite civil war in Athens!" He knew by this time of the gossip the clubs had started about his wife, and that she was one of the unnamed women mentioned in the accusations against Pheidias. His knowledge of the bitter falsity of those scandals fired his wrath to-day.

Pericles spoke again. "I appreciate your sympathy and indignation, my friends," he said, and his tones had never been more even. "But I insist that you do nothing rash. It would make matters worse—and they are bad enough. But I shall save Aspasia. Make no doubt of that."

There were more execrations and protestations, but they left in a few moments; they knew that, however intimate, their continued presence was an intrusion. Those two must long for solitude, and they had much to discuss!

Aspasia and Pericles walked as if by instinct to the thalamos, and there for a moment they clung to each other like two ship-wrecked beings on a rock surrounded by a hungry sea. There was a new passion in their straining arms, for they seemed destined to sound every phase.

"Can you save me, Pericles?" she whispered with chattering teeth, for there was no need for pretense here. "Shall I have to drink hemlock?"

"I shall save you. One way or another. I do not even contemplate life without you. I believe the dicasts will listen to me and I have many friends among them this year."

"But what can be said in my defense? I have never spoken of my disbelief to any but our intimate friends, who would not deliberately betray me; but they may have talked carelessly among themselves and been overheard. Even if you asserted there was no truth in the accusation those men will not believe! And it is equally impossible to disprove that other foul accusation—as impossible as it would be to prove it! They well know they can find no witnesses, for none of our slaves could be bribed—that is what terrifies me so. It is as if they had already made up their minds."

"If they will not accept my defense, then Phornio and his hoplites will surround you until you are safe in a galley and on your way to Miletus—"

"To leave you to fall a victim to the vengeance of which I am but a tool! . . . You would not flee with me?"

"I could not do that."

"Then I remain here. Far better to drink hemlock than drag out lonely years pursued by the furies of remorse, for they would execute you—"

"Put that thought out of your mind. I might be in danger in a time of assured peace, but not now. And although the separation would be intolerable I do not believe it would last long. When war comes and they think of nothing else, they will give an indifferent consent to your return. So take courage, dear head."

XV

Not even during the worst days of the Samian War had such an atmosphere of gloom pervaded the house. The servants moved about like shadows, weeping and wringing their hands, in spite of severe reprimands from Aspasia. Pericles Y refused to go to school and looked as if his arrogant happy boyhood had been blighted for ever. Paralus was at the breeding farm. Alcibiades did not leave the house. He was nearly eighteen and of age and about to enter the army and become master of his fortune. He stood for the most part with folded arms leaning against a pillar, frowning and speechless. It was his first glimpse of the stark realities of life, and he was not only bewildered but filled with shame that his great gifts, his wealth, and his increasing importance counted for naught in this terrible drama. One way or another his goddess would be sacrificed, and when he was not stifled with rage he was overwhelmed with self-pity that he should see her no more. He cuffed Pericles Y occasionally to relieve his own feelings.

Xanthias alone was cool and collected. He had been rehearsed for his own part in the escape, and would accompany Aspasia and the boy to Miletus. No one seemed to doubt the verdict.

Pericles had arranged to appear before the court in the afternoon, pleading pressure of work in the morning. The winter days were short, and Phormio and his troops would be waiting behind the house to spirit Aspasia away in the dusk before the police could arrive to arrest her. Hagnias would have a galley in readiness; indeed the entire Piræus would cover her retreat if need be. The popularity she had won on the day of Galatea's wedding had never diminished, and she had enhanced it by lunching at more than one Metic table.

Aspasia, in spite of Pericles' unruffled serenity, was persuaded that sentence of death would be passed upon her, and although she confided in no one but Agariste, she had made up her mind not to flee. She was convinced that if she did, even the Demos, keen though it was on self-preservation, and resting its hopes on Pericles, would yield to a fury kindled by superstition and consent to his execution. She was far too Greek to be imbued with a desire for martyrdom, and would have smiled at the thought of sacrificing herself for the sake of Athens, but to do Pericles a mortal injury would be an odd way of showing her own love, and he had still many years before him in which to prove his genius and add to his fame. Nor had she any wish to live without him. If her happiness were over let it end in death not in exile and remorse.

When she had confided her purpose to Agariste, that daughter of Xanthippus had agreed that if Fate demanded a victim she must offer herself. Alcibiades was to go to court with Pericles on the day of trial, and if an unfavorable verdict seemed imminent would slip out and give warning. Aspasia would then make some excuse to go to the thalamos, before putting herself under the protection of Phormio, and evade Xanthias by passing through the adjoining rooms—to meet the police at the front of the house.

"I feel like a Spartan!" cried Agariste wildly, when the plot was perfected. "But it must be, Aspasia. Pericles son of Xanthippus and First Citizen of Athens may not be sacrificed to a woman. I would be as inexorable with myself if I were in your place. And after all, you have had your day—and there is nothing but unhappiness ahead for any of us. Women will be of less account than ever, and you will be happier in your urn than many you leave behind full of health and desires. We have sons and husbands to fall on the battlefield, and follow, wailing, to the Ceramicus. But I shall weep bitter tears, Aspasia, for your noble contempt of death endears you to me more than ever."

XVI

It gave Pericles some measure of consolation that it was raining on the afternoon of the trial and the sky black as night. There would be no one abroad to detect the men who would assemble behind the house at the proper moment, and give warning of a well-matured plan. A police-slave stood on either side of his entrance door, but those at the back could be easily overcome.

The aula, that scene of so many distinguished gatherings, was a desolate sight. The rain fell in torrents and the wind dashed it against the pillars. Achilles, forgotten, took refuge in the colonnade, folded his tail, and looked as gloomy as Fate. Old Marcus bolted the door behind his master and returned to his bed to groan with rheumatism and woe.

There had been no parting between Pericles and Aspasia, although it might be years before they met again; but he must leave the house with his faculties in perfect order, and there were some things beyond human endurance. By mutual consent they had not alluded to the subject since the first day.

She awaited the verdict in the andron with Agariste, Socrates, Sophocles, Menippus and Pericles Y. Many had begged to spend these last hours with her and she had refused all but the few who loved her best. Glaucon and Menippus had sent their wives to the country. Phyrra, who took no interest whatever in politics and knew nothing of the clubs and their designs upon Pericles, was about to have her fifth child and concluded it were best to stay at home and read philosophy.

Aspasia had welcomed these few devoted friends, for she dreaded nothing more than solitude and she could always rely on her pride. She sat calmly in a marble armchair and endeavored to draw them into a discussion on some one of their favorite topics; but there was little response. Agariste stalked up and down muttering incoherently. Menippus stared gloomily at the door. Socrates sat with his head in his hands. Pericles Y stood by his mother's chair endeavoring to look as serene and lofty as his father. Xanthias had threatened him with a beating if he shed a tear, and he knew the weight of that hand. But he was a proud boy, and, only half-comprehending the danger, felt that if calamity invaded the house he was there to defend his mother. All wore their warmest mantles, for a fire on the central hearth would have filled the room with smoke, and the portable stoves in that large room were inadequate. But no one expected to be comfortable in winter. All the lamps were lit and the room, if cold, was brilliant in effect.

Only Sophocles, although he took a turn up and down the room occasionally, maintained his ordinary composure and managed to look almost genial as he endeavored to raise the spirits of the company.

"Come! Come!" he exclaimed. "The time is not yet for a funeral feast in this house. The greatest outrage in the history of Athens has been perpetrated but think how much worse it would be if our Aspasia were really to drink hemlock. She has only the winter seas to fear, and there will be no danger for her there with the skilled seamen Hagnias has chosen. A few days hence and she will be safe in Miletus in her own house—if the verdict is unfavorable, which is by no means certain. If she must leave us we shall be disconsolate at her loss, but how the knowledge of her safety will aid us to bear it! And when Athens is at war she will return. Then we shall all for ever dismiss this terrible episode from our minds—"

"Episode!" exclaimed Socrates bitterly. "It is a wonder you did not say 'act,' for you see all things in the terms of drama. I am not questioning your love for Aspasia, but can you deny that you are secretly thrilled at taking part in a great living tragedy instead of writing about ancient horrors?"

Sophocles flushed, but answered calmly: "I hope you are mistaken, Socrates, and I am sometimes reproached for being so much a man of the world in society and so little the poet. It is quite true however that if it were the fashion to write of our contemporaries I should make Aspasia the heroine of my next drama, and I am sure it would be the finest."

Aspasia deliberately summoned her Ionian levity. "Oh, write it and hide it away for posterity to discover, dear Sophocles," she cried. "And make me do valiant things. My life has been wonderful and happy but it has not been dramatic. I, who have been the spectator of so much drama here in Athens! But only a spectator. What can you think of, Sophocles? I, myself, can think of nothing, for I would not have my life other than it has been. But suppose I had never met Pericles, or had come as an unknown adventuress to Athens? Could you not cast me in the rôle of a villain?"

"Oh, yes, dear Aspasia," said Sophocles, smiling. "If Fate had been less kind you might have been a very wicked woman indeed. A little less intellect—a little more ambition—less pride and more love of excitement and change—shall we say a little less of the goddess and more of the Ionian— Oh, I shudder to think of the part you might have played in our poor Athens!"

"Then you will write it?" asked Aspasia gaily. "Promise me."

"Oh, Aspasia!" cried Socrates. "You give me courage for all my life! If my turn ever comes to fall under the ban of Athens I shall remember this day and be ashamed to do less than emulate you."

"You will have your own courage, dear Socrates," said Aspasia tenderly. "And no doubt will need it far more. Remember that I am to be rescued—"

"That again fills me with misgivings. Suppose Athens discovers your destination and sends a trireme to Miletus to demand your return? They would not dare refuse to give you up."

"You speak wisdom, Socrates. Perhaps it would be better if I went directly to Lampascus. Anaxagoras writes me that he is well and as happy as he ever can be out of Athens. We should have many subjects for discourse!"

"By far the better plan. You will instruct the captain of the galley, Menippus?"

"I agree with you, Socrates. The captain shall merely obtain fresh rowers in Miletus."

"Are you going away, mother?" asked Pericles Y in surprise. "I have not been told. But you will take me with you?"

"You may be told now," said Aspasia, and for the first time she turned pale. "That is the plan and of course I should not leave you behind."

Her levity had deserted her. She turned to Sophocles. "I fear we are not in the mood for conversation. But we rely upon you to keep us from thinking of the ordeal Pericles is undergoing at this moment. Will you not tell us of your new tragedy?"

"Tragedy!" muttered Socrates.

"I have but half finished my *Electra:* a great and remorseless character, whose possibilities, it seems to me Æschylus neglected. It will give me great pleasure to read what I have written if I may be permitted to summon a slave and send to my house for the manuscript."

His house was close by and when the slave returned he pushed a chair near one of the lamps and, holding the roll far from his eyes, began to read the great drama that was to enthrall audiences as far apart as the poles for centuries to come. No cultivated Greek, no matter in what dolour of circumstance, could resist intellectual display. Socrates forgot to brood. Agariste sat down abruptly, and even Aspasia, with Death at her elbow, throbbed with righteous hate and a cold desire for vengeance. That rough soldier Menippus growled at Clytemnestra's defense. Only Pericles Y was inattentive. His mind was filled with coming adventure and he finally slipped out to seek Xanthias and learn full particulars.

Then I will speak! Electra's tones could not have been more saturated with scorn and contempt than those of the poet who was about to give her immortality.

> *You say you slew him.*
> *Where*
> *Could there be found a confession more depraved*
> *Even though the cause were righteous? But I'll prove*
> *No rightful vengeance drew thee to the deed,*
> *But the vile hands of him you dwell with now—*

The door leading into the pastas was flung open violently and Thucydides stood before them. His hair and mantle were dripping with rain and the mud of Athens had splashed to his knees. His eyes were blazing with anger, his chest heaving as if he had been running, and even Sophocles dropped his manuscript and stared at him. The others had sprung to their feet with white faces and arrested breath, for he looked the bearer of ill tidings.

"What is it?" cried Menippus, whose right hand had gone to his dagger. "Cannot you speak?"

Thucydides regained his wind but not his usual air of gravity and contemptuous detachment.

"I slipped from the court before Alcibiades, who was still too enthralled to remember his orders," he exclaimed in biting accents. "I wished to be the one to tell you, Aspasia wife of Pericles, that you are free—and at what cost! Ah! You all look as if I had brought good news indeed. It may be good news that you are not to drink hemlock, Aspasia, nor to run ignominiously from Athens. But what of Pericles? O Zeus! I have spent the most agonizing hour of my life—"

"Pericles!" Aspasia grasped the back of a chair, trembling violently. "They could not make him suffer in my place—that is not the law—"

"No, he will not drink hemlock, nor be put to the sword. Fear not, Aspasia, he will return to you. But he has lost to-day what is dearer than his life. His pride, Aspasia—and for a *woman!* His pride! That glorious majesty and remoteness that the comic poets may well call Olympian and has

made him seem to us little short of the gods. He defended
you brilliantly, but those fifteen hundred dicasts were unmoved,
for he had no proof to offer. They might be made to believe
that one part of the accusation was slander, but they were convinced you had no respect for the gods and had corrupted
others. And then, when he saw that even he—the greatest
orator of any time—he, Pericles, who has moulded six thousand
minds on the Pnyx into one, could not convince them of your
innocence and knew that the sentence would be death—then
he suddenly broke out into a passionate plea that you should
not be taken from him. He begged them to remember that he
had given his life to Athens and asked only this boon in return.
That golden voice broke, he shed tears—he, *Pericles,* wept in
public, in the sight of three thousand men, for that courtroom
was crowded! He wept. He pleaded. He vowed he could not
live without you— O Zeus, that I should live to see this day!"

"What superb art!" cried Sophocles irresistibly. "Would I
had been there to witness it!"

"And you think naught of his humiliation?" Thucydides
looked as if he would spring upon Sophocles and strike him.
"But a poet is no better than an actor in a mouthing mask.
Pericles was made by the gods for the Bema, not for the
Dionysus. And although he has won—for the jury, too, wept
and went down before that terrible eloquence—his pride must
be shattered within him—"

"Nonsense!" exclaimed Sophocles, whose robust common
sense never deserted him, for he was unique among poets. "He
had a great part to play and he played it greatly. Pericles
never fails. He might not have chosen that part in preference
to others, but the case was desperate and he did not hesitate.
For he did not break down, Thucydides. That was calculated,
no doubt written out and committed to memory before he left
the house. Make no mistake about that." He turned to
Aspasia, who had sunk into a chair and covered her face with
her hands. "Do not weep," he said gently. "Or only over
an anticlimax. That is not the tragedy in real life it may be
for the poet in his study. I accept this great anticlimax without
a shudder, for it leaves you with us and your danger is over—"

"Danger, yes!" interrupted Agariste. "But Thucydides is right. Pericles has demeaned himself. Far better for Aspasia to have escaped from Athens. He said himself she would have been permitted to return in time." She forgot for the moment Aspasia's determination to give herself up.

"Far better as it is," said Sophocles. "For who knows what might have happened between here and Piræus? Pericles knew that the only real safety lay in acquittal. And others might have been executed for that rescue."

"Where is Pericles?" demanded Agariste. "It is significant that he did not hasten to bring the news himself."

"He was summoned to the prison," said Thucydides grimly. "Pheidias is dying."

Sophocles' humor deserted him at once. "This is ill news indeed! I too must go and bid farewell to Pheidias. This, at least, is no fault of yours, Aspasia. Give me a message for him. You must not leave the house for many days."

"Women are a curse!" cried Thucydides, and turned on his heel. Socrates sighed deeply and followed him, after awkwardly patting Aspasia's bowed head. He had been married to Xanthippe for three years, and agreed with Thucydides.

When Aspasia was alone with Agariste she raised her face for the first time. It was drawn and haggard but not tear-stained. "When Zenophile was dying," she muttered, "she told me to go back to Miletus. It would have been well if I had taken her advice."

Agariste gave a laugh that was more like a bark. "Let Pericles decide that! I do not understand this love that makes fools of mortals and drives even a Pericles to make an exhibition of himself in public; and I thank the gods for making me a sensible human being, if a woman. I am very fond of you, Aspasia, for I cannot help myself; the gods gave you an irresistible fascination; but I wish you had never come to Athens. And—I fear this may make Pericles hate you. The gods on Olympus are not prouder than he."

Aspasia shook her head. "You do not know his real pride if you believe that, Agariste. Not only has he made an art of life, but in the balanced development of all virtue he alone has reached the highest ideal of the Greeks. There is no room in that nature for petty rancor and mean resentment. He may be suffering now, but he will put that humiliating ordeal of to-day out of his mind to-morrow."

And when he came home to her late that night, he dismissed the subject briefly and talked only of Pheidias who had died an hour before. He had obtained permission to bury him in the Sacred Way, if without honors. Pheidias was not to be cast into the Barathrum, the common fate of criminals. But although they had much to be thankful for, they knew that the shadows were closing about them, and their old consummate joy in life and each other could never return.

XVII

Archidamus, the old king of Sparta—Pleistoanax was still in exile—was laboriously making up his mind that the time had come to make war on Athens; and although several of the ephors still hesitated, they were forced into final acquiescence by Sthenelaidas, the strongest among them. But the king still hesitated and sent an envoy to Delphi to consult Apollo. The ambiguous utterances of the Pythoness, sitting on the tripod in the cave of the temple and inspirationally intoxicated by the mephitic vapor rising from the cleft, were construed as a promise of the god to conduct them to victory.

But no power mortal or immortal could hurry the Spartans. While Corinth, fearful for Potidæa, fumed and importuned, they sent an embassy to Athens to demand the expulsion of Pericles. This seemed to them an opportunity too precious to be neglected, convinced as they were, by the persecution of his friends, that his power was waning. With him out of the way victory would be assured. In no ambiguous oracle-phraseology the ambassador was to stand on the Pnyx and order the Athenians to "drive out the curse of the goddess."

Athens herself had well-nigh forgotten that curse. Nearly two hundred years before an ambitious Athenian named Cylon, supported by a number of restless young aristocrats and encouraged by another ambiguous oracle, had seized the Acropolis while the great festival of Dionysia was going on in The

Marshes. He held the fort for a time, and the Athenians recovered from their excitement and went about their business leaving the Nine Archons to conduct the siege with a troop of horsemen. The First Archon was Megacles the Alcmæonid, a man ruthless and determined, who never erred on the side of mercy.

When the little garrison was on the verge of starvation Cylon and his brother managed to escape. The others, who had taken refuge at the altar in the temple, sent a herald to announce their willingness to surrender if promised immunity. Megacles and his men entered the Acropolis, whose gates had been left open, the rebels being safe in sanctuary. They were promised their lives, and issued forth. Megacles ordered them to be cut down to a man, the blood of several staining the sacred steps of the temple. Those who ran back were slain while clinging to the altar.

Megacles apparently was no psychologist. A fearful outcry arose. Suppliants were sacrosanct and the goddess herself had been insulted. Megacles was tried before the Areopagus and banished with the entire Alcmæonid clan. Nor were they recalled until they had rebuilt out of their own funds a part of the temple of Delphi, destroyed by fire. But the memory of the "curse of the goddess" lingered in the minds of their fellow-citizens until the Battle of Marathon, and no doubt inspired the story that an Alcmæonid had signalled the Persians from a height above the field; an accusation never proved and in this day forgotten by all but the enemies of Pericles.

When the embassy arrived in Athens it was greeted by a full Ecclesia, for all expected a declaration of war. But when the ambassador stated the purpose of his visit and demanded they "drive out the accursed thing," they burst into a roar of indignation. Antiphon, Thoron and Cleon endeavored to take advantage of this unexpected opportunity, but their arguments in favor of obeying the behest of Sparta were listened to with impatience and even derision. The embassy was told to go home and tell Sparta to remove her own curses—she had two— and Pericles' old popularity was restored in an hour. If the enemy both hated and feared him, so much more worthy was he of their honor and respect. Moreover, they felt he had been punished enough and their mercurial temperaments were in the usual state of reaction.

The insult to the embassy should be the last straw, cried the Corinthians, Megarians, Bœotians, Leucadians, Phocians, Ambraciots, Anactorians, Locrians, bombarding the ears of dilatory Sparta. But she would not listen and sent another embassy to Athens to demand that she raise the siege of Potidæa, rescind the decree of Megara, restore Ægina to independence, and, if she would avert war, dissolve the Empire, returning to all subject states their former independence and relieving the allies of their heavy yearly tribute.

Even the clubs were stunned at the last condition, for they had no desire to become the citizens of a poor City State, impoverished in purse as in importance. Cleon himself was undecided, and hesitated to risk his popularity by making an appeal to the Athenians to yield to the demands of Sparta and avert war; nor was he as enthusiastic as might have been expected at this opportunity to realize his ideal.

But the Oligarchs had more courage. They knew that the Athenians were appalled at the prospect of war, and argued on the Bema that no doubt if the siege of Potidæa were raised, and the Megarian decree rescinded, the Spartans would agree to withdraw their demand for the dissolution of the Empire. They spoke with eloquence and much speciousness, and were listened to not unwillingly, for these able men could be sent as ambassadors to Sparta to persuade that dreaded State to modify her outrageous demands.

Pericles let them talk for two days and then took his place on the Bema. No man had been driven to the Pnyx that day by the fear of red paint on his mantle. Even the surrounding hills were crowded, and Metics filled the road and the upper end of the Agora; for all knew that on this day their fate must be decided once for all.

Pericles, always the astute politician, gave no peremptory orders on this momentous occasion. He was there to convince, and his melodious voice was friendly and persuasive, his discourse logical and steeped in incontrovertible common sense.

He adopted the tone of a man among equals, discussing a topic of profound importance with reasonable fellow-citizens who could have but one opinion. His whole discourse was a subtle flattery that Cleon could never achieve.

"Athenians," he began, "I say, as I always have said, that we must never yield to the Peloponnesians, although I know that men are persuaded to go to war in one temper, and act when the time comes in another, and that their resolutions change with the changes of fortune. But I see that I must give you the same or nearly the same advice that I gave before, and I call upon those whom my words may convince, to maintain our united determination, even if we should not escape disaster. The movement of events is often as wayward and incomprehensible as the course of human thought; and this is why we often ascribe to chance whatever belies our calculations."

He went on to point out that while the designs of the Lacedæmonians had been clear enough, they had ignored the treaty in not asking for arbitration. He recapitulated the demands of the Spartans, so insulting in tone and so impossible to comply with, and once more the Athenians seethed with wrath. He impressed upon them the indubitable fact that if they agreed to any of those demands, others more oppressive would immediately be dictated. Only firmness would make the Spartans understand that the Athenians must be treated as equals. "Wherefore make up your minds once for all either to give way while you are still unharmed, or, if we are going to war, as in my judgment is best, then on no plea, small or great, to give way at all. Any claim, the smallest as well as the greatest, imposed on a neighbor and an equal, when there has been no legal award, can mean nothing but slavery."

His argument on the respective wealth of the two confederacies was sufficiently convincing to the Athenians. Their own, in gold, silver and treasure, was practically inexhaustible and augmented yearly. The Peloponnesians were little more than farmers and would be in a constant state of anxiety over their finances. Sparta exerted no such control over her allies as Athens over the members of the Delian League and must ever

wait on their assembling in Sparta and on votes, always cast
in their own interest, not in that of the confederacy. "Their
greatest difficulty will be the want of money which they can
only procure slowly; delays will thus occur, and war waits on
no man." He told them of his intention to ravage the Peloponnesian coasts and predicted that its navies would not, dare
meet the Athenian; they were not only inferior in number but
their men knew little of seamanship. "They are tillers of the
soil, not sailors. They will not be permitted to practice, for
a large fleet will constantly be lying in wait for them. . . . If
they attack our country by land we shall attack them by sea;
and the devastation of even a part of the Peloponnesus will be
a very different thing from that of all Attica. For they, if
they want fresh territory, must take it by arms, whereas we
have an abundance of land both on the islands and on the
continent; such is the power which the empire of the sea gives."

There was a slight stir of uneasiness at the words that followed, for they received their first hint of his intentions. "We
should not under any irritation at the loss of our property give
battle to the Peloponnesians, who far outnumber us. If we conquer we shall have to fight over again with as many more; and
if we fail, besides the defeat, our confederacy, which is our
strength, will be lost to us; for our allies will rise in revolt when
we are no longer capable of making war on them. Mourn not
for houses and lands, but for men; men may gain these but
these will not gain men. If I thought you would listen to me
I would say to you: "Go yourselves and destroy them, and
thereby prove to the Peloponnesians that none of these things
will move you.'"

Then he counselled them to send the ambassadors away, re-
fusing all their impertinent demands; and with the warning
"that we do not want to begin a war, but intend to defend ourselves if attacked."

There was more to the same effect, and an allusion to their
fathers who had fought and conquered the Persians, with far
fewer resources than their sons had to-day. "We must be
worthy of them and resist our enemies to the utmost, that we
may hand down our empire unimpaired to posterity."

When he left the Pnyx he had convinced the Athenians, and the Ecclesia voted to inform the ambassadors that they "would do nothing on compulsion, but were ready to settle their difficulties by arbitration upon fair terms according to the treaty." So the embassy went home, and there was nothing to do but await the final move from Sparta.

XVIII

There was one person in Athens who gave little thought to the coming war, and that was Alcibiades. His own great day was impending: he was of age and about to be the principal figure in ceremonies to which he had long looked forward with impatience. These ceremonies had been delayed owing to the pressure of more important events, but they were to take place on the day following the departure of the last embassy from Sparta.

"And shall you be glad to leave us, Alcibiades?" asked Aspasia. It was raining again but not cold, and they were sitting in the pastas.

"I shall be sorry to leave you, dear Aspasia, for no one is so dear to me." He had mastered his *rs* by slurring them over but retained a few *ls* for the sake of picturesqueness. "But—forgive me—not Pellicles. He is a hard master to all but you, and Xanthias is worse. Lemember that I am a man now and my spirit chafes constantly."

"As it has done for many years past!" said Aspasia gaily. "Dear Alcibiades! When did it not?"

His own smile was spontaneous. "Oh, yes, I hate discipline! And ever shall. You always have your own way, so even you cannot understand how a man feels."

Aspasia was too fond of him to laugh at his new importance, and merely asked: "How about the next two years? You must serve for a year in garrison duty at the Piræus, and another on the frontier—if the Peloponnesians permit!"

"That is true, and I wish those two years were over and I could enter the permanent cavalry as Pa'lus has done, and be my own master in my own house, but at least I have the satisfaction of knowing that I am master of my fortune and owe no obedience to any but the State. Many of my friends go with me to the Piræus and we shall find ways of amusing ourselves—and I shall not have to ask Pellicles for spending money. And I shall cut my hair!" He shook his bright mane in distaste. "It is ridiculous that one must still wear the hair like a school-boy when he is a man in all other ways."

"You are no longer the 'beauty,'" said Aspasia teasingly. "Your chin is already rough and your 'bloom' has departed. They will forget you for another."

"It is time, Aspasia. I shall never want to be any one thing too long. And I like women better than men."

"Ah?" She looked alarmed. "Where have you met women?"

"Not many of the kind that come here. But there are others, you know." He looked mysterious and important.

"You are too young to visit the hetæræ," she said severely.

"They do not think so—"

"How have you eluded Xanthias?"

He threw back his head and laughed. "That has been a great game!" he cried exultantly. "Xanthias must sleep, for I wear him out by day. It is safe to tell you that I have an under-standing with old Marcus—for I know that you will not tell on him, now that I am about to leave the house and it would do no good."

Aspasia shrugged. "I shall not even scold you, as that would do no good either, and if I did you would avoid me; but you must promise me that when my son is older you will not lead him along your own wild ways."

Alcibiades looked almost sober as he exclaimed earnestly, "Oh, no, dear Aspasia, I'll never do that. I still feel like a father to that boy and shall see that he behaves himself when he is older. The more I know of the world the better guardian I shall be. And I'll have more time to look after him than his father. Pellicles will have his hands full for many years, I fear."

"Yes! Oh, yes!"

Alcibiades looked at her critically. "I am rejoiced that all the terrible trials you have undergone, beloved goddess, have not marred your beauty, although you are a little too thin. I could not endure to have you lose your beauty, for I always find pleasure in looking at you."

"Thanks, dear Alcibiades! I am greatly relieved at your verdict, for I am sure you would *not* look at me if I became an ugly old woman."

"You could never be that, but you might lose your lovely complexion, and that would be almost as great a calamity as if you broke your nose. And I know you do not cry like silly women, for your eyes are still like stars."

"No, I do not weep. I do nothing so futile. And rest assured I shall keep my looks—as long as Pericles lives."

"He is more than twenty years older than you, but men do not grow old in Athens—not till long after his age. Sophocles is nearly sixty and does not look forty; no doubt, like Pellicles, he could still throw his man if he cared to wrestle in the gymnasium. I too shall be always young—and beautiful."

"Not if you drink at too many wild symposia, as many of these young men do—and spend too much time with low companions of both sexes. So be warned."

"Not I!" he said gaily. "You've found the weak spot in my armor, dear Aspasia. Like you I intend to keep my beauty, for no woman is vainer." He turned suddenly grave. "This war will come soon now. They are saying that Pellicles will shut up all the population of Attica within the walls. Do you think he will let none of us go out and fight?"

"There will be sallies, no doubt, but unless it lasts longer than we hope you will still be too young."

"Young! Young! How I hate that word! It has been flung in my face all my life. And yet youth should be the most desirable thing in the world, not a reproach. It is worth more than all else in life save only beauty."

"And wisdom? Do not let Socrates hear you."

"Dear Socrates!" Alcibiades smiled indulgently. "He told me the other day that I was an ignoramus and had learned less at school than any young man he knew. He asked me questions and bombarded my brains with dialectics until I felt like standing on my head in the Ilissus to cool it off. But I love him better than any one but you, and I like to go to him and be scolded. He has made me feel I need it, and quite often! Sometimes when I was the beauty he would not speak to me for months, and then I'd forget every one else and pursue him. Sometimes, thinking he has lost me, he chases me all over Athens —and I do my best to escape him. How strange life is, Aspasia."

"I doubt not you will find it stranger yet," she said drily. "But you cannot do better than to seek Socrates constantly. No one will ever love you more than he."

"He loves me more than you do! For you love Pellicles first and the youngster next. I am only third."

"But that is something!" She gave her old merry laugh, for she could always summon gaiety of spirit save in her darker hours. "Remember I have many friends and am fond of all of them."

"But I would always be first! I hate to think that any one I love loves another more."

"Well, remember that you love yourself more than all, and you have no rival there!"

"You mean no one will ever love me as much as I love myself? You are cruel, Aspasia."

"I fear it would be impossible. When a man has his armor on can he fit in another? But don't worry, dear boy. Many women will love you enough—to their own undoing, no doubt."

XIX

The skies were clear on the following day and the sun came out in all the glory of spring, an event which Alcibiades regarded as a personal attention and omen. Soon after daybreak he arrayed himself in a new white mantle and placed a garland on his curly head. At the same time he made a very boyish face at Xanthias, standing with folded arms beside him.

"You are rid of me and I of you," he said mockingly. "I wonder which of us is the more thankful?"

"You, no doubt, O Alcibiades," replied Xanthias, and there was mockery in his own voice; "for you will never know what is good for you, and I, at least, have been my own master for some years now. It has been in my power to leave this house

at any moment, and you are free for the first time to-day. I
wish you joy of that freedom."

"I'll taste it to the full; make no doubt of that, and not the
least of my delight will be that I am rid of you." But Alcibiades, save when crossed, was always amiable and generous. He
took a heavy gold chain out of a casket and threw it over the
head of the ex-slave. "I would not have you forget me, so be
sure you keep that and not give it to my good little cousin.
Will this garland stay in place, do you think, Xanthias? I
would not have it lop to one side and detract from my dignity.
Perhaps it would be better to get a hair-pin from Aspasia."

Xanthias bent the wreath deftly. "It will not move now
unless you get angry and fling your head about. And I thank
you for the chain. If we are forced to flee before the Spartans,
as your fathers fled before the Persians, no doubt it will buy
bread in a foreign land. But it is not meet I should wear it—
I hear voices without." He opened the door. "I think the
company is assembled. It is better you go forth. The Master
is there and you would not care to have him send for you."

Alcibiades ceased to regard himself in the mirror and stood
up. He was now almost as tall as Pericles. He had grown
rapidly, but there was no ungainly age for boys trained in
palæstræ and gymnasia. His long burnished hair was the color,
as he had often been told, of a bronze helmet, and his magnificent flashing eyes were so deep a blue they were almost purple,
the black lashes as thick and long as Aspasia's. There was a
constant play of expression on his high regular features, but
when he wished he could set them in a godlike repose; and before he left the room to walk forth in all the dignity of his
acknowledged manhood he paused a moment and arranged them
into a fair semblance of marble. As Xanthias closed the door
behind him he shrugged, and picked up combs, toilet articles,
and clothes, scattered all over the floor.

Between twenty and thirty men of varying ages stood near the
altar; the clan of Alcibiades was a large one and included the
Alcmæonidæ: his mother, Diomachè, had been the daughter of
Megacles, grandson of Agariste, daughter of Cleisthenes Tyrant
of Sicyon. Many of these gentlemen had not entered the house

of their most illustrious member for many years, but they put aside resentment and enmity for this august occasion, and arrived in their choicest mantles and bearing appropriate gifts.

Pericles introduced Alcibiades ceremoniously to the members of his phratry, many of whom he had never seen before; and congratulations were received with just the right shade of graciousness and reserve. His manners were pronounced faultless; and the least touch of insolence or of awkward shyness would have been severely criticized. Athenians were inexorable in their standard of manners if not of morals. They whispered that he must have had an excellent pedægogus, and was well fitted to take his place among them.

Once more Pericles had been forced to assume his priestly robes, but he was so glad to get rid of Alcibiades that he did not even murmur a humorous protest to Aspasia—banished to the women's quarters; when a young man came of age even the mother who had given him life was excluded from the ceremonies.

Pericles sacrificed a sheep, and the meat, sliced and wrapped, was presented to the members of the phratry. The priest of the clan received a cake, two quarts of wine, and a bit of money. Alcibiades stood like a statue beside the altar, concealing admirably his consciousness that all eyes were upon him. When the time came to receive his gifts his courtesy was so charming that all present forgot the stories of his disobedience and propensities, and congratulated themselves. His transcendent gifts still slumbered, but all felt themselves in the presence of a remarkable personality; and, as ever when he wished to ingratiate himself, he used his lisp freely; it gave the proper touch of boyish ingenuousness. These tiresome relations might be of use in the future, and it always amused him to charm people who looked as if they were inclined to disapprove of him.

They marched with him to his house; a mansion not as large as that in which he had spent his childhood and youth, but handsomely furnished and kept in order by his father's slaves retained by the late tenants; and was placed in formal possession by Pericles. He accepted his new honors in a graceful speech of appreciation for all he owed his "dear guardian";

and when the company had departed turned a double somersault in the aula.

That night he gave a banquet to his friends, and his cousin Axiochus cut his hair as soon as the wine was brought in, and the flute girls were seducing the ears of the guests—but it were best to draw a veil over that symposium.

The next day he went with his friends, also recently come of age, to the temple of Aglaurus and took oath to be a loyal citizen of Athens all his life; that he would not disgrace his arms, nor desert his companions in battle; that he would obey orders and assist in their observance by others, and defend and honor the shrines. All were then invested with the mantle and hat of the soldier and marched down to the Piræus.

Alcibiades was a man at last.

BOOK IV

I

In the dawn of a day in Skirophorion when the corn was ripe, Pericles, accompanied by Aspasia, mounted to the summit of the north wall and entering one of the towers that flanked the Acharnian Gate, gazed out over the plain. It was alive with a mass of men, women and children moving toward Athens. All were laden with household goods, and some of the men carried doors on their heads, others bedding, portable stoves, and sacks of food. Those of the women unencumbered by babies had their arms full of bundles, and even the little boys and girls bore their burdens. It was a melancholy and silent procession, but they moved rapidly, for it was their last day of grace.

Pericles had prevailed once more on the Bema, and all but those who lived high on the mountains had consented, after much grumbling and protest, to desert their homes and take refuge in the city, but they had delayed until the last moment.

The Pelopennesian army, sixty thousand strong, had, nearly half a month since, entered the northwestern corner of Attica and laid siege to Œnoe, one of the strongest of the border fortifications. The Generals had chafed at the inaction, but Archidemus had argued that when the Athenians saw his army actually on the soil of Attica they would defy Pericles and insist upon going out to meet the enemy; their bravery and fiery impatience were well known. It was only when it became evident they would be permitted to do nothing of the kind, and the fort appeared to be impregnable, that the Generals won permission from the King to march south.

A spy had brought in the news to Pericles the night before, and mounted messengers had dashed to all corners of Attica to give the alarm. With heavy hearts the out-living citizens of Athens had taken up their burdens and moved with the break of day.

The country had never looked more fair! The golden corn, the silver olive orchards, the green vineyards, and a peace that it hardly seemed possible to violate! But they gave no thought to the beauty that would shortly disappear under the ruthless hand of the invader. They were leaving all their material wealth behind them, wealth that had been slowly wrung from the reluctant soil of Attica after the Persian devastations, and with long days of unremitting work during forty-eight years. They had driven their herds and flocks over to Eubœa, but they had no other consolation. The inhabitants of the little towns were equally disconsolate, but some of these had gone to the islands.

Pericles, like his father before him, enjoyed the personal friendship of Archidemus, and fearful that he might give orders to spare the estate of the First Citizen, or his more astute councillors should conceive the plan of ignoring it in order to excite the indignation of the Athenians against their leader, he had told the Ecclesia that if this policy were carried out he would present all his lands to the State. Nothing more had been needed to cement the confidence of the Demos and convert it to his policy.

He had offered the inner quarters of his house to as many of his own farmers as they would accommodate. Clinias had been sent with Zopyrus to the house of Alcibiades, and Pericles Y and Xanthias moved into rooms on the outer court. His farmer friend Pyrilampes would be his guest, but had received orders to leave his peacocks to the Persians or send them to Eubœa. Pericles never wanted to see a peacock again, and Achilles had preceded Clinias.

"So they must have looked when they fled before the Persians," said Aspasia. "Poor refugees. So, I suppose, it must be in every generation. Do you think the time will ever come when war will cease?"

Pericles' voice and smile were grim. "Not until envy and greed are exorcised from human nature. And there are no traits man cherishes more. One country might grow in wisdom —or a few men in it—but that would give the greater encouragement to its enemies. Archidemus, left alone, might have hesitated a few years longer, but not for ever. That race bred to war and with little else to think of has been eager to attack us since the Delian League was formed; the more ambitious men among them have never ceased to talk of the day when the old supremacy of Sparta in Hellas shall be restored. War would have come in the end—as well now as later."

"Could nothing have averted it?"

"Nothing but another Persion invasion—and you with your political wisdom know that as well as I. . . . The irony of it is that all Hellas looks upon Sparta as the champion of the oppressed! She has talked to some purpose, and she was ever an expert in righteousness. But our allies and subject states must confine themselves for the present to sympathy and admiration. With the Athenian navy on the seas they will not dare revolt—nor send aid to our enemy."

Aspasia took his arm and leaned more closely against him in the narrow embrasure whence they looked out on those marching thousands, now beginning to enter the gates.

"Will they hate you for this?" she asked.

"Possibly; later if not now. But I am indifferent to their hatred as long as they obey me; and that they are wise enough to do—thank the gods they worship. If they had refused to desert their farms I should have sent out troops to drive them in, and they would hate me more. But they know that I am acting for the best, that there is literally nothing else to be done. At least I am thankful I am not called upon to govern fools. And Athens, apprehensive as she is, is in an excellent temper. Now that the worst has come they are resigned and cheerful, and willing to do what they can for these poor refugees. But it were better to return before the streets are congested."

They were congested enough in the hours that followed. Some had friends in the city, but few, even of the more prosperous, had town houses, for they preferred the life of the country the year round, and there was rarely a house for rent in Athens. Friends gladly made room for as many as could be accommodated, even in the poorer quarter, but thousands roamed the streets looking in vain for shelter. They pitched their tents in the Agora and all open spaces, and finally received permission to establish themselves in the temples and shrines, always excepting the Eleusinion, sacred to Demeter, and those on the Acropolis. Others took possession of the towers on the walls, many erected little huts between the Long Walls, and finally invaded the Piræus. The wall between Athens and Phaleron had fallen into disrepair, and they were forbidden to camp in the wide meadows. But there would always be an abundance of food, for the protected trading ships brought corn from the Chersonese, and the fishermen were uninterrupted in their daily excursions. But the crowding was frightful and children wailed incessantly.

Pericles did not go to the walls again. Hundreds of young men stood there day after day grinding their teeth and shouting curses as they witnessed that vile army of Peloponnesians and Thebans devastate their country. It had begun by ravaging the land about Eleusis, and was now at work systematically destroying the vineyards, cornfields, and ancient olive orchards of the Attic plain.

They shouted curses on Pericles, for not to fight an invading army was beyond all reason in the minds of courageous young men. That mass of glittering helmets at their very gates maddened them; they leaped from the walls, and, led by Xanthippus, ran to the house of Pericles shouting to him to come forth and lead them to battle. But old Marcus would not open the doors, and they tramped, still shouting, through the streets and besieged the Council Chamber, demanding the assembling of the Ecclesia. But Pericles had given orders that no Ecclesia should be called for the present, and the four regular monthly meetings were suspended. He permitted columns of flying horsemen to go out occasionally and harass the enemy, but nothing more.

Acharnæ, seven miles from Athens, was the most populous of all the Attic demes, and its inhabitants, some twelve thousand in number, exclusive of slaves, peculiarly enterprising and irritable. It drove them frantic to imagine the destruction of their property, and their voices were loudest in wrath and execration of Pericles. The other refugees accepted their fate in a more amiable spirit and gave no trouble, thankful for the safety of their bodies, and for the good food provided by the State.

But many of the Athenians proper were as distraught as the

Acharnians as they looked on at the destruction of so much wealth, particularly of the olive trees, slower of growth than ilex or pine. Had they not twelve hundred horsemen and horse-bowmen, sixteen hundred foot-bowmen, and twenty-nine thousand hoplites? To be sure some were at Potidæa and others at sea, but the forces left were not insignificant, and, combined with the invincible spirit of their race, would surely strike terror into the enemy if they issued in a combined sally on a dark night.

They stood in angry discussion on street corners, or wherever they could find space, and assembled before Pericles' house, and on the hills of the Muses and the Nymphs; but their respect for the law kept them away from the Pnyx. Cratinus wrote scurrilous rhymes denouncing Pericles as a coward, which were copied by the scribes and distributed. Soothsayers and diviners ran about the city quoting oracles to this and that effect, and when news came of a great earthquake—the first in its history—on the sacred island of Delos, the birthplace of the League, cried out that it portended the wrath of Apollo unless Athens showed her courage to the enemy.

Cleon was everywhere, denouncing Pericles as a coward and a traitor, calling on the Athenians to defy him; and Xanthippus and Thoron were as active, demanding an Ecclesia with or without his consent. But the bulk of the Athenians, excited as they were, had too much regard for their democratic institutions to act without authority, and only the Council of Five Hundred, and Pericles, as President of the Board of Generals, had the legal right to convene the public assembly.

Pericles, imperturbable, went forth when it was necessary and did all that could be done to make the refugees comfortable. He had already dispatched a fleet to join the Corcyrean navy and it was inflicting grave damage on the Peloponnesian coast, killing many of the troops sent out to meet the invaders, and capturing the Corinthian town Sollion. It then took Artacus, expelling its despot and enrolling it in the Athenian Confederacy. Later the large district of Cephallenia, with its four cities, was subdued without bloodshed and entered the Delian League. Another fleet went up the Euripus—past the neglected but still

unravaged estate of Pericles—-to sack the Locrian towns on
the coast, and a garrison was planted on the island of Atalantè
to prevent egress. On the whole, if Attica lost much, the honors
rested with the Athenians.

At the end of the summer, when the enemy withdrew to attend to pressing domestic affairs, the farmers went back to the
ruins of their little estates, patched up their walls, and replanted
their crops, in the fond hope that all would be settled before
the following summer. The congestion in Athens was diminished, the Agora was cleaned, and once more men gathered there
to exchange a multitude of opinions. Nobody was cheerful, for
many men had fallen, and there was little hope that the enemy
would not return. But at least there was no more loud talk
and gathering before the door of Pericles. The young men who
had not gone with the fleet were sullen and relieved their feelings in the clubs. Taking what vengeance they could they circu-
lated the story that Pericles had poisoned Pheidias, fearing that
the sculptor in his weakness might confess what he had denied
before the court; and the comic poets prepared to call him names
in the Dionysia and ridicule him for discarding his Olympian
frigidity and shedding tears in public.

II

The large aula of Pericles' house had been a refuge for his
friends during those summer months when Academe and the
Lyceum, now, alas, in ruins, were no longer a resource, and one
could not even walk through the Agora without tripping over
women and children. As there were generally crowds before
the door, and Marcus was rarely induced to lower the bars, they
entered at the back, picking their way past refuse and sprawling
bodies. They came in the afternoon as well as in the morning,
for have social intercourse they must, and although they saw
little of Pericles they were always sure of a welcome from
Aspasia. Socrates was with the army at Potidæa, all the Generals were on duty, and the younger men avoided the house of
Pericles; but there were many eminent citizens, lovers of discourse, who found much to console them in that peaceful aula.
They disregarded the heat, and philosophically dismissed their

regrets for the leafy woods and seaside breezes of their usual summers. Aspasia was obliged to send them home at midday, for all must feed themselves who could afford it, and those in the inner court were a heavy drain on diminished resources, but they returned after siesta.

Aspasia was glad of their company, for it gave her less time to think, and Pericles occasionally mingled with them; unscowling faces were a pleasant relief. He could close his mind to his terrible responsibilities whenever he chose and engage in philosophical discussion with as much concentrated ardor as Damon or Zeno. And he had his evenings with Aspasia, for when night fell even the clubs ceased from activity. The watchers were alert on the towers and hoplites at the gates. There had been no attempt to rush the city, for the enemy well knew that its walls were impregnable and archers stood on it by day.

His office was filled more often than not from dawn until dark with citizens striving to turn him from his purpose, or with messengers come in from the fleet, and he was consulted as commissariat-in-chief by the officials whose duty it was to feed the refugees. But in the back of his mind was always the thought that when his duties were over the peace of his home awaited him. Paralus was in one of the frontier forts and safe enough; he put him out of his mind. He enjoyed his occasional discussions with the philosophers, and his youngest son amused him at dinner. But it was his evenings with Aspasia that he looked forward to—that friend who never failed him, whose counsel inspired him, whose beauty enchanted him, and in whose conversation he could always find distraction. The old days of intense almost blind happiness were over, but it seemed to him that they were more one than ever. In spite of unremitting work he had not begun to feel his age, but he knew the time must come when those twenty odd years between them would open her eyes to the fact that while still a young woman—and her youth appeared to be as persistent as that of the more or less fabulous Helen—she was married to an old man; but such an idea had not yet entered her head. If his spirit was oppressed he had changed little in appearance and his magnificent constitution had defied all mental and physical strain. The reverses of fortune he ignored, and whether through force of will or habit his sleep was rarely disturbed, no matter what the cares of the day or the portent of the morrow. He was convinced that three years would see the end of the war, for the Lacedæmonians and their allies would realize the futility of sitting down in a barren land summer after summer. Another would complete the ruin of Attica, and the devastation he wreaked on their coasts must bring them to terms in time. They would gain nothing by the prolongation of the war and their losses would appal them.

Then a few more years of peace—would it be the peace of old age for him? Would he begin to crumble when the strain was over? Must he live to witness Aspasia's love change to that of a dutiful daughter? She, whose love had seemed to deepen with the years and who still regarded it as immortal? He had satisfied every need of that consummately endowed nature, as she of his, and he shuddered to think of the day when she would still think him interesting to talk to, but look back upon the time of their complete union as a pleasant and possibly receding memory. The day might come when he would pray to the gods to deliver him from life.

But he had little time for brooding, and dark as was the present, with perhaps worse to come, and their afflictions had saddened them, they were still too closely knit for anything but death to sever. The time might come when he would long for the tomb of his fathers on the Sacred Way, but not yet!

After the retirement of the enemy he was still besieged by men importuning him to meet the Peloponnesians in the field when they returned in the summer, and patiently reiterated his purpose. He sent troops into the Megarid to lay it waste, for no Athenian would have consented to let that traitor state go unpunished. Not a stone was left upon another in the town, and its fields and orchards were destroyed. Ægina, that beautiful island just south of Salamis in the Saronic Gulf, always bitterly rebellious of its conquest by Pericles after the Persian War, had secretly conspired with Sparta before the outbreak of the present war, and to it also he meted judgment. The inhabitant were ordered to move out bag and baggage and find refuge if they could with the friend on whom they had rested their hopes. He could send several thousand refugees there, and the congestion in Athens during the following summer would be less unbearable.

III

It was six months before the Spartans returned and Athens fell insensibly into her old ways. The philosophers and sophists held their classes in the porticoes of the Agora, and although the palæstræ without the walls had shared the general destruction, that of Tauræus near the King Archon's Stoa was crowded daily. Socrates returned from Potidæa to find Charmides, the son of Glaucon and Constantia and another young Apollo, the beauty of Athens. When not improving the mind of this promising youth, he attended Aspasia's morning levees, and was in time to hear the great Funeral Speech of Pericles.

If there was little evidence of war in Athens, now that the enemy had departed, the walls of more houses than one sheltered heavy hearts. Many had fallen before Potidæa and in the raids on the coasts, young cavalry officers during the skirmishes on the plain. The bodies had been burnt wherever convenient, and the usual custom was observed of burying them collectively and inviting some orator to make the funeral speech before the late autumn rains.

Pericles was chosen for this mournful occasion, and although he never spoke without "arranging his ideas" beforehand, never did he take greater pains with an oration than this. It was his mission not only to glorify the dead but to put courage into the living, to revive their pride in their city if they had lost it, and make them as determined as himself to preserve the monuments of Athens intact, no matter what further sacrifices and miseries they might be called upon to meet.

The court door of the thalamos had been closed during the refugee invasion and the window enlarged; at present, however, the inner aula was deserted, for the farmers had gone back to the still unmolested estate on the Euripus: the enemy had confined their depredations to the plains. The breezes wandered as freely through the large beautiful room as of old and Pericles and Aspasia frequently sat there when alone.

For three successive evenings he walked up and down dictating his speech. She revised it by day and he revised it again when they were together, adding and rejecting. There were moments of irresistible cynicism but he let them stand.

"This speech will be a noble monument to you, Pericles," she said when he finally gave it the seal of his approval. "I shall give a copy of it to Thucydides. Even though he hates me he will receive it gladly from my hand. But no doubt if he copies it into his history he will leave out all you have said of the debt of Athens to our great men of genius. He seems to hate any that is not displayed exclusively in statesmanship and war."

Pericles shrugged. "Thucydides is a man of great talent himself, but limited. He has none of the even development which is the pride of the best of the Athenians; but such mental virtues as he has could hardly be more distinguished, and he is brave in war, loyal in friendship, and dispassionate in his judgments of all whom he condescends to notice. That is much to say of any man, and I forgive him his lack of appreciation in art."

"And of me?" asked Aspasia gaily.

He smiled down upon her. "You have so many admirers you can afford to forgive poor Thucydides for hating all women. It is much that he is without malice and has never sought to inflict injury upon you with his harsh tongue. Even if I were out of the question he would never stoop to that. Now I must commit that speech to memory. Read it to me slowly and pull me up sharply if I leave out a word. Each has been calculated and weighed, as no one knows better than yourself."

IV

Once more Athens gave herself up to a day of mourning. A tent had been erected in the Agora where the bones of the dead rested on a table for three days. Relatives and friends brought garlands and offerings of all sorts; the rich valuable gifts, the poor what they had. The bones were then placed in ten cypress coffins, one for each of the ten tribes into which Cleisthenes had divided the population of the State, and these were lifted on to wagons, draped with black, that served as hearses. They were preceded to the Ceramicus by an empty litter covered with a black pall, eloquent of bodies vanished as completely as the brave spirits that had driven them. Athenians and Metics, wearing the mourning himation, followed the sad procession to its destination without the walls; oppressed not only by the wailing of the bereft but by the most melancholy occasion in which any but the very old had ever taken part. No woman carried a garland to-day.

Again Aspasia stood with Agariste at the foot of the platform erected on the highest point of the Ceramicus, and looked down over a mighty throng. Those silent men and women had come to hear Pericles speak as well as to honor the dead, but their faces were pale and set, and it was doubtful if any recalled that former assemblage where only decorum had prevented them from cheering the returned hero and showing their exultation in assured peace and prosperity.

There were many sullen eyes, and Aspasia picked out the scornful faces of Cratinus, Hermippus, Telekeides, and Thoron. Thasson stood with his arms folded, leaning against a stele, his noble countenance stern and disapproving. Aspasia wondered why he had condescended to come. Beside him, his handsome face disfigured by a sneer, stood Acestorides, with Phyrra, handsome and matronly, clinging to his arm. As she caught Aspasia's eye her thin lips curved into a brilliant smile; no occasion was mournful to Phyrra that involved no personal loss. Socrates and Charmides stood together, looking like Silenus and a faun. Young Pericles had come with his mother but made his way to the side of Socrates, who, meeting him frequently in his father's house, had been fascinated by his still girlish beauty and lively manner, and shown him much attention.

Alcibiades stood conspicuously at the left of the tribune and threw all young immature beauties, even Charmides, into the shade. Few glanced at youths or women when the gorgeous Alcibiades monopolized the field of vision. He looked like the legendary heroes of the *Iliad*, and it was his pride that he had never been styled an Apollo nor likened to any other tiresome god, but recalled to men their mental images of Achilles or Hector. As he stood there facing the greater part of that vast audience, his eyes flashing and his mien as authoritative as if he were about to lead them to battle and victory, the Athenians conceived for him one of those sudden passionate adorations to which they were peculiarly liable, and longed for the time when he would coruscate in public life It was significant that no one ever argued whether Alcibiades would or would not have a great career. He was one of the chosen.

This was the first time that the women, save the few that had indulged in a passing flirtation with him at Aspasia's levees, had seen him, and their eyes wandered toward him constantly.

"I don't see Elpinike," said Agariste. "No doubt she has succumbed to old age at last."

But Aspasia was not interested in Elpinike. She was noting the response in Alcibiades' expressive eyes to those of certain young women, restless and filled with vain longings, and wondered if they would find ways of inviting him down new paths of misconduct. Then she shrugged her shoulders, a common habit when speculating about Alcibiades. A mind as fertile as his needed little guidance in devious paths; already an affair with the wife of a Piræan had created a scandal barely hushed up by Ariphon.

There had been a low murmur of conversation, but it ceased abruptly as Pericles appeared on the platform. He drew all eyes irresistibly; whether men hated him or not they saw no one else when he rose to speak. Alcibiades shrugged his own shoulders and sat down on a corner of the rostrum.

The libation was poured and Pericles began at once.

"Most of those who have spoken here before me," he began, his voice faintly ironic, "have commended the lawgiver who added this oration to our other funeral customs; it seemed to them a worthy thing that such an honor should be given at their burial to the dead who have fallen on the field of battle. But I should have preferred that when men's deeds have been brave they should have been honored in deed only, and with such an honor as this public funeral which you are now witnessing. Then the reputation of many would not have been imperilled by the want of eloquence of one, and their virtues believed or not as he spoke well or ill. For it is difficult to say neither too little nor too much; and even moderation is apt not to give the impression of truthfulness. The friend of the dead who knows the facts is likely to think that the words of the speaker fall short of his knowledge and of his wishes; another who is not so well informed, when he hears of anything that surpasses his own powers, will be envious and suspect exaggeration. Mankind are tolerant of the praises of others so long as each hearer thinks that he can do as well or nearly as well himself, but, when the speaker rises above him, jealousy is aroused and he begins to be incredulous. However, since our ancestors have set the seal of their approval upon the practice, I must obey, and to the utmost of my power shall endeavor to satisfy the wishes and beliefs of all who hear me.

"I will speak first of our ancestors, for it is right and seemly that now, when we are lamenting the dead, a tribute should be paid to their memory. There has never been a time when they did not inhabit this land, which by their valor they have handed down from generation to generation; and we have received from them a free State. But if they were worthy of praise, still more were our fathers who added to their inheritance, and after many a struggle transmitted to us, their sons, this great empire. And we ourselves assembled here to-day, who are still, most of us, in the vigor of life, have carried the work of improvement further, and have richly endowed our city with all things, so that she is sufficient for herself both in peace and war. Of the military exploits by which our various possessions were acquired, or of the energy with which we or our fathers drove back the tide of war, Hellenic or Barbarian, I will not speak; for the tale would be long and is familiar to you. But before I praise the dead, I should like to point out by what principles of action we rose to power, and under what institutions and through what manner of life our empire became great. For I conceive that such thoughts are not unsuited to the occasion, and that this numerous assembly of citizens and strangers may profitably listen to them.

"Our form of government does not enter into rivalry with the institutions of others. We do not copy our neighbors, but are an example to them. It is true that we are called a democracy, for the administration is in the hands of the many and not of the few. But while the law secures equal justice to all alike in their private disputes, the claim of excellence is also recognized; and when a citizen is in any way distinguished he is preferred to the public service not as a matter of privilege, but as the reward of merit. Neither is poverty a bar, but a man may benefit his country whatever may be the obscurity of his condition. There is no exclusiveness in our public life, and in our private intercourse we are not suspicious of one another; nor angry with our neighbor if he does what he likes. While we are thus unconstrained in our private intercourse, a spirit of reverence pervades our public acts; we are prevented from doing wrong by respect for the authorities and for the laws, having an especial regard for those which are ordained for the protection of the injured, as well as for those unwritten laws which bring upon the transgressor of them the reprobation of the general sentiment.

"And we have not forgotten to provide for our weary spirits many relaxations from toil; we have regular games and sacrifices throughout the year; our homes are beautiful and elegant; and the delight which we daily feel in all these things helps to banish melancholy. Because of the greatness of our city the fruits of the whole earth flow in upon us; so that we enjoy the goods of other countries as freely as our own. We have carried art to the highest pitch in the history of the world, and our great poets, sculptors, painters and architects have immortalized Athens and themselves even while they live. From all parts of Hellas and from farther still men come to witness their achievements or to learn their secrets. And the same may be said of our philosophers—who light the path of all that would penetrate the mysteries of nature and the souls of men. Such works of art as we may export—in statues, pottery or metal-ware—are eagerly bargained for in distant countries. Not the least part of the history of Athens is her achievements and her preeminence in art.

"Then, again, our military training is in many respects superior to that of our adversaries. Our city is thrown open to the world, and we never expel a foreigner or prevent him from seeing or learning anything of which the secret if revealed to an enemy might profit him. We rely not upon management or trickery, but upon our own minds and hands. And in the matter of education, whereas they from early youth are always undergoing laborious exercises which are to make them brave, we live at ease, and yet are equally ready to face peril when it comes. And here is the proof. The Lacedæmonians come into Attica not by themselves, but with the whole confederacy following; we go alone into a neighbor's country; and although our opponents are fighting for their homes and we on foreign soil, we have seldom any difficulty in overcoming them. Our enemies have never yet felt our united strength; the care of a navy divides our attention, and on land we are obliged to send our own citizens everywhere. But they, if they meet and defeat a part of our army, are as proud as if they had routed us all, and when defeated pretend to have been vanquished by us all.

"If, then, we prefer to meet danger in a cheerful mood but without laborious training, and with a courage which is gained by habit and not enforced by law, are we not greatly the gainers? Since we do not anticipate the pain, when the hour comes we can be as brave as those who never allow themselves to rest; and thus too our city is equally admirable in peace and in war. For we are lovers of the beautiful, yet simple in our tastes, and we cultivate the mind without loss of manliness. Wealth we employ, not for talk and ostentation, but where there is a real use for it. To avow poverty with us is no disgrace; the true disgrace is in doing nothing to avoid it. An Athenian citizen does not neglect the State because he takes care of his own household; and even those of us who are engaged in business have a very fair idea of politics. We alone regard a man who takes no interest in public affairs, not as harmless, but as a useless character; and if few of us are originators, we are all sound judges of policy. The great impediment to action is, in our opinion, not discussion, but the want of that knowledge which is gained by discussion preparatory to action. For we have a peculiar power of thinking before we act and of acting too, whereas other men are courageous from ignorance but hesitate upon reflection. And they are surely to be esteemed the bravest

spirits, who, having the clearest sense both of the pains and
the pleasures of life, do not on that account shrink from danger.
In doing good, again, we are unlike others; we show our friendship by conferring, not by receiving favors. Now, he who con-
fers a favor is the firmer friend, because he would fain by kindness keep alive the memory of an obligation; but the recipient
is colder in his feelings, because he knows that in inviting another's generosity he will not be winning gratitude but only
paying a debt. We alone do good to our neighbors not upon
a calculation of interest, but in the confidence of freedom and
in a frank and fearless spirit. To sum up: I say that Athens
is the School of Hellas, and that the individual Athenian in
his own person seems to have the power of adapting himself
to the most varied form of action with the utmost versatility
and grace. This is no passing and idle word, but truth and
fact; and the assertion is verified by the position to which these
qualities have raised the State. For in the hour of trial Athens
alone among her contemporaries is superior to the report of
her. No enemy who comes against her is indignant at the reverses which he sustains at the hands of such a city; no subject
complains that his masters are unworthy of him. And we
shall assuredly not be without witnesses; there are mighty
monuments of our power which will make us the wonder of this
and of succeeding ages; we shall not need the praises of Homer
nor of any other panegyrist whose poetry may please for the
moment, although his representation of the facts will not bear
the light of day. For we have compelled every land and every
sea to open a path for our valor, and have everywhere planted
eternal memorials of our friendship and of our enmity. Such
is the city for whose sake these men nobly fought and died;
they could not bear the thought that she might be taken from
them; and every one of us who survives should gladly toil on
her behalf.

"I have dwelt upon the greatness of Athens because I want
to show you that we are contending for a higher prize than
those who enjoy none of these privileges, and to establish by
manifest proof the merit of these men whom I am now commemorating. Their loftiest praise has already been spoken.

For in magnifying the city I have magnified them, and men like them whose virtues made her glorious. And of how few Hellenes can it be said as of them, that their deeds when weighed in the balance have been found equal to their fame! I think that such a death as theirs has been gives the true measure of a man's worth; it may be the first revelation of his virtues, but is at any rate their final seal. For even those who come short in other ways may justly plead the valor with which they have fought for their country; they have blotted out the evil with the good, and have benefitted the State more by their public services than they have injured her by their private actions. None of these men was enervated by wealth nor hesitated to resign the pleasures of life; none of them put off the evil day in the hope, natural to poverty, that a man though poor, may one day become rich. But deeming that the punishment of their enemies was sweeter than any of these things, and that they could fall in no nobler cause, they determined at the hazard of their lives to be honorably avenged, and to leave the rest. They resigned to hope their unknown chance of happiness; but in the face of death they resolved to rely upon themselves alone. And when the moment came they were minded to resist and suffer, rather than to flee and save their lives; they ran away from the word dishonor, but on the battlefield their feet stood fast; and in an instant, at the height of their fortune, they passed away from the scene, not of their fear, but of their glory.

"Such was the end of these men; they were worthy of Athens, and the living need not desire to have a more heroic spirit, although they may pray for a less fatal issue. The value of such a spirit is not to be expressed in words. Any one can discourse to you for ever about the advantages of a brave defense, which you know already. But instead of listening to him I would have you fix your eyes upon the greatness of Athens, until you become filled with the love of her; and when you are impressed by the spectacle of her glory, reflect that this empire has been acquired by men who knew their duty and had the courage to do it, who in the hour of conflict had the fear of dishonor always present to them, and who, if ever they failed in an enterprise, would not allow their virtues to be lost to their country, but freely gave their lives to her as the fairest offering which they could present at her feast. The sacrifice which they collectively made was individually repaid to them; for they received again each one for himself a praise that grows not old, and the noblest of all spectacles—I speak not of that in which their remains are laid, but that in which their glory survives, and is proclaimed always and on every fitting occasion both in word and deed. For the whole earth is the sepulchre of famous men; not only are they commemorated by columns and inscriptions in their own country, but in foreign lands there dwells also an unwritten memorial of them, graven not on stone but on the minds of men. Make them your examples, and, esteeming courage to be freedom and freedom to be happiness, do not weigh too nicely the perils of war. The unfortunate who has no hope of a change for the better has less reason to throw away his life than the prosperous, who, if he survive, is always liable to a change for the worse, and to whom any accidental fall makes the most serious difference. To a man of spirit, cowardice and disaster coming together are far more bitter than death striking him unperceived at a time when he is full of courage and animated by the general hope.

"Wherefore I do not now commiserate the parents of the dead who stand here; I would rather comfort them. You know that your life has been passed among manifold vicissitudes; and that they may be deemed fortunate who have gained most honor; whether an honorable death like theirs, or an honorable sorrow like yours, and whose days have been so ordered that the term of their happiness is likewise the term of their life. I know how hard it is to make you feel this, when the good fortune of others will too often remind you of the gladness that once brightened your lives. And sorrow is felt at the want of these blesssings, not which a man never knew, but which were a part of his life before they were taken from him. Some of you are of an age at which you may hope to have other children, and you ought to bear your sorrows better; not only will the children who may hereafter be born make you forget your own lost ones, but the city will be doubly a gainer. She will not be left desolate and she will be safer. For a man's counsel cannot have equal weight or worth, when he alone has no children to risk in the general danger. To those of you who have passed your prime, I say: 'Congratulate yourselves that you have been happy during the greater part of your days; remember that your life of sorrow will not last long, and be comforted by the glory of those who are gone. For the love of honor alone is ever young; and not riches, as some say, but honor is the delight of men when they are old and useless.

"To you who are the sons and brothers of the departed, I say that the struggle to emulate them will be an arduous one. For all men praise the dead, and, however preëminent your virtue may be, hardly will you be thought, I do not say to equal, but even to approach them. The living have their rivals and detractors, but when a man is out of the way, the honor and good-will which he receives is unalloyed.

"I have paid the required tribute, in obedience to the law, making use of such fitting words as I had. The tribute of deeds has been paid in part; for the dead have been honorably interred, and it remains only that the children shall be maintained at the public charge until they are grown: this is the solid prize with which, as with a garland, Athens crowns her sons living and dead, after a struggle like theirs. For when the rewards of virtue are greatest, there the noblest citizens are enlisted in the service of the State. And now, when you have duly lamented, every one his own dead, you may depart."

v

A frown had displaced the sneer on the faces of the comic poets and their ilk, and their eyes, darting over that great audience—motionless for a moment after Pericles turned and left the platform—saw that its expression had changed. These men and women still looked sad, but subtly comforted, proud, and even hopeful. All evidence of dissatisfaction or hostility had vanished. For the moment they seemed to have merged into one vast composite mind, unconscious of all but the words of the speaker and of the solace he had given them.

"By Zeus, he knows how to handle the Athenians!" exclaimed Alcibiades as he joined Aspasia and Agariste. "I've heard sev-

eral of his orations but that was the cleverest. He's a regular
doctor of souls! And I'll wager my best horse that he wrote
a good part of that speech with his tongue in his cheek."

"He did nothing of the sort!" said Aspasia indignantly.
"Do you imagine he does not really feel for these poor mourners
—and for all whom this war must afflict?"

"Quite possible. But Pellicles never wrote a speech under
the drive of his emotions. He would have said exactly the same
things if he had despised them. I'll never love Pellicles but
I shall always admire him superlatively for his cleverness in
manipulating men, and for the cold calculating judgment that
never fails him. Even when he 'thunders and lightens,' as the
comic poets say, he has weighed every word beforehand. When
I too am in public life I shall take him as a model—"

"Much good it will do you," interrupted Agariste, who liked
him no better than when as a small boy she had caught him
making faces at her. "You'll be brilliant enough, no doubt, but
you'll always think of yourself first and of the people little at
any time; and unless you learn better—which I doubt—you'll
fail in the end."

"And would you deny that Pellicles thinks of himself first—
that he is the most ambitious of men?"

"A man may be ambitious—what man worth a pinch of Attic
salt is not?—and yet have a mind great enough to include love
of his people as well of himself."

"I do not believe that he loves these Athenians who hate him
one day and adore him the next. They are his puppets and it
amuses him to pull the strings and make them dance—as I shall
one day. He only loves power—and Aspasia. What have you
to say to that, dear goddess?"

"That you show a little perspicacity but not too much! If
Pericles does not love the Athenians he never forgets his duty
to them and his concern for them. He uses his power for
their good not for their ill. And he has much human sympathy
—something you would do well to cultivate, dear Alcibiades,
if you would one day dominate the Athenians, for they are very
sharp. You now despise all who are not your equals in intelli-

gence, and he has achieved that true greatness which is above contempt for the meanly endowed."

Alcibiades laughed. "The most remarkable thing I know about Pellicles is that you still think him wonderful after being married to him for so many years."

"That is more than you will ever be able to say for your own wife when one is so unlucky as to have you for husband." Agariste's tones had never been tarter.

"Well, I'll have a much more amusing life than Pellicles, for I'll love many women, not one. Even if there were another Aspasia I'd not blind myself to the charms of others—"

"You couldn't if you tried. You are what you are—and you'll never be another Pericles—not in anything. You may dazzle the Athenians when your time comes, but you'll never hold their allegiance as Pericles has done for nigh on to forty years. You will merely use them and they will find it out."

Alcibiades turned a rueful face to Aspasia. "Is this female Socrates right?" he asked plaintively. "How familiar this all sounds! But you are wiser than both of them. Am I doomed to failure because I never can love these Athenians to distraction?"

"I am not a prophetess," she said coldly. "And I do not enjoy speculating upon a time when Pericles shall have resigned in your favor."

"But time does not stand still," said Alcibiades lightly, as they walked through the Ceramicus, deserted now by all but the mourners lamenting about the public tomb that had been raised to cover the indistinguishable dead. "The kind gods have ordained that man is not immortal and must give way in due course to the generation behind him."

"So be it," said Aspasia. "Let us talk of other things."

VI

The enemy returned with the wild flowers of spring and Athens once more was crowded beyond capacity. Ægina seemed to have afforded little relief. Salamis not only had a large population of her own but was forced to receive some two thousand slaves from the mines of Laurion. But although the summer came early and was very hot, the Etesian wind as ever brought relief, and there was little sickness in the city, even among the children and old people accustomed to the fresh air of the country.

They had not yet begun to suffer from the dearth of fruit and fresh vegetables. Corn, honey, olive oil, and fish were abundant. They ate little meat at any time. It was served at banquets as a mark of hospitality, and sacrificed sheep and goats were cooked for dinner; the animals offered up before the public temples were distributed among the people; but neither health nor palate was dependent upon it, and during this time of forced abstinence their only lament was the lack of living offerings for public and private altars.

Commerce was uninterrupted, and the shops did a thriving business, for many of the farmers had money. Those who would enliven their misfortunes with conversation met in the aulæ of friends or on the roofs in the late afternoon.

The Athenians had made up their minds to be cheerful. The invading army was now ravaging the coast lands and approaching Laurion, but after this summer there would be nothing left to destroy, and the enemy must see the folly of continuing the war. If Pericles could hear of the destruction of his estate and remain tranquil it behooved them to follow his example. Only the younger men disdained philosophy, but they no longer wasted their time besieging Pericles' house; they sat in the clubs and denounced him, or paced the walls, as there was no room for exercise in the city.

Pericles had not dared to remove his heavy hand from Athens during the preceding year, for anything might have happened in his absence. But in its present mood he felt that it could be left to the care of faithful and capable magistrates—he had permitted the Ecclesia to be called for purposes of election only —and fitted out a fleet of one hundred triremes which he intended to command in person. Chios and Lesbos received orders to contribute fifty more. He would take four thousand hoplites with him and three hundred cavalry; and he took care to include a large number of his malcontents.

"This is the only time I shall be resigned to your absence," said Aspasia one evening as they were dining; it was a family gathering, for they entertained little in these days, and Paralus and Pericles Y were present. "I shall rejoice in the knowledge that you are breathing fresh air once more, and have long since made up my mind that you bear a charmed life."

"I shall certainly be glad of sea breezes," he said; "but I should like to know that you too were out of Athens. Why not go to Miletus for the summer?"

"Not I! I shall await you here. The city is safe and healthy, and I can receive news promptly."

"Why not go to Delos if Miletus is too far? I have friends there. A number of families who are fortunate enough to have friends on the islands are visiting them."

But Aspasia shook her head. "I shall need distraction, not change, and here the house is always filled with the friends who interest me most."

"I cannot wait to start!" cried Paralus; his company was going with the fleet. "Would that we sailed to-night!"

"Well, you have but four days to wait," said his father; "and you will find enough to do between now and then. I can at least be certain that you have seen to the well-being of the horses!"

Paralus had grown tall and strong, and if he had escaped being a "beauty," was a handsome young man and magnificently healthy. Pericles had never been demonstrative to his children, but Paralus was comfortably sure of his affection, and, removed from the influence of Xanthippus, had given no further trouble. After his recall from the north he had spent the winter months at the breeding farm on Eubœa, and was now excited at the prospect of action. His younger brother looked at him enviously.

"Why am I not five years older?" he demanded gloomily. "And a soldier, not a mere boy to be ordered here and there by Xanthias?"

"Your time will come," said his father smiling. "But not in this war. Another year will see it ended."

The door opened and Hagnias entered.

"Salutations," said Pericles cordially. He liked this young

Metic, who had done him good service more than once, and was a man of much influence in the Piræus. "You are in time for the wine—but to what do we owe this pleasure?"

Hagnias exchanged a word with Aspasia, nodded to the others, and disposed himself on a couch pushed forward by an attendant before he answered his host. "I hope I do not bring bad news," he said; "but I have worried all day and thought it best to consult you—"

"The Peloponnesians have not undermined the walls in the night?" Paralus sprang to his feet. "But surely that would be impossible—they are too well guarded—"

"The city is safe enough from the Peloponnesians. Sit down and drink your wine in peace." He turned to Pericles. "I have apprehensions of another enemy. Six men have been stricken to-day in the Piræus with a singular disease. They were all as well as you or I, when suddenly they ran about as if distracted, complaining of violent heat in the tongue and throat, sneezing, and coughing as if they would tear their chests asunder, finally falling down in violent convulsions. Have you heard, O Pericles, that the plague is raging in Æthiopia, Egypt, Persia, and Carthage? Trading ships came in from Carthage three days ago and I hear that men died on the voyage."

"Great Zeus!" muttered Pericles. "I fear it is nothing else. I was in Lemnos during an epidemic of plague, and recognize the symptoms. What do the doctors say?"

"Their remedies are ineffective; their patients get worse instead of better, and their theory is that the cisterns have been poisoned by the enemy. I hope they are right—but not one of them has ever been out of Attica."

"I shall send Acron down there to-night. He went to Lemnos during that epidemic to study the disease. Athens crowded and filthy! If it had come at another time I should have sent every one out into the country, and now they must stay here and poison one another. The enemy will think they have the gods on their side!" He rose and sent a slave for his mantle and helmet. "It may be possible to isolate any fresh cases and prevent an epidemic. I shall go for Acron now and take him with me to the Piræus."

He went out and Hagnias shook his head. "With all those sailors from a plague-ridden city loose in the town I doubt if the plague—if it be the plague—can be suppressed. Surely you will go to Miletus, Aspasia? And I shall ask you to take Galatea and the children with you."

She had turned very pale but she felt that nothing but physical force would drive her from Athens. "My place is here, but Galatea is welcome to my house, and the boy and Xanthias shall accompany her. Athens will be no place—"

"The boy" burst into loud remonstrance. Ever since the danger that had threatened his mother he had looked upon himself as her protector-in-chief. Alcibiades had told him of the proud position he had filled at the age of ten when Pericles was absent at Samos, and at thirteen he felt himself equal to defending her against the entire Peloponnesian army. "I will not go!" he cried. "I will not go!"

"You will do as you are told," said Aspasia with more severity than he was accustomed to from her lips, but she was filled with dire forebodings. "I shall speak to your father as soon as he returns."

But when Pericles returned late that night, his own forebodings justified, he refused his consent. "The head of the State may not send his own son to safety while other fathers are in no position to do so. Young Pericles must stay here and take his chances with the rest. And do not worry, for Acron thinks the distemper may be arrested before it spreads further."

The plague spread slowly and the swift mortal disease was still believed to be the fiendish work of the Peloponnesians, who must have agents in the city. People for once drank their wine undiluted, and the magistrates of Athens gave orders that no water should be used save in cooking. Acron assured Pericles that the disease was well in hand, and he sailed with the fleet.

As he was leaving the harbor an eclipse of the sun occurred, and a shout went up that this was a terrible portent and should not be disregarded.

Pericles, whose ship led the fleet, took off his mantle and threw it over the head of his shivering helmsman, who had been loudest in his protests against sailing when an omen had taken pains to warn them.

"Do you think this a terrible portent?" asked Pericles.

"No—but—" answered a muffled trembling voice.

"What then is the difference between it and an eclipse of the sun, except that the eclipse is caused by something larger than my cloak?"

Anything in the nature of logic always made an irresistible appeal to the Athenian mind, and the helmsman, cheered, resumed his duties. The other ships must perforce follow, although Pericles heard loud grumbling in the rear. But he knew the men were too well disciplined to defy his authority, and did not trouble to look behind him as the fleet sailed across the Saronic Gulf to lay siege to Epidaurus.

VII

Dinner was over and Pericles Y had gone for a walk on the walls with Xanthias. Aspasia went to the thalamos, but left the door of the andron open, for a light in her own room would draw the mosquitoes. The night was suffocatingly hot. The window was open, but admitted little besides the snores of people sleeping in the street and the crying of children. Through the closed door of the court she heard the screams of a woman in travail. There was a distant rumble of thunder, but if a storm came to cool the air it would but add a drenching to other discomforts.

She walked up and down, oppressed not only by the loneliness and the misery about her but by nameless fears. Her spirit had been heavy often enough during the past two years, but she had always had Pericles to comfort her. Her long association with so strong a character had robbed her of much of her old independence. She felt as if some vital part had gone out of her, and smiled faintly as she thought of that other long separation when Pericles had been away at Samos for nine interminable months. She looked back to that period with a physical ache of longing, for it seemed to her that in that far-off time she had been not nine years but a lifetime younger than she was to-day. Her buoyant nature had been but temporarily depressed, nor had she grown so dependent upon him. If she had lost him then the arrogance and insolence of youth would have triumphed in time, and, with fewer memories, she would have turned her face to the future. Nothing had happened then to sadden her spirit incurably and to demonstrate that she and Pericles were really one, not merely a man and woman passionately in love.

And if he were the stronger she doubted if he would be able to put her out of his mind during this separation as he had when he too had been younger. In a more subtle way he had grown to be as dependent upon her as she upon him. Neither had ever failed the other! It was much to say, but it gave her little consolation now. She must spend long lonely evenings for months without him, bereft and stranded, and oppressed with the fear of worse to come.

She heard a girl give a low contented laugh under her window, and for a moment wished she were twenty once more and safe in Miletus. But she moved her head with slow unconscious emphasis. Not even for peace of mind or her old gaiety of spirit would she exchange the saddest of her memories with Pericles.

There was a step in the andron and she turned to see old Marcus.

"A slave has come from the house of Simonides, O Mistress," he said. "Agariste is ill and would see you?"

"Agariste? Ill?" If he had announced that Hermes at the door had thrust out feet from his pedestal and walked down the street she could not have felt more astonished. Agariste, like Pericles, had never been ill in her life, and looked as if she would outlive her great-grandchildren. But she went hastily to the inner room for a light mantle and veil.

"Has Xanthias come in?" she asked.

"But a few moments ago, Mistress."

"Go quickly and tell him to attend me."

The house of Simonides was at the other end of the street, but hurry as they would it took them some time to pick their way past and over recumbent bodies. Xanthias held her elbow firmly and prevented her from slipping. He did not speak until they were close to the house, and then his voice was gloomy.

"I hope it is not this new and terrible disease, O Mistress.

When Young Pericles and I were returning from the walls we saw two men spin about clutching their throats and fall to the ground, foaming at the mouth."

Aspasia stopped abruptly, feeling as if she had been turned into marble. "The plague!" she whispered. "In Athens!"

"I fear it is, Mistress. I remember it in my boyhood. I saw men fall in the street like that. If it has entered the house of Simonides I would have you turn back."

But Aspasia's muscles had relaxed and she went on as swiftly as was possible. The door of the house was opened by a pale and trembling slave, and Simonides ran forward to meet her.

"O Aspasia!" he screamed. "Come quickly! Agariste is dying! Agariste!"

He was an ineffective little man, although intelligent, and he loved his authoritative wife much as a dog loves a stern master.

"How long has she been ill——"

"Five days now, but Acron would not let me send for you before, although when she can speak she asks for you. But when he was away just now I sent for you. She is suffering frightfully——"

Aspasia waited for no more and ran through the pastas into the thalamos. Then for a moment she shrank back at the horrible sight before her.

Agariste, naked, her body livid and covered with ulcers, her staring eyes as red as if swimming in blood, was sitting up on a hard cushionless bed, a slave supporting her, and drinking greedily from a large krater held to her swollen lips by Acron. She suddenly thrust the bowl aside, attacked by a terrible retching, and then went into violent convulsions.

When they passed she opened her eyes and caught sight of Aspasia, who had dragged herself close to the bed and stood staring down at her.

"Oh, Aspasia!" she gasped out faintly. "Cannot you help me? I am dying. . . . I never thought about death at all . . . and to die like this. . . . O Zeus, how I suffer!" And she twisted herself from side to side beating the bed with both hands.

Aspasia caught Acron by the shoulders and shook him. "Can

you do nothing?" she cried furiously. "What are doctors good for?"

"Calm yourself, Aspasia," he whispered. "It is the plague, and nothing can save her. . . . This, I fear, is the last." For Agariste had been seized with another violent paroxysm. It lasted but a moment. The body turned suddenly limp, the face black. The maid ran out screaming and Simonides fell to the floor tearing at his hair.

"Come away," said Acron. "They sent for you against my orders. You must not expose yourself further—"

"I shall stay with Agariste. It is the least I can do for her—and she sent for me!"

"Think of Pericles and your son," he said sternly. "You can do nothing for her now."

She ceased to resist and he led her from the room.

"Are there other cases?" she asked, and wondered she could speak at all. "Has the plague come to Athens?"

"It began to rage in the Piræus yesterday, and I have had seven cases here. Agariste's was one of the first. Thucydides has been attacked, but will recover. Now, do not leave the house again no matter who sends for you. The doctors have kept their council so far, and assured the afflicted households that the attacks were caused by poisoned cisterns. But if the disease spreads, as I feel sure it will, there will be a terrible panic in Athens. If any of your friends are smitten I will come and tell you—I will call daily for a moment in any case. Will you promise me that for your husband's and son's sake you will not leave the house?"

"I promise," muttered Aspasia.

She stumbled along beside Xanthias, blind with tears and shaken with horror and grief. Agariste! What would life be without that faithful strong friend? The loss of Anaxagoras and Pheidias seemed trifling in comparison. One more friend gone out of this terrible world—loathsomely dead!

"Do not weep, Mistress," said Xanthias, who was supporting her with his arm. "I cannot bear it, for I have never seen you weep before. And do not fear the plague, for fear invites it."

"I have no fear—and neither had Agariste."

"No, Mistress, it attacks whom it will and often the strongest, but to fear adds to the danger. And you must keep vinegar in all the rooms you frequent and smell of it constantly. I shall keep a rag wet with it about Young Pericles' neck."

"The boy!" she cried, forgetting Agariste for the moment. "The boy! He was with you when those men were attacked."

"I shall go to-night to one of the temples and offer sacrifice to Ascelpius and Athenè for him and for you and for all the household—of the gold chain that Alcibiades gave me. Let us believe that the gods will protect us."

When they reached the house Aspasia ran into Young Pericles' room, but he was sleeping quietly. She went on to her own to pace it, wringing her hands and weeping for Agariste until fatigue overcame her and she fell on her bed and slept.

VIII

When she awoke she was calm and felt that all her old strength had returned to her. This was no time to mourn the absence of her husband and dwell on the past. She mattered little in this terrible calamity that had overtaken Athens. If her own household were spared she would have much to be thankful for. If not she must meet further tragedy with all the firmness she possessed. She thrust Agariste out of her mind.

She forbade Pericles Y to leave the house. Xanthias put him through many of the exercises to which he was accustomed in the Palæstra, then doused him with water, rubbed him down with olive oil and scraped it off. It was not only exercise that made the Athenians supple. He was a studious boy, and when he could escape from Xanthias found a cool spot and read his Hesiod and Homer.

Certain of the slaves were obliged to go out daily and buy fish and bread, but Aspasia isolated them in the garden and they passed their purchases through the door to the cook. They were given no reasons and it was not for slaves to ask questions nor dispute the will of their masters. Euangelos and Xanthias alone were in her confidence at first, and ably seconded her efforts, but in a day or two she decided to inform the four farmers whose families occupied the inner quarters that the plague was in Athens, for she guessed they were in the habit of seeking amusement abroad. Terrified as they were, they readily promised to keep as far from danger as possible. She ordered them to use vinegar freely and to keep the aula clean.

Acron called daily to inquire for the health of the household, but when Aspasia was sent for she met him at the entrance door which he held between them, speaking through the crack. He gave her news of the progress of the plague and that news was daily more appalling. Few households escaped and men fell constantly in the streets. The temples were charnel houses. Panic reigned. None left the house who could avoid it and gathered about the altar offering sacrifice. The disease was raging among those herded in the Agora. They died like poisoned dogs, cursing the gods. The survivors burned the bodies until they were weary, then left them to rot. Those there and in the streets who could reach the fountains to quench the mortal thirst that consumed them fell in and infected the water. Several of the doctors had died, but a number of calm spirits had offered their services to those who were left, and went fearlessly about giving what aid they could. But others had deserted the stricken and left them to die alone. They hid in distant rooms or on the roof, and would have left the house if they had known where to go. Others whose families had been wiped out or recovered went to the bedside of their friends. There were many instances of heroism, if more of cowardice.

Funeral pyres were erected in the courtyards. None was sacred in the open, for distracted men dragged their dead there and cast them into the flames. Acestorides was dead and many of his slaves, but Phyrra, at the first alarm, had gone with her children to Delos; Hagnias had provided her with a galley. As Thasson had persuaded Acestorides to remain and help the doctors, she had made her father go with her. His sons were all on military duty—at Potidæa, the frontier, or with Pericles —and he went not unwillingly. The family of Hagnias was safe in Miletus.

She heard this bit by bit, for Acron had no time to linger. It was only his affection for her that made him come at all. And there were things he did not tell her. The people were cursing Pericles as the cause of the war and therefore of the plague, which would never have become an epidemic if the countrymen had remained on their farms and others could have left Athens at the first sign of danger. And word had come that although he had ravaged the country about Epidaurus, the plague had broken out among the troops and he had failed to take the city. He had not turned back, however, but gone on to inflict damage on the territory surrounding Trozen, Halieis, and Hermione.

She received no messages from the fleet this time, for he had no orders to give her. Acron reflected she would hear of his reverses soon enough.

One day he told her that Xanthippus was dead. He had been stricken in the house of his hetæra, and she too had died, cursing him. The revelry in that part of the city had been scandalous, for men went there to forget the horror about them. But if she thought of Xanthippus at all it was to be thankful that Pericles had one enemy the less.

None of her other friends came even to the door of the house. Socrates had gone back to Potidæa and Alcibiades with him. Sophocles sent a slave daily to inquire for her health, but he thought it wise to remain in his own house and divert his mind with a new play to be called *Ajax*. Pyrilampes had remained as the guest of Pericles but a few weeks; he felt himself out of place in that rarefied atmosphere and had persuaded a friend of his own class to make room for him. Aspasia was thankful she did not have him to entertain at table.

She went daily among the people living in the rear quarters, quieting their fears as best she could and on the lookout for symptoms. But although they were pale and silent they seemed well enough. Two of the slaves sent out for food had not returned and she could only infer they had fallen in the street and died untended.

Horrible sounds came through her window and over the walls into the courts. Shrieks; the despairing groans of those just attacked; coughing and retching as if soul and body were being torn asunder. And the stenches were abominable.

She had three tents erected on the roof, for herself, Young

Pericles, and Xanthias, and they slept there at night. But although she burned frankincense it did little to mitigate the reeking atmosphere, and the hooting of owls could hardly be heard for the screams of the afflicted. But she forced her mind to tranquillity and managed to sleep. She knew that Pericles must be well, for if he had been attacked the news would have come swiftly to Athens.

One day she was surprised by a visit from Constantia. She knew that this faithful friend had had the disease but recovered; she had sent messages to her by Acron but had no expectation of seeing her until the epidemic was over. She was leaving the andron when she caught sight of a veiled woman in the aula and ran forward.

"It cannot be Constantia!" she cried. "But of course—"

"Don't come too close—although all the clothes I had been wearing have been burned and these were in a chest upstairs. And I cannot carry the infection in my hair!" She laughed with little of her old mirth and threw off her veil. Her head was bald, and eyelashes and eyebrows had disappeared. She looked like something taken from a tomb and terribly provided with a pair of black living eyes.

"Constantia!" Aspasia's legs gave way and she dropped on a bench. Constantia seated herself opposite and covered her head.

"Acron says my hair will come back in due course and I'm thankful to be alive. No one else in the house took it and I'm still hoping they'll be spared. I knew my appearance would shock you but I could not resist bringing you good news."

"Good news? What could be good news for Athens? And I have no wish to hear that Pericles is on his way home. I only pray he will not return before the plague has passed."

"I have heard little of Pericles, but my news is really good. The enemy is leaving Attica. The Generals suspected something wrong when they saw so many fires in Athens. A terrified wretch managed to slip out of the city two nights ago, and when he confirmed their suspicions they packed up in haste."

"Well, I hope the deserter will infect the entire army," said

Aspasia, with no attempt to be noble. "But Fate is on their side so far. What a city for Pericles to come back to!"

Constantia knew of his failure at Epidaurus and the attitude of the Athenians, but she had no intention of adding ill news to good, and said warmly: "I cannot tell you what a relief it has been to me to be assured daily by Acron that all is well in this house."

"Dear Constantia!" Aspasia's eyes filled with tears; but she sternly banished any tendency to melt. She had hardened her spirit and hard it must remain. "You cannot tell how much good your visit has done me," she said smiling. "It seems as if years had passed since I had any one to talk to. Give me what news you have."

"Olympias has recovered but I suppose she still mourns for Xanthippus. She was as fond of him as she could be of any one, no doubt because he was so much like her and had nothing of Pericles in him. Thasson is doing good work, but inconsolable over the loss of his Acestorides. I hear he nursed him, although poor Acestorides was a thing to run from before he died. He was a supercilious weak creature, for all his intellect, but I would he could have kept his beauty to the last. The slaves had deserted the house and Thasson built the pyre in the courtyard and burned him. I hate Thasson for the ill he has done Pericles, but it is impossible not to admire him."

"He has many virtues," said Aspasia coldly, "but I will say with candor that I wish the plague would claim every one of Pericles' enemies. What of Cleon?"

"Neither Glaucon nor Acron has told me aught of him. But if he had died we should have heard of it. Perhaps he is with the fleet. Have you heard that old Zopyrus is dead?"

"No!"

"It was yesterday. But he had long ceased to have any influence over Clinias—who spends his time in the worst quarter of the city. He tries to imitate Alcibiades in his vices—and with nothing to redeem them. The moment Zopyrus was stricken he ran from the house and has not returned."

"Have you heard anything of Elpinike—and my old Aunt Daphne? I have not thought of her for years."

"I should think they were both too old to die of anything but age, although Acron says many of the old have been stricken. The plague seems to be impartial—and democratic enough to satisfy even Cleon. If the poor have suffered so have the rich. Oh, Aspasia! Why should Athens be so afflicted? What has she done to deserve it? It was not she who wanted this terrible war. The gods must hate us, and who has done more to honor them?"

Aspasia shrugged. "Futile questions. We are the victims of unhappy chance. If Athens did not deserve affliction neither did many who have died horribly. If your gods were just and impartial Sparta not Athens would have been stricken—and only the wicked among us attacked. It is idle to question or speculate."

Constantia looked at her keenly. "You have changed, Aspasia. You were always cold in your intellectual moods, but this is different. You seem—is it harder?"

"I would turn myself into marble if I could. But at least I have composed myself to meet whatever befalls. For the first time in my life I have had to stand alone. Perhaps it has done me good!"

"Perhaps—but I wish Pericles need not have left you to bear this ordeal alone."

"It is the only thing I have to be thankful for—that and the continued well-being of the boy. How glad I am that your beautiful Charmides has escaped. You will send him to the country now, of course?"

"We shall all go as soon as the enemy has disappeared—to live in tents! That is another reason I felt I must see you." She rose and lowered her veil. "Pray that I may have my eyebrows and eyelashes back when we meet again," she said, with something of her old lively humor. "Shall you not go to the country too?"

"I shall remain here."

"I feared so—but for you I have never feared. You know I always said you were at least half a goddess. Until better times, then, dear Aspasia."

When she had gone Aspasia carried the good news to the inner quarters. Three days later that aula was deserted by all but the slaves. She sent Xanthias and Young Pericles to the breeding-farm on Eubœa and ordered them to remain there until the city was healthy again.

IX

There was an occasional cool day in summer and on one of them Aspasia went up to the roof to refresh her weary eyes with the beauty of the Acropolis.

The workmen had deserted it long since and no one remained there but the citizen-archers guarding the treasure. If the plague attacked them others were sent in their place—thankful, no doubt, to be elevated even so slightly above the city.

Those marble temples must have resounded with the groans and shrieks of the stricken, but from where she stood it would seem as if nothing could disturb their serene and lofty repose. They had been built by mortal hands, conceived by mortal minds, but themselves they looked as immortal as the gods— and as indifferent. So they would look a thousand years hence, when generation after generation of mortals had fallen to dust, forgotten, their futile lives over. What would this terrible visitation matter then: when one's remote descendants would neither know nor care who had died of a plague or been assailed by his enemies in an ancient city of which naught but her monu- ments remained? They would read of Pericles in their history- books, but what would he be to them save a name? For a moment, as she projected her mind far into the future, she seemed to stand with them, idly unrolling a history—Thucydi- des' perhaps—on which the name of Pericles meant nothing more to her than that of any of the great names of the past. She lost all sense of that vital body and quick pulsing brain out there on the sea making history at this moment, and recalled a line of Pindar:

For man is the creature of a day, the dream of a shadow.

What were they all but shadows? Drifting through their little parts among other shadows, few to survive on the page of history!

She recalled herself and looked down over the city; that

lofty columned beauty on the Acropolis no longer soothed her tired spirit, for it seemed to mock at the desires and the ambitions of the pigmies that crawled at its base. The streets were deserted now, and the Agora had been cleaned once more; no doubt men gathered there as of old, for although the plague had not abated panic had passed. The magistrates had been active, cleaning up the streets and burning the huts occupied by the refugees; and all bodies left unburied had been carted out of the city by slaves under the lash and burned on one vast pyre, the bones buried in a deep trench.

The people, although bitter and gloomy, were stoical. Those who had been spared so far looked upon themselves as the chosen of the gods, and some had caught the distemper but recovered. They went about their business doggedly and took up the burden of daily existence. The Areopagus—what was left of it—assembled on the hill of Ares. The Council of Five Hundred met daily, and the dicasts were active, trying once respectable citizens, who, lost to all sense of law or decency, had broken into houses where the last man to defend his possessions had been burned in the courtyard, and seized whatever they could lay hands on. Nor had they spared the sacred vessels in the temples and shrines. To them the end of the world had come, and they fought and killed over a bag of drachmæ that they might drink out their lives in wine houses. But many survived and they seemed to take a mean delight in accusing one another.

Acron, tired out, had been persuaded to enter the house the day before, and rest, and remain for luncheon. He had given Aspasia another piece of information and one which she knew would be unwelcome to Pericles. The Council had sent a herald to Sparta offering to open negotiations for peace; and been repulsed with disdain. But he told her nothing of the hatred he heard expressed on every side for Pericles, who was still looked upon by Athens as the author of all her woes.

Aspasia, however, knew Athens well enough to guess at its temper and gave a quick impatient sigh as she turned to go below. And then she stopped short and looked toward the west with straining eyes. A fleet was sailing across the Saronic Gulf toward Piræus. Pericles had returned!

No joy shook her. He was coming to expose himself to the plague, and to the ghost of the Athens he had left. She had hoped he would continue to ravage the coasts until the winter rains set in. Of course he must have heard that the plague had spread to Athens, but as he had been constantly moving it could have been nothing more than an unconfirmed rumor, and there had been little communication between the Council and the fleet. But she had fortified her spirit to some purpose, and she went down the stair to order a house slave to dust and air the office and set out vinegar in all the rooms.

x

Pericles walked up and down the thalamos as Aspasia related the terrible story of Athens. Hagnias had met him at the quay and briefly prepared him for the worst. He had ridden alone from the Piræus, and through the deserted streets of the city. The few men he had passed had averted their heads, and one had run after him shouting invectives.

"It is all to do over again," he said with a sigh when she had finished. "There shall be no more heralds sent to Sparta; and iron must be poured into the Athenians. They have suffered a terrible visitation, and one no man could foresee—it has upset all my calculations. But if they can be made to remember they are men, and of a race that has suffered many vicissitudes, and that Athens must be preserved at all costs, we shall come off victors in the end. I doubt if the Spartans will return next summer. There is little left to destroy and they will still fear the plague. We shall go on inflicting damage with our navy."

He told her of his failure at Epidaurus. "In three days more we should have taken the city, but the plague suddenly broke out with virulence. There was nothing to do but abandon the poor wretches and get away as quickly as possible. The rest must be protected, and by good fortune we had no further cases. I am sending a part of the fleet to Potidæa, but I shall not leave Athens again. How many of my friends have been taken?"

She gave him a long list of his contemporaries, some of whom he had once known intimately.

"And so few of my enemies! But if the tide of my fortune has turned I am still strong enough to swim against it. And you have been spared—you and the two boys. I cannot grieve for Xanthippus, for if he had lived it would have been but to disgrace himself further. But I should grieve for the friends I have lost—and for Agariste!—if this were the time for anything so personal as grief. How many Athenians have gone back to their estates?"

"A few like Glaucon are living in tents or huts, but Acron told me that after the enemy left many rode out to look at their properties and returned in a state bordering on distraction. Every house in Attica without the walls has been burnt, the trees of the parks cut down, the statues and fountains and shrines smashed to bits. They are too disheartened to face their ruins again, and try to forget in Athens."

"There they could have expected nothing else, and if the plague had not come no doubt they would have endured the loss of their material wealth in a better spirit. But they must be taught they are to endure all things without yielding to the enemy. I shall call the Ecclesia six days hence, and begin to compose my speech at once."

He attended the funerals of two of his friends during the interval; friends of whom he had seen little of late years but with whom he had wrestled in the gymnasium in his youth, and who had served him willingly when called upon.

Funerals attracted little attention in these days, but as Pericles was noticed among the male relatives and friends preceding a couch on its way to the Outer Ceramicus, many paused and stared at him, wondering that his calm should remain unshaken amid all the calamities that had overtaken him. Something of their old admiration stirred; but others resented that Olympian aloofness and would have given a part of their remaining wealth to see it shattered. All looked forward to his appearance on the Pnyx, and with mingled feelings. It would be a distraction at least, and there was much curiosity as to what he would have to say. Several went to his house to warn him that the Athe-

nians held him responsible for their bitter misfortunes; perhaps
with the hope of shaking his confidence in himself, and of creating a distress and confusion of mind that would cause him for
once to be weak and ineffective on the Bema. But Pericles
listened to them calmly and replied that he would reserve his
arguments for the Ecclesia.

Cleon and Thoron had served with the fleet but were not
detailed to Potidæa. They as well as other members of the
reorganized clubs, notably Sammias and Lacritides, both of the
extreme democratic party, ran about Athens lighting the fires of
hatred in minds grown apathetic to all but personal loss, feeding others with tales of Pericles' cruelty at Epidaurus in throwing out men from the ships to die like dogs on the enemy's
shore. They feared he would regain all his old influence now
that he was back in Athens to seduce with that golden voice
of his and his infernal cleverness. However these Athenians
might blame him for their sufferings they were likely to reflect
that they had no other leader. They would be taught another
lesson in the future, but it was the present these ambitious
young men feared. When they heard that his favorite son
Paralus was down with the plague they rejoiced.

Paralus, not unnaturally, had longed for a little amusement
after months of hard service, and had gone with some friends
to the house of a popular hetæra; no other than Samantha of
Megara, who possessed courage as well as liveliness and gave
nightly banquets. He had returned late and very drunk, and
been grumblingly but not unsympathetically put to bed by old
Marcus. He awoke sneezing and coughing, and ran out into
the aula screaming that he was on fire inside. Pericles was on
his way to the entrance. Paralus fell at his feet groaning with
the terror and despair that clutched at the vitals of all victims,
and lessened their chances of recovery.

Pericles, feeling as if his world was sinking under him, carried him back to his bed and sent in haste for Acron. That
indefatigable wiry little man, who often wondered if he had
seven lives, ran to the house. A glance told him that the young
man had taken the distemper in its worst form, but he assumed
a cheerful manner and ordered the bed taken out into the

portico and a bonfire of pine wood and myrrh to be kept burning constantly beside it. For three days and two nights Pericles and Aspasia sat by the bedside of Paralus, witnessing his terrible sufferings and gazing with dry despairing eyes at his hideous face and body. They administered the futile remedies and gave him the water he screamed for when not in convulsions. Euangelos and Hagnias tended the bonfire, and Thera and old Marcus helped as they could. The other slaves huddled in the inner court and several deserted the house.

On the third night Pericles went to the thalamos and slept, for he must speak on the Pnyx in the morning. He put his dying son out of his mind, and left the house at the rear.

XI

The Pnyx was packed with men standing, and all knew of the fresh affliction that had visited him. Some were filled with pity, for they had lost sons of their own or feared for them. Others stared at him with hard curious eyes. All had wondered if he would come, and those who did not hate him gazed at the calm majestic figure that faced them on the Bema, after the usual preliminaries were over, with awe and admiration. There was no trace of grief or anxiety on that lofty countenance. His enemies felt a sinking sensation of apprehension. Was this man a god that nothing could move him? They had built their hopes on the presumably fatal illness of his son, and he looked as if he had not a care in the world, although his calm face was stern. The sight maddened them and many others and they burst into shouts and wild invectives, shaking their fists and looking as if they would press forward and tear him limb from limb. In vain the President called for order and the Scythian archers hit them over the heads with their staffs. It was their first chance to relieve their feelings in public and tell him what they thought of him.

Pericles stood immobile and waited for the tempest to pass. He knew their desire to hear him speak would overcome their hatred, and ran his mind hastily over his oration. He had composed it with his usual care, and with a view not only to the psychology of his Athenians, but to their circumstances of the moment. This was no time for an assumption of friendly sympathy and an air of intimate understanding. They must be brought to their senses before they had time to invite the final disaster. He would encourage and raise their spirits, but as citizens of Athens, not as men suffering unduly under the lash of fate. When the men had exhausted themselves and their voices died away in a low grumble he began to speak, and his own voice was cold, quick, and authoritative. At times there was scorn in it, but never a hint of apology nor compromise.

"I was expecting this outburst of indignation," he said. "The causes of it are not unknown to me. And I have summoned an assembly that I may remind you of your resolutions and reprove you for your inconsiderate anger against me, and want of fortitude in misfortune. In my judgment it would be better for individuals themselves that the citizens should suffer and the State flourish than the citizens should flourish and the State suffer. A private man, however successful in his own dealings, if his country perish is involved in her destruction; but if he be an unprosperous citizen of a prosperous city he is much more likely to recover. Seeing that states can bear the misfortunes of individuals, but individuals cannot bear the misfortunes of the State, let us all stand by our country and not do what you are doing now; who because you are stunned by your private calamities are abandoning the hope of saving the State, and not only condemming me who advised, but yourselves who consented to, the war. Yet I, with whom you are so angry, venture to say of myself, that I am as capable as any one of devising and explaining a sound policy; and that I am a lover of my country and incorruptible. Now, a man may have a policy which he cannot clearly expound, and then he might as well have none at all; or he may possess both ability and eloquence, but if he is disloyal to his country, he cannot, like a true man, speak in her interest; or again he may be unable to resist a bribe, and then all his other good qualities will be sold for money. If, when you determined to go to war, you believed me to have somewhat more of the statesman in me than others, it is not reasonable that I should now be charged with anything like crime.

"I allow that for men who are in prosperity and free to choose it is great folly to make war. But when they must either submit and surrender at once independence, or strike and be free, then he who shuns and not he who meets the danger is deserving of blame. For my own part I am the same man and stand where I did. But you are changed for you have been driven by misfortune to recall the consent which you gave when you were unhurt, and you think that my advice was wrong because your own characters are weak. The pain is present and comes home to each one of you, but the good is as yet unrealized by any one; and your minds have not the strength to persevere in your resolution, now that a great reverse has taken you unawares. Anything which is sudden and unexpected and utterly beyond calculation, such a disaster for instance as this plague coming upon other misfortunes, enthralls the spirit of a man. Nevertheless, being the citizens of a great city and educated in a temper of greatness, you should not succumb to calamities however overwhelming, nor darken the luster of your fame. For if men hate the presumption of those who claim a reputation to which they have no right, they equally condemn the faint-heartedness of those who fall below the glory which is their own. You should lose the sense of your private sorrows and cling to the deliverance of the State.

"As to your sufferings from the war, if you fear that they may be very great and after all fruitless, I have shown you already over and over again, that such a fear is groundless. If you are still unsatisfied I will indicate one element of your superiority which appears to have escaped you, although it nearly touches your imperial greatness. I have not mentioned it before, nor would I now, because the claim may seem too arrogant, if I did not see that you are unreasonably depressed. You think that your empire is confined to your allies, but I say that of the two divisions of the world accessible to man, the land and the sea, there is one of which you are absolute masters, and have, or may have, the dominion to any extent you please. Neither the great King nor any nation on earth can hinder a navy like yours from penetrating whithersoever you choose to sail. When we reflect on this great power, houses and lands, of which the loss seems so dreadful to you, are as nothing. We ought not to be troubled about them nor to think much of them in comparison; they are only the garden of the house, the superfluous ornament of wealth; and you may be sure that if we cling to our own freedom and preserve that, we shall soon enough recover all the rest. But if we are the servants of others we shall be sure to lose not only freedom but all that freedom gives. And where your ancestors doubly succeeded you will doubly fall. For their empire was not inherited by them from others but won by the labor of their hands, and by them preserved and bequeathed to us. And to be robbed of what you have is a greater disgrace than to attempt a conquest and fail. Meet your enemies therefore not only with spirit but with disdain. A coward or a fortunate fool may brag and vaunt, but he only is capable of disdain whose conviction that he is stronger than his enemy rests, like our own, on grounds of reason. Courage fighting in a fair field is fortified by the intelligence which looks down upon an enemy; an intelligence relying, not on hope, which is the strength of helplessness; but on that surer foresight which is given by reason and observation of the facts.

"Once more, you are bound to maintain the imperial dignity of your city, in which you all take pride; for you should not covet the glory unless you will endure the toil. And do not imagine that you are fighting about a simple issue, freedom or slavery; you have an empire to lose, and there is the danger to which the hatred of your imperial rule has exposed you. Neither can you resign your power, if, at this crisis, any timorous or inactive spirit among you is for thus playing an honest man. For by this time your empire has become a tyranny which in the opinion of many may have been unjustly gained, but which cannot be safely surrendered. The men of whom I was speaking, if they could find followers, would soon ruin a city, and if they were to go and found a state of their own would as surely ruin that. For inaction is secure only when arrayed by the side of activity; nor is it expedient or safe for a sovereign, but only for a subject state, to be a servant.

"You must not be led away by the advice of such citizens as these, nor be angry with me; for the resolution in favor of war was your own as much as mine. What if the enemy has come and done what he was certain to do when you refused to yield? What too if the plague followed? That was an unexpected blow, but we might have foreseen all the rest. I am well aware that your hatred of me is aggravated by it. But how unjustly, unless to me you also ascribe the credit of any extraordinary success which may befall you! The visitations of the gods should be borne with resignation, the sufferings inflicted by an enemy with manliness. This has always been the spirit of Athens, and should not die out in you. Know that our city has the greatest name in all the world because she has never yielded to misfortunes, but has sacrificed more lives and endured severer hardships in war than any other; wherefore she has the greatest power of any state up to this day; and the memory of her glory will always survive. Even if we should be compelled at last to abate somewhat of our greatness (for all things have their time of growth and decay), yet will the recollection live, that of all Hellenes, we ruled over the greatest number of Hellenic subjects; that we withstood our enemies, whether single or united, in the most terrible wars, and that we were the inhabitants of a city endowed with every sort of wealth and greatness. The indolent may indeed find fault, but the man of action will seek to rival us, and he who is less fortunate will envy us. To be hateful and offensive has ever been, at the time, the fate of those who aspired to empire. But he judges well who accepts unpopularity in a great cause. Hatred does not last long, and besides the immediate splendor of great actions, the renown of them endures forever in men's memories. Looking forward to such future glory and present avoidance of dishonor, make an effort now and secure both. Let no herald be sent to the Lacedemonians, and do not let them know that you are depressed by your sufferings. For those are the greatest states and the greatest men, who, when misfortunes come, are the least depressed in spirit and the most resolute in action."

XI

As he left the Pnyx he saw Cleon forcing his way toward the President, and before he was out of earshot heard the man shouting—with an accent of terror in his voice! He was joined a moment later by Thucydides, who had hastened after him.

"That was the right speech, Pericles," he said. "Every word weighed, as ever. I think it will have due effect. The Athenians are distraught, but the majority are reasonable and only ask to be told what to do. That Cleon and others like him will shout in vain." He turned his head. "Look! They are already leaving the Pnyx. They are in no mood to listen to any one else."

But Pericles had forgotten the Athenians. "Paralus is ill of the plague," he said. "I must hasten to the house."

"I am grieved to hear of this affliction, Pericles." Thucydides spoke awkwardly. He had little human sympathy and was poor at expressing what he had. But he feared the effect of this favorite son's death on the First Citizen. If that strong spirit should break he shuddered to think of what would happen to Athens. "I hope for the best," he continued. "I had the disorder myself and recovered, although I feel its effects yet. And he is young and very strong."

"I hope, of course," said Pericles, and there was little in his voice. "But if the worst comes I can do no less than follow the advice I gave the Athenians."

Thucydides changed the subject. "There was one point in your speech that Cleon will not fail to make the most of. When the Athenians after the Samian War wished to use their navy to conquer the world you scolded them roundly. And yet to-day you encouraged them to hope for conquest in the future."

"That future is far off, and my business to-day was to infuse them with hope and with pride in the Empire. When we have conquered the Lacedemonians they will think of nothing but rebuilding their houses and replanting orchards, vineyards, and crops; others of increasing their fortunes. If the time ever comes when they remind me of my words I shall speak to them as circumstances dictate."

"Here is your house, Pericles, and I shall enter if you permit, and assist you in nursing Paralus. I have much knowledge of the disease and should have come before but have been with a friend mortally stricken."

"That is like you, Thucydides, and I shall be grateful for your help."

But no help served for Paralus and he died on the eighth day, tormented to the last and an awful sight to look upon.

When it was over Pericles and Aspasia went to the thalamos and did not leave it again until the funeral, which took place on the following morning.

Thucydides and Hagnias performed the last offices and laid the body on a couch in the aula, covering it with one of Aspasia's purple quilts. Marcus went out to order the pyre to be built near the Dipylon Gate, and Euangelos, as in duty bound, left the death news at the houses of all members of the two clans.

The Alcmæonidæ and Bouzygæ put aside their hatreds, and in that gray depressing hour before dawn assembled in the aula of Pericles' house on the morning of the funeral. They covered the body with their garlands, but hardly veiled the curiosity in their eyes as they watched Pericles and Aspasia walk down the court from the pastas. Aspasia, white and exhausted, sank into a chair at some distance from the altar, but Pericles came forward to lay an olive wreath on the bier. His face was bleak and hollowed from his long watch, but his step was firm and he held himself as proudly as ever.

Whispers ran through the company. "Olympian!" "Of course." "What did you expect?" "He has no love for any but Aspasia." "And no son to carry on his name!" "So much the better." "No doubt he thinks it fitting his line should end with himself."

Pericles laid the garland on the body, and then, as unexpectedly to himself as to his startled relatives, he broke down. His calm during those long days and nights, when he had slept but an hour at a time, had been an unnatural strain, and he was exhausted in body as in mind. He buried his face in his hands and sobbed uncontrollably.

Aspasia threw her veil over her face and hastened forward and stood beside him. Thucydides was horrified and resentful. But in that moment of insufferable agony Pericles won back the affection and allegiance of those proud men and women whom his arrogance had alienated in the past. It took them a moment or two to recover from their incredulous astonishment, and then they crowded about him, murmuring their sympathy and forgetting their love of cynical criticism. One of the women took Aspasia's hand and held it firmly.

He recovered himself quickly, and told Thucydides to form the procession and start for the Ceramicus at once. Six slaves, threatened with sale by Euangelos if they disobeyed orders, came in and raised the bier on their shoulders, the women followed behind it, and Paralus passed out of the house of his father to lie beside Xanthippus on the Sacred Way. The direct line of Pericles was extinct.

Pericles had forbidden Aspasia to go to the cemetery and as she turned from the door she found that one of the women had remained also. She recognized her vaguely as the one who had held her hand during that moment when she had longed to be alone with Pericles.

"I am Clearista, the wife of Pericles' cousin, Euryptolemus," said the funeral guest, smiling. "It is many years since I have been in this house, and although I attended the wedding and the reception you would not remember me."

"No," said Aspasia listlessly. "I do not remember, but you are kind to have come to-day."

"This is the time to bury resentments, and Pericles has been sadly afflicted. We are all sorry for him, and if he meets us halfway, we shall be friendly with him again. Families should cling together as never before. Now I shall take you to the thalamos and put you to bed."

"Oh—but—" Aspasia threw back her veil and looked with a slight frown at this stranger who would intrude upon her sacred privacy. But Clearista's broad face beamed with so much kindliness and good-nature that annoyance flickered out. "You are kind," she said, "but is it wise to linger in this plague-smitten house?"

"We have had three cases among the slaves; my youngest son had it and recovered. What fear I had of the distemper has left me. It flies over the walls into the court; why apprehend taking it through the front door?"

She was a woman of ample proportions and she encircled

Aspasia with a thick but friendly arm. "Were Agariste alive she
would be with you to-day and I shall take her place as well as
I can. I shall remain with you until Pericles' return and then
leave you. But you must rest meanwhile and be ready for him.
Let us be grateful that in these days there is no funeral feast,
and even his enemies will let him alone for a few days."

XII

The Athenians, despite the passionate protests of Cleon, concluded to obey Pericles, and sent no more heralds to Sparta.
But although the ancient habit of deference to the wisdom of
their leader had asserted itself once more, they still believed
they hated him and were in a mood to find some practical vent
for their long resentment. Cleon, Thoron, Sammias, Thasson,
and Lacritides knew it was their moment to strike. They laid
before the archons an accusation of "pecuniary malversations,"
and the dicasts too were in a temper to humble him. He was
ordered to appear before the court and give a stricter account
of his public expenditures.

This blow was not unexpected, for Pericles knew his Athenians to the core. He went before the dicasts with even more
than his usual calm arrogance and defended himself with cold
precision. But they were not prepared to listen to reason and
fined him ten talents. He replied that the fine should be paid
as soon as his famous blooded horses could be sold, and as money
was scarce in Athens he suggested they take the horses over
and send them to Syracuse. To this they consented, and he
left the court knowing that worse would come. It came two
days later when the Ecclesia met to elect the Strategi for the
year. For the first time in nearly forty years he was not
reëlected.

Alcibiades, who had returned wounded from Potidæa shortly
after the funeral, brought the news to the house pale with rage.
He did not love Pericles, but deeply resented this affront to the
head of his clan, and still more the triumph of the enemy.
Moreover he feared for the safety of the State with its head cut
off, and he wanted no disaster to the Empire until he was old
enough to assume its leadership himself. He would have had

Pericles in firm control during the interval and then retire gracefully in his favor.

He found him sitting with Aspasia in the pastas arguing over Protagoras' *Truth,* which Pericles held open in his hand.

"How calm you both look!" he exclaimed irritably. "I believe if the truth were known you were both born in the Pentelic quarries. And I have ill news for you, Pericles. Can you guess what it is?"

Pericles lowered his lids and pressed his lips together. But he answered calmly. "I think I can guess. The Ecclesia has not reëlected me. Is it not true?"

Alcibiades sat down on the step of the pastas and looked at him curiously. "How can you take it so coolly, Pericles? Are you really indifferent?"

"No, I am not indifferent. But of what use to strive all one's days for the rhythm of life if it will not support one in adversity? I have endeavored to meet life at all points with serenity and I should be a poor thing if it failed me now. And I have had nearly forty years of power. Perhaps no man should ask more."

Aspasia, when Alcibiades delivered his news, had risen hastily and left the room.

"Our goddess feels these harsh and undeserved blows, O Pericles," said his young relative with a shrug. "She has kept up well, but she looks sad and tired, and if she is not careful will lose somewhat of her beauty."

"Which you would think the greatest misfortune of all! But Aspasia has a strong spirit and will not succumb to adversity."

"Well, I doubt if this phase of it lasts long, for the Athenians will soon realize they cannot do without you."

Pericles gave a quick involuntary sigh. "I shall care little if they do not," he said. "I feel as if some prop had fallen within me. I have no more desire for public life and should be content to spend the remaining years of my life at the farm in quiet and seclusion. The house is being rebuilt and all that was destroyed replanted. I shall live there with Aspasia, and my friends will be welcome. If the Athenians are firm the war will be over in another year. What Generals were elected?"

"Phormio, Hagnon, Thucydides—the others I do not recall."

"Phormio is an able and daring General. He will inflict damage enough to bring the Peloponnesians to terms. I have some hope, for Cleon and the rest are not yet men of sufficient influence to determine a policy. Nicias is rising to influence among the Oligarchs, but that party is still weak."

"You do not seem natural to me, Pericles," said Alcibiades crossly. "It is all very well to be resigned—and Olympian. But I see no trace of ambition left in you, and that is unnatural enough!"

"It is true, Alcibiades, that something seemed to go out of me with the death of Paralus. I never gave a thought to my age before, but I feel it now."

Alcibiades looked at him appraisingly. "You are gray only on the temples, which is rather becoming. But—yes—in some subtle way you look older. You have many years before you still however, and when the Athenians come begging it will be your duty not to repulse them."

Pericles smiled slightly. "It affects my sense of humor to hear you preach duty to me! Here comes Thucydides. You will have a strong advocate there."

Alcibiades rose hurriedly. "I cannot abide that virtuous young man. He bores me as much as Thasson." And he walked with great dignity down the aula, giving Thucydides a lofty nod. Thucydides took no notice of him whatever.

XIII

If Pericles had called upon all the resources of a mind and character trained through so many changing years to lofty purposes, he had hours of profound dejection. But this was the one thing he did not confide to Aspasia. She too had schooled herself to endure all things, but he had no wish that she should be tried too far. And he would have her look up to him until the end.

Alcibiades' prediction was justified. The Athenians, satiated with their own vengeance, underwent a quick reaction. They bitterly regretted his loss to public life, and although he could not be reëlected until the following summer, the magistrates and

Generals went constantly to his house to consult him. He found little of the repose he had anticipated.

Phormio, Thucydides and the other Generals came to him for advice before going out with the fleet. The heads of different departments in the government were after him continually. Even the magistrates of the Piræus visited him daily, and as for the expenditures for the following year, it seemed to him that he was forced to determine every obol of them.

The morning receptions were resumed, although on a sadly reduced scale. Many who had been faithful in attendance were dead, others were away superintending the reconstruction of their estates, for they believed that the Spartans would not return. Those who, like Sophocles, had ceased to think of the infection, were glad to forget Athens in that famous aula once more.

Good and bad news came from Potidæa. The city surrendered, but many of the besiegers had been killed or died of the plague. When the northern fleet returned to Athens there was another public funeral, but Pericles declined to make the oration. He dared not trust himself as far as that. He did not brood over the loss of Paralus, but he invited no reminders.

The clubs gnashed their teeth, for there was no question of Pericles' reëlection when Hekatombaion came round again. They had accomplished nothing after all. Cleon, Simmias, Thoron, Hermippus, Lacratides, Thasson, put their heads together but could think of no further way of discrediting him. Even the fine had not been pressed, and the Alcmæonid horses were still nibbling the grass on Eubœa. It was maddening, and to no one more than to Thasson. He felt that the death of Acestorides had not been avenged. But when Thoron suggested assassination he recoiled in horror, and even Cleon shook his head. He feared the vengeance of the Demos that was extolling Pericles as never before. They had heard that he intended to retire from Athens as soon as his new country house was finished, but this seemed too good to be true. It was damnable that the plague had not taken him when he was exposed to it during the illness of that booby Paralus, but there was hope of that solution yet. Thasson felt that nothing less would content him.

When Hekatombaion approached and the news spread in Athens that Pericles would not suffer reëlection, the Demos was deeply uneasy, and ambassadors visited him daily, imploring him to reconsider his decision and resume the leadership of the Empire. Alcibiades gave him no peace and Sophocles dared to lecture him.

It was not only a certain apathy of spirit that made him indifferent to a return to power; he was sensible of a curious lowering of his vital forces, and although he had been accustomed all his life to exercise he found himself disinclined for even a walk up and down the porticoes. This he could not conceal from Aspasia and she persuaded him to go with her to the farm and camp in the half-finished house. But it was a melancholy time for both of them, for that once beautiful estate was haunted by too many memories of poignant happiness.

That visit however decided his return to public life. His young son came over with Xanthias from Eubœa, and as Pericles looked with delight on this handsome and promising youth he suddenly realized that now was his opportunity to mend the break in the severed line of his house. He hastened back to Athens and asked to be heard before the dicastery.

A panel of fifteen hundred jurors was hastily called, and the courtroom was crowded, for all were aflame with curiosity to hear the explanation of such a request. Cleon *et al.* were present, hoping that he was come to beg off from his fine and they would enjoy the pleasure of seeing him properly humiliated; the dicasts might dilly-dally about collecting that fine until the whole episode was forgotten, but they hardly would dare cancel it publicly and slap the face of the law they professed to revere.

Pericles when summoned by the herald walked into the courtroom with his usual firm step and lofty dignity of carriage, but those staring eyes saw a change in him. Always slender, he looked really thin for the first time in their memory, and his face, if calm, was drawn and of an unhealthy yellow tint. There was a profound silence as he began to speak.

"I have asked to appear before you to prefer a singular request, Men of Law," he began, and there was a curious hollowness in his rich voice, although his tones were unfaltering.

"Many years ago I proposed the passing of a law to deprive all aliens of citizenship, decreeing that all children not born of two Athenian parents should be declared illegitimate, and ineligible to any office of the State. I am here to ask you to make an exception to that law in my favor, inconsistent as it may seem. I have, as you know, lost my two legitimate sons. There remains only my son Pericles the Younger; born under the ban of that law. I ask you to legitimate him that my name may be carried on in Athens and my line remain unbroken. It is not meet that the great name of Bouzyges should be disgraced in the future by the stain of bastardy. And if this boy is the son of Pericles who has served you faithfully, he is also the grandson of Xanthippus whose deeds you have recognized by a statue on the Acropolis.

"It is for you to decide, Men of Law, and I feel that I am entitled to have my request granted if I comply with your demand and return to public life. If you refuse I shall continue to live in retirement, for I can have no faith in your protestations without this pledge."

He spoke with a simple dignity that impressed the dicasts if not his enemies, and the threat manifest in his concluding words impressed them equally. They put the matter to the vote, and if there were a few who would have been glad to defeat the measure, they dared not gratify themselves and incur the wrath of the Demos.

Pericles the Younger was declared legitimate and could be enrolled at once in the phratry.

Two days later Pericles was elected a Strategos with acclaim, and cheering crowds surrounded his house for an hour. But they never saw him again.

XIV

Pericles lay on his narrow bed in the thalamos and heard little of the constant murmur of voices about him. He was dying of a low wasting disease for which Acron had no name, unless, indeed, it were some strange variant of the plague. He had not been called in until the morning after the scene in court, when, attempting to rise at the usual time from his bed, Pericles had sunk back overcome by weakness.

The doctor, to conceal his alarm, had scolded Aspasia, who, almost in a state of collapse herself at the sight of Pericles helpless on the bed, had protested she had asked her husband several times to visit him, but he had always refused. He had seemed better of late.

Acron, although he was at the head of his profession, called in several other doctors for consultation. They shook their heads solemnly and pronounced it the plague. What else could it be? The distemper was expiring, and no doubt the Strategos had taken it in this attenuated form. It was a matter for congratulation, not for alarm, and he would soon be as well as ever.

But three months had passed and he had steadily grown worse instead of better, so weak that he rarely raised his heavy eyelids, and had ceased to speak at all. Aspasia knew however that he was rarely unconscious of her presence.

She had summoned her fortitude again, and although she was too relentlessly clear-sighted to delude herself and hope for his recovery, she sternly put the future out of her mind and gave no thought to anything but his needs of the moment. But if she was rarely away from his bedside she obeyed the doctor and slept on the broader couch at night; it now occupied the corner, and Pericles' bed the middle of the room. Clearista had taken up her abode in the house and proved herself to be a sound and practical nurse. She was not Agariste, but Aspasia was thankful for her companionship, and when Clearista ordered her to take a walk in the aula did as she was told.

The other women of the two clans came in frequently to render what service they could, and when they begged permission to hang amulets and charms on Pericles, Aspasia gave an indifferent consent. The ridiculous objects could do him no harm and the act gratified them, so what matter? Pericles, before he became too weak to care what any one did to him, agreed with her, and indicated the talismans to Sophocles and Hagnias one day when he awoke to find them sitting at his bedside. "You see what I have come to!" he murmured with the phantom of a smile.

Once, as Aspasia, alone for the moment, stood staring down at him, wondering if this emaciated form and shrunken skull-like head could really belong to the man who for so many years had been her friend and companion and lover, he opened his eyes suddenly and met her wide, horrified, but pitying gaze.

"Yes, it is I, Aspasia," he said. "It is over—all that we have known together. . . . But you once said that nothing could take the past from us, and I think of that as I lie here dying. And I go without regret, dear head, for this is better than years of old age during which you would forget I had once been your lover. I would I could have gone suddenly, not been for so long a poor thing in your sight . . . that I could have died far away and only my decently covered bones returned to you. But you must forget—remember only—" His voice trailed off and his eyes closed.

He had resented his approaching death bitterly, when, for the first time he realized that he had been attacked by a disease that would yield to no treatment. There was more to leave than Aspasia. He knew now that he never would have contemplated retirement if his old vigor had not deserted him. It was not the death of Paralus, cruel a blow as that had been, which had induced that singular apathy. The seeds of the disease had been in him then; and later he would have hailed his return to influence and power with both triumph and joy. The Peloponnesians would be reduced to beg for terms and he would be the head of a greater Empire than ever, for Sparta and Corinth would be subject states, and those that had rallied about them in humbler case still.

Without him, and with those unprincipled and inexperienced demagogues in control, Zeus only knew what fate awaited the Athens he had loved and toiled and suffered for. Mercifully he was spared the prophetic foresight that the war would last twenty-seven years and his worst forebodings be realized.

But he had long ceased to think of Athens or to care what became of her. He was too weak to think, to regret, even to long for death. Sometimes vague thoughts or memories flitted through his mind and he made a feeble effort to hold them: it was as if Reason, pushed from her throne by the vile humors of the body, made vain efforts to regain it. But for the most part he lay in a stupor.

To-day he felt a trifle stronger and his brain was singularly clear. He became conscious that many men surrounded his bed and were talking about him. He recognized the voices of Sophocles, Zeno, Alcibiades, Phormio, Thucydides, Menippus—it must be late autumn and the fleet in harbor. There were other voices also, those of his relatives; he had heard them infrequently these last twenty years.

And then he found himself listening to their words, and smiled to himself as he realized they were discussing his many good deeds and famous achievements. He was a great patron of art, said Sophocles, and would live in history for that if for nothing else; but Menippus interrupted him angrily.

"He was the greatest of our Generals," exclaimed that old warrior. "No one else has erected so many trophies." And he recited the names of the battles in which Pericles had led his armies to victory or subdued rebellious cities.

"He could have been as great a philosopher as any of us," said Zeno when Menippus had finished. "He should have left war and the State to care for themselves. As it was, few could argue him into a corner—"

It was Thucydides who interrupted. "All that is as nothing to his statesmanship. You say he was the greatest of Generals, Menippus. It is true that he seldom failed, but there are others to take his place. But as a statesman he was unrivalled, in this or any time. He combined every gift the gods could bestow on a mortal selected for the greatest of all destinies. We shall never see his like again and I tremble for Athens."

There was a sharp discussion over these several virtues, for they believed him to be unconscious and were carried away by their love of argument. Suddenly Alcibiades made himself heard.

"We will put it to the vote," he cried. "All who agree with Thucydides lift your hands. Now for his greatness in war. For his merits as a philosopher. For his certainty to live in history as a patron of art. Statesmanship has it!"

Sophocles shrugged his shoulders. "The majority may be

right," he said amiably. "But statesmanship after all is but a name when a man has left this world for the realm of shades. These great monuments he has raised in Athens, the many men of genius he has encouraged—whose fame is also immortal—will be far more than a name to posterity."

"I maintain," said Menippus obstinately, "that it is as a great soldier he will go down the ages. Do you not agree with me, Phormio?"

"I do, Menippus—but look! His eyes are open! He has heard us—he looks as if he would speak."

He bent over the couch. "You have heard naught but good of yourself, Pericles," he said. "I hope we have not disturbed you and that you do not resent this discussion at your bedside."

Pericles smiled faintly, and his voice was clear as he spoke. "I have listened with surprise and some amusement to your words," he said. "What you praise in my life belongs partly to good fortune, and is, at best, common to me with many other Generals. But the peculiarity of which I am most proud you have not noticed: no Athenian ever put on mourning through any act of mine."

These historic words were his last. He lapsed into unconsciousness, and the men, awed, stole from the room.

XV

Aspasia, alone in the thalamos, slept for twenty-four hours. Pericles died in the early morning and his body was taken out into the main aula, where the women of the Bouzygæ performed the last offices for the dead. When they had finished, every member of the two clans, save only the youths and girls, assembled about the bier and stood for hours chanting the family dirge.

Young Pericles, who had been sent for several days since, stood among them endeavoring to look as calm and dignified as became the head of his house, but not daring to sing lest his voice break. He longed for the support of his mother or even Xanthias, but had been told by his stern mentor that on this day he must stand alone and do credit to his bringing-up. Aspasia had forbidden him to approach her until the ceremonies were over.

Just before nightfall Euangelos took the will of the dead man from the Master's Chest and handed it to Ariphon, who led the way into the andron to read it in the presence of the men of the clans. The women were sent home. Aspasia would have been invited but Euangelos refused to disturb her. She would need what strength she had left for the funeral on the morrow.

Ariphon sat under one of the high lamps and unrolled the parchment; holding it far from his eye as Sophocles had held his *Electra* in another tragic hour. But there was no one present to recall that scene. Agariste was dead, and the rites just performed were sacred to the family.

They stood in heavy silence waiting for Ariphon to begin; tired and oppressed. They had not loved this powerful and haughty relative but they were filled with apprehension for the fate of Athens, as well they might be. Pericles' death had signed her death-warrant, as far as her enduring greatness was concerned.

The will was brief and had been drawn up after the death of Paralus.

" 'This is the will of Pericles the Athenian,' " read Ariphon in a quavering voice; and then followed the usual formula: "May it be my lot to live in health and manage my own property, but should anything happen to me . . . I set free my faithful slaves Euangelos and Marcus. I bequeath my racehorses to Alcibiades son of Clinias, their progeny to be equally divided between himself and my son Pericles the Younger. To my friend Menippus I bequeath my helmet. To Thucydides son of Olorus my gold stilus. To Phormio my spear. To Hagnon my dagger. To Damon and Zeno each a volume from my library. To Sophocles any work of art in my collection he may prefer. To Hagnias of the Piræus my signet ring. To my son Pericles the Younger my shield. To my brother Ariphon the scarlet and white vase from Crete he has always coveted. To him also I bequeath my entire fortune in trust for my wife Aspasia daughter of Axiochus of Miletus and my son Pericles the Younger. I appoint my brother Ariphon son of Xanthippus and my friend Menippus son of Hippocles executors of my estate.

(Signed)
"Pericles the Bouzyges son of Xanthippus."

Alcibiades had looked sombre and depressed, but the bequest of the famous Alcmæonid horses raised his spirits; he knew they would never be claimed by the State. Ariphon, who was deeply afflicted by his brother's death, could not refrain from darting a glance at that ancient work of art still brilliant in color, that once may have graced the table of Minos. It had been saved from the conflagration that had laid the great palace of Knossos in ashes, perhaps by some appreciative revolutionist. At all events it had turned up in Carthage whence it had wandered to Athens and the house of Xanthippus.

The men went home to rest for the funeral of the morrow, leaving Ariphon to watch beside the bier with Thucydides, who had asked for that privilege. They cast a last glance at the shell of Pericles as they crossed the aula on their way to the entrance door of the house. Pericles dead! He had had the strongest body among them, as the mightiest brain and the most awe-inspiring presence. And now one part of him lay a shrunken corpse on that hard narrow couch, the great spirit that had animated it but a shade in the dark realm of Pluto. The mere mention of death had always oppressed them, but the death of Pericles made their souls faint. He was only sixty-four and should have lived for many years yet. What were all the deaths Athens had numbered during these last terrible years to the extinction of this great citizen to whom she owed more than life itself? Never before had they so bitterly realized the inevitability, the casual remorselessness of death. They went forth with dragging feet. Even Alcibiades was gloomy and forgot his bequest.

XVI

"It is time to awake, Mistress."

Thera, holding a lamp, stood by the broad couch whose soft violet cushions had been so often renewed. Aspasia opened her eyes and glanced quickly, as was her habit, in the direction of Pericles' bed. It was gone, and as she struggled up from the heavy sleep to which exhaustion had succumbed, she understood, uttered a faint cry, and shrank among her cushions. Thera set down the lamp and began to wail and beat her breast.

Aspasia sprang from the bed. "Keep quiet!" she exclaimed harshly. "Have I time for my bath?"

"Yes, Mistress. I thought of that. It will be more than an hour before the sun rises, and the bath is prepared."

"This is no time for tears," said Aspasia more kindly. "They may be indulged later, but I need all my strength now. If I should look weak and faltering they would not let me follow him to the pyre, and that would make me weep all my life."

She took her bath, and Thera dressed her in a white linen chiton, and a new black himation thoughtfully provided by Clearista. She twisted up her hair hurriedly, for the long black veil would cover it, although not the face. Her body felt as empty of its lamp as that of Pericles on its bier, but she knew she should go through the morning's ordeal with the calm and lofty composure he would have asked of her. Nor would the others expect her to wail, for in a recent conversation with Clearista she had requested that the women of the clans emulate the silent dignity of the men.

Before she left the room she took from its pedestal the bust of herself Pheidias had created for the pleasure of Pericles, and wrapping it in a piece of black cloth, encircled it with the arm that should have held a lekythos.

Sophocles, Alcibiades, Clearista, and Constantia met her in the pastas, and she saw that the aula was as crowded as on the night when the citizens of Athens had come to congratulate him on the result of the ostrakismos. All the dignitaries of State were there; the archons, the fifty Presidents of the Council of Five Hundred, the prytanes, the more important of the lesser magistrates, and even the members of the Areopagus; representatives of all the great families of the Eupatridæ save the extreme Oligarchs, all prominent Metics, besides relatives and friends. All wore the mourning himation, and above that black mass white faces shone dimly in the light of four lanterns Euangelos had attached to the pillars.

But her eyes were blind to details. She failed to detach even the woebegone countenance of Socrates and the cold regular profile of Phyrra, who was stifling a yawn. The aula was as silent as if it had been empty. The body of Pericles was obliterated under wreaths of olive and laurel and garlands of flowers. Euangelos had placed a coin between the gray lips of the dead man, although he would have omitted this convention had he dared to face the indignation of the clans, for few had known Pericles better than his steward. He felt as if he were insulting that proud spirit that had stood alone always, asking nothing of gods, and holding superstition in contempt.

Public marshals had been summoned to arrange the funeral procession in order and get it out of the house and on its way to the Ceramicus in good time. As soon as Aspasia appeared they signalled to the dignitaries to assemble at the door and march out two by two.

"I would I could walk with you, Aspasia," murmured Sophocles, while Alcibiades caught her hand and Constantia and Clearista looked at her anxiously. But she moved her head slightly.

"Go," she said. "My place is behind him, and I would walk alone." And she made her way to the bier which the slaves had lifted to their shoulders.

The torch-bearers were before the house, and Scythian archers to keep the crowds assembled there from pressing forward too closely. Ariphon and Young Pericles walked directly before the couch, Aspasia behind, followed by the women. The long procession was closed by slaves bearing a table covered with lekythoi, garlands and votive offerings. Xanthias, although no longer a slave, had taken his place among them, as he felt it more his duty than ever to watch over the daughter of Axiochus.

The population of Athens was sadly reduced, for twenty thousand citizens had succumbed to the plague alone, although many had not been residents of the city; but the streets and Agora were crowded by men and women in mourning, and others stood on the roofs to watch the last journey of Pericles as so often they had stood to cheer him as he rode forth to war. The silence was profound, for no voices were raised in lamentation. The people were too oppressed by the calamity that had befallen them to be demonstrative in their grief.

The procession moved slowly past the Pnyx, the scene of so many of his triumphs, through the Agora and out the Dipylon Gate. The bier was lifted to the pyre and Aspasia summoned Alcibiades and handed him the bust.

"My arms are not long enough," she said. "Place this beside him."

Alcibiades guessed immediately what was hidden within that black cloth and recoiled from the sacrifice of a great work of art, and the only portrait of Aspasia in existence. He doubted if she would ever sit again.

"Aspasia! Aspasia!" he exclaimed. "This is nonsense. Who ever heard of such a thing? And I believe—I know—he would not have had this destroyed—"

She interrupted him sternly. "Do as I ask, Alcibiades. This is no time for argument."

And Alcibiades obeyed reluctantly; he had intended to possess that bust himself in due course.

Aspasia took a lekythos from the table and poured the libation. The torches were applied and the flames sprang upward, the resinous wood crackling as merrily as if it were consuming the humblest of citizens, not all that was left of the greatest of Athenians. The relatives and friends raised their voices in a high monotonous chaunt, but the crowds that had climbed up among the cypresses and tombs and stood on the walls, preserved their heavy silence. It was not their privilege to intrude upon this solemn ritual, and they could only listen to the melancholy volume of sound that seemed but a part of that cheerless gray hour before the dawn. Even Thasson, who had deliberately placed himself on the high point where Pericles had made the Funeral Speech, felt none of the bitter triumph he had anticipated. That dark pillar of smoke looked a harbinger of evil, and he felt suddenly humble and helpless as the clouded eyes of his spirit strove to pierce the future. Pericles may have been a Tyrant in all but name, but he had left pigmies behind him. Acestorides was avenged but what of Athens?

Aspasia stood apart, staring at the flaming pyre. Her body felt a mere lump of clay, but her mind darted about in erratic flights, pouncing on pictures briefly lit, and vanishing as suddenly. . . . The funeral of her father when she had fancied herself acquainted with grief, but reminded herself that death was death and she was a Greek . . . her first glimpse of Pericles, on the Bema. . . . The night she had met the Spartan envoy among these tombs. . . . That moonlit night on the Acropolis when she had guessed for the first time what love with Pericles would be. . . . That other night when he had returned suddenly from Samos. . . . The bluff above the shore where she had listened for the splash of oars and the first glimpse of his helmet. . . . Nightingales and the warm scent of roses . . . her wild adventure with Constantia in the gorge. . . . Sophocles reading his *Electra* as she waited for her fate to be decided. . . . His return that night. . . . Hours . . . hours . . . hours. . . . She had thought him a god and he had died at the last a pallid withered old man huddled in his bed, pride and passion gone out of him for ever. That memory persisted, putting others to flight. Could she ever recall them . . . dwell on them . . . forgetting, as he had asked . . . as that arrogant passionate spirit would will and desire? . . .

She became aware that the pyre had fallen to ashes and the bones were being gathered. Alcibiades lifted out the seared and darkened bust and laid it on the table. She looked on dully as they transferred the fragments of Pericles to the large stone urn, and her thoughts, vagrant once more, remembered that Athenians, less luxurious than Ionians, had not yet been persuaded to bury their dead in marble.

The urn was placed on the table among the votive offerings and garlands and carried down the Sacred Way; past the high eminence which Thasson had suddenly deserted; and, a moment later, the bearers turned aside and came to pause a short distance from the street of tombs.

Pericles was not to be buried with his father and sons. His friends, when convinced he would die, had demanded that a man so much greater than any of his ancestors should lie alone, and had seen to the building of a handsome dignified tomb, with no carving on it but the word PERICLES.

The doors were opened and the urn placed within by reverent hands. The votive offerings followed; objects of great value brought by every member of the clans and many friends; none, surely, of such supreme importance as the sacrificed work of Pheidias. A libation was poured, and the tomb sealed by Ariphon.

The sun rose above Hymettus, flooding the Ceramicus with a rosy light. The procession re-formed and walked back to the dead man's house to partake of the funeral feast. The crowd dispersed. Sophocles and Alcibiades would have lingered, but Aspasia motioned them to go. They looked back as they turned into the Sacred Way. She was standing alone in the path, her arms hanging listlessly, her sad eyes, wearing a faintly puzzled expression, fixed on the sealed door of the tomb.

THE END

Following are the authorities consulted for THE IMMORTAL MARRIAGE.

Ancient: Herodotus, Thucydides, Xenophon, Plato, Aristotle, Plutarch, Pausanias. Tragic, comic, and lyric poets.

Modern: Evelyn Abbott, Bury, S. H. Butcher, H. B. Cotterill, Stanley Casson, Maurice Croiset, G. Lowes Dickinson, J. G. Frazer, Arthur L. Grant, Charles Burton Gulick, Gustav Glotz, E. A. Gardner, Grote, Maurice Hutton, Jane Harrison and M. de G. Verrall, B. Jowett, R. W. Livingston, William Watkiss Lloyd, F. L. Lucas, Marshall MacGregor, Gilbert Murray, J. P. Mahaffy, J. W. Mackail, E. B. Osborne, Walter Pater, Adolf Schmidt, John Addington Symonds, T. G. Tucker, F. A. Wright, Alfred E. Zimmern.

For valuable suggestions I am indebted to Professor Oeconomon, Director of the Numismatical Museum of Athens; M. René Pinon of the Revue des Deux Mondes, Paris; Professor Maurice Hutton, Principal of University College, Toronto; Professor Edward Delavan Perry of Columbia University, New York; Professor Ivan Linforth of the University of California; H. W. Parker of the Mechanics Institute, New York, and T. R. Smith.

NOTE: If I have alternated somewhat arbitrarily the c and k of proper names (Pericles—Elpinike), and the original Greek spelling with the Latin transliteration (Sunion—Miletus) I have, after all, been no more self-indulgent than many scholars. My normal preference is for k, but I recalled the forbidding pages of Grote, and as Greek proper names are often long and difficult, and my book necessarily full of them, I concluded not to discourage the reader further. I therefore only used the k occasionally as a guide to pronunciation, and not as often perhaps as I should have done. There is only one way to pronounce Pericles, but as much cannot be said for Alcibiades. I refrained in the latter case because he is essentially an intimate character and the k (in type) seemed to banish him to some remote pedantic region wholly unrelated to so gorgeous and vital a creature. Such eclecticism as I have employed in terminations I based on usage.

Note: As to Aspasia I have accepted the conclusions of modern scholars, who have made her social status a matter of exhaustive research. While her irregular marriage with Pericles may have made her a hetæra under the law she was not one by profession. Her position was much the same as that of the morganatic wife of a prince in subsequent times. Adolf Schmidt seems to have settled the question once for all. The attacks of the comic poets—who were allowed more license than our yellow press—were directed partly by hatred of Pericles, partly by resentment that a member of a thoroughly despised sex should possess the "virtues" of a man. In all ancient literature there is no authority for the prevalent belief, so facilely accepted, that she was a professional hetæra except these same comic poets. Plato and Xenophon speak of her with the greatest respect. As the glory and prestige of Athens declined, her men of genius were forgotten; to be resurrected later by the Romans. When interest in those great poets, architects, sculptors revived, as well as in their patron, Pericles, Aspasia too was remembered, and libidinous minds accepted without question the savory libels of the comic poets. Plutarch was the most careless offender. On one page he states that her house was full of young harlots, on another that Pericles never left the house nor returned to it without kissing her; which certainly intimates that she lived under his roof. Is it to be imagined that the First Citizen and virtual ruler of democratic Athens kept an assignation house? It is astonishing that for twenty-four centuries scholars seem to have done no thinking for themselves where this remarkable woman was concerned. But I refer the curious to Adolf Schmidt's "Pericles and Aspasia" for something like twenty-seven refutations of this ancient and vicious tradition regarding the first intellectual and "emancipated" woman of whom history, barring the periods of matriarchial rule, has any account.

Note: No extant "bust of Aspasia" is authentic. Nor is it possible that she could have sat for any of them. They do not bear the slightest resemblance to any description of her that has come down to us. True her name is on them but Aspasia was not an uncommon name in Ancient Greece.

MAP OF ANCIENT GREECE